HALF A WORLD AWAY

MIKE GAYLE

HALF A WORLD AWAY

HODDER &
STOUGHTON

First published in Great Britain in 2019 by Hodder & Stoughton
An Hachette UK company

1

A CIP catalogue record for this title is available from the British Library

Hardback ISBN 978 1 473 68733 2
Trade Paperback ISBN 978 1 473 68734 9
eBook ISBN 978 1 473 68735 6

Typeset in Plantin Light by Palimpsest Book Production Limited, Falkirk, Stirlingshire

Printed and bound in Great Britain by Clays Ltd, Elcograf S.p.A.

Hodder & Stoughton policy is to use papers that are natural, renewable
and recyclable products and made from wood grown in sustainable forests.
The logging and manufacturing processes are expected to conform to the
environmental regulations of the country of origin.

To Claire for everything

THEN

30th November 1992

Dear Jason,

 I've done a lot of mad things in my life but I definitely think writing a letter without knowing if it'll ever get read has to be one of the maddest! And yet here I am doing just that!

 The reason I'm writing to you is simple. My name's Kerry Hayes and I'm your sister and even though I haven't seen you since you were tiny, I love you more than anything in the world.

 Yesterday I turned eighteen, which means I'm an adult and I'll be leaving Milread Road soon. (Milread Road, in case you don't know, is the children's home I've lived in for the past six years. It's okay, I suppose, but I'm not going to miss it.) Anyway, because I'm leaving care the social is going to set me up with a flat and everything, and I'll be able to do what I want when I want (not that I don't already!).

 In a perfect world, getting a place of my own would mean that you could come and live with me. But you and I both know that the world isn't perfect. I don't know where you are. No one's ever told me. When I asked my social worker to help me find you she said that because of some stupid rule they've made up, she's not allowed to tell me where you are. I don't know if you're in London or in Liverpool. Or even if you're still in the country. The only thing I can do is write letters to something called the Adoption Contact Register and they won't even pass them on to you. Instead I have to wait until you get in contact with them and that might not be for years.

 You must be ten now, and living with your new parents. Have you got any brothers and sisters? Part of me hopes not because

I hate thinking that you might have forgotten me. You haven't, have you? You still remember me, don't you?

We used to have so much fun together, Jason, you and me. I used to make you laugh all the time pulling silly faces and playing the clown. You were never happy unless I was with you. You used to call me 'Keh-wah' when you were small because you couldn't say my name properly. If I wasn't with you, you'd run around the flat shouting, 'Keh-wah!' at the top of your voice until I came.

Anyway, I'll write and let you know my new address as soon as I move in.

I miss you, Jason.

I miss you so much.

Please, as soon as you get this, write back so that I can know for sure that you're safe and happy.

It's all I ever want for you.

All my love, always,

Kerry xxx

PART
1

I

Kerry

Friday, 26th February

I'm belting out 'All I Want For Christmas Is You' at the top of my lungs as I pull up in front of the house. I absolutely love that song. It's such a banger! I don't care that it's the end of February, that Christmas is nothing but a memory and that we're now closer to Easter than the festive season. It could be Mother's Day, Saint Patrick's Day or even Yom Kippur for all I care because whenever that song comes up on my *Best of Mazza* playlist, it's officially Christmas again. I forget all about how hard it was to get out of bed this morning, the miserable drivers who cut me up left, right and centre on my way over here after school drop-off, in fact I pretty much forget about every crappy little thing that tries to rain on my parade. Instead I belt out my favourite song in the world proper diva-style: all-in, no shame, hogging the limelight like there's no tomorrow. I love Mariah Carey, I really do. She. Is. Amazing. She don't take no crap from anyone, does what she wants the way she wants and no one says a word to her because do you know what? She. Is. Mariah. Bleedin'. Carey!

Waving my hands in the air and squeezing my eyes shut like they do on *X Factor*, I'm giving the final chorus my all when I hear a knock on my side window. I get a right shock when I open my eyes to see some old dear with her face pressed right up against it. She looks really miffed.

I wind down my window.

'You all right, love? You lost or something?'

She gives me the evil eye. 'I know exactly where I am, thank you very much, young lady! I've been trying to get your attention to tell you that you're blocking the way!'

I look around and sure enough she's right. I've been so lost in Mariah Town, I've completely forgotten to open up the gates.

I apologise to the old dear, then dip my hand into my bag, whip out the remote and press the big button on it. Hey presto – the huge black metal gates in front of me slide back just like magic.

With Mariah still crooning away I give the old woman a little wave, mouth 'I'm really sorry,' and then pull up on to the drive, grab my things out the back and practically skip to the front door. Rummaging around in my bag again, I pull out the front door keys and do a little Mariah-style dance as I step inside. Unbuttoning my jacket, I start slipping it off my shoulders but as I catch sight of the state of the hallway Mariah shuts down sharpish.

The place is a tip.

There are kids' toys strewn across the floor, a mountain of coats draped over the bottom of the banister, piles of stuff on the stairs and even a half-eaten plum on top of the radiator.

I edge myself along the corridor towards the kitchen, scared of what I might find, and as I enter the room my worst fears are confirmed.

In spite of its handleless German engineered cupboards, polished granite work surfaces and – I kid you not – fifty-odd grand's worth of oven and hob – it looks like a bomb's just hit it. The counter is covered with spilled cereal, dirty bowls, half-drunk glasses of milk and a load of newspapers and magazines. The huge gloss-white eight-seater dining table has half-eaten bits of toast on it, half a dozen dirty wine glasses, three empty juice bottles and – get this – a pair of designer stilettos lying on their sides showing their bright red soles for all the world to see.

The cat's litter tray at the end of the kitchen island is so full that even the cat looks a bit disgusted by it, the open dishwasher is stuffed to the gills with dirty pots and pans, and there's a child's roller skate in the sink. As I fish it out and set it on the counter, my eyes come to rest on a handwritten note that's been weighed down with a tall bottle of extra-virgin olive oil.

'Hi Kerry,' it reads. 'So, so, sorry about the mess! Had a bit of a party last night and we were in such a mad rush this morning that I didn't get round to any of the tidying I wanted to do. I'm sure with your super skills it won't take too long to sort out! All best wishes, Cathy. PS The loo in the en suite is blocked. Could you possibly work your magic on it? PPS We seem to have run out of bathroom cleaner but I'm sure you'll have some of your own.'

I take a long look around me and let out a huge sigh. I can't believe how happy and positive I'd been just a few minutes ago, and now I wish I hadn't bothered dragging myself out of bed this morning. I'm suddenly so, so, tired. Tired like I always seem to be these days. It could easily take me all the time I've got just to clean up this mess, let alone do the rest of the house. Reaching down, I pick up the note and toss it in the kitchen bin that is, of course, full to bursting. Mariah has well and truly left the building, I think to myself, and right now I feel like she's never coming back.

Like most women – and in all the years I've been doing the job I've yet to meet a single man doing this – I got into the cleaning game because I could fit it around childcare. Being a single mum with a young child made it virtually impossible for me to go out to work, but I told myself that as soon as my Kian was old enough to start nursery I'd look for something. People round my way thought I was mad when I told them my plans. What did I want to go looking for a job for, when my lad was still so little, especially when I'd probably end up worse off than if I did nothing? I told them straight though, it was exactly because he was so young that I wanted to get a job. I didn't want him growing up like some of the wasters from our estate, hanging out on street corners, nicking things to order or selling a bit of weed on the side. Some of them have never done a day's work in their lives and neither have their parents. I wanted better for my Kian. I wanted him growing up knowing that there's a right way and a wrong way, and the wrong way is sitting on your backside all day long thinking the world owes you a living. And as for being worse off, I couldn't give a monkey's. To me, showing my son that there's another way, a better way, that he doesn't have to waste his whole life on the dole has always been far more important than being able to keep him in the latest Nikes or whatever. To me, the most important thing in the world is that he has pride in himself.

When the time came for me to start looking, it turned out that the only jobs I had a chance of getting were in retail or wait-ressing. Every interview I had, the bosses made out like the positions were flexible but that was rubbish. They were either all that zero-hours nonsense or they'd ask if I was prepared to work late nights and weekends as if I hadn't just told them I was a single mum with a young kid! Just as I was beginning to tear my hair out, a mum of one of Kian's friends at nursery told me about a gig she'd got working for a cleaning company, and apparently they were looking for people to cover staff holidays and the like. To be honest, it didn't sound ideal. Most of it was last-minute-can-you-go-to-such-and-such-a-place-in-the-next-half-hour type stuff, but it was cash in hand and it could fit around childcare so I asked her to give them my number. Sure enough, the following week, after a quick five-minute interview, they sent me off to my first job.

I remember it like it was yesterday. It was a two-bed flat in a beautiful stucco-fronted mansion in Maida Vale. I'd never been anywhere quite like it in my life. It was all white walls with horrible-looking modern-art paintings on them, stripped floor-boards, and furniture that looked like it was straight out of *Star Trek*. Though none of it was to my taste, you could tell it was all dead expensive and I was almost scared to breathe in case I accidentally broke something. Still, cleaning was what I'd come to do and so that was what I did and by the time I'd finished, even the loo seat sparkled. It was a nice feeling, doing a good job like that, my little contribution to making the people who lived there just that little bit happier.

Six weeks on I was doing such a good job that they officially put me on the books working all the hours I wanted when Kian wasn't home, and I loved it, really loved it. I felt like I'd finally found my thing. My place in the world. Then about a year in I happened to see a client invoice on my boss's desk. I couldn't believe how much they were charging people for three or four hours of cleaning. I was so outraged, I wasn't sure who was being ripped off more: us girls or the clients. Still, it gave me a few ideas of my own and that same week I put up a card in a news-agent's window just around the corner from Notting Hill Tube: 'Reliable and trustworthy female cleaner available, reasonable rates, and references on request.' Within a few days I'd booked my first gig, and within the month I had enough clients to be able to hand in my notice and be my own boss, just like Mariah Carey.

When it comes to where to start when you're cleaning a house, most girls I know have rules. Some say you should always start at the bottom and work your way up because the bottom of the house is where people do most of their living and so it tends to be messier. Others say you should start at the top and work your way down because that way you can ease yourself into the job and pick up speed as you go. I've never much been fussed one way or the other, because at the end of the day it all needs doing, so I tend to let my mood decide. Today, given the state of down-stairs, I'm in a top-down state of mind. Grabbing my bucket, mop, floor sweeper, dusters and the vacuum cleaner from the under-stairs cupboard, I haul my way up both flights of stairs to the Pryors' master bedroom suite up in the loft, and then promptly have to sit down on the edge of the bed to catch my breath.

The room is decorated in what I suppose you might call a modern fashion. All the walls, floorboards, bed linen and furnish-ings are white, which is stylish but a bit too cold for my liking. I like a bit of colour and sparkle in a room, something a bit cheerier like orange or yellow or even a nice lime-green. Rather than normal windows, the room has got these fancy bi-fold jobs that look out right across west London. Sometimes when I've finished cleaning the house I like to come up here and stand for a minute or two enjoying the view. I like to think about the lives of all the people whose homes I can see right into, wondering who they are, what they do and if they're happy. Today, though, I won't have time for any of that. Today's going to be hard graft right up until it's over and I'm not looking forward to it at all because my back has been aching something rotten for the past few days. I give it a rub with the heel of my palm and then stand up, pop *Absolute Eighties* on my phone, plug in my earphones and slip on my Marigolds: it's time to get down to business.

All it takes to unblock the en-suite toilet is a couple of goes with a plunger. After that I give it a good clean, followed by the sink and shower. I tidy up Mrs Pryor's make-up and perfumes on the bathroom counter and as I do, I catch sight of a middle-aged brunette looking back at me from the mirror. I look tired and my roots need doing again, but other than that I quite like what I see. I don't look half bad for a woman the wrong side of forty. Okay so there are a few little lines around my eyes, and when I tilt my head to one side in the morning to dry my hair my face does look a bit like it's about to slide off, but my skin's pretty clear, my teeth are nice and straight, and when I do get the chance to get dolled up, I reckon I could easily pass for someone five years younger. Not bad, all things considered.

In the bedroom, I run my floor sweeper over the painted hardwood flooring, make the bed (even though I've told Mrs Pryor that's not my job), and tidy away the clothes draped across the armchair in the corner of the room (also not my job). When I finally finish, the room looks like the sort of upmarket hotel suite you see in glossy magazines, which I suppose is the look they were going for, but it's taken me the best part of an hour to get it like this and I've still got three kids' bedrooms, the hallway, the family bathroom and, not forgetting, the apocalypse in the kitchen-diner to deal with too.

As much as I'd like to stop in an hour's time and just leave

the kitchen in whatever state I've managed to get it to by then
– or even better, invoice for the extra time it will take to get it
looking spick and span – I know from experience that it's not
worth the hassle. The Pryors are exactly the sort of people who,
in the same breath as justifying spending a fortune on organic
coconut water, will fight tooth and nail for the right not to slip
me an extra tenner for cleaning up a mess I shouldn't even be
asked to deal with. But I can't afford to start losing clients right
now, no matter how useless they are. Recently I've had a few
things come up at the last minute that have meant I've had to
take either a morning or an afternoon off work, so I'm down
quite a bit on my money this month. And on top of all my usual
bills and outgoings, it's Kian's birthday soon. I want to get him
something special, something he really wants, that will really
knock his socks off, and if I know him, that won't come cheap.
So if tolerating clients like the Pryors is what I've got to do to
make that happen, then that's what I'll do.

While I tackle the kids' bedrooms I try and keep in mind that
actually most of my clients aren't pigs. The majority are somewhere between okay – no small talk, pay on time, not too untidy
– and lovely – tidying up a bit before I arrive or at the very least,
realistic about just how long it actually takes to get a home clean.
My favourite clients, as well as tidying up a bit before I get to
them, go the extra mile. They're the sort who leave out biscuits
on the kitchen counter, or put a little extra in with my regular
money if the place is unusually messy, and of course, they always
remember to tip at Christmas.

It's a funny thing cleaning people's houses and seeing all the
things up close that they'd much rather keep hidden away. I've
lost count of the times I've accidentally seen things I'm sure I
shouldn't have. Everything from certain battery-operated items
tucked under pillows, to packs of anti-depressants hidden away
inside books. The most surprising thing I ever came across was
at the home of a really quite recently married couple, both big-shot
lawyers in the City. One morning I found the husband's phone
on the kitchen counter and just as I picked it up to move it out

of the way, he got a text from his bit on the side asking him how the meeting with his divorce lawyer had gone. For three whole weeks I knew before his wife that he was planning to leave her and probably had never even loved her in the first place.

That's why cleaning is such an intimate job. You get to see behind closed doors where people let their guard down. You get to see who they really are. I suppose that could be why Mrs Pryor is so mean and demanding. Because for all her airs and graces, private education, good-looking tax-accountant husband, picture-perfect children and designer wardrobe, I know exactly who she is. Then again, it could just as easily be that she's a jumped-up bitch with a *Downton Abbey* complex. With women like her it's just so hard to tell.

By the time I'm finally finished at the Pryors' I'm running late for my next job, which of course has a knock-on effect for the rest of the day. I have to text Mrs Greig, my last client of the day, to let her know I'll take her ironing home tonight and drop it back first thing tomorrow while Kian is at karate. Unlike Mrs Pryor, Mrs Greig is one of my lovely clients. Even though she's a senior manager at a big telecoms company with more than enough on her plate, somehow she still manages to text me back before I've even put my phone away: 'No problem at all. I'm just grateful you're doing it. It's the one job I can't stand! x.'

After I load the last of my things into the boot of my car, I send out a few texts to rearrange my work for the following week, lock up at the Pryors' and set the alarm, before heading over to Ladbroke Grove. Parking as near as I can to Kian's school, I nip across the road to the Tesco Metro, pick up a few things for tea, and am walking through the school gates just as the bell goes.

To be honest, at ten Kian's probably a bit too old for me to still be picking him up from school. At his age I'd been walking myself to school for at least three or four years. Plus he's not the little boy who clung to my legs sobbing on his first day at school any more. He's a big lad now and streetwise with it, and most of his mates have been making their own way home alone since the beginning of the school year. But even though he's asked me a million times if he can join them, I always say no. I tell him it's because there are too many dangerous roads to cross, or dodgy people to avoid, or kids causing trouble, even though I reckon he could handle those sorts of things standing on his head. The thing is, while he might be nearly eleven he's still my baby, and it's just been him and me for so long that it's hard to let go. I know I'll have to one day soon – we should be hearing whether he's got a place at Melbourne Park the month after next – and he can't have me picking him up from secondary school in front of all his mates – but I'm just not ready yet. One day I will be, but not yet.

He greets me with his usual question: 'Have you got anything to eat?'

I roll my eyes and ask him if he thinks I was born yesterday as I dip into my bag and, like a magician, pull out a packet of salt and vinegar crisps, his favourite. He's wolfed down the lot by the time we get to the car and so he spends the rest of the journey home rummaging through the shopping on the back seat. He keeps grabbing stuff and asking if he's allowed to eat it and time after time I tell him, 'No, that's for tea,' or 'No, that's for breakfast,' or 'No, that's for your packed lunch.'

Finally he gets a cheeky glint in his eye and pulls out a box of Weetabix. 'How about one of these?' he asks, knowing full well I'll say no. So when I say he can have one his jaw drops, proper cartoon-style. 'Really?'

'Yeah,' I say with a grin, 'but if I find any crumbs back there, it'll be your job to clear them up!' I know some people might think letting your kid eat cereal straight out of the box in the back of a moving car is bad parenting but I prefer to think of it as keeping him on his toes. Every time he thinks he knows what I'm all about, I'll do something to surprise him and keep up the mystery.

If it were up to Kian we'd eat every meal on the sofa in front of the TV, but today like most days we eat tea at our tiny dining table in the kitchen. I like sitting across from him, watching him eat, seeing all the weird and wonderful faces he pulls as I grill him about what he's been up to at school. Meal times are my favourite parts of the day, they're when we're most *us*. Our little family comes together. They're when I find out what he's really thinking or feeling, even though sometimes he doesn't say more than a few words. A mum can tell a lot about her son just by sitting across a table from him. Sometimes he tells me off for studying him like he's a tiny insect under a microscope and when he does, I always joke, 'Too right, mate! You'll never be able to hide anything from me: I see everything!'

After tea Kian heads off to his room, even though it's his job to clear the table, but before I can call him back my phone rings. I'm half expecting it to be Mrs Pryor with a complaint about something or other, because she's an ungrateful cow and that's just the sort of thing women like that love to do, but it's not Mrs Pryor. In fact it's not one of my clients at all.

When the call's finally ended, I stand by the sink shaking my head over and over again. I want to cry. I want to shout. I want to smash something and watch it shatter to pieces. But in the end I just stand there thinking how from now on, nothing is ever going to be the same again.

2

Noah

'Yeah, yeah, yeah . . . I understand all that, mate . . . GBH . . . blah, blah, blah . . . very serious crime . . . blah, blah, blah . . . let's see what we can do about getting you bailed . . . blah, blah, blah . . . But before we get into all that just explain one thing for me, yeah?'

As he pauses, my brow furrows in anticipation.

'You're my brief, innit?'

'I am indeed your legal representative.'

'And that means I can ask you anything I like, yeah?'

My brow furrows further. Soon my entire upper face will be one huge wrinkle.

'Is there some specific aspect of your case you'd like to talk about, Mr Nazeeb?'

'Not about my case, about you, blood. No offence but . . . how comes you, a black geezer, talks like a posh white geezer? Is your mum the queen or something?' He laughs heartily as though this is the funniest joke he's ever heard. 'Dude, you don't sound nuthin' like any of the black geezers from round my ends and it's proper doing my head in. What's your story?'

One might assume that given Mr Nazeeb is being held in custody for attacking a rival drug dealer with a baseball bat, is looking at a five-year sentence, has already had an appeal for bail turned down and is facing a second in just twenty-five minutes, he would be a tad more focused on his current situation. But to make such an assumption about the twenty-seven-year-old Asian man sitting across the table from me (dressed head to toe in his drug-dealing street uniform of baseball cap, black North Face jacket, grey sweatshirt, matching jogging bottoms and bright white box-fresh trainers), one would need to be ignorant of a truth of which I have long been painfully aware: that little frustrates the human brain so much as an inability to immediately pigeonhole complete strangers. And for the man sitting across from me in a dingy conference room at Westminster Magistrates Court the question of why I, as a thirty-four-year-old criminal barrister with light-brown skin, Caribbean heritage and a three-piece pinstripe suit, don't drop my aitches is, it would appear, of greater priority than even personal liberty.

It is a phenomenon unbounded not only by race but by class too. I have witnessed it in career criminals like Mr Nazeeb, pupils in the playground of my prep school and even senior teaching fellows at Oxford. For as long as I can remember I have been asked Mr Nazeeb's question many times, in many guises. Sometimes it's posed subtly: 'So tell me, where exactly are you from?' and sometimes delicacy goes completely out of the window: 'I don't get it, you're black, so why do you talk like a white dude?' But rarely, if ever, does the question remain unasked, which I believe perfectly illustrates a long-held theory of mine that when it comes to the employment of specious, insulting and downright racist stereotypes, no social class or indeed race has a monopoly. Everybody, whether rich or poor, black or white, educated or uneducated, is as guilty of this behaviour as everyone else.

'I was adopted at two and a half and my parents are white,' I explain perfunctorily, having learned the hard way that offering individually tailored lectures on race and social class to all I encounter is indeed the shortest route to madness.

'That explains it then, bruv,' exclaims Mr Nazeeb, and he gives me a deliberately exaggerated nod of recognition that is as smug as it is irritating.

'Right then,' I announce, returning my gaze to the brief open in front of me. 'Now that's settled, how about we return to the matter in hand: what I can do to prevent you spending the next one hundred and eighty days of your life on remand.'

While I'd always wanted to work in law, it had never been my ambition to be a criminal barrister. I grew up in Islington, attending a nearby prestigious private school that was in truth little more than a sausage factory for the establishment, and when the time came for me to select one of the array of professional careers on offer to my peers and me (future fund managers, City whizz kids, academics, lawyers, medical professionals, senior civil servants, politicians and policy makers), it was law that seemed the best fit for me. Not only did it suit my personality (growing up I liked nothing more than a good debate), it also seemed incredibly lucrative, as confirmed by a school friend's father who worked in commercial law. Once he took his son and me out for lunch at Chez Bruce in Wandsworth and casually announced as we waited for our starters to arrive that he was now earning in excess of a million pounds a year.

So when I went up to Oxford to study, it was commercial law I had in mind to practise once I was qualified, and nothing else, because I very much liked the idea of earning a great deal of money. But then during my training for the bar I got a taste for criminal law that only increased during my pupillage. By the time I was called to the bar I had abandoned all interest in commerce and had fallen head over heels with criminal law.

The reason was simple. When it came to law, the criminal arena was not only where the stakes were highest but also where words like 'justice' and 'liberty' ceased being abstract concepts. Their application could mean an innocent person gaining their freedom and a guilty person receiving just punishment for their crimes.

Over the course of my ten-year career I've acted as a junior in murder cases where the evidence against a client has seemed so incontrovertible, only to have that very same evidence fall apart under scrutiny. I've prosecuted cases of horrendous violence and cruelty that due to my efforts have resulted in those responsible receiving the highest sentences the law allows. In short, whether defending or prosecuting I have given my all to each and every client I have represented (even the Mr Nazeebs of this world). And I do so because as hopelessly naïve and idealistic as it sounds, I believe in justice, in the law, and in the fundamental human right to have someone defend your cause at a time in your life when you are at your weakest.

Emerging from Westminster Magistrates Court an hour and a half after my conference with Mr Nazeeb, I feel somewhat victorious, having not only secured bail for my client but also an admonishment from the judge against the Metropolitan Police for the late disclosure of some of their evidence against him. As if to temper any feeling of bonhomie, however, the bright crispness of the late February afternoon that I'd enjoyed on entering the building has given way to a cold, damp evening. With the kitbag containing my wig, gown and collar, along with a number of case files in my hands, I join the heads-down, umbrellas-up shuffle of the homeward-bound masses trudging through the rain towards Marylebone. All thoughts of my victory dissipate as I consider my destination: my home in Primrose Hill; and recall the most recent whispered row between my wife Rosalind and me this morning, while our daughter ate breakfast in the next room in blissful ignorance. It seems lately as though Rosalind and I are always arguing. It seems lately as though everything I say and do only serves to exasperate her.

Peeling off before I reach my bus stop, I duck into an upmarket florist's decorated with zinc buckets of flowers stacked on vintage wooden crates and staffed by two impeccably turned-out young women sporting striped canvas aprons. It feels like a huge cliché buying flowers in the hope of appeasing an angry wife but I'm not sure exactly what else I can do. The taller of the two women, speaking English with a heavy French accent, asks how she might help and I reply in her native tongue that I'd like some flowers for my wife. Surprised, she asks me whereabouts in France I'm from and she is further taken aback when I explain that I'm actually English. 'My father is half French,' I explain, 'and I studied French at school but the only reason I'm any good is because my wife and I regularly holiday at my in-laws' villa in Cavalaire-sur-Mer so I get lots of practice.'

We chat about Cavalaire-sur-Mer for a while (she has family there) and eventually circle back around to the question of flowers. Still conversing in French, she asks me whether my wife has any floral preferences. I shrug and tell her that she's fond of white and cream and she makes some suggestions that mean little to me in either French or English. I say that she should do whatever she thinks is best and when she asks what sort of budget I have in mind, I reply, somewhat decadently, 'The sky is the limit.'

I leave the shop carrying a bouquet made up of white roses, freesias and lilies, which to my eyes at least looks wonderfully impressive. I imagine handing them to my wife, her accepting them in the spirit in which they've been offered, and the anger of this morning, of many recent mornings, vanishing in an instant. It feels good to believe that things will return to normal between us, to imagine the tension that's lingered these past few weeks might disappear forever.

Whether it's because of the flowers, which provide such a cheerful contrast to the rain, or because I know it's Friday evening and I won't have to think about work again until Sunday, when I'll have to continue preparing for the aggravated burglary case I'm prosecuting first thing on Monday morning, I'm not sure, but my spirits feel sufficiently lifted that on the journey home, rather than mull over my troubles, I allow myself some time off. On the bus I manage to flick through most of the *Evening Standard*, and on alighting I even listen to most of a legal podcast that a number of colleagues from my chambers have been recommending to me for months. In fact, I'm so pleasantly distracted for the entire journey that it's only when I finally arrive at the front door of our Primrose Hill home and remove my headphones that my earlier anxiety returns.

Clutching the flowers tightly, I stand on the pavement for a moment looking up at my home, a four-storey Georgian townhouse. We had the painters in just two weeks ago and with its gleaming black front door, railings and dazzling white façade, its aesthetic appeal is undeniable. It's so pristine that I'm sure passers-by imagine the inhabitants must live similarly perfect lives. If only they knew.

I enter the house and call out from the hallway as I close the front door behind me. While there's no reply, I can hear the sound of the TV coming from the front room. Kicking off my shoes, I leave the flowers on the antique side table and pop my head around the door. My daughter Millie is sprawled out on the sofa, her long mane of wavy black hair spread out behind her like a cloak. Her big brown eyes are glued to the screen and she's watching some sort of reality TV programme starring unfeasibly handsome twenty-year-olds that I'm pretty sure – given that she's only twelve – she isn't supposed to be watching. She mutes the sound and tips her head back, allowing me to place my lips gently on her forehead. Even after all these years it's a delight to see myself in another human being, albeit partially. She has my cheekbones, eyes and colouring, but the rest is pure Rosalind.

'Good day?'

She shrugs. 'It was okay. Mrs Eliades freaked out in chemistry because Zoe H was watching YouTube videos on her phone under the desk, and for lunch I had vegetarian paella, which was really lovely.' She pulls a face and adds, 'Oh, and someone was sick on the bus home from school and the smell was so rank I thought I might die. How about you?'

'All good thanks, sweetie. Is Mum around?'

'I think she's in her study.'

'Have you eaten?'

She shakes her head. 'Just some fruit. Mum said something about us maybe getting a takeaway later.'

I glance at the TV again. Two handsome bare-chested young men appear to be having an in-depth conversation with two equally gorgeous young women wearing tiny bikinis.

'You do know you're too young to be watching this, don't you?'

'Everybody at school watches it,' she replies wearily, as if this is all the justification she needs. She grins cheekily and adds, 'And yes, Dad . . . if everyone at school jumped off a cliff I'd probably do that too.'

In spite of myself I laugh. It was a good tactic: attempting to negate my argument by pre-empting my admonishment, thereby rendering me more likely to leave her alone. Despite her current desire to be 'a social media influencer' or to perhaps 'do something in fashion' when she grows up, maybe I might still make a barrister of her yet. 'All right then. Just don't spend the whole night watching this rubbish, okay.'

Returning to the hallway, I pick up the flowers and walk down the single flight of painted concrete stairs to Rosalind's basement study. She's an interior decorator by trade, and a very good one. I've lost count of the times our home has featured in some magazine or other, and once we even had a TV crew here interviewing her about her work. In the past her clients have included hotels, restaurants, a couple of bars and the occasional rock star and supermodel. Rosalind and her business partner, Aoife, have a studio space in nearby Camden but when she's got a lot on she'll often work from home.

Rosalind is at her desk staring at her computer screen, her long blonde hair swept up into a ponytail. Even though she's been working from home today and is dressed more casually in an oversized white shirt, faded skinny jeans and Converse, she looks as chic and sophisticated as always.

Finally sensing my presence, she lifts her gaze from the screen towards me but says nothing. No hello. No how was your day. Nothing. This is who we are now.

'For you,' I say, holding out the bouquet. She looks weary and defeated, and I'm suddenly conscious of the inadequacy of my floral gesture. 'I'm . . . well you know . . . about this morning.'

She doesn't speak, or take the flowers; instead she looks past me into the mid-distance, as if searching for the answer to a question she has yet to ask out loud.

'Flowers aren't going to fix this, Noah.'

Her voice is measured and quiet. So quiet, in fact, that when she stops I have to ask myself whether she's actually spoken or if it was a trick of my mind.

I place the flowers on her desk gingerly, almost as if this current situation is their fault and not my own. Rosalind continues to sit but her fists are now clenched on her lap and her eyes are looking anywhere other than at me. Her gaze comes to rest briefly on the flowers and then finally, taking a deep breath, she looks up at me.

'I've been thinking all day . . . about you . . . us . . . where we are . . . and I think . . . well, I think that perhaps we should . . . we should take a break.'

A wave of relief crashes over me. The thought that this whole situation could be cured by something as simple as a holiday seems too ridiculous to believe. I'd book a thousand holidays if it meant we could put this behind us. I only wish I'd thought of it, rather than her having to say.

'Of course,' I say all too eagerly, 'wherever and whenever you'd like.'

She shakes her head but says nothing and as a deafening silence fills the room the message sinks in, even though it makes little sense at all.

'It was just an argument, Rosalind. One little argument. Surely you can't—'

'It wasn't *just* anything,' she says firmly. 'It wasn't just about this morning, this week or even this year. It's about us, Noah. The way you've been these past few weeks, the way I suppose you've always been. I love you, really I do, but I think we both need to work out what we want from this marriage and I don't think we can do that living under the same roof. And I know you'll think I'm overreacting, that I'm blowing things out of proportion, that this is all to do with the miscarriage. But I'm completely serious about this, Noah. First thing in the morning if your bags aren't packed, then I'll pack a bag for Millie and me and we'll go to my parents'.' She pauses then adds, 'I know you think I'm overreacting, I know you think I'm being unfair, but

I'm not, I'm not at all. This is the only way I can think of to get through to you just how serious this is, Noah. This is the only way I can get you to understand that we can't carry on another day just pretending that we haven't got a problem.'

For the rest of the evening Rosalind and I don't say another word to each other. Instead I tell Millie I won't be able to watch TV with her as I've got too much work on, and Rosalind takes that as a cue to suggest to Millie that they go out for noodles. Ironically I then do spend the whole of my evening working because I'm so desperate for the distraction, and when they return two hours later Millie pops her head around the door of my study, tells me I work too hard and then kisses me goodnight.

That night I sleep on the futon in my study and when morning comes around I get up early and go for a run so that Millie doesn't get suspicious. As I run I tell myself that Rosalind isn't serious about us separating, even if it is only temporarily. I tell myself she's just upset. I tell myself she's probably spent the whole night regretting everything she said yesterday. I tell myself that things will be better when I return home.

But when I do get home, soaked through with sweat because I've somewhat overdone it, rather than being better, things are actually worse. I go upstairs to our room to take a shower but I've barely got my top off when Rosalind comes in, takes out her overnight bag from the bottom of the wardrobe and starts packing.

'Stop,' I tell her, shocked by the look of steely determination on her face. 'Just stop, you've made your point, I'll go.'

And that's just what I do. I pack a bag, explain to Millie that something has come up at work and that I'll be away for a night or two, and then with as little fuss as possible I load my things into the back of the car and drive.

3

Kerry

Saturday, 27th February

There's no Mariah Carey blasting out of the car as I drive through the gates of Kensal Green cemetery the day after the call. In fact there's no music at all. Instead there's just the whir of the car heater working overtime, that weird rattling noise the engine has been making for the past couple of weeks, and the sound of my own thoughts.

I pull into a space next to one of those depressing wire bins that are neither use nor ornament. It's half full of dead flowers, crisp packets and empty pop cans, which only makes me wonder who brings snacks along with them on a visit to a cemetery. It doesn't seem right somehow, shovelling pickled onion Monster Munch into your gob on a visit to see dear old Granny's final resting place. But then again, what do I know about being respectful when I had to learn in a call from a total stranger that not only is my mum dead, but that I missed the funeral too?

I switch off the engine and sit for a minute looking out across the cemetery. If it wasn't quite so rammed full of dead people, I suppose it would be quite a relaxing place. It's like a big field with loads of trees and shrubs, and although it's a bit bare right now, in a few weeks as spring starts up I can imagine it looking really nice with plenty of leaves on the trees and bright yellow daffodils dotted about. Right now it just looks a bit weird, like a park where nobody's allowed to play, no kids, no bikes, no ball games, just a collection of sad-looking people standing in the cold, staring at slabs of granite poking out of the ground.

Pulling my scarf a bit tighter around me to keep in the warmth,

I think about Kian. He's at his Saturday morning karate class right now, he doesn't know I'm here and I'm not going to tell him. I want his head full of skateboard tricks and video games and action heroes like it should be, not cemeteries and headstones and misery.

Grabbing my bag from the passenger seat, I get out of the car, close the door behind me and then stop. I don't exactly know what to do next because . . . well, I've come empty-handed. It feels a bit off, visiting a grave without bringing anything with me, like turning up at someone's house for tea without bringing a present. I mean, even if you know the food's going to be rubbish and you didn't really want to accept the invitation anyway, you've still got to bring a box of chocolates or a nice bottle of wine with you. Turning up empty-handed just seems rude.

That said, it's not as if I've actually forgotten to bring any flowers for Mum's grave. I pulled up next to some young bloke with tattoos on his neck and hands, selling flowers out the side of his van in a layby just down the road. But as I stared at all the sad bunches of carnations, roses and lilies stuck in black plastic buckets dotted around him, it suddenly seemed so point-less, so hypocritical, to be buying flowers for a woman who I deliberately chose not to see for over a decade. In the end I got back into my car without buying a single thing. It might seem harsh but it was the right thing to do. While I'm guilty of being a lot of things, the one thing no one can accuse me of being is a fake. Yes, she was my mum. Yes, I was her daughter. But we definitely weren't a family.

It doesn't take long to find the plot; she's right there next to Nan and Granddad, which is nice for her, I suppose. It's a shady spot, and there are a few snowdrops poking their heads through the tall grass in the verge nearby. Mum's headstone is really plain, some sort of white stone with gold lettering on it. Not something I would've chosen myself but it must have cost a bit, which at least means that when she passed away she must have had someone in her life who cared enough to cough up for it. According to the inscription, Mary Anne Hayes was a beloved mother and friend – all of which is news to me but there you go. To be fair, though, it has been a very long time since we last saw each other, so there's always the possibility that before she died she had a complete personality transplant.

I was thirty-two and six months pregnant the last time I saw Mum. Out of nowhere, she just knocked on the door to my flat and asked if we could talk. It was the first time I'd seen her in about three years, and because I was so used to her drifting in and out of my life whenever she wanted, I was about ready to tell her where to go. It was because of her that Jason and me were taken into care. It was because of her that I ended up in a children's home. It was because of her that for the longest time I felt nothing but anger and bitterness towards the world. I didn't need her in my life to feel loved any more, especially now I had a baby growing inside of me. But she was different this time, or at least that's what I thought. She seemed . . . I don't know . . . changed somehow . . . full of remorse about everything she'd put me through in the past. She practically begged me to let her be part of my life again and I suppose I felt sorry for her. She told me she didn't have any friends, money or anywhere to live. I was her last hope.

Maybe it was being pregnant that made me a bit soft in the head. Then again maybe it was because she was saying all the right things about us finding Jason and being one big happy family together. Whatever it was I couldn't help myself. I totally believed her. I fell for her every last word. I think it's what they call a triumph of hope over experience. Thing is, she knew exactly what she had to say to get me on side so basically I was putty in her hands, and in no time at all I was making plans for her to move in with me.

As living situations go, it wasn't exactly ideal. At the time I only had a one-bed flat, which to be honest was more of a bedsit than anything: a kitchenette, shower room and loo, a single sofa and a bed. I had absolutely no idea how it was all going to work once the baby arrived. There wasn't enough room to swing a cat, let alone for two adults and a baby. But even though I knew in my heart of hearts it couldn't work, I really was over the moon. For the first time since I was a little girl, Mum and me were back living under the same roof, and for someone like me who hasn't exactly had much happiness in their life, this felt like the beginning of a new chapter. Maybe she'd finally love me like she should've done, maybe my little bean would bring out the best in her. Maybe she'd do a much better job of being a nan than she ever had being a mum.

Maybe.

Maybe.

Maybe.

After about a month of living together, I came home from work to find Mum gone and the money I'd been saving up for a pushchair (hidden away in an old ice-cream tub at the bottom of my wardrobe) missing. I know people like to throw around the word 'heartbroken' like it's confetti, but that's exactly how I felt staring into that empty ice-cream tub. I felt like my heart had literally shattered, like she'd scooped it right out of my chest and stomped all over it. Right there and then, I told myself I was done with her. If she ever came near me again, it would be the last thing she ever did. As far as I was concerned she was dead to me. I think she must have known she'd gone too far because she never did come back, not to beg my forgiveness, not even to see her own grandson. I never heard a word from her, and now she's gone, of course, I never will.

Staring at Mum's headstone, I try really hard to think of one happy memory but even though I know I must have some somewhere, it's like they're hiding. Instead all I find as I rummage around inside my head are the bad memories, the ones I've kept hidden for a reason. Like the time she forgot my birthday and didn't remember until a week later. Or when I came home from school to find that she'd sold the TV, even though we didn't own it in the first place. Or the time she let the social take my baby brother away from me and didn't do a damn thing to stop them.

Time after time all she did was let me down, time after time all she did was put herself first. So why is it I feel so guilty? Why is it, as I stand here, all I can do is wonder what must people have thought of me not being present at my own mother's funeral? They must have thought I was a terrible daughter, that I was selfish and self-centred, that I was some kind of monster. Maybe they were right. Maybe I am. I'm a monster that loves its son more than anything else in the world. A monster that is prepared to do anything to make sure he's happy.

Out of nowhere, I start apologising to the headstone as if it's her. Even though I know it's nuts, I just do it anyway. I tell her I'm sorry, that from now on I'll be a good girl, that I'll do things differently if only she'll forgive me. But when she doesn't say anything back, the need to get on her good side disappears and a stream of loud and hateful abuse comes out of my mouth, and I almost scare myself. My last words to her are these: 'I'll never make the same mistakes as you. I'll always put my child first. Always.' And then I turn around and leave.

Kian acts like I've lost the plot when I hug the life out of him as he comes out of karate. He wriggles in my grasp like I'm trying to kill him, but I just can't help myself, I love him so much. I want to hold and kiss him forever and tell him how proud I am of him, so he's never in any doubt just how amazing he truly is. When he finally escapes my clutches, he demands to know what's wrong with me. 'You're acting like a nutter, Mum.'

He wants me to be embarrassed, but the huge grin on my face shows him that I'm anything but. 'A mum doesn't need an excuse to give her son a little cuddle every now and again,' I tell him, as his friends from karate look on. 'It's the law, I can do it any time I like.'

For lunch we have salmon because it's good for you, but Kian hates it and does nothing but moan.

'Why are we having boring food on a Saturday?' he whines. 'We always have nice food at the weekend.'

He's right of course, we do normally have 'nice' food at the weekend: sausages, burgers, fish fingers and the like. But I suppose I'm trying to make a point, to him, my mum and myself. I want him to know that being a good parent isn't easy. I want him to know that sometimes it involves having to make difficult decisions. I want him to know that life isn't always about giving those you love what they want, but what they need. And I'm trying to make this point through a piece of frozen salmon. Maybe I am losing my mind after all.

'It smells weird.' He curls up his nose at the food on his plate. 'And what's that white stuff coming out of it?'

His disgust is written all over his face; he doesn't get it and I'm not sure he ever will.

'It could have shooting stars coming out of it for all I care. You're eating it because it's healthy, and that's all the reason you're going to get.'

Sure enough, he does eat it all – not without making a right song and dance about it, mind – and only then do I let him leave the table.

Before now, people have said to me that my parenting style is a little bit old-fashioned and it is, I guess, especially when most parents these days seem to want to be their kid's best friend. But I know first-hand what it's like to have a parent who doesn't do their job properly. I know what it's like not knowing what life is going to bring from one day to the next, and do you know what? I'd sooner die than have any child of mine feel like that even for a single second. So if old-school is what they call me then yes, old-school is what I am.

Once Kian's cleared the table, I do the washing-up and then go and join him in the living room. He's sitting on the sofa, his face inches away from the laptop screen on the coffee table, watching the antics of boys old enough to know better playing video games on YouTube. He doesn't look at me once, even though I'm standing right next to him. Sometimes I worry how engrossed he gets in stuff. I mean, if there was a fire in the flat, would he even notice? But then again, he seems to get so much pleasure from the things he does, so much joy, that sometimes I wonder if the grin on his face will stay there forever. I suppose it's good to be able to get out of yourself every now and again.

It's good to be able to leave your problems behind, even if it is only for a short while. And that's partly why the very next thing I do is pick up my phone from the table, take it to my room and call Jodi, my oldest and closest friend in the world.

I was fifteen and had been in the care system for five whole years when Jodi arrived at the children's home where I lived. She was thirteen and a bit of a newbie at being in care, while I was two years older and something of an expert. Before Jodi, I'd found it quite hard to make friends and mostly kept myself to myself, but there was something about her I liked straight away. She was small, and thin, with light-brown skin and curly black hair. She was so shy she looked like she wouldn't say boo to a goose, whereas I was loud and angry and in trouble all the time. On paper we shouldn't have got on at all, but in reality it was love at first sight. She was wise and clever and daring, and made me laugh like nobody else. In no time at all we were best friends. Every day after school the first thing we'd do was catch up on each other's news: the highs, the lows and everything in between, and we'd make each other laugh, and encourage each other and promise to always be there for one another.

One of our favourite things to do was make plans for the future: what we'd do once we'd left care, what we'd do once we were free. Our plans went like this: when I turned eighteen I'd get a job and a flat but still see Jodi every day. Then when she turned eighteen she'd come and live with me and then later we'd get a bigger flat in west London. By day we'd work in cool clothes shops and use our staff discounts to buy each other presents and by night we'd go clubbing and chase boys. It was going to be brilliant, we were going to take over the world, maybe even get talent-spotted by Mariah along the way and become her backing singers. In reality it didn't really matter what happened, so long as we were together.

Of course, things didn't turn out anything like the way we planned. When I turned eighteen the social set me up with my own place and gave me some money to get myself sorted. That was it: I pretty much went mental and forgot all about Jodi. I started drinking loads, smoking loads and getting into stupid fights and arguments. I wasn't interested in getting a job and instead I spent all day every day shoplifting – clothes and make-up mostly – and then selling it on. One time I even nicked a car, though I'd never had a driving lesson in my life. It was madness really. I was completely out of control. I was just so angry, at the world, at social workers, at Mum. I didn't care what happened to me. All I cared about was having a good time.

By the time I finally did clean up my act I thought I'd lost contact with Jodi forever, but then Facebook happened, and it seemed that suddenly overnight you were only ever a click away from being reunited with everyone you'd ever lost touch with. She lives up north now, Newcastle-upon-Tyne to be precise, in a tiny three-bed terrace she shares with Mark, her fella, her kids from a previous relationship, Stacey and Mason, and her and Mark's two kids, Marley and Paige. Oh, and let's not forget two Staffies called Bo and Luke, and a hamster called Barry.

'Babes!!!!' screams Jodi at the top of her voice, in that weird Brixton/Geordie accent of hers. 'It's so good to hear your voice. How are ya?'

'All the better for being able to chat to you. Is now a good time?'

'For you, anytime is a good time. It feels like ages since we had a catch-up and I've got loads to tell you.'

And she's not joking either. She tells me about the nightmare next-door neighbours, Mark's mum's dementia, Mason's dyslexia, her worries that Stacey might have bulimia, problems with the younger kids' school and the ongoing saga of her fallen arches. And that's on top of an endless cycle of coughs, colds and ailments that all the younger kids have been through. I tell her it's almost as if every part of her life is like some mini drama, and all she does is laugh and say, 'And do you know what, Kez? I love this madhouse, and every time I think about moaning about my life, I remember Milread Road and think about how this is everything we missed out on.'

When it's my turn I don't know why exactly, but I don't tell her about the phone call. Partly it's because I know if I did, she'd drop everything like a shot and be with me, and I know she's already got enough on her plate. But mostly it's because I don't feel ready to talk about it yet. It's all still a bit too raw, too real. So instead I tell her about the small stuff that's going on in my life. About how Kian's getting on at school, ideas I'm thinking about for his birthday present and plans I've got to redecorate my bedroom. It's so lovely, having a good old gossip like this, to talk over everyday problems with a mate, knowing full well that the world's not going to fall apart even if we don't come up with any solutions. It feels safe being in the middle of a conversation like this, as if the real world is somewhere else, and couldn't get to me even if it tried, and once again I think about Kian in the next room with his face glued to the laptop. I want to stay here forever, my head resting on my pillow, and Jodi's voice in my ear.

Left to our own devices I'm sure we would've carried on chatting until midnight, but as it is we have to stop when Stacey yells that Marley has been sick all over the kitchen floor.

'And just like that the spell is broken,' laughs Jodi. 'I'm so sorry, babes. Maybe we can chat again later in the week?'

'That would be lovely. But don't you worry if you can't. I know how it is, you do what you've got to do, I'll be here whenever you're ready.'

Plugging my phone into the charger by my bedside table, I return to the living room, chase Kian off the laptop and tell him to go and find something else to do that doesn't involve staring at a screen. He pulls a face, and begs me for five more minutes but I tell him no, and while he's packing away I sort through the dirty clothes basket in the bathroom, take a load to the kitchen and start putting them into the washing machine. After Kian killed the last machine by leaving a ton of Lego figures in his pockets, I always check everything twice before it goes in. And while I don't find any Lego, I do fish out a pack of chewing gum, some football stickers and a handful of pebbles.

As I empty it all into a saucer on the draining board I find myself thinking about this morning. It feels like a dream, like it didn't happen. I visited Mum's grave, I touched her headstone with my own hands and I felt guilty for not being there when they put her in the ground. Next, I think about Jodi. About her crazy, messy, never-a-moment-to-herself life, and her home that's full to bursting. And then I think about my beautiful boy, growing up and changing with each passing day but still picking up random pebbles off the ground just because he likes the look of them.

I close the washing-machine door with a click and start the programme, and as the drum starts to fill with water I suddenly realise what needs to be done. Grabbing a pen from my bag and the posh writing-paper I'd bought a few years back from the drawer in the sideboard, I sit myself down at the kitchen table, take a deep breath and start writing a letter.

4

Noah

Wednesday, 2nd March

The judge is looking at me expectantly and I realise that I have no idea what she's just asked me. Searching for clues, I look across to Mr Lucas, my client in the dock accused of aggravated burglary, then at opposing counsel, and then finally, having managed to glean no valuable intelligence from either source, return my attention to The Right Honourable Lady Justice Peak.

'Your honour,' I begin. 'Please accept my most sincere apologies but might it be possible to hear your question again?'

Peering over the top of her glasses, she looks at me sternly. 'Well, Mr Martineau, within reason anything is perfectly possible but given that my diction throughout this morning's hearing has been nothing but precise I can only conclude that the problem lies with you.'

'Forgive me, your honour, but over the past few days I've been struggling with a severe ear infection, which has considerably reduced my ability to hear,' I say quickly, thinking on my feet.

To my relief, rather than reprimanding me for my failure to pay attention in court, Lady Justice Peak proceeds to recommend several home remedies for me to try, which have apparently worked wonders for her husband, Lord Chief Justice Peak, himself a martyr to glue ear.

Feeling slightly guilty about my feigned affliction, I scribble down each and every one of her recommendations and then, as I frantically check my notes trying to work out where I am, Lady Justice Peak finally repeats her question.

'For the benefit of those in court today suffering from

temporary hearing loss, my question, Mr Martineau, was this: Does counsel have any objection to the adjournment of these proceedings until tomorrow morning to allow the prosecution to make new arrangements for an interpreter for their next witness?'

I breathe a huge sigh of relief. 'No, your honour, I have no such objection.'

As I leave court, I remove my wig and upbraid myself for my lapse in concentration. Moments like this have been happening all week but this was by far the worst slip so far. I'm distracted, of this there is no doubt, and it's all because of Rosalind, or rather because of the problems between us.

It's been five days since she asked me to leave, and it's taken me all of this time to realise that this is not the temporary arrangement I'd believed it to be. I had thought that by moving out for a night or two and giving Rosalind a little breathing space I was paving the way for a road back to how we used to be. That by keeping my distance I'd not only demonstrate that I was taking her seriously, but also give her time to calm down. She couldn't want this to be a permanent separation, she just couldn't. Who in their right mind ends a perfectly good marriage just because of a blip like this? But I had thought that given a little time, a little patience, she would come to see that she had acted rashly, hadn't meant what she'd said and would see that in order to work things through we needed to be together. But having tried everything these past few days, having called, texted, and even emailed, I haven't been able to talk her into letting me move back in. It's as though having made up her mind, she's determined not to allow herself to have it changed. She wants the problem between us fixed once and for all and to do this she says she wants us to live separately and seek professional help. If I return home she wants it to be the beginning of a new era for us, not a continuation of the past. I can't believe any of this is happening. I can't believe that things can have got so out of hand quite so quickly. I can't believe that, tragic though it was, a miscarriage can have such far-reaching, devastating effects.

★

With my afternoon unexpectedly free I decide to take the opportunity to return home, albeit briefly. Right now Rosalind is at her studio, Millie at school, and by rights I should be in chambers but as I'm in court first thing tomorrow morning I'm in need of fresh clothes.

As I enter my home for the first time since moving out I feel a lot like a burglar, a sensation not alleviated by the fact that it's the middle of the day, the house is empty and in my right hand I'm carrying an empty holdall. Heading upstairs to the master bedroom, I go to my wardrobe, take out two suits, half a dozen ties and the same number of crisp white shirts and carefully pack them into my holdall. From the large antique chest of drawers next to it I take enough socks and underwear to last me a week, and then scan the room one final time to see if there's anything I've forgotten. That's when I catch sight of a silver-framed photograph lying face down on Rosalind's dressing table. Normally it lives on top of the chest of drawers and I can only assume that Rosalind has moved it because she's been looking at it closely, something I now feel compelled to do too. It's a black and white wedding photo taken just as we were leaving the church. The air around us is thick with confetti and we're both grinning from ear to ear.

I pick it up and sit down on the edge of the bed. We look so young, so happy, so utterly pleased at the prospect of spending the rest of our lives together that it's impossible not to wonder exactly how we've got from there to here: from being overwhelmed with happiness to this point only twelve years later where my wife has ejected me from the family home, leaving me to sleep on my sister's sofa without a clue as to how we're going to get through all this.

Rosalind and I met at a college ball during our first term at Oxford. I was studying law and she art history and within a few short moments of being introduced by mutual friends we were shamelessly flirting with one another. It wasn't just that she was beautiful, she was also completely and utterly open about every aspect of her life. Within an hour of being in her company she had not only told me when, where and with whom she'd lost her virginity (two years earlier, on a skiing holiday in France, to Édouard, her handsome ski instructor some five years her senior) but also that she had been treated in the past for depression and anorexia, was slightly deaf in one ear due to a childhood illness and the previous summer had been sexually assaulted by a boy who she had considered a friend. She was the very definition of an open book, a creature born without the compulsion to hide who they were or how they felt from those around them, and I could only wonder how it was that she had managed to survive in the world until that point.

In contrast to Rosalind's openness that night, I was the complete opposite. I barely told her anything about myself beyond my name, rank and number. I suppose, looking back, she must have mistaken my reticence for mystery and thought it romantic somehow, because in no time at all we were an item and we were blissfully happy together. And so it's been ever since. Throughout the course of our relationship we've hardly ever argued but if we do, it's only ever about this one aspect: my inability to share, to open up, to talk about my feelings.

Of course, it doesn't take a genius to work out that I am the way I am because I'm adopted. The fact that my life had undergone such a dramatic change so early on couldn't have failed to impact me, even if I can't remember anything about it. To take a child in its formative years out of one family situation and drop it into another is clearly going to influence how that child develops. For an infant to experience such upheaval at such a key stage is bound to shape them in some way, even more so as it grows up and discovers the truth. The knowledge that the people who were supposed to love you unconditionally, to protect you, to care for you, blithely relinquished their responsibilities is indeed a weighty burden to bear, even for the most balanced of individuals.

I know all this and more, and yet awareness that an issue exists is not in itself a solution. At some point in my childhood I must have made a decision to turn my back on the past, and instead turn my focus completely to the present. And I suppose over the years it's become a survival mechanism of sorts, one I'm so accustomed to employing that now, as an adult, it's part of who I am. Unlike Rosalind I can't see the value of dwelling in the past. I can't see how spending time there would help anybody. As the only thing I can have any influence on is my present and my future, that is where I direct all my energies. And while this works for me, I understand that for someone like my wife, someone whose understanding of the world and her place in it comes from doing the opposite, my way of being isn't just a mystery, I'm sure at times it can be rather hurtful. But what can I do? How can I possibly unlearn everything I've spent a lifetime teaching myself?

It was the week before finals when Rosalind discovered that she was pregnant with Millie. Of course, it wasn't what we'd planned but somehow it just felt right and so we married that same summer. Shortly afterwards we found ourselves in the very privileged position of being able to buy our home in Primrose Hill using a combination of money Rosalind had inherited from her great-uncle and a small loan from my parents. Millie was born the following January and this new life, this family we'd become was everything we'd hoped it would be and so much more. For the most part we were happy, really happy, but from time to time the old argument would resurface.

Over the years I've tried to address this problem. I've read books, digested articles and even listened to the well-being podcasts Rosalind has suggested. For a short while I saw an actual human being, a counsellor, one to one, just me and a funky grandfatherly figure with white hair and frameless Scandinavian-style spectacles sitting in the front room of a large house in a residential street in Kentish Town. For six consecutive weeks I spent an excruciating hour talking about myself in an attempt to locate what he described as 'the missing part of me'. But after those six sessions I gave up because Rosalind felt that it had made things worse not better, that I was drifting further away from her not closer. So I stopped going, and things went back to normal, or so I thought. But then the miscarriage happened and everything started falling apart.

The letterbox rattling downstairs, followed by the sound of the post landing on the doormat, suddenly breaks the spell and standing up, I put the photograph back exactly where I'd found it, pick up my holdall and hurry guiltily from the room.

Descending the stairs, I make my way to the front door, scoop up the pile of letters from the doormat and sort through them, exchanging those addressed to Rosalind with the few addressed to me on the antique side table. Zipping away my post in the large side pocket of my holdall, I take in my surroundings one last time and as I step out into the thin spring sunlight and pull the door closed behind me, I can't help wondering when or indeed if I'll be allowed to return.

Later that evening, following an afternoon spent in chambers preparing my opening argument for court the next day, I return to my sister Charlotte's mansion flat in leafy Hampstead.

'You were a while coming up,' she says as I enter the room with my holdall and case files. 'I was beginning to think I hadn't buzzed you in properly when you didn't appear. Where have you been all this time?'

'I ran into a neighbour of yours,' I explain. 'Old-ish woman, probably in her late sixties, violently red hair, speaks with a bit of an accent. She gave me a real grilling, and insisted on knowing who I was visiting and how long I was staying.'

Charlotte throws back her head and lets out her trademark deep, rich laugh. 'That'll be Mrs Mazur, or The Maz as I like to call her. She's already quizzed me several times about you but I remained irritatingly elusive because I'd already heard from my friend Ally, at number five, that The Maz thinks I've taken a "brown gentleman" as a lover.'

I have two siblings: Phillip, who is a tax lawyer and lives in Hong Kong with his wife Cassie and their two small children, Emily and Arthur; and Charlotte, who is a professor of Medieval and Early Modern History, and the author of a highly regarded biography of Martin Luther. Of the three of us, I'm the youngest and Phillip the eldest.

When I turned up at Charlotte's flat on Saturday morning she didn't grill me for information as she knows how I am. Instead all she said was, 'You can stay as long as you like,' and then she gave me a huge hug and offered me a glass of wine. It took me two days before I felt able to explain to her what had happened and even then I didn't go into detail. Having been through marriage difficulties herself, however, which sadly ended in divorce, Charlotte didn't offer any advice, unsolicited or otherwise. All she said was that whenever I was ready to talk, she was ready to listen.

Filling a kettle, Charlotte continues to make jokes at her neighbour's expense. She has something of a dry sense of humour and for reasons of her own amusement has always liked to leave people guessing about the true nature of our relationship. In her teens she reasoned that just because she was a plump, short blonde with pale skin and green eyes and I, a tall skinny seven-year-old boy with coffee-coloured skin and dark-brown eyes, this didn't give strangers the right to ask questions that she considered both ignorant and rude. Those who asked about me soon regretted having done so, especially when she informed them with all seriousness that I was her son. Both then and now, Charlotte has always been my champion.

For supper Charlotte makes a large bowl of pasta with salad and as we sit down to eat, she opens a bottle of red and tells me about her day at work, taking great pleasure in regaling me with tales of the interdepartmental feuds and extramarital indiscretions of academic life. Her conversation makes me feel at ease and allows me, at least for a short while, to stop thinking about how much I miss Rosalind and Millie.

Later, after we've cleared up, we decide we could both do with another drink and head to the Oak Tavern, a pub less than a ten-minute walk from the flat. Two glasses of Merlot deep into our conversation, Charlotte reveals that Mum has been asking after me again.

'You didn't say anything though, did you?'

Charlotte laughs. 'Of course not! I may be an academic but I do have some degree of common sense. She was worried because you haven't been returning her calls and she's desperate to re-arrange that Sunday lunch you cancelled. I told her I'd spoken to you and that you were busy at work, so that should buy you some time before she sends out a search party.'

I breathe a sigh of relief. 'I know I've got to tell her sometime but I just can't face it at the moment. Hopefully things will sort themselves out sooner rather than later and there will be no need for Mum or Dad to know anything about this.'

Charlotte takes a sip from her glass. 'When's your first coun-selling session?'

I shrug. 'I don't know yet. Rosalind's still sorting it out.'

'And how are you feeling about it?'

A second shrug follows the first. 'To be honest, I'm trying not to think about it. You know I don't have much faith in counsel-ling but I'm just hoping against hope it does the trick this time.'

'I wish that Bill and I had had counselling,' she says wistfully. 'I actually looked into it but he absolutely refused to go. I suppose that should have told me all I needed to know: he wasn't inter-ested in sorting out the problem, he just wanted to get out of our marriage as fast as he could so that he could be with her.' She takes another sip of her drink and raises her glass. 'Well done you, for agreeing to try. At the very least, I'm sure Rosalind will appreciate the gesture.'

It's late when we finally decide to return to the flat and Charlotte is more than a little merry as we make our way home. While I'd stopped at two glasses, Charlotte has put away several more during the course of the evening and though she is a sweet and highly amusing drunk, I am more than a little worried that she is back to her old habits. Although she puts on a brave face, I can see how lonely she is, and drinking is her way of coping.

I know if I say anything, she'll laugh it off and tell me I'm worrying about nothing, because that's exactly what happened when she was going through her divorce. Thankfully then she eventually got her drinking under control by herself and I'm hoping this time she'll do the same.

Back at the flat, I make her a coffee to help her sober up a little but she's fast asleep in the armchair before she's even taken a sip. When I wake her up to try to coax her to go to bed, she looks at me and in a moment of clarity says, 'Do you remember how even when you were small you used to pretend that everything was okay even when it wasn't? You thought you could hide how you felt but I always used to know, didn't I? You never could hide anything from me.'

I help her into bed, then brush my teeth at the kitchen sink and make up the sofa bed in her study-cum-spare room as quietly as I can. As I lie underneath the duvet I stare at the ceiling, listening to the sound of passing traffic and far-off police sirens. Despite my best efforts, however, sleep doesn't come and, if the past few nights are anything to go by, won't arrive for a good few hours more. Switching on the lamp next to me, I reach into my holdall for my case notes but then recall the post I picked up from home and opt for that instead. Most of it is junk, offers from estate agents to value our home, invitations to receive new credit cards, and brochures for exotic holidays, but among it all is a small blue handwritten envelope that stands out a mile from the rest. My curiosity piqued, I tear it open. I have to read through the letter inside three times before it makes any kind of sense to me, and even then I'm still not fully convinced that it does. 'Dear Mr Martineau,' it begins. 'My name is Kerry Hayes and although you may not be aware of this, I am your sister.'

5

Kerry

Thursday, 3rd March

From the minute I woke up it's like everything that could go wrong did. First I overslept because I forgot to set my alarm, then the car wouldn't start because the battery was dead and so I had to talk some bloke I'd never spoken to before into giving me a jump-start, then because of that I was late dropping Kian off at school, so not only did I have to find somewhere to park (nearly impossible at that time of the day) but I also had to sign him in at the school office and get a telling-off from Mrs Curtis, his school's witch of a secretary. Then for no reason at all it was like every road in west London was completely gridlocked. By the time I got to my first job of the day at the Singhs', I was already running an hour and a half behind and I was in such a fluster that I ended up setting off their alarm. And could I remember what the code was to turn it off? Of course I couldn't, even though I've been cleaning for them for a good five years. In the end I had to call Mrs Singh, a dental surgeon, up at work and ask her for it. I felt like such an idiot! She was lovely about it, and told me that she forgets it all the time but still, I felt so stupid and just couldn't apologise enough.

Now I'm just finishing off at Mrs Ryman's. She's a lovely old dear and one of my favourite clients, which is why, along with cleaning her house twice a week, I also do her shopping and run errands for her whenever I can. She's as posh as you like but somehow down to earth with it and although she's in her eighties and her neatly cut bobbed hair is pure white, she holds herself ramrod straight. What's more, even though her arthritis means she doesn't get about much, that doesn't stop her from dressing as if she's still going out to work every day – smart blouses, tailored skirts and the like. I've never seen her dressed down; in fact I'm not sure she even owns anything you might call casual.

Her house is lovely, Victorian with all high ceilings and original features, but not in some poncey decorating-magazine type of way. She told me once she was actually born in this house and she's never been one for knocking things about. She's just loved it and looked after it and it shows, even though she can't do as much herself any more as she'd like.

I give the sink in her main bathroom a final wipe round, then breathe a huge sigh of relief as I chuck the cloth in the bucket with the rest of my cleaning gear. For a while there I wasn't sure I was going to get everything done before picking up Kian, but I've managed it somehow. There's plenty of time to spare and at this rate I might even be able to do a bit of shopping before I get him too.

Collecting together my cleaning stuff, I go downstairs, load it all into the back of the car and then just as I'm about to head back inside to find Mrs Ryman to say goodbye, my phone rings. It's my bank. Apparently my credit card has been cloned and some git has spent two and a half thousand pounds on it. It's as if I suddenly realise I can't take any more and in seconds I'm proper sobbing. The next thing I know, Mrs Ryman is standing in front of me. She puts her hand gently on my shoulder.

'Oh, my poor dear,' she says. 'Whatever's wrong?'

I take one look at her lovely kind face, so full of concern, and it just makes me want to cry even more. Before I can say anything, she's giving me a hug and leading me back into the house. She sits me down at the kitchen table, presses a sheet of kitchen roll in my hand, and tells me that she's going to make us both a cup of tea. By the time she sets mine down in front of me, I feel a bit calmer but embarrassed that she's seen me in a state like this.

'I'm so sorry, Mrs Ryman.' I wrap my hands around the mug for comfort. 'You must think I'm a right idiot.'

'Nonsense, dear,' she says, 'we all need a little cry sometimes.

When I worked at the Foreign Office I used to regularly take myself off to the stationery cupboard for a little sob before getting back on the job. I think a good cry is like a safety valve: it releases the pressure before it builds up. I'm sure if some of the chaps I worked with had done that, then there would've been quite a few less whisky bottles stuffed at the back of departmental filing cabinets. Now, come on, tell me what the matter is.'

I sniff and wipe my nose on the folded kitchen roll. 'It's a long story.' I take a sip of my tea. 'I don't know where to start.'

Mrs Ryman smiles. 'Well, I don't want to be funny but I usually find that the beginning is the best place.'

I'm not sure what to do for the best. I'm quite a private person really. I like to keep myself to myself, but I don't want to lie to Mrs Ryman because she's so lovely. Then again, I don't want to tell her the full truth either. I don't want her knowing the ins and outs of everything – to be honest, sometimes I wish I didn't know myself – so I'm going to have to pick and choose what I tell her, to gloss over when gloss is what's needed.

'I suppose it's all to do with my brother,' I begin. 'Well, I suppose he's my half-brother, if you want to be technical about it. We've got the same mum, but different dads. But that's never mattered to me, to me he's just my baby brother Jason, and before Kian came along . . . well . . . I don't think I'd loved anyone more in the entire world.' Feeling vulnerable, I pause and take another sip of tea, not sure if I should say anything more, but Mrs Ryman nods at me encouragingly. 'I was eight when Jason was born. Growing up I'd always wanted a little brother or sister and so from the moment he came along my dolls and teddies didn't get a look-in. He was lovely, really smiley, and he was so loving too. Of course, he loved Mum, but I was definitely his favourite. I knew exactly how to get him off to sleep, how to cheer him up and stop him crying. Didn't matter what time of day or night, I was there for him. Mum used to call me her little helper.'

'I'm sure you were an enormous support to her, as you are to me,' says Mrs Ryman with a smile.

I grip my cup of tea tightly in my hands. 'The thing was,

though, Mum had problems. My dad wasn't in the picture and neither was Jason's, and she didn't really get on with my nan and granddad so basically everything that needed doing was down to her, and she found it hard. Long story short, after a while she found she couldn't look after us any more and Jason and I got taken into care.'

Mrs Ryman puts her hand on my arm. 'Oh, my dear, that's dreadfully sad. How old were you?'

'Ten,' I reply, 'and Jason was coming up to two. The thing is, if we'd been allowed to stay together it might not have been so bad, but we weren't. They either couldn't or didn't want to find us a place together, so to start with we were put in separate foster homes. For weeks I begged and screamed for them to let me see him but they wouldn't even tell me where he was. Well, I was just a little kid so I didn't have any choice but to accept that this was the way things were. I felt so guilty about it. Absolutely awful. It was my job to keep him safe.'

'Oh, Kerry, you mustn't blame yourself. As you said, you were just a child, powerless to do anything else. Still, it must have had a tremendous effect on you.'

'It did. It made me very angry for a very long time. In the end, I either ran away or got kicked out of so many foster placements that they eventually gave up on me and dumped me in a children's home.'

'And how was that? You hear such dreadful things about those places.'

I spare her the gory details of Milread Road: the kids off their faces on cheap drugs, the girls getting involved with blokes twice their age and ending up pregnant at thirteen, the constant screaming arguments, police visits and slamming doors.

'For all its faults, I actually preferred it. At least in the home no one pretended to be my family. That's what used to really set me off back then. "I've already got one family," I used to tell them. "I don't need another." Anyway, the home was fine, the people there were okay and over time I even made a couple of good friends, but I never forgot about Jason. Not for a second.

I thought about him all the time and I told myself one day we'd be together again, one day I'd find him.'

'No small task, I imagine,' says Mrs Ryman. 'Where would you even begin?'

'Well, I figured Jason must have been adopted – he was so cute, always smiling, so he must have been snapped up by some nice family or other. But the thing is, once kids get adopted it's a nightmare of red tape, which I found out when I turned eighteen. I got in touch with social services and they pointed me in the direction of the Adoption Contact Register. They said that even though I was his sister, they couldn't tell me anything, the only thing I could do was leave them my details and if Jason ever contacted them wanting to know about his birth family, they'd pass them to him. But of course, I was eighteen and he was only ten, so the chances of that happening any time soon were non-existent. Even so, whenever I moved flats the first thing I did before I unpacked a single thing was write to the Adoption Contact Register with my new details. I used to write letters to him as well, telling him what I was up to so that he'd always know I was still thinking about him. I got really excited the year he turned eighteen because I knew he was practically a man, and I convinced myself that he'd come looking for me. But even though I carried on writing my letters, I never heard a word from him. Not when he turned eighteen, twenty-one, or even twenty-five.'

Mrs Ryman gently touches my hand again. 'You poor, poor thing,' she says. 'I had no idea.'

I blow my nose on the piece of kitchen roll again, and give her a small smile. 'Well, it's not the sort of thing you like to broadcast, is it?'

Mrs Ryman smiles. 'I suppose not.'

'Well anyway, recently something happened and it's made me think about family and how important it is and so I decided that I didn't want to sit around waiting for him to get in touch a minute longer. I wasn't sure how to start looking for him. I even wrote into that TV show where they reunite long-lost relatives but I never heard anything back. So then – you'll never believe this – I actually hired a private detective like they do on the telly. Looked one up on the Internet, made an appointment and went to see him. I could've died when he told me how much he wanted to charge to find Jason. There was no way I could have afforded it on the money I earn, so thinking on my feet, I made him an offer: six months free office cleaning in exchange for Jason's address. It only took him a week to find my brother. He said it would've been quicker but apparently he's changed his name. He isn't Jason Hayes any more, he's called Noah Martineau.'

Mrs Ryman raises her eyebrows. 'My goodness, what a story!'

'And that's not the end of it,' I say. 'My baby brother is now this posh barrister type with a massive house in north London. He's married too and he's even got a daughter. Can you believe it? I've got a niece out there I've never met.'

'That's all very lovely,' says Mrs Ryman. 'There's a "but" coming though, isn't there?'

I nod, and take a swig of tea. 'To cut a long story short, I wrote to him on Sunday. I explained who I was, how I wanted to meet him and gave him all my contact details. I even pushed it through his front door myself just to make sure it didn't get lost in the post. But it's Thursday now, four days since I sent him the letter and I haven't heard a word. That can't be right, can it? Who gets a letter from their long-lost sister and doesn't answer straight away?'

Mrs Ryman squeezes my hand. 'You poor girl. No wonder you're in such a state. But there could be any number of reasons for him not having contacted you yet. It's only been a few days after all, and if he's a successful barrister as you say, he may well have to travel for work. He and his family could even be away on holiday.'

'But they're not,' I say. 'I checked first thing this morning. I called his office pretending to be his cleaner and they told me he was in a meeting.'

'Still, that doesn't mean he doesn't want to meet you. Given what you've told me he might not even know he was adopted, let alone that he has a half-sister. He may simply be still digesting what he's learned. It could just be a question of giving him time.'

Time.

I put my head in my hands, running my fingers through my hair.

'But how long?' I ask after a while. 'How long should I wait? It's torture. I want to believe he'll get in touch, Mrs Ryman, really I do, but I can't help thinking he's just not interested. That he doesn't care. That all he wants is to leave the past in the past.'

Still holding my hand, Mrs Ryman takes a deep breath and sits up straight. 'I know I'm just a silly old woman now but I have been around for a long time and if there's anything I've learned, it's that the past rarely stays buried for long. I've always found that things have a habit of coming to the fore. Don't give up hope, Kerry. I'm sure your brother has very fond memories of you, even though he was so young when you were separated. You never forget a love like that, no matter how long it's been. He will contact you, I'm certain of it, you just have to hold on a little while longer.'

6

Noah

Friday, 4th March

As I watch the sharp shadow of concern fall across Mum's face,
I can't help recalling how difficult she'd found Charlotte's divorce.
For Mum it's not just important that all her children are happy,
it's vital.

'But it's not over, is it?'

'Of course not.' In an effort to reassure her, I make myself
sound considerably more optimistic than I actually feel. 'It's just
a bit of a hiccup, that's all. We're working on it and we'll get
through it.'

'Of course you will,' says Dad, speaking for the first time.
'These things happen but I know you two will get it sorted.
There's simply too much at stake not to.'

'How's Millie holding up? Does she know what's going on?'

I nod and think back to yesterday, Rosalind and me standing
in front of our tearful daughter attempting to explain that although
I'd moved out, it was only a temporary measure, that her mother
and I were working on solving our problems, that I would be
back home soon.

Mum lifts her hand to her mouth, stifling a deeper outpouring
of emotion. 'Oh, poor Millie,' she says after a moment. 'Is there
anything your father and I can do at all? We could have her for
the weekend, if you'd like. It would give you and Rosalind a
chance to talk. Patch things up.'

'Thanks, Mum,' I say, 'but for now we just want to keep things
as normal as we possibly can for Millie. But I promise I'll bring
her for that Sunday lunch we spoke about soon. She'd like that,

I'm sure.' Keen to shift the focus away from my crumbling relationship, I attempt to change the subject. 'Anyway, how are you both? How's your research coming on, Dad?'

My father allegedly took early retirement some years ago, although you'd be hard-pressed to notice. As well as continuing to mark undergraduate exams and taking the occasional seminar group in the English department that he was once head of, he is also working on the second volume of his biography of Jonathan Swift.

'Oh, you know,' he says, sounding very pleased with himself. 'It's like the man himself says, "When a true genius appears in this world, you may know him by this sign, that the dunces are all in confederacy against him."'

Mum looks at me pointedly, no doubt having heard this rant several times today already.

'Which dunces are we talking about this time?' I enquire. Barely a week goes by when my father isn't at war with some academic or other, and growing up I learned quickly that the best thing to do when he embarked upon one of his rants was to look equally outraged and then make a hasty exit.

'Wells has produced another of his ridiculous papers calling into question some of my assertions about Swift,' says Dad. 'Not to worry though, I have a rebuttal in progress that will knock his argument into a cocked hat.'

I turn back to Mum. She's still wearing the same look of concern she'd had when I broke the news to her about Rosalind and me. 'And how about you, Mum? How's that landscape you were working on last time I was here?'

Mum frowns, but at least she's stopped looking worried. 'Oh, that old thing,' she says offhandedly. 'Not finished yet, I'm afraid. There is just something wrong about it. I've gone back to still life for the time being. There's something splendidly therapeutic about spending an afternoon staring at a pomegranate. I'll show you some of them after supper, if you like.'

These are my parents. Geoffrey and Margaret Martineau. Dad is half French but can't cook to save his life. Mum was born and raised in Islington and with the exception of three years spent at Cambridge (where they met) has only ever lived within the M25. They both came from very comfortable middle-class backgrounds: Dad's father was a banker while Mum's was the headmaster of a small private school in St John's Wood. My parents married soon after they graduated from university and a year later my brother Phillip was born, followed eighteen months later by my sister Charlotte. After two children of their own they decided to adopt me because, in their eyes, it wasn't just the right thing to do but the only thing to do. In addition to having opened their home to a complete stranger, my parents regularly give considerable amounts to charity, are so concerned about the future of the planet that they sold their car and donated the proceeds to Greenpeace, and now they're retired and seem to have more going on than ever they still somehow find time to volunteer twice a week at a local homeless shelter. And while Dad can be quite pompous at times and Mum more than a little scatty, they are both undoubtedly the very definition of good people, which makes it all the more difficult to believe the assertion that for the past thirty-two years they have effectively been lying to me.

Even now, it's impossible to fully describe the range of emotions I felt upon reading the letter from the woman claiming to be my half-sister. It just seemed too fantastical to take seriously. Strange though it sounds, I'd never once imagined the possibility. If I thought about my early life at all, I'd always imagined that I was an only child, that I was a mistake, a one-off, a lesson to be learned from, not part of a bigger family, or a more complicated story. And yet here was a new proposition, one I'd never explored, and it felt bizarre and unsettling to countenance it.

The author of the letter told me that her name was Kerry Hayes and she was my half-sister. Not only did she know the precise time and location of my birth (2.22 p.m. on 8th September 1982, at Hammersmith Hospital), but she also made reference to my birth name (Jason Lewis Hayes) and the date I was taken into care (23rd March 1984). She then went on to conclude her missive with the hope that having tracked me down we might meet in person as soon as possible, furnishing me with not only a mobile phone number and a landline number but an email address too.

As I sat up late into the night reading and rereading the letter in Charlotte's sitting room, I reasoned that it had to be some sort of scam. After all, my parents had always striven to be open and honest with me about my adoption. From as far back as I could remember they had told me I was special because they had chosen me. They used to call me their 'little gift'. And when anyone seemed surprised or chose to remark upon the colour of my skin, my parents' response was always a very swift affirmation that I was very much their son, and anyone who didn't like it wasn't welcome in their home. Whether or not this closing down of any questions from outsiders had an impact on me growing up I'm not sure, but I'd never felt the need to press them about the circumstances surrounding my adoption, or indeed the details of my life before they'd taken me in. The little I knew was borne out partly by the letter: I'd come into the world as Jason Lewis Hayes in south London and was indeed taken into care in March 1984. But these facts could've been discovered from my birth certificate or social work files, and certainly didn't in themselves verify the story put forward by the letter in my hand.

That night I did a lot of thinking about this other life of mine, the one about which I had no recollection. I wondered about the parents who had given me life only to hand me over to strangers and, of course, about this woman claiming to be my blood relative. Growing up I'd often look in the mirror and wonder which of my birth parents I resembled, whose temperament I'd inherited, as my siblings were quite clearly my parents' birth children. Charlotte shares my mother's build and colouring and Phillip is a carbon copy of my grandfather on Dad's side. He's tall and thin, with striking blue eyes which are somewhat undermined by the hawklike nose of Dad's forebears. And then there was me, part white, part black, light-brown skin, dark curly hair and an athletic frame, looking nothing at all like any of the people I called family.

Despite these differences, I'd always been happy being a Martineau. I had loving parents, wonderful siblings, and the best start in life any child could ask for. And even before I fully understood what being adopted actually meant, I was conscious on some level that I was lucky, that things could have been different, that this life I had been blessed with was somehow better than the one I had left behind. But now that security I'd once enjoyed felt as insubstantial as smoke. I was no longer certain what was real and what wasn't. Given that my parents were so open with me about my adoption, why wouldn't they tell me the truth about my sister? What else would I discover if I started digging deeper? What would my siblings think if I agreed to meet with this woman who claimed to be my sister? And if this woman wasn't telling the truth, what was it exactly she hoped to gain by peddling such a lie? I needed answers not questions, which is why the very first thing I did the following morning was arrange a visit to my parents in Islington, hoping to kill two birds with one stone: tell them about Rosalind and uncover the truth about my past.

While Mum makes some final adjustments to our meal, Dad puts some Mahler on the stereo and begins to lay the dining table. All offers of help from me are cordially declined and so as Mum cooks, I stand next to her at the stove and catch up on family news. She tells me about her most recent conversation with Phillip that took place only yesterday. Apparently he's well but working too hard, Cassie is getting homesick for the Monmouth countryside where she grew up and the children are getting taller by the second. Mum misses them a lot, and I know she wishes they were closer but accepts that they have to live where they do for work at the moment.

When Mum announces that supper is ready, I hang my jacket on the back of my chair and instinctively take out my phone and turn the sound off. During the second six of my pupillage I once forgot to turn my phone off in court and the roasting I received from the judge when it rang was so fierce that eleven years later it's still vivid in my memory. Suffice it to say, it has never happened since.

As I flick the switch at the side of the handset I notice I've missed a call from Millie. Not wanting to be any more absent from her life than I already am, I excuse myself from the table and call her back from the hallway. Her line rings out several times before going to voicemail. I leave a message asking her to call me back and for a moment I think about going back in to eat with my parents, but then, though I know she's safely at home, I feel that need, the need that every parent has, to double-check, to be sure.

I dial the landline, aware that there's a fifty-fifty chance Rosalind will answer the phone. We haven't spoken directly since I left. Every necessary conversation, every arrangement, so far has been made in a functional fashion by text. Not to worry, I tell myself as the phone rings, Rosalind almost never answers the house phone.

'Hello.'

It's her. For a moment I consider hanging up like some schoolboy prankster. Aside from the fact that it would only be a matter of pressing a couple of buttons to find out that it was me who had called, I remind myself that I am an adult, she is my wife and in spite of everything we still love one another.

'It's me. Sorry to ring like this but I had a missed call from Mills and when I rang back she didn't answer. Everything okay?'

She lets out a groan of annoyance. 'That girl! I told her to wait until I'd had the chance to talk to you but she never listens. The forms are out for the hockey team's tour. It's to Canada of all places and Mills is desperate to go despite the fact that she's missed the last three practices because she wasn't sure hockey and her were and I quote, "a good fit".'

I laugh in spite of myself. After having to break the bad news about Rosalind and me to Millie, it's good to be talking about something ordinary, something less emotionally charged for a change.

'That sounds so like her. Well, whatever you think is best, I'll back you up.'

'Thanks.'

There's a pause, and suddenly the ease of the last few moments disappears, only to be replaced by awkwardness and uncertainty.

'How are you? How are things at Charlotte's?'

'Fine, I think she's glad of the company, to be honest. I'm at Mum and Dad's at the moment, just for supper. They send their love.'

There's another pause and then she says, 'So you've told them?'

'Only in the vaguest of terms. All I've said is that we're having a bit of a tough time but we're working things out.' And then with more than a degree of hopefulness in my voice I say, 'That's right, isn't it?'

'Of course it is,' she says, making an effort to sound upbeat. 'In fact while I've got you, how does a week on Wednesday sound for our first counselling session?'

'Perfect.' Even if it isn't, I'll move things around.

'Good,' she says, 'I'll text you the details and so I guess I'll see you then.'

I think once again about all the things I'd wanted to tell her when I saw her last: about my strange letter, how confused I am and how much I miss her. 'Yes, see you Wednesday.'

Mum has always been an amazing cook, but of late she's taken to being a little more experimental with her flavours and the Moroccan dish she's served up is out of this world. At least I think so. Dad, however, fishes out any apricots he comes across and leaves them untouched at the edge of his plate, as if to make it clear that in his opinion fruit should only ever make an appearance at the dining table unadorned or, at the very least, encased in short-crust pastry and served with cream.

Later, when the meal is over, the table cleared and we've all retired to the sitting room, it occurs to me that now might be the right time to ask my big question. No matter how hard I try, however, I can't quite bring myself to do it. Instead I find myself mulling the whole situation over again. What if asking this question makes my parents angry or leaves them thinking me ungrateful? What then? And anyway, even if they hadn't exactly told me the whole truth about my past, what did it matter? It wasn't as if I'd ever been all that interested myself. Whenever they'd raised the subject of my adoption, I'd always shut down the subject straight away. I was desperate not to have what I felt was the most embarrassing conversation possible with my parents of all people. Growing up, whenever anyone tried to speak to me about my being adopted, all I did was shut down the conversation immediately. I didn't want to talk about it, I didn't want to examine my feelings, all I wanted was to get on with my life.

'Mum . . . Dad . . . would you mind if I asked you both a question?'

The words sound strange on my lips as I finally force them out into the open. As a barrister I've lost count of the times I've had to ask difficult questions in court, about sexual preferences, about moments of intense intimacy, about things people would much rather have kept hidden. Not once in my entire career have I baulked at doing so. Yet here I am, a grown man, a practising barrister, struggling to ask my own parents a question.

My odd behaviour grabs both their attention and refuses to let go. Dad stops his searching through endless shelves of CDs and looks at me expectantly. Mum stops flicking through the canvasses she's brought in to show me and fixes a full beam gaze on me.

'What's wrong, darling?' she asks. 'Is it something more to do with you and Rosalind?'

'No, nothing like that.' I pause, wondering briefly if she thinks I'm about to confess to having had an affair, and then consider how easy this would be to do compared to what I have planned. 'It's nothing really, I . . .'

I stop, unsure of how to proceed. I don't want to tell them about the letter, at least not until I know more. So for now I need them to believe that I'm asking because . . . well . . . because I've had what . . . a personality transplant? That's the very least they're going to need to hear, in order to believe for a single moment that I'm asking this question out of mild curiosity. I need something better, something more concrete. Something credible.

'Well, with everything that's been going on lately it's made me do a lot of thinking about life, about my past . . . about my adoption . . . about who I am.'

I feel terrible using the state of my marriage as a disguise, like this. It feels awful and cynical. But it's all I've got.

'Go on,' says Mum. 'We're listening. What exactly would you like to know?'

'Well . . . it's going to seem like a bit of an odd question: I know one of my parents was white and the other black but which was which? Someone asked me this the other day and it seemed strange to confess that I didn't know.'

While it's true that a mixed-race clerk at Woolwich Crown Court had actually asked me this a few weeks ago, the only reason I am bringing it up now is because it's a seemingly innocuous question that will lull them into a false sense of security. Hopefully they won't notice the significance of the question I really want an answer to. It's a classic technique, one that I use in court all the time and which I'm now employing on my parents. It's offical: I'm a terrible person.

Just as I hoped, Mum visibly relaxes. 'I believe your birth father was black,' she says matter-of-factly, 'and your mother white. That's right, isn't it, Geoffrey?'

Dad nods and seems more at ease too. 'I believe so, such a long time ago though, that it's hard to recall. I'm sure we could have a little dig around and see what that throws up.'

'That would be great,' I say. 'It's such a basic question. I felt quite odd not knowing.'

'Of course,' says Mum. 'It's only natural. To be honest, your father and I have always hoped you'd be more curious about your past but you never seemed to want to talk about it. Anyway, we're both more than happy to answer whatever you'd like to know, although I must say we never had a great deal of information ourselves. Back then social workers rather liked to keep you in the dark about things.'

'Thanks,' I say, 'that's it for now . . . although . . . now I think about it, I do have another question. You probably won't know the answer but: do you know whether my birth parents had any other children besides me? I expect they didn't, given what happened, but . . .'

As I deliberately leave my sentence unfinished, my parents' faces switch from open to uncomfortable in an instant. Mum shifts in her seat while Dad moves his weight on to the balls of his feet nervously. Something's not right here, something's not right at all.

Mum looks at Dad anxiously. 'We always said we'd tell him if he asked, didn't we, Geoffrey?'

'True,' says Dad. 'Although I feel it's important to make it clear that it wasn't actually our decision . . .' He corrects himself. 'Well, of course, ultimately I suppose it was . . . but in our defence we were simply going on the advice of the professionals at the time. Advice we didn't feel confident to go against.'

I feel myself getting impatient. 'Of course, Dad, I understand. They were different times. I am just curious, that's all.'

He casts one last forlorn look in Mum's direction, as if checking for permission, and she gives him a barely perceptible nod. He clears his throat. 'Yes,' he says. 'As far as we know you do have a sister.'

7

Kerry

Monday, 7th March

I'm usually quite a morning person. I like nothing more than pottering about while everything's nice and quiet and Kian's still fast asleep in bed. It's my little bit of peace, time to get my head together before I'm catapulted into the day proper. But today is different. When the alarm screeches at me at six o'clock sharp, I feel like I've been woken from the dead. I can't believe it's time to get up already. All I want to do is roll over, close my eyes and go back to sleep.

I haven't been sleeping well for quite a while now, but last night was the absolute worst. I'd already had a long soak in the bath *and* a mug of warm milk beforehand, and because they say that blue-light stuff can affect your sleep, I didn't even touch my phone, but as soon my head hit the pillow, next-door started up with their music again and that was it, I was awake.

It's a Somali family next door, the mum and dad are lovely but they both work late and their kids are complete tearaways. I banged on the wall as usual but they just ignored me, so I had to get out of bed, put my dressing gown on and go round there. To start with they gave me a bit of lip, but by the time I'd finished tearing into them they were practically in tears. Of course, when I got back to the flat I was too wound up to sleep, but too tired to read. I just lay there in the dark with my thoughts.

In the dark everything seems so much worse than it really is; even the smallest thing seems like a mountain you've got to climb. I tried to tell myself that I was just tired, blowing things out of all proportion, and that everything would seem better in the morning, but what use is that when the morning's so far away? In the middle of the night, waiting for daylight feels like forever, a forever where you're stuck going over every bad thought in your head with a fine-tooth comb.

I kept thinking how everything would be so much better if only I'd heard from my brother. But it had been over a week now, without so much as a text or a call. *So that's that*, I told myself. *He's not interested. He doesn't care. He doesn't want to know you. You're in this on your own.*

I must've eventually drifted off, most likely cried myself to sleep somehow, but I can't have been unconscious for long because when the alarm went off it was a real shock. And so now here I am – body aching, head feeling like it's full of cotton wool, feeling like I could sleep forever – and now I've got to get up.

Some mornings I wonder what would happen if I didn't get out of bed every day like I do. Some mornings I wonder what it would be like to just roll over, go back to sleep, and wake up when I'm ready. But then again, being a single mum I already know the answer. My savings would dry up, we'd end up in rent arrears, get evicted and then the social would probably put us in temporary accommodation at the back end of nowhere: me and Kian in a single room, with a toilet and shower between five families.

And all because I didn't get out of bed.

That's the thing about being a single parent: the buck stops with you. You can't opt out, take a day off, or give up, even if that's all you want to do. You've got to carry on whether you feel like it or not. And that's what I do, day after day. Most days I don't mind. To be honest, most days I don't even notice. But every now and again on a morning like this, after a night like I've had, I can't help thinking how nice it would be to have someone there to share some of the load. But there is no one else, there's just me.

I did think about dating for a while. I even got as far as putting up a profile on one of those free dating sites, but all the messages I ever got were from sleazy blokes wanting one-night stands. All

I wanted was a bit of companionship, someone to cuddle up to, talk to and tell me everything was going to be all right. In the end I deleted my profile and treated myself to a fifty-quid mani-pedi at the beautician's up the road. Life's too short to settle for second best. Sometimes you just have to make your own happiness.

Rubbing the sleep out of my eyes, I yawn so massively I feel like my head's about to crack open. Then I have a long stretch and, just like that, I switch on, ready to take on the day. To begin with I haven't got a clue where I'm getting this energy from, because I'm pretty sure my batteries need charging. But wherever it's coming from, it's enough to get me out of bed, into the shower, and dressed. But later, when Kian and I are on the way to school, and he's chatting away ten to the dozen about some level he's just cracked on some game or other and I'm struggling to keep my eyes open, I realise it isn't fear, habit, or plain old grim determination that keeps me going. It's love, pure and simple. My love for Kian is the engine that keeps me moving, his are the only hugs I really need. Without him I doubt I'd bother getting out of bed at all, but with him I can do anything.

After dropping him off at school I head over to my first client of the day, Mr Tonkin in Notting Hill. He owns a mansion flat that apparently once belonged to Noël Coward. It's a beautiful place with loads of old features, but Mr Tonkin is not exactly the tidiest man I've ever met. I spend half my time folding things up and putting them away before I can get down to any actual cleaning.

Once I've finished there, I'm so shattered I stop for a quick cuppa in a nearby café before heading off to the Edwards, who live in a smart Victorian terrace about ten minutes away. They're a really lovely couple and Mrs Edwards, or Jane as she insists I call her, is especially nice. Jane is some sort of financial wizard and her husband is a solicitor. They haven't got kids and I've never asked why, but then last week when I was cleaning, I noticed a box of tablets next to the sink with the brand name Clomid, and I don't know why but it rang a bell somehow. Later that night while I was watching some old rubbish on TV it suddenly popped into my head exactly what sort of drug it was: it's a fertility treatment. I knew that because it was part of the plot of some thriller novel I read a few months back. It was the curse of the cleaner all over again: try as you might to mind your own business, you end up learning more than you want to know anyway. I left her a bunch of flowers and a card on the kitchen counter after my last clean. In the card I said they were because she was such a lovely client, but the truth was I felt bad for her. Having my Kian was the best thing I ever did, and I couldn't begin to imagine the ache she must feel wanting to start a family so badly and not being able to.

The Edwards' country cottage-style kitchen is spotless, there's not a single crumb on the counter or splash of wine to wipe away, so I do a quick sweep of the floor, empty the bins, re-organise the cutlery drawer and unload the dishwasher, before turning my attention to the oven. Jane said the other day she was ashamed about how filthy the inside of her cooker was, and so I get out the special oven cleaner I ordered off the Internet just for her, and decide to surprise her by giving it the clean she's always dreamed of. As I read the instruction leaflet (six whole pages of health warnings and disclaimers) my phone buzzes with a text. I reach into my bag and fish out my phone. I'm not really concentrating when I start reading the message, but then I blink, and I blink again, and I'm so shocked that the can of cleaner just falls out of my hand with a clatter.

I can't believe it.

I really can't believe it.

It's a text message.

A text message from my brother.

His first words to me in over thirty-two years are these: 'Dear Kerry, it's Noah/Jason here. I'm so sorry to have taken so long to reply to your message. It took me somewhat by surprise, given that until you made contact I hadn't even been aware I had a sister. I'd love to meet up as you suggested. How does this Saturday at 11 a.m. sound? There's a place in Soho called Collette's on

Dean Street and we could meet there. If the time or location aren't convenient please let me know and we can make alternative arrangements. Of course, I'm assuming you live in London (is that right?). If not, I'm more than willing to travel somewhere closer to you. I look forward to meeting you soon. Warmest wishes, Noah.'

For the longest time after reading this, I'm just a complete mess of snot and tears. I'd given up all hope of him ever replying. I'd convinced myself that he didn't care. But now that he has, I'm faced with a new problem: how exactly to reply. I'm scared of saying the wrong thing, doing something stupid that will make him change his mind. I tell myself that I'll reply when I'm calmer, when I can trust myself not to act like a fool, but not now. I'm still so nervous and I'm liable to go over the top thanking him for his reply if I do it now.

I make myself a cup of tea to calm my nerves and sit clutching it to my chest at the Edwards' kitchen table, with a massive grin plastered right across my face.

It's still too incredible to believe.

After all that waiting and worrying, my baby brother doesn't hate me after all. He hadn't even known I'd existed.

The poor thing, no wonder it's taken him so long to get back to me. There he was, going about his business, happy as Larry, only to have me throw the mother of all spanners in the works. It's a wonder he's replied to me at all, let alone agreed to meet. But he has.

He wants to meet me.

And oh, oh, oh, do I want to meet him.

I think about what it will be like, our café meeting. The two of us in the same space, sitting face to face . . . it's just too much.

When I pick up my phone to send my reply, my hand's trembling so much that I have to put it back down again. It takes me three goes before I can hold it without losing my grip. I start typing, not really knowing where I'm going from one word to the next: 'Dear Noah, thank you so much for getting back to me. It was lovely getting your message. It has absolutely made my day. You should see the size of the grin on my face. Saturday would be perfect. I don't know the café you mentioned but I'll find it for sure, and yes, eleven is good for me too.' I stop and reread to make sure I haven't been too gushy, too overbearing. I don't want him thinking I'm a nutter. In the end I decide it sounds okay, so then I type, 'See you Saturday xxx!' but it just looks wrong somehow. I look again at the way he ended his message: 'Warmest wishes.' Warmest wishes isn't very me. But this must be how the sort of people Jason knows talk to each other. In my experience posh people don't like to show emotion if they can help it. They downplay everything. I remember I had this client once, and while I was cleaning I noticed these 'Sorry for your loss' cards on the mantelpiece. When I finished the job I said to her, 'Oh, I am sorry about your sad news,' and I pointed to the cards. From the horrified look on her face you'd have thought I'd just caught sight of her on the loo. She bustled out of the room muttering that she was fine, but she avoided me like the plague after that and gave me the push by text a couple of days later.

Anyway, the last thing I want is to scare Noah off by being too emotional, so I delete the last bit and type, 'Warmest wishes, Kerry,' instead, and then because it still doesn't feel right I add a kiss, but just the one this time. I reread the message twice. It looks okay to me but I think about sending it to Jodi to check it over for me, just to be on the safe side. In the end I tell myself not to be so silly, read it through one last time just to make sure it makes sense, and then press send.

For a minute I feel good.

Then for another I'm sick with nerves.

Then for another after that, I'm convinced that I've said the wrong thing.

I keep remembering the bit in Jason's message where he asked me if I lived in London. I start to worry that he might think . . . I don't know . . . that I'm deliberately not answering his question. I tap out another message: 'Btw, yes, I do live in London.'

I press send and feel better for all of twenty seconds . . . and then straight away I'm back to feeling weird. I sit staring at my phone, imagining my messages flying through the air to him. Then I imagine him opening the texts and trying to picture me, the person who wrote them. Who does he think I am? What does he think I'm like?

My phone buzzes in my hand and I practically jump out of my skin.

It's a reply. A reply from Jason.

Opening the message, I hold my breath as though if I dare to make a sound things will fall apart. His text says: 'Sorry to bother you again, but it's just occurred to me that I don't know what you look like. How will I recognise you?'

I get a lump in my throat straight away, but at the same time I'm smiling because I'm just so happy. I picture the Jason I remember: his chubby little face, that killer smile of his that could light up a room and oh, those huge dark-brown eyes.

'Don't you worry about that,' I type, feeling strangely confident now. 'You were my baby brother and I adored you. Thirty years or not, I'd recognise you anywhere.'

8

Noah

Saturday, 12th March

The young woman behind the counter with the shocking pink hair and a nose ring hands me my coffee and, spotting a free space, I weave through the forest of occupied tables to the back of the café. When I'd chosen this location for our meeting I'd assumed that it being a Saturday, the Soho media types who colonised it during the week would be absent, so Kerry and I would be assured some degree of privacy. Instead, however, they've been replaced by brunching weekend hipsters – boys with beards, pretty girls in ugly clothes – and consequently there are only two tables left.

I look at my watch.

I'm half an hour early.

Half an hour early to meet the sister who, until ten days ago, I never even knew existed.

I'd experienced a visceral, almost physical shock when my parents confirmed the existence of my half-sister. Hearing them say that I had a sibling, combined with the letter, had literally taken my breath away and I'd had to work hard to conceal my reaction.

'I feel absolutely wretched that we've never said anything about this until now,' Mum had said, placing her hand on mine. 'It's unforgivable.'

'Of course it isn't,' I'd assured her firmly. 'You've never been anything but open and honest with me about my adoption and I'm sure if I hadn't been so closed off about it over the years, this would've come up well before now.'

'But we were the adults,' Dad had said. 'We should've known better, we should've done better by you. You're our son. We should have pushed to find out more.'

Mum had squeezed my hand, while I'd wondered briefly exactly why they hadn't pushed harder. Was it because they hadn't wanted to make waves or perhaps, unconsciously, because they, like me, hadn't wanted to know?

'We're so sorry, Noah,' Mum had said tearfully. 'Please say you forgive us.'

'There's nothing to forgive,' I'd said, and I meant it.

Dad had put a comforting hand on my shoulder. 'Clearly, this is a lot for you to take in. And you must feel free to come back to us with any questions you might have about your birth, your former family, anything at all. And whatever you decide to do next, your mother and I will support you one hundred per cent. You don't need to worry about anything.'

They were assuming this information would mark the beginning of a new journey for me, a journey to find my birth family, a journey that in one way or another they had always expected me to take.

'There won't be any further action.' As open as they were trying to be, I could see that bringing up the subject had already caused enough distress as it was. I couldn't imagine how they'd react if they knew my birth sister had already been in contact. And anyway, what would be the point? 'What's done is done,' I assured them. 'It wasn't your fault, it wasn't anybody's really, and anyway I've already got all the family I need.'

They seemed comforted by my words, which pleased me because more than anything I want them to be happy. My parents are good people, they'd done a good thing in adopting me and I wasn't about to give them a hard time for a single bad decision made with only the best of intentions.

A few sips into my coffee a blonde woman, eyes framed by a Sixties-style flick of eyeliner, wearing a white fur coat, green suede skirt, cowboy boots and her hair in pigtails strides confidently into the café. I scan her face for some flicker of recognition and as I do so, I recall Kerry's last text to me. '*You were my baby brother and I adored you,*' she'd written. '*I'd recognise you anywhere.*' There was so much to unpack in those words, so many questions her response left unanswered. I had no idea if she was black, white or dual heritage; in truth, I had no idea what I was expecting at all.

At a guess, I'd say the blonde woman was in her early thirties but she could have been older. I've never been all that great at guessing people's ages. I've lost count of the times when I've gone to meet a client expecting them to be young, only to be faced with a person who looks middle-aged, or gone expecting to meet someone older, only to be presented to somebody with the face of a child.

The blonde woman's eyes briefly alight on me and she gives me a smile, and for a moment I stop breathing. But then she shifts her gaze towards a table of twenty-somethings dressed like extras from *A Clockwork Orange* who are sitting at a table to my left and who, as one, rise to their feet as she approaches, smothering her in a flurry of hugs and air kisses.

Time passes.

I try to read an abandoned *Independent* left on the seat next to me but I find it impossible to concentrate beyond reading the headlines. At the slightest movement in the café, from staff cleaning tables to patrons walking to and from the toilets, my eyes automatically lift up from the newsprint, searching for my sister.

With five minutes to go before Kerry is due to arrive, I abandon the newspaper altogether and think instead about Rosalind and Millie. Typically on a Saturday morning, Millie and I would watch TV together in the snug while Rosalind pottered around in the kitchen. Then later we'd go out for a nice lunch somewhere local, perhaps going on to explore some farmers' market or other. Loaded down with all manner of delicious delicacies, we'd finally head home, where Rosalind would magic the food we'd bought into a spectacular supper to be enjoyed by visiting friends and their children.

Just a few weeks ago that used to be my typical Saturday, and now everything's changed.

Spurred by the pang of loss deep within me, I reach for my phone and, desperate to feel some sort of connection with my family, tap out a message to Millie with all the urgency of an SOS. I ask her how she is and what she's up to, and tell her how much I'm looking forward to our shopping trip this afternoon. I press send, then look towards the door of the café to see if anyone new has arrived, but my view is blocked by a woman walking towards me. She's white and is in her late thirties or perhaps early forties. She has light-brown hair and is dressed smartly, as if she's on her way to a job interview, in a black woollen coat with matching tailored trousers and court shoes. It's the urgency in her gaze that gives the game away; there's a longing and sadness there as our eyes lock that can only mean one thing.

I try to stand but my legs buckle the moment I ask them to bear my weight. Only on my second attempt do I make it to my feet and then, having done so, I freeze. She's reached my table now, and is standing only centimetres away from me.

'Jason.'

Her voice sends a shiver down my spine because of its quiet intensity and the use of my former name.

'I'm so sorry . . . I mean Noah . . . Noah, it's me . . .'

I automatically hold out my hand, as if she's a colleague or a client, and the moment I do so, I know it's the wrong thing to have done. She hesitates for a moment and then, as if not to offend me, she takes it. By turns it is both woefully inadequate and comically British, and for a moment after we let go we both stand staring at each other.

Her face changes and she shakes her head, as if having come to some sort of conclusion. 'I'm really sorry,' she says, 'and please say no if it makes you uncomfortable, but do you think . . . would you mind if . . . if I gave you a hug?' Her request is quietly spoken and delivered in a manner that makes me think she is choosing each and every word carefully. And as she awaits my reaction, she pulls a face nervously, her eyes searching mine for disapproval. 'Is it a weird thing to ask? It is, isn't it?'

'Not at all,' I reply, even though I have my reservations. I want to put her at ease, but at the same time I'm not sure I'm the right person to do it.

I step around the table towards her and she throws her arms around my waist, burying her face in my chest. It is at once both awkward and uncomfortable, all the more so because it is so utterly one-sided.

'I'm sorry,' she says when it's all over. 'I promised myself I wasn't going to be over the top. I told myself I wasn't going to do or say anything to embarrass you, and now look at me. It's just that . . . it's just that . . . well . . . I've dreamed of this moment for so long, I think I would've died if I hadn't . . .' She starts to cry again and as she does so, she dabs at her eyes with a tissue and I find myself reaching out to this stranger and touching her very gently on her arm in an effort to comfort her.

'It's okay,' I say. 'Really it is. Please take a seat and let me get you a drink, and something to eat. Hopefully that will help us both calm down a bit.'

At the counter I order an English Breakfast tea for Kerry and another coffee for myself, and as I return to our table I wonder what her initial impressions of me are. I feel bad about the handshake and worse still about the one-sided nature of our embrace.

'This is a nice place,' says Kerry, looking around as I take my seat opposite her. Her eyes are dry now and her make-up re-applied. She sounds calmer too, more composed. 'I've never been here before. Are you a regular?'

'Not exactly, just the occasional meeting if I'm in the area.'

Her eyes flit briefly down to the table and she self-consciously tucks a stray strand of hair behind her ear.

'So what is it you do?'

'I'm a barrister, for my sins. How about you?'

There's a pause and then she says, 'I'm a . . . well . . . I'm a cleaner.'

A barrister and a cleaner, I think. We couldn't be more different if we tried.

She shifts in her seat, eyes averted. 'It's not very impressive, I know. But someone's got to do it.'

'Believe me, there's nothing impressive about being a barrister,' I say, hoping to play down the differences between us. 'Mainly I just spend my time filling in paperwork and trawling through case notes, not exactly the stuff of TV dramas.'

'Do you have to wear those funny wigs and the robes and all that?'

I nod. 'It's not a great look, I'll admit.'

She laughs, and I feel pleased to have set her at ease if only for a moment. 'I bet they make your head really itchy.'

'They do, but you get used to it.'

She thinks for a moment. 'And how did you get into it, being a barrister, I mean? Did you do it at university?'

'Yes, I read law as an undergraduate, and then I had to undertake lots of training afterwards to become fully qualified.'

Kerry smiles shyly. 'That sounds really impressive. I could never do anything like that. What made you go into that line of work? Are your parents barristers too?'

At the mention of my parents I immediately feel both guilty and disloyal.

'No,' I reply, 'they're both academics, actually.'

'Oh right,' she says. 'But you didn't fancy that?'

'No, not really, I suppose the law speaks to the performer in me. Even though I say so myself, I made a quite excellent Joseph in my infant nativity play.'

She smiles but then suddenly looks serious. 'But what about murderers, rapists, child molesters and the like? How can you defend someone like that? Doesn't it churn your stomach?'

I think for a moment. This is the question every criminal barrister gets asked, if not quite every day then somewhere close. 'I decided to be a barrister because . . . well . . . because I suppose I believe everyone, no matter who they are or what they've done, deserves to be treated fairly by the law. My job isn't to say whether or not my client is guilty, my job is to give them the best defence I possibly can. Believe me, if you'd seen as many cases as I have where the seemingly guilty are proven innocent beyond the shadow of a doubt, then you'd be as glad as I am for the system we have in this country.'

She thinks for a moment, digesting my words, and then smiles proudly. 'I hadn't thought of it like that,' she says. 'But you're right. Innocent until proven guilty, isn't it? Without that, we're all stuffed.'

She studies my face and smiles. 'I bet you're good at your job, aren't you?' she asks, and for the first time I recognise the hint of the rhythmic swagger of west London in her accent – half Jamaican patois, half cockney tearaway – that's been there in her speech all along, although it's almost as if she's trying to hide it from me. I wonder what she makes of my own accent, whether like some of my clients she thinks it out of place coming from someone with my colour skin. For a moment I think about trying to modify my speech, toning it down somehow, but I realise it's too late to turn back now without seeming to patronise her. Even if my motivation is to make her feel more comfortable around me, changing my accent suddenly would seem odd and offensive. No, for better or worse, this is how I speak, this is who I am.

Kerry regards me carefully and I realise that I have still to answer her question. 'I try,' I reply. 'For each and every client, I try to give of my best.'

The couple at the table next to us stand up to welcome a friend, and for a moment Kerry and I fall silent as they greet one another.

'How about you?' I ask after a moment. 'Your line of work? How did you get into it?'

Kerry smiles. 'When I was really little I wanted to be an air hostess, but I think that was probably more about the outfits and getting to travel places than anything else. But then you grow up, don't you? You move on. Mostly all I've ever done is work in retail or restaurants. It was only when I had Kian that I finally went into cleaning.'

She has a child.

All this time I've been so focused on adjusting my mind to the idea of having a sister that it hasn't even occurred to me that she might have children, that unbeknownst to me, I might be the uncle of a child I've never met.

'Kian is your son, I take it?'

Kerry nods. 'He's ten and can be a right bundle of trouble sometimes, but I wouldn't be without him. Have you got kids?'

'Just the one: a daughter, Millie. She's twelve. She's funny, and cheeky and my absolute world.'

She nods towards my wedding ring. 'And you're married?'

'Twelve years now, but we've been together fifteen.'

Kerry laughs. 'Congratulations. I couldn't even manage six months with Kian's dad, you're really lucky.'

I consider all the people I still haven't told about Rosalind: colleagues, university friends, extended family members, people who I've known and trusted for years. 'Yes, I suppose we are.'

We fall silent and I don't know why, but for some reason I feel compelled to tell the truth to this stranger, this woman I have no recollection of knowing.

'Actually . . . we're currently separated.'

A strange mixture of concern and surprise flashes across her face as if she hadn't thought such a thing was possible. 'But what . . . what happened?' She corrects herself quickly. 'I'm sorry, that's none of my business. Just ignore me and my big mouth.'

'It's fine, honestly. To be truthful, I'm not even sure what the problem is myself. I've moved out for now but I'm confident we'll work things through.'

'I really hope you do,' she says. 'It's horrible when things go pear-shaped, but like you say, you'll get through it.'

Our waitress arrives with our drinks and the two slices of cake I ordered. I gesture to the plates she places before us. 'I wasn't sure what you'd like, so I thought I'd give you a choice: Black Forest or some sort of cheesecakey thing.'

'You choose,' she says. 'I'm not fussed really. I know I've calmed down a lot but I think I might still be too nervous to eat.'

While she's adding sugar to her tea and searching around for a spoon, I think again about how strange all this is. All around us people are having everyday throwaway conversations, discussing weekend plans, gossiping about mutual friends and interesting articles they've read, and yet here we are, my sister and I, sitting across from each other with three decades of history to catch up on.

There are so many things I want to ask her, about our mother, about our past, about her life. And yet at the same time, these are the very same things I don't want to know. It's a conundrum: how to explore the past without wreaking havoc on the present. If only I could pick and choose. The one question I am certain I need to know the answer to, however, is the one I've been asking myself ever since I received her letter, and it's this: Why now? Why after thirty years of silence has my sister come to find me?

I coax Kerry into sharing some of the cake with me, and in between forkfuls I ask her about her journey to the café this morning. She tells me how she normally uses her car to get around for work but today she took the Tube, which she found quite relaxing compared to being nose to tail in traffic. I ask her where she got the Tube in from and when she says Ladbroke Grove, I immediately think about all of the times I've been in that area, whether to visit the market, the carnival, or friends in and around Notting Hill and Westbourne Grove. Had I ever walked past her and her son? Had we ever been in the same shops at the same time? Had we ever missed bumping into one another by a matter of hours, or minutes or even seconds? It all seems too fantastic to contemplate.

In return, she asks me about my own journey today and while I tell her I'm staying in Hampstead, I make no mention of Charlotte: it seems inappropriate somehow. Instead I make her laugh, telling her about the woman I was wedged up against on the bus ride in, who kicked off her shoes as soon as she sat down next to me and proceeded to have an extremely loud conversation on her phone for the rest of the journey without pausing for breath.

As we chat and work our way through both pieces of cake, I

decide that now is as good a time as any to ask my question, but I take so long formulating it that she looks over at me, her face full of concern.

'Are you okay? You look like you've got something on your mind.'

'I have, but I'm not quite sure how to say it.'

'Have I said something to upset you? Because if I have I—'

'No, it's nothing like that,' I say quickly. 'It's just that I keep wondering . . . well, why now? What exactly made you choose to get in touch now after all these years?'

She looks down at her hands, not speaking. And even though she's a grown woman, I find it all too easy to imagine what she must have been like as a child. She looks small and vulnerable and I immediately wonder if I've said the wrong thing.

'I'm sorry. That was rude, wasn't it? I don't know what I was thinking. Of course you don't have to answer that.'

She shakes her head. 'It's okay, really. I do want to answer it. It's just difficult.' She pauses as though carefully weighing up not only her response, but also my potential reaction to what she's about to reveal.

'I'm sorry to be the one to have to tell you this,' she says finally. She looks briefly down at her hands again and then back at me, 'but I've got some bad news about Mum . . . our mum. I know you probably feel like you never knew her, but I just thought you ought to know that she died.'

9

Kerry

Saturday, 12th March

It breaks my heart watching Noah taking in the news about Mum's passing. Even though he's sitting across from me in his expensive shirt and smart shoes, I can still see the little boy I used to cuddle and sing to sleep when he was upset, even more so now. Perhaps I should've dressed it up a bit more, told him in a gentler way. After all, it's a lot to take in.

I reach across the table to take his hand but stop myself at the last minute. I tell myself to remember that right now, to him, I'm as much of a stranger as any of the other people in this café. Instead I rest my hand on the table, my fingertips a hair's breadth from his. I don't say anything. There's nothing worse than someone yapping on when you're trying to get your thoughts together. Instead I look down at my hand, willing it to stay where it is, insisting that it doesn't try to comfort him, even though that's all it wants to do.

Moments pass. I lift my eyes from my hand to his face. He seems a bit more together now, as if he's ready to talk.

'What was she like?'

What a question. How can I possibly explain who Mary Anne Hayes was in a couple of sentences, especially when there were so many different versions of her? How about fun Mary, who was full of laughter and jokes? Or sad Mary, always crying and never leaving the house? Or how about reckless Mary, who didn't give a thought to her own safety or that of her kids? The list is endless. So which one am I supposed to tell him about? Which one am I supposed to say: this is what our mum was like? It's a big responsibility, a big moment, and I want to get it right. I don't want to make her out to be a monster, but I certainly don't want to make her a saint either.

I reach into my bag, take out the three photos of Mary that I've brought along with me and place them one by one on the table in front of Noah. The first is a black and white one of Mum as a teenager. She's sitting on a park bench, pulling a face and holding her hand up as though she's embarrassed. The second is a Polaroid of me and Mum taken when I was about five. We're at a farm and she's holding me up while I stroke a pony. The third photo is a blurry snap of Mum sitting on a brown corduroy sofa with Jason on her lap. Even though she's smiling, she looks thin and tired.

I point to the last photo. 'This is Mum . . . and that baby on her lap . . . is you.'

He takes in the photos, not saying anything, and even though I tell him he can pick them up, he doesn't touch them.

'Mum was . . . how can I put it . . .?' I search around for the right word but it won't come and so I have to make do with: 'She was . . . complicated.' Even as I say it, I feel myself groan. Everyone knows 'complicated' is shorthand for difficult. 'She could be loads of fun,' I carry on in spite of myself, 'she could make you laugh until you thought you'd wet your knickers, but she had problems too. In her own way she did love us both very much, but she just wasn't always very good at being a mum.'

Without going into too much detail, I tell Noah that Mum and I had a falling out. I tell him how someone I'd never met before had rung and told me that not only was Mum dead but because they hadn't had contact details for me, she'd already been buried too. Then finally I tell him that it's taken me a long while to get my head around it all, but that I thought as her son he ought to know.

Everything I say is the truth, but not exactly what you might call the whole truth. I suppose it's a kind of truth. A version of the truth that I hope will give him a little bit of comfort without weighing him down with a whole bunch of stuff he doesn't need to know, at least not yet.

When I finish talking, he stares at the photos a little while longer. Occasionally he glances up at me awkwardly but says nothing. I feel like I've overwhelmed him, and I'm scared any minute he's going to just stand up and leave. I know I probably would if the tables were turned. I know if it was me I'd be thinking: Why couldn't you have just kept all this to yourself?

I have an idea, a way of lifting the dark cloud that's settled over our table.

'I don't suppose you've got any photos of your Millie, have you? If you have, I'd love to see them.'

'Yes, yes, of course,' he says in that voice of his that sounds like he's reading the news. Sitting up, he rubs his hands over his face as if he's trying to wake himself up and then reaches for his phone, while I pick up the photos of Mary and put them back into my bag. He flicks a finger across the screen a few times and then turns it towards me. It's a photo of a girl a bit older than Kian with light-brown skin, huge dark-brown eyes and a smile to die for: Noah's daughter, my niece. She's beautiful, really beautiful and the shocking thing is, although he wouldn't be able to tell from the photos I've just showed him, her smile, that twinkle in her eyes, is pure Mary.

'She's gorgeous.' I feel myself getting a bit worked up. He doesn't need to know his little girl reminds me of Mum. He doesn't need that burden. 'You must be really proud.'

'I am, very. She's a great kid.'

There's a smile on his face as he says this. Like he can't quite contain the love he feels for her. It's such a relief to know he's a good dad. It's such a weight off my mind when so many men I come across simply couldn't care less.

He looks up at me. 'How about you? Do you have any photos of Kian?'

I have to smile. My phone's stuffed full of them. 'Er . . . I think I might have a couple.'

The photos on my phone are like a potted history of the past few months: Kian in the park playing football; Kian dressed up like a mummy for Halloween; Kian opening presents at

Christmas; Kian in his school uniform at the start of term. And in between those moments are a million cheeky-faced selfies he's taken whenever he can get hold of my phone. In every photo I see his face changing, getting leaner, less childlike, more grown-up.

'This is a good one.' I show Noah my phone. I took it last week when he got an award at karate. When I got my phone out to take a picture, he kept pulling faces until I threatened him and this is the first good shot I managed to get.

Noah grins as he studies the picture. 'I can see he's quite a character.'

'Oh, he's that all right. One minute he's making your heart melt and the next he's making you want to throttle him.' I rummage round in my bag and take out a folded-up sheet of paper. It's a card that Kian made for me last week. One night, for no reason at all, he took himself off to his room and then he left this on my pillow without saying a word. On the cover is a picture of me and him as *Minecraft* characters that he's drawn in pencil crayon and inside it says: 'To Mum, You are the best Mum in the world xxx.'

'See what I mean? From throttling to heart-melting in sixty seconds!'

'It's lovely,' says Noah. 'You must be really close.'

'We are,' I say. 'Very. It's what happens when it's only the two of you. We've only got each other.' I tuck the card back inside my bag and think about Kian and Millie, and how different their childhoods have been to mine and Noah's. Almost thinking my thoughts aloud, I say, 'At least our kids have had a better start in life than we ever had.'

I regret it the moment I say it. It's too much, too soon. A worried look flashes across Noah's face and there's an awkward silence, until he says in a voice that's barely a whisper, 'Was it . . . was it . . . bad?'

I freeze. I have no idea what he knows, what he's been told or even what he can remember.

'It wasn't great,' I admit, and I wait for him to ask a follow-up question, to reassure me that he really wants to know. But it doesn't come. Why would it? Why would anyone want to know bad things about their past if they didn't have to?

He glances at my half-empty cup. 'Would you like another drink?' he asks, but it feels more like, 'Please, can we talk about something else?'

'I'd love one,' I say. 'Same again, if that's okay.'

I watch as he walks over to the counter and starts chatting to the barista. I wonder what he thinks of me now we've met. He's so handsome, so well-spoken and educated, that I can't help but think he's disappointed. How could he not be? Even though I've tried really hard with my hair and make-up, I can't imagine I've turned any heads today. Even though I've tried my best not to drop my aitches, it's not as if anyone would mistake me for being posh. And as for being clever, I haven't even got a single GCSE to my name, let alone a degree or anything fancy like that. I can't imagine how he could be anything but disappointed. I can't imagine he's thinking anything apart from: *How can I be related to someone like her?*

When he gets back to the table, I try my best to put the thoughts I'm having out of my mind. I tell myself that even though he's posh, he seems like a decent sort. And I tell myself that he doesn't care about superficial things, that he's deeper than that. But the thing is it's hard, really hard. When we talk about our kids, all I can think is how different their lives must be. When we talk about plans for the weekend, all I do is imagine the fancy places he'll be taking his daughter while me and Kian are stuck on our estate.

'Where are you going to go?' I ask, when he tells me about his plans to take Millie shopping this afternoon. 'Bluewater or Oxford Street?'

'Haven't even got that far, but knowing Millie, chances are she'll demand the impossible and want to do both.' He smiles and then looks at his watch, the first time he's done so since I arrived. I know what's coming next. 'Actually . . . if I'm not going to be late to pick her up . . .'

'Of course,' I say, even though all I want to do is cling on to him and beg him to stay. 'You should get off. You don't want to be late.'

At the counter we argue over the bill. I tell him it has to be my treat, but before I can stop him he's handed over his credit card. I try to give him some money but he won't take it. In the end I say, 'Okay, but next time is on me.'

I'd said it to be nice. Not to push him into a corner or guilt him into seeing me again. But it's out there now, only he doesn't say a word. Instead he carries on paying the bill as if he hasn't heard me, and I can't tell if he's saying nothing because he's concentrating on what he's doing or because he's made up his mind that there definitely won't be a next time.

Outside it's cold, and he zips up his jacket and shoves his hands deep into his pockets. This is it, I realise, he's getting ready to leave.

'I don't want to sound like an old lady,' I say, 'but you really have grown up into such a proper young man, Jason.' I notice my mistake straight away. *What an idiot! I've done it again.* I shake my head and apologise. 'I really am sorry, Noah. You must think I'm brainless. It's just . . . well, it's just so hard for me to stop thinking of you as . . . you know . . . Jason. I bet you can't even remember being called it, can you?'

For a moment I think he might tell me about how he came to change his name, because it's something that's been bothering me ever since I found out. Who adopts a kid at the age of two and then changes their name? You might do that with a baby, but not a toddler who already knows its name. It doesn't seem right somehow. But he doesn't say anything about his name, he doesn't even make a joke about me having called it him again, instead he says, 'Not really,' and leaves it at that, and then just when I think it can't get any more awkward, he holds out his hand again like I'm some bloke he's doing business with. I think I must have made a face or something, because the next thing he does is pull his hand away and open himself up for a hug. I don't need to be told twice, I'm in there like a shot and squeeze the life out of him. He hugs me back this time, but it's just as stiff and awkward as it was the first time.

'It was lovely to meet you, Kerry,' he says in that smooth voice of his, when it's over, and I'm struck again by how he talks the same way most of my clients do, no trace of an accent, just nice, clear and posh, the complete opposite of my own voice.

'And it was lovely to meet you too,' I say, only just about stopping myself from adding, '*I hope we can do it again soon.*'

He gives me a little smile and a wave, and that's it. He starts walking away towards Oxford Street and I just stand there staring after him like a right lemon, fighting the urge to run after him, hoping he'll turn around and come back.

Everything was riding on today being a success.

Everything was riding on us making a connection.

And I've messed it all up.

Not once the entire time I'm watching him does he look back, not even to wave; he just keeps on walking until finally, reaching the end of the road, he's swallowed up by the crowds of Saturday shoppers. Even then, I don't move. Standing in the middle of the pavement, people tutting at me as they walk past on both sides, I carry on waiting, hoping he'll change his mind and come back. It's only when I feel a few spots of rain on my face that I finally come to my senses, turn around and start making my way back to the Tube.

I'm still thinking about Noah as I go down the escalators.

I'm still thinking about him as I stand on the westbound platform of the Central line waiting for the next train.

And I'm still thinking about him as I squeeze myself into the last empty seat on the end carriage.

As the train leaves the station I look down at my outfit, and wonder if it hadn't been a bit over the top, especially when he'd just been wearing a casual jacket, nice shirt and smart jeans. I'd bought my outfit brand new from Next and put the whole thing on my store card so I didn't have all that expense straight away. But Next don't have a things-to-wear-when-you're-meeting-your-long-lost-brother-for-the-first-time-in-thirty-years range, so I went for their workwear section instead. I can't think when I'm ever going to wear this outfit again, unless it's to court or to a funeral.

The train stops in a tunnel just outside Marble Arch, something to do with a signalling error they're trying to fix. A young Indian guy sitting opposite me stands up and I catch sight of my reflection in the train window. I feel like I'm seeing now what Noah must have seen: a tired, desperate, middle-aged woman, with bags under her eyes, wearing clothes that don't suit her.

I want to cry.

Right here on the Central line, I want to let it all out.

I've dreamed of this day for so long, imagined how perfect it would be, how it would be the answer to everything. And now it's in the past and nothing has gone the way I wanted. Today was my one and only chance and I've screwed it up. He doesn't want to be related to someone like me, let alone see me again and who could blame him? He's got everything he needs: an amazing career, a beautiful kid, and parents who, though he didn't really talk about them, clearly love him. Why would he want to mess all that up for a total stranger? Why would he want to ruin his happy life to make room for a sister he doesn't even know?

10

Noah

Wednesday, 16th March

The young woman behind the desk smiles and tilts her head to one side in a manner I suspect she imagines is disarming.

'Hi there, can I help you?'

I want to say, 'No, you can't, thank you very much.' I want to say, 'I'm only here because my wife is making me.' I want to say, 'Look, I get it, I'm sure this sort of thing helps some people but let me tell you right now, it's not going to help me.' But in the end, what I actually say is, 'Yes, my name's Noah Martineau and my wife and I have a seven-thirty appointment with . . .' and it's at this point I realise I've completely forgotten the name of the relationship counsellor Rosalind has booked us in to see. 'I think it's Ellie . . . or Evelyn something or other.' The young woman frowns. 'Do you mean Elspeth?' she asks. I want to say yes, but I'm not sure and the last thing I want to do is end up crashing some other poor couple's counselling session, so I search through all my texts from Rosalind until I finally find the right one. '. . . Elspeth Greene,' I say, scanning the text for the relevant information. 'I'm here to see Elspeth Greene.'

The young woman tilts her head again but this time in the opposite direction, and smiles. 'Thought so.' She scans the computer screen in front of her and taps the keyboard several times. 'That's lovely, I've booked you in, just take a seat and I'll call you through when Elspeth is ready.'

I sit down on a hard plastic chair in the corner of the waiting room and realise for the first time just how exhausted I am. Today's been non-stop, a blur of last-minute prepping, grumpy judges, cases being dropped in my lap from nowhere, and with a mid-morning ham sandwich counting as my only sustenance for the day, I'm fast running out of energy.

As my stomach rumbles loudly I look around for something to distract me. On the coffee table in front of me are the obligatory dog-eared magazines and a pile of leaflets about self-care during depression. Ignoring them, I lean my head back against the wall and close my eyes but it's not Rosalind I think about, or even what the next hour of my life is going to be like. Instead all I think about, in fact all I have thought about since our encounter four days ago, is Kerry, and the news she's given me about my birth mother.

It has really shaken me, shaken me in a way I hadn't thought possible. Although, of course, I'd wondered about my birth mother from time to time over the years, what she looked like, whether she thought about me at all, or ever regretted giving me away, I'd never met the woman and have no memories of her. And so it came as something of a surprise that her passing registered with me on an emotional level. After all, how can a person miss what they've never had? And yet there I was, feeling like I'd just experienced an underwater earthquake, like a fissure had opened up in the earth's crust somewhere deep down and hidden, and I wasn't quite sure what it meant. The photos of my mother hadn't helped; in an instant they'd transformed her from a faceless ghost to something more substantial, more real. This ambushing of my emotions has unsettled me, all the more so given the current turmoil in my personal life. My every instinct has been to put as much distance as I can between me and anything connected to it, which I suppose is why, even though it's been four days since my meeting with Kerry, I have yet to contact her, and I'm not sure I ever will. I feel terrible about this, of course, especially after she's opened herself up to meeting me, but I've been so overwhelmed by everything she told me, so unsettled by it that all I want to do is relegate this whole episode to the past, draw a line in the sand, move on and never look back.

At the sound of the automatic doors in the front entrance, I open my eyes to see a damp Rosalind coming in from the rain. Taking off her coat, she glances briefly in my direction, her expression set to neutral. The receptionist books her in, and then she comes and sits in the next-but-one chair to me, placing her bag in the empty space – a physical reminder, if such a thing were needed, of the distance between us. She looks windswept and tired, and my instinct is to wrap her in a comforting embrace. But I can't rely on instinct any more, at least not yet. For now I have to hold back, I have to show her that I'm listening, that I've understood.

'Tough day?'

She nods, running her fingers through her hair. 'Just work stuff.'

'Is it that new restaurant messing you around again?'

She shakes her head. 'It's a long story. Would you mind if we talk about it later?'

I want to say no, let's talk about it now, because I care about everything that happens to her from the smallest thing to the biggest. But then it occurs to me that the reason for Rosalind's abruptness might be that she's mentally preparing herself for confrontation, for battle. Even as a barrister going up against a friend, you don't engage in chitchat with opposing counsel when you're about to go head to head in court. For all its piped classical music, pastel paint colours and boxes of tissues, this place is little more than a battleground, and you don't make small talk before stepping into the arena.

We sit in silence until our names are called and then follow the receptionist along a narrow corridor and into a small room. Inside are three brown leather armchairs positioned around a low coffee table, and standing next to one of them is a small, smartly dressed middle-aged woman with cropped grey hair and round tortoiseshell glasses.

She greets us with a beaming smile. 'You must be Mr and Mrs Martineau,' she says. 'My name's Elspeth.' She invites us to take a seat and starts by telling us a little about herself. 'I've been working with couples like yourselves for the past twenty years, and ten of those have been at this practice.'

The room suddenly seems hot and cramped, as if we're practically sitting on one another's laps and somebody's just turned up the thermostat. Next to me, Rosalind clears her throat but says nothing.

'Before we begin, I think it's important from the outset to make it clear that I'm not here to take sides, pass judgment or tell you what to do. My role here is simply to facilitate a discussion between the two of you, and enable you to identify any issues you might be having and work with you to find a pathway towards resolving those issues. Everything said in this room is confidential and for the process to work, you must both feel as if you're able to speak freely. Agreed?'

Rosalind and I nod in unison. Elspeth smiles. 'Good, then let's begin. What would you say has brought you here today?'

I look at Rosalind expectantly. Usually I know exactly what she's thinking but her face proves impossible to read. Does she want me to go first, to tell our counsellor what I stand accused of, or would she rather bear witness to our judge and jury in her own words?

Rosalind clears her throat again. 'I can't speak for Noah, but in my opinion the reason we're here is because I feel like we don't communicate properly. If I'm honest, I don't think we ever have. And if I'm being really honest, I think it's largely to do with him being adopted. Which is, of course, something he never ever wants to talk about.'

Elspeth nods encouragingly, but it seems that's all Rosalind's going to say for now and so after a moment all eyes are on me.

'And Noah, what would your response be to what Rosalind has just said?'

I shift my gaze from Elspeth, to Rosalind, then to the coffee table in front of me. It's a difficult question. The barrister in me wants to tear apart Rosalind's argument if only because I can, but the husband in me knows better. 'On the whole I'd agree with her assertion,' I say, trying my best to sound reasonable, but then I add: 'That said, I'm not sure what I can do about it.' I'd meant it to be more of an observation than an attack, but that's exactly how it sounds. 'Of course,' I add quickly, 'that's what I'm here to learn.'

Elspeth leans forward in her chair, her face, much like that of a judge, expressing neither condemnation nor approval. 'Thank you for that, both of you,' she says. 'What I'm hearing is there's an issue to do with communication and it's causing problems in your relationship. I suppose my next question would be whether there's been one particular incident that has brought you here today to seek help, and if so, what is it?'

Rosalind looks at her hands and though she doesn't say a word, I feel that she's willing me to answer for the both of us.

'The miscarriage,' I say, in a voice so quiet that I barely hear it myself. 'We're here because at the beginning of last month we both lost the baby that we very much wanted.'

'No,' says Rosalind firmly. 'We're *not* here because of the miscarriage. We're here because of your refusal to talk about it.'

It had been a chilly but bright December morning and I'd been on my way to Blackfriars Crown Court to defend a client against a charge of credit-card fraud when Rosalind called with the news that she was pregnant.

'I've got something I need to tell you,' she'd said, but before she could say any more she'd burst into tears and it was several minutes before I fully understood what it was she had been trying to tell me.

'You're pregnant?' I'd replied, wanting to make certain I hadn't misunderstood.

'Yes,' she'd exclaimed through her tears. 'Noah, isn't it wonderful? After all these years we're finally going to have another baby.'

Because of the ease of our first pregnancy, I think we'd simply assumed that adding to our family when we were ready would be straightforward. So when Millie turned four we started trying, but a year on nothing had changed. We sought medical advice, each undergoing a battery of tests that were frustratingly inconclusive. The phrase 'secondary infertility' was an unhelpful one but it was all the explanation the medical professionals seemed able to offer us. IVF was suggested as a possible solution, but it was one about which Rosalind had grave reservations. She was only too aware from friends and relations, in particular Effie, her closest friend, of the strain that such a process can put on a relationship. 'After all,' she'd said, 'we have Millie and each other. Why put all we have in jeopardy for something that may or may not work?'

So six years on, the news that Rosalind was pregnant had left us both reeling. This baby was clearly a miracle, something we'd given up hoping for, but once the initial shock had receded we allowed ourselves to fully give in to the joy and excitement we were both feeling.

Then just two weeks after confirmation of the pregnancy, Rosalind experienced some bleeding, which our GP confirmed was a miscarriage. Rosalind of course had been very sad about it, we both were, but thankfully we hadn't told Millie, so for the most part we were able to keep this sadness to ourselves. In an effort to lift Rosalind's spirits I booked a weekend away in Barcelona for us, while Millie stayed with my parents. But although the weather was surprisingly warm for February and we ate some wonderful food and visited some breathtaking art exhibitions that ordinarily Rosalind would have loved, the weekend was a disaster. No matter what I did or said, I couldn't seem to coax her away from her sorrow.

The moment we returned home, things went from bad to worse. It was as if everything I did irritated Rosalind. If I brought home a takeaway for the family, it would be the wrong one. If I suggested she go out and see friends, she'd accuse me of not wanting to spend time with her. And if I had to stay late at work, she'd accuse me of neglecting her and Millie.

One morning, desperate for a solution and reasoning that this had to be about the miscarriage, I'd even suggested we ought to reconsider IVF. This, I can see in retrospect, was the straw that broke the camel's back. An argument ensued that wasn't so much about the IVF as it was about me. Rosalind accused me of being cold, of being heartless, of refusing to mourn with her or talk to her about the effect the miscarriage was having on me, and so it was that evening I returned home brandishing a vastly inadequate bouquet of flowers, desperate to make things up between us, only for Rosalind to ask me to leave.

'And what makes all this so much more difficult to bear,' says Rosalind, once I've finished speaking, 'is the fact that I feel like I'm still stuck in the depths, while Noah is determined that we just focus on moving forwards. It's the way he's always dealt with things he finds uncomfortable, it's the way he's always been. He just closes the door on things he doesn't want to deal with.'

Everything Rosalind says is true.

I'm not very good at talking about my feelings, I never have been. It's not that I don't have them – I'm not made of stone – I was just as upset about losing the baby as she was. But I've always found it difficult to talk about my emotions. I think in one way or another it's been the defining theme of our relationship ever since we got together: her wanting me to be more open and me struggling to give her what I know she needs.

Elspeth turns her attention to me, her gaze still non-accusatory, but it's clear she expects a response. 'And what, Noah, would you say to Rosalind's assessment of your situation?'

I think for a moment, about how difficult this must be for Rosalind, about how even though I want this to be over as quickly as possible, she at the very least deserves my honesty.

'Again she's right,' I say. 'Right about everything.'

'This is what I'm up against,' says Rosalind. 'He knows there's a problem but he refuses to explore it and I'm always left on the outside looking in, trying to see behind the curtain, trying to discover just who he really is.' She laughs. 'Do you know Noah didn't even tell me he was adopted until after I'd met his parents for the first time? What kind of boyfriend takes their girlfriend home to meet his family and neglects to mention the fact he's adopted? I spent the whole of that Easter Sunday afternoon trying to work out the relationships. Was my boyfriend the only black man in the centre of a very white family, the product of an affair no one ever referred to? Or was he the reappearance of some long-forgotten gene from his parents' family tree? It's ridiculous really, almost comical. I kept going over all the logical possibilities in my head because I couldn't quite believe the truth: that the man I loved would omit to share something so central, so fundamental about himself with me.' She pauses and looks at me briefly. 'We recovered from it and from time to time I even laughed about it with girlfriends, and at the time I convinced myself that this was just an anomaly, a one-off, caused by a charming sort of awkwardness that I told myself would fade as we grew closer, but it wasn't at all. It wasn't a one-off, it wasn't anything of the sort. It's how he is, it's how he's always been. Sometimes I feel like he's got this whole secret world going on inside his head. And of course, that sort of thing is attractive when you're young – what girl doesn't like a challenge? – but we're not students any more, we're adults, adults who've built a home and a life and have a daughter together too.'

She stops for a moment, clenches and unclenches her fists in her lap before continuing. There's a new layer of sadness in her voice when she speaks. 'There shouldn't be any secrets between us any more, no part of ourselves we keep hidden. Day after day I feel like I present myself to my husband as an open book, but when I look at him all I see are fragments. It's as though he'll reveal parts of himself, but never the whole story.'

11

Kerry

Saturday, 19th March

Standing outside Mrs Ryman's house, I feel a rush of excitement from my head right down to my toes as I spot Noah coming towards me behind the wheel of a flash motor: silver, and sporty-looking, all sleek lines and polished chrome. I don't know anything about cars – they're not my thing – but even I can tell it must have cost a fortune.

He gets out of the car. He's dressed like he was the last time I saw him, in jeans and a nice shirt and jacket, casual but somehow managing to look smart at the same time. I think about my own outfit: jeans, boots and a knock-off Barbour jacket that I got off eBay and even paid extra for next-day delivery. All of it's new. I couldn't help myself. I hated the idea of him being embarrassed by me. On the plus side, though, I feel less trussed-up than I did the last time we met, although still not as comfortable as I would in my usual gear.

'You look smart. Just the right sort of thing for a day at the beach in March.'

I feel myself going red. I've never been great at taking compliments. 'Thanks,' I say quickly, hoping he hasn't noticed. 'You look nice too.'

'Was work okay this morning?'

My cheeks flush from crimson to scarlet. I nod guiltily towards Mrs Ryman's. 'It was fine, thanks.'

Given that I hadn't heard a single word from Noah since we met up, I'd given up all hope of ever hearing from him again. So when late on Wednesday night my phone buzzed as I was sitting in front of the TV feeling sorry for myself, I didn't think much of it. Probably one of the school mums asking about spelling lists, or Jodi checking to see how I was after I'd phoned her in tears telling her what a mess I'd made over trying to see my brother. When I checked and saw it was a message from Noah, I had to put my hands over my mouth to stop myself screaming. Happy didn't even begin to cover how I felt, especially as we texted back and forth most of the night.

Him: '*Hi Kerry, sorry to text so late . . . and for leaving it so long to get back in touch. I've had a really crazy week but that's no excuse. Hope things are well with you. All best, Noah.*'

Me: '*Hi Noah, no need to apologise about anything, it's just so great to hear from you no matter what time it is. And anyway, I'm a bit of a night owl these days. Everything is good with us, how about you? K xxx*'

Him: '*I'm well, thanks. As I said, work and life in general have been a bit manic but I'm hanging in there. I was thinking we should get together again sometime soon, if you're free. Let me know when is good for you. N.*'

Me: '*That would be amazing. I know this might be a long shot with you being so busy but I don't suppose you're around this Saturday? Kian's staying over at his mate's house after karate so I'm free all day. We could grab another coffee if you like or even a bite to eat? K xxx*'

Him: '*Or how about we make a day of it? Funnily enough I'm free all day Saturday too. We could drive down to Brighton, get a bit of sea air and maybe a cone of chips too? N.*'

Me: '*That sounds amazing! Yes please!*'

A whole day at the seaside, just him and me!

I literally had to pinch myself to make sure I wasn't dreaming. This was better than anything I'd ever dared hope for.

Over the next couple of days we texted back and forth about the arrangements and even though I'd offered, he'd insisted he wanted to drive and told me he'd pick me up at eleven on the

Saturday morning. That's when I had a bit of a panic. Truth is, I didn't want him picking me up from the estate. On the best of days it isn't exactly much to write home about, and the last thing I wanted was to give him an even worse impression of myself than he'd already got. I solved the problem by telling him I had to work for a bit on Saturday morning and it would be easier if he picked me up from in front of one of my clients' houses in Notting Hill. It wasn't exactly a lie – I did actually drop in a few bits of shopping Mrs Ryman had asked me to pick up – but I could have easily done it on Monday.

As I slide into the passenger seat of Noah's car, I practically have to stop myself from letting out a little groan of pleasure. No word of a lie, these have to be the most comfortable seats I've ever sat in. It's like being perched on a cloud, or floating on a bed of feathers. Honestly, if it wasn't for the company and the fact that I'm so excited, I could just close my eyes and drift off to sleep. Believe me, after this the seats in my old banger are going to feel like sandpaper.

He gets into the driving seat. 'All buckled up?' I nod. 'Next stop Brighton.'

He's about to start the engine when I remember I've got something for him. 'Could you hold on a sec?' I reach into my handbag, take out an envelope and hand it to him. 'These are for you. I had the photos of Mum copied for you. You don't have to hang on to them if you don't want to, but I thought you should have them.'

'Thanks, that was really thoughtful of you,' he says, and then he takes the envelope from me and slips it into the glove box without looking at them. 'Right,' he says, 'let's get going,' and then he presses a button on the dashboard and just like that, the car roars to life. For a moment I feel like I'm in a jet about to take off, leaving all my problems behind.

Noah asks me what music I like to listen to. I tell him I don't mind, even though that isn't exactly the truth. Back in the day,

I used to be a bit of a raver, and I still like that sort of thing now, along with some jungle, hip hop, drum and bass, and of course, Mariah. But I'm guessing the things I like won't exactly be his cup of tea, so I tell him he should choose. He puts on some old Motown, which is a little bland for my taste but I don't mind, and for a while we drive along listening, neither of us saying much of anything.

'What are Kian and his friend up to today?' he asks two songs in. 'Anything fun?'

'After karate, I think they're going to Laser Quest, which is right up Kian's street. How about Millie?'

There's a little pause before he answers and then he says: 'Er . . . she's away skiing with school.' He smiles awkwardly and looks embarrassed.

'That's nice,' I say cheerily. I know he's got money, I don't want him to feel awkward about it.

'Thanks,' he replies with a sigh. 'It's her first time without us, but she's very experienced so I'm not too worried.'

It doesn't surprise me in the least that Noah and his family go skiing. Virtually all my clients go at least once a year, some even twice. I can't quite see the attraction myself, bombing down some hill, in the freezing cold, with two planks of wood tied to your feet. I'd be too worried about breaking my neck or catching pneumonia to enjoy myself. But people with money just can't seem to get enough of it. It's weird, like some sort of cult they all have to sign up to, or else get kicked out and forever be like the rest of us.

'I suppose I've got all this school trip stuff to come when Kian gets to secondary,' I say. 'I think the furthest he's been without me is Whipsnade Zoo, and even then I couldn't rest until he was home safe.'

'It's not easy, letting them go, is it?'

All at once my deepest darkest fears rise up to the surface. 'No,' I say, stuffing them all back down where they came from. 'I don't suppose it is.'

It doesn't matter how often I've been to the seaside, I still get a little thrill when I catch sight of the sea for the first time. It's so breathtaking, just a big line of sea and sky stretching out for miles and miles. It reminds me how big the world really is, how there are so many places I've never been and things I've never done.

After parking the car, we walk towards the beach, cross the main road, then go down some steps and crunch over the pebbles until we're right at the water's edge. I turn to Noah, a big grin on my face, and I see he's smiling too.

'This is lovely, isn't it?'

Noah nods. 'Really blows the cobwebs away, doesn't it?'

'It's always been a bit of a dream of mine to live by the sea,' I say. 'Maybe Cornwall or something, in one of those tiny little cottages you see on the telly.'

'It would be amazing, wouldn't it? To wake up to a view like this every day?'

'Yeah, but of course I'd have to win the lottery first. Even the tiniest of little cottages don't come cheap in Cornwall.'

I don't know what comes over me, but right there and then I want nothing more than to be in the sea and I start taking off my boots and socks, even though I've completely forgotten to paint my toenails.

Noah laughs. 'Are you really going in? It'll be freezing!'

'It's got to be done,' I say. 'You can't come all this way and not get your feet wet.'

I try to coax Noah to join me but he's not having any of it. Then, after a while of me splashing around, I turn to look at him and he's taking off his boots and socks too. I watch, laughing, as he rolls up his jeans and steps into the freezing cold water, inching his way forwards until he's right next to me. We stand looking out to the horizon, watching a tanker way out in the distance, but then out of nowhere a massive wave crashes right in front of us, spraying icy water right up my coat. I scream, and stumble backwards, and Noah grabs my arm to keep me steady. In an instant I've travelled back thirty years: me, Mum and Jason paddling in the sea at Margate. Jason in the middle, holding both our hands, giggling and screaming every time a wave soaks him through.

Noah lets go of my arm and we walk back up the beach and sit on some rocks, drying our feet off.

'I bet you don't remember the day you, Mum and me went to the seaside,' I say as I dab at my toes with a tissue. 'You must have been about a year old, and had just started walking. You yelled your head off whenever me or Mum tried to put you on the sand – you didn't like the feel of it on your feet – but you loved being in the water. Mum said you were a proper water baby.'

Noah doesn't speak for a minute. He just sits staring out to sea. 'You're right,' he says in the end. 'I don't remember it. I don't remember anything about those days, to be honest.'

He looks so lost I just want to hug him. 'It's to be expected. You were only very little.'

He nods thoughtfully. 'What was I like . . . you know, as a baby?'

A huge grin springs up on my face as I remember. 'Beautiful. A real smiler. Whenever Mum or me took you down the shops, total strangers would come and coo over you, and you were a right charmer, you'd lap it up.'

Noah looks at me for a moment, but when I look back he turns his head towards the sea. 'Sometimes I wish I could remember more than I do. Sometimes I wish I didn't feel like there were so many blank spaces where my memories should be.'

'I shouldn't worry. I can't remember anything from being a baby. Mum could've taken me to Disneyland, for all I know, and I wouldn't have a clue.'

'But it's different, isn't it? It's not so much that I can't remember being that age, nobody can. It's more that all these years I've had no one to tell me the stories like the one you've just told me.'

I don't know what to say after that, and he doesn't either. So we just put on our shoes and socks, and decide to go and find something to eat.

We search for a café to get out of the cold, but then we pass a couple eating fish and chips. The warm vinegary smell is so delicious that we decide we want some too, and minutes later we're sitting in one of those bus shelter type things on the front, protected from the worst of the wind, looking out to sea, stuffing our faces with hot, salty chips.

We're just finishing off, when Noah gets a text. I look away while he checks his phone, but when he's done I can feel his mood has changed.

'Everything all right?'

'It's nothing, just a text from Rosalind. She's heard from school and everything is going well with Millie's trip.'

'Just say if you don't want to talk about it, I won't be offended, but how are things with you and your wife? Any better?'

He shakes his head. 'Much the same,' he says. 'We've started counselling, but I can't say it's helping much.'

He sounds really sad, and while I don't want to push too hard, I'm desperate to help if I can.

'What's the problem, if you don't mind me asking?'

He thinks for a moment, eyes fixed on the waves. 'Me, I suppose, and the way I am, the way I've always been.'

'How do you mean?'

He frowns, thinking. He really likes to consider what he says before he says it. Like he's weighing up his words.

'I'm not really one for talking about my feelings, never have been, but Rosalind's been through a tough time recently, and she's wanted, or rather needed, me to be more open, and I just haven't been able to manage it.'

'You seem pretty open to me.'

He laughs. 'Maybe the counselling is working better than I thought it was.'

'I know what you mean about talking though. I've never been all that great at it. Kian's dad used to say I had a mind like a bloke when it came to that sort of thing. He could never get me to talk about what was bothering me. To be fair though, most of the time it was him so there wasn't much point.'

'How long has it been since you split up?'

'It's hard to say really, it was always a bit on and off, but then once I got pregnant it was over for good.'

'And does he keep in contact with Kian?'

'When he feels like it, which isn't that often.'

'That's a shame. I can't imagine not being part of Millie's life.'

He looks away for a minute. I'm guessing he's thinking about everything that's going on with his family. I want to hug him again, but instead I put my hand gently on his back. 'Everything's going to be all right, you know. I'm sure you and your wife will work things out.'

'I hope so, I really do, but the thing is, if the problem is me and I don't know how to fix myself, then how will we ever get over this?'

I think about all the mistakes I've made over the years, how many times I'd thought I'd messed things up for good, and yet here I am, still standing. 'You might think you're always going to be like this, that people can't change, but that's not true. We can all change if we really want to, you've just got to have the right motivation. For me it was Kian, and for you, it's that beautiful family of yours. Because that's the thing about family, when it's done right, there's nothing in the world that you wouldn't do for them, no obstacle you wouldn't climb, no sacrifice you wouldn't make, just to see them be okay.'

12

Noah

Saturday, 19th March

'Are you sure I can't get you a pudding?'

Kerry shakes her head. 'No, I'm stuffed, thanks. But you go ahead if you want one.'

'Actually, I'm stuffed too. Perhaps it's time we hit the road back to London.'

Kerry nods. 'It's like they say,' she smiles. 'All good things must come to an end.'

Having walked and talked around the Lanes for much of the afternoon, we took refuge in the nearest pub when the weather took a turn for the worse. We'd only meant to stay until the rain stopped, but with the warmth of a roaring log fire and a menu replete with the tastiest comfort food imaginable, we'd found it impossible to tear ourselves away.

As we walk back to the car, I can't help but feel disappointed that the day is drawing to an end. It had definitely been the right decision to get back in contact with Kerry. I had instinctively wanted to keep the door to the past firmly closed, the door that had been kicked open so violently when Kerry had got in touch, but having met her, I found I couldn't hold it shut any longer. She had piqued a curiosity in me that I'd worked hard my entire life to suppress, and I wanted nothing more than to get to know her. Even though we couldn't be more different if we tried, the fact remained that she was part of me and I was part of her, and for someone who, in spite of the best efforts of his family, still, on occasion, had moments where he felt like the odd one out, the cuckoo in the nest, it was a surprising and yet sweet relief to finally feel connected to my past.

I've really made a connection with Kerry, although I'm aware we were both careful to keep the topics of our conversations fairly neutral as we wandered in and out of the shops around the Lanes, and sat nursing our coffees in the pub. She told me more about what I was like when I was small: how my favourite toy had been a purple stuffed parrot that I took everywhere. How my first solid food had been some mashed potato straight from her plate, and how I would regularly escape Houdini-style from my cot when put down for a nap. So many stories, a past revealed in anecdotes, which Kerry delivered with such animation, it was clear that those times had meant a great deal to her.

As we approach the multi-storey car park that is our destination, I find myself filled with the urge to honour her candour with some of my own.

'You know the other day, when you asked me whether I remembered being Jason?' Kerry nods. 'Well, I think you ought to know that my response to your question wasn't . . . well, it wasn't entirely truthful.'

'How do you mean?'

I think about the guilt I'd felt when she'd asked me about this when we first met. I'd felt awkward and uncomfortable, so had deliberately avoided talking about it. 'Well, the truth is . . . I actually was called Jason. In fact, it was my name right up until the age of ten when I told my parents I wanted to change it.'

'Oh right,' she says, and then she looks away from me. 'I just thought it must have been the people who adopted you who changed it.'

I think about how, back then, I'd wanted so desperately to belong, to fit in with my peers. 'No. It was all my doing. I didn't like the name very much. Jason . . . well it wasn't the sort of name the boys at the school I attended had.'

In my head these words had sounded pretty awful; said aloud, however, they seemed even worse. That's the thing about shameful confessions: whether in the courtroom or at the kerbside, actions once removed from their context and examined in the cold light of day can seem harsh, dark and unfeeling.

There's a long silence as we both let my prepubescent act of class betrayal sink in.

'I don't know what I was thinking, really,' I continue awkwardly. 'I suppose, because I knew I used to have a different surname, it made some sort of sense in my little head to go the whole hog. To cut all ties with a past I couldn't remember.'

I wonder what she must think of me, what must be going on behind those grey-green eyes of hers, but I can't tell. Like the most inscrutable of jurors, the ones you can't tell whether you've managed to get completely on side or have lost to opposing counsel, she gives me nothing.

'And what made you choose Noah?' Her tone is non-accusatory, almost as if she really wants to know the answer, rather than score points or share her hurt, and so I tell her the story, even though it makes very little sense.

'Years ago we used to have an old wooden Noah's ark that had belonged to my father when he was young. I really loved playing with it, and would spend hours marching the animals on and off. So when I sat down with my parents in front of the *Oxford Book of First Names*, looking for a new name for me, it just sort of jumped off the page.' Forgetting myself, I can't help but smile as I recall the moment. 'My parents aren't the slightest bit religious, so I don't think anyone was more surprised than they were, but they went along with it because they thought it would make me happy.' I look over at Kerry and smile apologetically. 'I'm sorry I wasn't more honest with you. I just didn't want you to be offended.'

She takes my arm. 'We all do what we need to do to get by,' she says gently. 'And you can't blame anyone for that, can you?'

Our return journey seems a lot quicker than the outward portion. Gone are the long awkward silences and nerves, and the conversation between us flows naturally. As we reach the outskirts of the city I realise I don't know where Kerry actually lives, but when I enquire she seems reluctant to tell me.

'Oh, just drop me off anywhere near a Tube, it won't take me long to get home.'

'It's no trouble at all, and as a gentleman I'd much prefer to see you to your door. I'm nothing if not gallant.' I grin, hoping she knows I'm joking.

'Really, Noah, I'm fine, I don't want you going out of your way.'

'To be honest, you'd be doing me a favour. I really only ever get the chance to drive at the weekends, it would be nice to have an excuse to be behind the wheel a little bit longer.'

'Honestly, Noah, like I said, I'm fine with the Tube.'

There's an edge to her voice I haven't heard before, and suddenly I realise what might be behind her reticence: she doesn't want me to see where she lives. I open my mouth to reassure her but before I can say anything, she apologises.

'I'm sorry, I didn't mean to snap like that, it's just the estate where I live it's . . . well . . . it's a bit of a dump, really.'

'And you think I'd judge you for that?'

'No, of course not . . . well . . . I don't know . . . we've had such a lovely day, and I feel like we're getting on really well. I just don't want anything to spoil it.'

'Good,' I reply firmly. 'Then let me take you home.'

My familiarity with Kerry's neighbourhood begins and ends with Portobello market but as I follow her directions, the landscape changes dramatically from grand stucco-fronted Edwardian houses costing millions, to boarded-up shop fronts covered in graffiti. Kerry's home is a flat in a low-rise development in the shadow of two huge tower blocks.

'This is me,' she says flatly, as we pull up. 'Like they say, it's not much but it's home. I'd invite you in for a cuppa, but I don't like the idea of you leaving your motor on its own. They'll nick anything around here.'

Although it's dressed up as concern about my car, I sense that she's still suffering the same embarrassment about where she lives and I'm determined not to let this come between us.

'I'm not going to worry about it. I'm sure it'll be fine. And besides, I really could murder a cup of tea.'

Kerry shakes her head. 'You don't know this area like I do. A flash car like yours will stick out a mile.'

'It'll be fine.'

Kerry smiles. 'You're not going to let me say no, are you?'

I shake my head. 'It's my persistence that makes me good at my job.'

'Fine,' she says. 'But let me try something first.' She takes out her phone and, moving out of earshot, makes a call.

'What was that about?' I ask when she returns.

'Me making sure no one nicks your car.' She raises an eyebrow mysteriously. 'Sometimes it's not what you know, but who.'

We don't pass a soul as we make our way up the stairs to Kerry's flat, but there is evidence of people having been here in the form of empty lager cans and discarded takeaway boxes. Sensing Kerry's anxiety, I make no comment about the mess and instead regale her with the tale of a persistent car thief I defended in the early days of my career. 'He was a lovely guy,' I tell her, 'but not very bright. He used to spend all night stealing cars and all day sleeping, but one night he must have stayed up a little too long because he ended up falling fast asleep in the very car he was stealing. He woke up not only to discover that he was still on the owner's drive, but also that he was surrounded by police officers.'

Kerry's still laughing as she opens up the door to her flat. In contrast to its surroundings her home is pristine, and tastefully decorated, albeit with a strong glittery motif. There's a gold glitter-framed mirror in the hallway, a metallic silver sideboard and matching coffee table in the airy living room, and purple sequined cushions on the sofa.

'So you like sparkle then?'

Kerry grins sheepishly.

'Just a bit,' she says. 'I think everybody needs a bit of shimmer in their life sometimes. It cheers you up.'

Kerry leads me to an immaculate kitchen with walls painted

bright yellow. It's not a huge space by any means, but somehow, along with the usual cupboards and cooker and washing machine, she's managed to squeeze in a small dining table and four chairs.

'I know it makes it a bit crowded in here,' she apologises, catching my eye, 'but I've always loved the idea of families sitting down around a proper table at meal times. It just feels right. Do you do that?'

'When we can,' I say, only aware of my mistake in speaking in the present tense when it's too late. 'Most nights I don't get home until late, by which time Millie has eaten and is up in her room doing homework. Rosalind and I usually eat together though.'

She fills the kettle for our tea and I look around the room. I catch sight of a photo of Kian stuck to the fridge, and examine it closely. It's a classic school photo pose and I'm struck once again by the knowledge that, in addition to my niece and nephew in Hong Kong, I now have another nephew right here in London.

'Did you tell Kian about today?'

Kerry is taking two mugs out of the cupboard next to her. She looks over at me and shakes her head.

'He's always known I have a brother that I don't see, but I want things to be more settled before I let him know I've finally found you. Is that okay?'

'To be honest, I've still not said anything to anyone either, not even Rosalind or Millie. Is that terrible?'

Kerry smiles. 'Of course it isn't. We will tell them, I'm sure. We're just waiting for the right time.'

We move into the living room, but before sitting down, Kerry checks on my car from the window. I look around the room again, keen to reassure her that she's made the right decision inviting me up.

'I really like what you've done here, it's lovely.'

'Thanks, I just wish I could pick it up and take it somewhere else,' she says, tucking her feet up beneath her on the sofa next to me.

'How long have you been here?'

'About eight years now, I was in a much smaller flat on the other side of the estate when Kian was born, and when this came up, I jumped at it.'

'So have you always lived around here?'

'Yeah, mostly. I suppose I've always thought of it as home because it was the first place I was dumped after getting kicked out of Milread Road.' She registers the look of puzzlement on my face, before adding, 'The children's home where I ended up.'

I'm immediately struck dumb. I feel guilty and angry, all at once. Stupidly it hadn't occurred to me that Kerry might not have been fostered or adopted like me. And yet she hadn't. While I'd been saved, she'd been left behind. While I'd been rescued, she'd been abandoned. It all seemed so cruelly arbitrary, so outrageously unfair, and though I know intellectually that, being a mere child myself, there was nothing I could have done, that doesn't stop me feeling culpable, responsible somehow for who knows what horrors she's suffered. I think about all the terrible things you read about that happen to children in care and feel sick to my stomach.

'How old were you . . . you know, when they sent you there?'

Kerry takes a sip of her tea but doesn't look at me. 'Twelve.'

Twelve.

Millie's age.

'But . . . but . . . why weren't you adopted or fostered? Surely someone somewhere could have done something?'

'I wasn't exactly the easiest of kids to look after.' She shrugs. 'I was fostered for a couple of years, but I think after getting kicked out of one place too many, they must have decided I wasn't worth the effort. Milread Road wasn't that bad though, if that's what you're thinking. No one hurt me or anything.'

'But still, you were only twelve, you should've been with a family, with people to love and care for you.'

'It was fine, honestly, Noah. I had a roof over my head, I had food, and I had Jodi.'

'Who's Jodi?'

'My best friend. She lives in Newcastle now but we're still

dead close. In fact, me and Kian are going up to stay with her for a bit over the Easter holidays.'

Despite the picture she's painting, I still can't shake the overwhelming sense of guilt I feel. Young people who have been in care are six times more likely to enter the criminal justice system, more likely to experience homelessness, develop drug and alcohol dependencies, and have children before the age of eighteen. I can't even begin to imagine the struggles Kerry has had to face and I'm not entirely convinced she's telling me the whole truth either, that she's not playing down the awfulness of it for my benefit.

'And so what happened when you turned eighteen? Did they just kick you out and leave you to fend for yourself?'

'Not exactly, they did at least kit out a little flat for me. But like I said, I don't suppose I was the easiest person to help back then.'

'How do you mean?'

We lock eyes briefly, then she looks away. 'I was quite an angry kid, and reckless with it. By the time I left Milread Road I was probably at my worst. I dropped out of college, got into all sorts of trouble, and wouldn't listen to anyone I thought was trying to tell me what to do. To be honest, when I think about those days I can't help but shudder.'

'So what changed? You don't seem like that any more to me.'

For a moment she reflects, a dark cloud of sadness temporarily shrouding her face. 'I woke up one day, in a strange flat in a part of London I'd never been to before, sick all down my front, with a bunch of people I didn't remember meeting. And that's when I realised.'

'That you had to stop?'

She shakes her head. 'That I was turning into Mum.'

I can see it's taken a lot for her to open up like this and I don't want to upset her by asking any of the questions that are flooding through my head right now. Was that what our mother was like? Was this sort of behaviour the reason we were taken from her care? Is Kerry implying that she's inherited our mother's sense of self-destruction and if so, what does that mean for me? There is so much I want to ask, but I can see she needs a moment so, when she stands up and offers to make us another cup of tea, I thank her and let her go into the kitchen on her own.

I'm still trying to make sense of everything I've just heard when I hear the sound of the front door opening, followed by a young boy's voice calling out Kerry's name. Realising Kian must have come home early, I get to my feet just as he walks into the room. He's wearing a navy-blue hoodie pulled up over his head, ripped jeans and white trainers. We stare at each other in silence for several moments.

'Who are you?' His features brim with outrage, while his fists clench by his sides.

'Never mind that.' Kian and I both turn our heads to see a stern-looking Kerry standing in the doorway. 'The only question that matters right now is why aren't you at Callum's?'

Kian blinks anxiously several times but says nothing.

Kerry puts her hands on her hips as if she means business. 'I'm waiting.'

Finally Kian relents. 'I'm here because Callum is a di—'

Kerry angrily cuts him off. 'Kian! What have I told you about using that sort of language?'

He looks down at his shoes. 'Well, he is,' he says sulkily. 'And he's an idiot too. He keeps going on about how he's getting this and that for his birthday, and saying my phone is rubbish and my trainers are no good and I just got sick of it.'

'So you made his mum bring you back at this time of night?'

Kian bites his lip but doesn't explain further. Putting two and two together, Kerry explodes and it's a truly frightening thing to behold. She's like a force of nature.

'Are you seriously telling me you just upped and left Callum's and walked home across the estate on your own in the dark?'

He pulls a face. 'I just had to get out of there. He was doing my head in.'

'Right, I don't want to hear another word from you,' Kerry barks, pointing to the empty sofa. 'Sit down there while I call

Callum's mum and explain what you've been up to.' She's so angry as she leaves the room in search of her phone that I daren't say a word, even though this is probably the worst introduction to my nephew I could imagine.

As I sit down, Kian glares at me as if I'm responsible for all the trouble he's in, but when Kerry sweeps back into the room in an instant I cease being the focus of his attention.

'I'm so angry with you right now, Kian. Have you any idea how embarrassing it was having to explain to Callum's mum that you'd done a runner?'

Kian says nothing but Kerry isn't about to let it go.

'Come on, then,' she demands. 'Have you?'

Kian shakes his head.

'I can't hear you!'

Kian mutters a barely audible, 'No.'

'I didn't think so,' she snaps. 'Otherwise you wouldn't have done it. What have I told you about dealing with idiots?'

Kian sniffs, his eyes already wet with tears. 'Ignore them.'

'And if you'd done exactly that, do you think you'd be in this trouble now?'

Kian shakes his head.

'Listen, son, the world is full of people like Callum West trying to wind you up for a laugh.' Her voice is lower now, softer. 'It's the only power they've got. But if you show them you can't be wound up, they'll soon realise you're the one with the power, not them.'

It's a properly old-fashioned scolding, the likes of which Millie, even at her very worst, has never received. But with the little I know of Kerry, I can see its severity comes from love not anger. Kian is her only son, and she's not going to let anyone accuse her of not bringing him up properly.

'Right,' she says finally. 'To bed, and no arguments. I'll let you know in the morning what your punishment is going to be, but I can tell you now, I'm taking the plug off the PlayStation.'

A chastened Kian heads towards the door but then stops, turns around and thrusts his hand in the air as if he's at school.

'What now?'

'Can I ask a question?'

Kerry narrows her eyes in suspicion. 'If this is you just messing about I'm going to really—'

The boy points to me. 'Who's that, Mum?'

Kerry and I exchange glances. With everything going on, it appears that she's forgotten to introduce us.

'This . . . darling . . . well, this is . . . my brother,' she says, looking from her son to me and back again, 'your Uncle Jason. After all these years he's finally come back to me.'

PART
2

21st May 1996

Hi Lovely,

Hope life is treating you well. I'm writing to let you know I've moved from my old address. Well, not just to do that! I always love catching up with you, even if I don't hear back. Writing to you makes me feel close to you somehow. It makes me feel like you're there, even if I can't see you.

I'm moving because I need a fresh start. It's been four years since I left Milread Road and well . . . let's say I've made a lot of mistakes in that time: ones that I'm not very proud of. You don't need to know the details. The only thing you need to know is that I'm not going to carry on that way any more. I'm going to change. I'm going to get a job, and settle down and try and be someone you'll be proud to call your sister.

I promise I'll write soon when things are more settled.

Love you so much,

Kerry xxx

PS Wish me luck!!!

13

Kerry

Friday, 25th March

'Which one do you think he'll like?'

Kian and I are at the supermarket and he is scanning the huge wall of Easter eggs in front of him. His eyes are wide and he's practically drooling.

'I could eat them all.'

'I know that, son. You could eat Easter eggs for England. I'm talking about Uncle Noah. Which one do you think *he* would like?'

Accepting the challenge, he screws up his face in concentration. It takes him a while but eventually he makes his decision. He reaches up and takes down a box with pictures of Spiderman plastered all over it.

'Do you really think Uncle Noah is going to want a superhero Easter egg? He's a grown man.'

Kian shrugs. 'So is Spiderman and anyway, if he doesn't like it, I'll eat it for it him.'

'You're all heart, aren't you?' I give his hair a ruffle and then take the egg and drop it into the trolley along with all the other nice things I'm getting in for the weekend.

'Come on, you,' I say, pointing him in the direction of the tills, 'let's go home.'

It's been six days since Kian met his Uncle Noah, but from the way he's been going on about him all week you'd think he'd known him all his life. 'I think Uncle Noah will get a Ferrari for his next car,' he'd said to me out of nowhere on Monday morning on the way to school. On Tuesday, when he should have been brushing his teeth for bed, he just barged into my bedroom without knocking on the door and said, 'I think if Uncle Noah ever came with us for a McDonalds he'd have a Big Mac and a Coke.' Then on Wednesday (and this is my favourite) he said to me as we were having our tea: 'I don't think Uncle Noah's mum ever makes him eat yucky salmon.'

Thinking back to the night when Kian met Noah, they weren't exactly what you'd call ideal circumstances, what with me shouting at Kian for coming home early on his own and him not having a clue who this strange bloke was standing in the living room. Thankfully, in the end it didn't seem to matter because once the awkward introductions were out of the way, for Kian at least it was pretty much love at first sight. Noah kept making him laugh and as he talked to him about video games and football and stuff, I could see that Kian was loving every second. He was totally in awe and couldn't get enough of him. It was such a lovely thing to see, because love him as I do, I don't kid myself that I can be everything to my son. Obviously there are times when I wish I could be, especially when he's missing that waste-of-space dad of his, but what can I do? That's why I take him to football, that's why I take him to karate, because I know he needs strong male role models in his life, men to show him how a good bloke is supposed to be. I mean, I can tell him until I'm blue in the face that he needs to be careful crossing roads but if his football coach or karate teacher mentions it once in passing, he'll quote them back to me chapter and verse. And now, of course, it's Noah's turn to be idolised.

In the end, the only way Kian would let Noah go home that night was if he promised to come back again soon. Of course I told Kian he was being out of order, that Noah was a very busy man, but Noah was having none of it. He said to Kian, 'How about next weekend? I'm with my family Easter Sunday, but we could do something on Easter Monday if you're free.'

Kian's eyes lit up and of course straight away he started going on about the skatepark and how he wanted to show Noah some tricks on YouTube that he and his mates had been working on.

I told Noah he didn't have to agree to anything but he said that the skatepark sounded like a great idea, and he told Kian a story about how he used to skateboard when he was a kid. He showed him a scar on his elbow where he'd fallen off and chipped a bone in his arm. Well, that was that: Noah couldn't have been a bigger hero in Kian's eyes if he'd popped on a red cape and flown out of the window.

Before Noah left, he shook Kian's hand and told him he'd see him again soon. I insisted on walking him down to his car, partly because I wanted to make sure it was still there and partly because I wanted to thank him properly for such an incredible day.

'So are you going to tell me who it was you called?' he asked when we got downstairs to discover that not only was his car still there, but so were all its wheels.

I laughed guiltily. 'It was one of the mums at Kian's school,' I explained. 'Her two eldest kids are pretty much behind ninety per cent of the car crime around here. So I told her that the car belonged to one of south London's biggest drug dealers who also happens to be my brother, and unless they wanted trouble they should leave your motor well alone.'

Noah raised an eyebrow and laughed. 'You're nothing if not creative, Kerry. Have you ever considered a career in crime prevention?'

'I'll stick to cleaning, thanks. It's a lot less messy.' Then I gave him the biggest hug I could manage and unlike last time at the café, it wasn't all stiff and awkward; it was strong and full of warmth and seemed to last forever. It made me feel so good that I almost poured out everything I felt in my heart, but at the last minute I stopped myself. I didn't want to overwhelm him or scare him away.

As we unload the shopping from the boot of the car back at the estate, Kian and I chat about what we fancy for dinner. I'm in the mood for a cheese toastie because it's been ages since I last had one, but Kian fancies a bacon sandwich, even though he had one last night. Normally, I'd only do one or the other because I don't like to make work for myself, but I'm in such a good mood about all the things I'm looking forward to this weekend that I agree to make both, and Kian's so chuffed he even lets out a little cheer.

As we climb the stairs up to the flat, carrying the shopping, I start singing a silly song that's popped into my head from one of those daft YouTube videos Kian's always watching. Straight away Kian's in stitches because I'm doing all the funny voices too and he starts to join in, but then we reach our floor and he stops suddenly. I follow his eyes as he looks down the walkway to where a stocky bloke with a fake tan and blond highlights is leaning against our front door, looking for all the world like he owns the place. My heart sinks. My brilliant day is about to take a nosedive.

'Dad!' screams Kian at the top of his lungs. He drops the shopping like it's radioactive and runs straight into the open arms of Steve, my ex.

I'd known Steve for about six months before we got together. He was in the warehouse at the Tesco where I used to work. Back then he was okay-looking if a bit vain. He had nice hair and wore nice clothes, and was good to have a laugh and joke with. At the time I was pretty down on myself; I'd just split up with yet another bloke and promised myself that I'd take a break from dating for a while. But what no one tells you is that when you get your life together for the most part it's pretty boring. You get up, go to work, come home, watch a bit of TV, go to bed and then start all over again the next day. So when Steve came along, it was something a bit different, a bit of excitement. It wasn't the world's greatest love affair or anything, but he was funny, straightforward, and anyway I didn't expect it to last.

Six months in we were still together and even though we'd not talked about it, he'd all but moved in with me. Useless as he was, I liked it. I liked having him around. I suppose I hadn't realised just how lonely I was, and for the first time in a long while I was happy, really happy, right up until the point that I woke up and realised my period was so late it could only mean one thing.

Finding out I was pregnant was a shock. I'd never wanted kids of my own, never thought I was up to the responsibility. I'd always thought I'd be hopeless at being a mum, just like Mary. But once I began to get my head around it, I realised this was the best news I could have had. Overnight I felt like I had a purpose, a job to do, and somewhere deep down I knew I could do it. When I told Steve I was pregnant the next day, I hoped he'd be as happy as me but, that said, I wasn't the slightest bit surprised when he wasn't. This was far too serious, too grown-up for Steve who, even though he was in his thirties like me, was little more than an overgrown child himself. He was gone by the end of the week and living with another girl from work by the end of the month. Not that I cared. I was too busy thinking about the future. Thinking how this was my chance to get things right, to love a child the way it is supposed to be loved, to raise it to know that it is cherished and valued, not just another problem to be solved.

Since then, Steve's not been a big part of Kian's life. He wasn't there at the birth, and in fact didn't even see his son until he was six months old. In ten years he's never once offered any money or help, not that I've asked for it. Everything Kian has is because I've gone out and earned it myself, and I'm proud of that. Now and again, though, I think Steve's conscience must play him up a bit, because out of nowhere he rocks up, acting like he's only been gone five minutes, arms full of presents, making out like he's dad of the year.

The moment I open the front door Steve and Kian disappear off into the living room, leaving me to put the shopping away and make dinner on my own. Every now and again I hear them laughing, in between the sound of a crash or an explosion coming from whichever game they're playing on the PlayStation, and I feel my blood boil. It's galling the way Steve acts sometimes, swanning into my home like he owns the place and picking up Kian like he's some sort of forgotten toy. It's enough to make me want to spit. But I've always told myself I'm not going to be one of those mums who turn their kids against their dads. I've always told myself that it's Kian's feelings that come first not mine. So even though I'd sooner wipe the smug grin Steve's always wearing off that stupid face of his with the business end of a frying pan than be nice to him, I pop my head around the door and, sweet as you like, ask him if he wants to stay for something to eat. Of course, the last thing I want is him hanging around the place all day, spoiling all the fun things I had planned. But what can I do when Kian is so happy now that his dad is here? So when Steve says, 'Yeah, I'd love a bacon sarnie, but I want my bacon extra crispy and I could murder a cuppa while you're at it,' I don't tell him where to go, or punch him in the face or act out any of the other fantasies that go through my head. Instead I shut my mouth, add a couple of extra slices of bacon to the pan and flick the kettle on.

It's weird when all three of us finally sit down to eat at my tiny little table in the kitchen. To anyone watching, we'd look like a regular happy family – father and son teasing each other over the table, slightly harassed mum looking on, tolerating their terrible table manners. But the fact is, we're not a regular happy family. We're . . . I'm not sure what we are . . . two adults connected forever through their child? A single-parent family, and some random who shows his face once in a blue moon? I'm not sure there's a proper word for what we are but if one exists, I know for certain that it's not family. Not even close.

Kian bolts down his food like he hasn't eaten for days and then asks me if it's okay to leave the table.

'There's a new game that's just come out and I know Logan's got it and he said he might lend it to me so Dad and I can play it.' The words flood out of him like water from a fully open tap. 'Can I go and see if he's in, Mum? He's only in the next block along. I won't be long, I promise.'

While most of the kids on this estate are left to wander around at all times of the day and night, Kian isn't. I don't really like letting him out on his own. There are too many bad things that can happen. You read in the papers about kids not much older than Kian getting mugged, beaten up, or even worse, stabbed. Still, he'll be at secondary school next year, and whether I like it or not, I need to give him the chance to be a bit more independent.

'All right, but phone first to see if he's there and if you're gone longer than ten minutes, don't think for a second that I won't come looking for you.'

While I clear the table, Steve just sits there like a big lump playing with his phone, never once thinking that after eating my food the very least he can do is give me a hand clearing up.

'He's in and he says I can borrow it,' says Kian, grabbing his coat, and before I can say anything he's slammed the door behind him, leaving me and Steve alone for the first time in probably about a year and a half.

Though we might have a son together, that doesn't mean we have much to say to each other. For instance, I don't know where he's living or who he's living with and I don't ask. As Kian is never there I don't see it as any of my business, really. But my son is my business, and while he's out of the way I think this might be a good time for me and Steve to talk.

Steve barely looks at me as I sit down at the table. He just carries on playing with his phone. He looks older than when I saw him last. He's put on a bit of weight and his hair's receding badly, but none of that stops him dressing like he did when we were together: tight T-shirt, designer jeans and expensive trainers. Not that I'm impressed any more.

'So how have you been?'

He still doesn't look up.

'I'm all right. Can't complain.'

He carries on staring at his phone. I slap my hands down sharply on the table in front of him and he nearly jumps out of his skin.

He finally looks up at me, his face all screwed up with annoyance. 'Easy!' he says, almost dropping his phone. 'What's wrong with you?'

'I'm fine, thanks, Steve, thanks for asking.' My every syllable is dripping with sarcasm but it goes straight over his head, and once again he starts playing with his phone. This time I'm so outraged that I don't bother to bang the table. Instead I just grab his phone, march over to the open window and dangle it outside.

He's on his feet in a flash. 'Are you mental? That phone cost more than anything in this crappy flat.'

The closer he comes towards me, the further I push my arm out the window. 'One step closer and I'll drop it.'

He stops in his tracks, scowling at me hatefully.

'I knew it was a mistake coming round here.' He holds out his hand. 'Stop messing about, Kerry, just give me my phone.'

I shake my head. It feels good to have a bit of power for a change. 'You can have it back once you've heard me out: I want you to see more of Kian.'

He lets out a groan like I've just asked him to take out the bins for me. 'Not this again! What's wrong with you? I'm here, aren't I?'

'And when was the last time? Kian never has a clue when you're going to pop up next. He's always asking me where you are and what you're up to, and I just have to tell him I don't know. I don't think it's fair.'

'I see him when I can, which is more than most blokes I know.'

'And what a bunch of charmers they must be! Listen, I don't ask for anything from you, not money, not help with Kian, nothing. I even lied to keep the CSA off your back. So why can't you just do this one thing for me? In fact, don't do it for me, do it for your son. Take him out for the day, show a bit of interest, ask him how he's feeling, what he wants to be when he grows up, anything, just pay him some attention.'

Steve's face is like thunder – he hates being told off by anyone, least of all me – and I know he's going to try to grab his phone back.

'Come on then,' I say, waving the phone in the air. 'Just try it and I swear I'll let go. And if you don't believe me, just keep on moving.'

Just like that, he freezes. It's like he loves this phone more than he loves his own son. I try one last time. 'Listen, I'm not trying to get in your face, or involved in your business. I just want you to be a proper dad to your son, one he can rely on if he needs you.'

'Bloke tries to do something nice for his kid and ends up getting it in the neck!' spits Steve. 'Well, I've had enough of it. Once I've got my phone, I'm out of here. And you can be the one to explain to Kian why I've gone.'

Every time I think my opinion of Steve can't get any lower, he finds some new way to surprise me.

'You really don't care about our son, do you? Kian means nothing at all to you, does he?'

I feel myself filling with rage. I can't believe Steve would treat his own flesh and blood like dirt. I want to hurt him. I want to hurt him badly. I pull the phone back inside, as if I'm going to give it to him, but then at the last moment I whip it forwards with all my strength and let go, sending it flying. Steve rushes to the window, his face white with shock, and we both stand and stare, neither of us able to quite believe what I've just done, as the phone makes a perfect arc through the air, before crash-landing on to the pavement and smashing into a million tiny pieces.

14

Noah

Saturday, 26th March

At Millie's summoning, Rosalind and I turn around to see our daughter posed halfway down the stairs. For a split second I struggle to make sense of what I'm seeing: a young woman in a long blue chiffon dress and matching heels, with immaculate make-up, her hair piled artistically on top of her head. She looks sixteen, at least, if not older.

'So,' says Millie. 'What do you think?'

I turn to Rosalind and we exchange looks of bewilderment at the sight of our baby, all grown up.

'You look amazing,' says Rosalind, recovering herself before I do.

'Yes, absolutely,' I echo, as Millie makes her way down to us. 'Amazing.'

She performs a little twirl in front of us. 'Mum did my hair,' she says shyly. 'But the make-up was all me.'

I cast a quick look at Rosalind again over the top of Millie's head. 'YouTube,' she mouths silently, by way of explanation at my daughter's seemingly miraculous acquisition of the skills of a professional make-up artist.

'Well, you've done a brilliant job,' I declare, and then check my watch, only to see that the cost of her transformation has been that we're now running twenty minutes late for the restaurant. 'Anyway, we'd better get a move on, Mills, everyone will be wondering where we've got to.'

Millie slips on a long black coat, then kisses her mother goodbye. Seeing them standing side by side, I can't help but notice the contrast between them. Millie dressed up for a night out in all her finery and Rosalind, dressed down in yoga pants and an old cashmere sweater.

'Are you sure you won't change your mind? Mills and I can wait.'

Rosalind shakes her head. 'Thanks, guys, that's really sweet of you but as I said, I'm just not really feeling a hundred per cent and the last thing I want to do is be a wet blanket on Nana and Papa's big night. Nope, tonight is just going to be about me, some hot lemon and Netflix.' She kisses Millie again, then ushers us out of the door. 'You two have a great time and take plenty of photos so I don't miss a thing.'

As Millie and I walk towards the car, I look back at the house and feel a stab of sorrow as I see Rosalind waiting to wave us off. Things are different between us, that's for certain, and it's all because of what happened in our second counselling session on Wednesday.

Having lulled us into a false sense of security in our first session by allowing us to talk in relatively general terms about what had brought us to seek help, Elspeth now wanted to drill down to specifics.

'From what I gather, your daughter Millie was unplanned,' she observed. 'How did you both feel about that?'

'It was a shock,' confessed Rosalind. 'Particularly coming as it did so close to finals. But Noah was amazing, so supportive and calm that somehow it just seemed to make sense.'

Elspeth nodded thoughtfully, then turned her attention to me. 'And how about you, Noah?'

'I can only echo Rosalind's comments,' I said. 'It was a shock . . . but a wonderful one.'

'I imagine it would have had an even more special significance for you, given the fact that you're adopted.'

I knew exactly what she meant but that didn't stop me from saying, 'How so?'

She took a moment to clean her glasses. 'Because this baby was to be the first blood relation to appear in your life,' she said, on returning her glasses to the bridge of her nose. 'That must have brought a lot of emotions to the surface for you.'

Of course it had. The knowledge that I was to be a father, that there was to be another living, breathing part of me in the world, someone who shared my DNA, someone who would look and perhaps even behave like me, had a huge impact on me. How could it not? But that didn't mean I wanted to talk about it.

'Only in the way it would for anybody,' I reply. 'I'm not special in that regard.'

'You know exactly what she's talking about,' snapped Rosalind. 'Just stop being a barrister for one second and answer her question.'

But I didn't. I couldn't. No matter how hard I tried. Instead I found myself being vague and evasive at every turn, and it wasn't as if I didn't know that I was doing it. I was well aware. But it made no difference. This was my survival instinct at play, and asking me to ignore that instinct was like asking me to hold my hand above a flame and not flinch; I simply couldn't do it.

After the session Rosalind had been angry with me, and as we stood outside on the pavement she'd accused me of not taking our counselling seriously.

'You can't just keep avoiding the issue,' she'd said. 'One way or another, if you want this marriage to survive, you're going to have to find a way to talk about your adoption.'

She'd stormed off towards the Tube and it was clear she didn't want me to follow. Later that same evening, as I sat chatting with Charlotte, I received a text from her informing me that she wouldn't be attending my parents' golden wedding anniversary celebrations, celebrations that she had planned single-handedly for months. 'I just don't think I can face everybody at the moment,' she'd written, but I knew it was more complicated than that. This was her hardening her heart, doubling down in the face of what she saw as my belligerence and making it clear that this time, no matter what, she wasn't going to let me get away with it.

★

As Millie and I drive to the restaurant, I determine to put these thoughts out of my mind for the time being. Instead I focus on Millie's constant stream of chatter. She talks about everything from school dinners to the antics of her best friend's new kitten. It's oddly comforting, like listening to the World Service in the middle of the night when you're unable to sleep, as has been my own experience of late, and I'm grateful for the distraction.

My family are seated at the largest table in the restaurant, and are making the most noise by far. As we approach them, my brother Phillip leads a small cheer for our arrival, and the next few minutes are taken up by a flurry of greetings from not just my parents and siblings, but nephews, nieces, uncles, aunts and cousins too. They all comment on how grown-up Millie has become, and express their sadness that Rosalind hasn't been able to join us. It doesn't take a genius to work out that they have all been briefed about the situation between Rosalind and me, most likely by my mother, but we all choose to go along with the pretence, even raising a glass of champagne to her health before we order our food.

Phillip has flown over from Hong Kong with his family especially for the occasion. He's five years older than me, and two years older than Charlotte, a fact he never lets us forget. Not that he's overbearing or boorish, more that as the big brother he has always felt that his role in the family is to sort things out. Whether defending me from bullies at school or taking care of Mum when Dad had his heart by-pass, Phillip was always in the thick of things when any of us were in trouble.

'Just thought you ought to know that I've talked it over with Cassie and we've decided not to renew the lease for our nightmare tenants, so you can have our old Bayswater flat,' he says. 'I'm sure it won't be for very long, but even so, you'll need space to have Millie over while you work things out at home.'

I don't know what to say. Charlotte has been nothing but kind to me, but of late I've begun to wonder whether I should make alternative arrangements. Renting somewhere of my own, however, seems too permanent somehow, an admission of defeat.

But staying where I am has made it difficult for me to spend one-on-one time with Millie, which in the light of everything going on is particularly important.

I look at Phillip, his pale-blue eyes full of concern. 'Are you sure?'

'To be honest, you'd be doing us a favour. This lot of tenants have been nothing but trouble from the moment they moved in. I found out from the downstairs neighbours that they've been leasing out the flat on Airbnb! Can you believe the cheek of it? It's not just breaking the rules of their tenancy agreement but also incredibly rude, considering the lengths Cassie and I have gone to make them comfortable in what is still, let's not forget, our family home.'

I open my mouth to thank Phillip and Cassie for their kindness, but I'm interrupted by the arrival of our starters. Keen to curtail my expressions of gratitude, Phillip makes us charge our glasses once again, and this time raises a toast to our parents. 'To Mum and Dad,' he says. 'Here's hoping the next fifty years are just as good!'

Fifty years.

Such a rarity in this day and age, and I hadn't even managed fifteen. My parents' marriage has always been so solid, such a firm foundation for us all. This is partly why they adopted me in the first place. They've always told me that because they were so happy together, and had so much love to give, even with two children of their own, they'd known that they wanted to share the good things of their life with a child who might otherwise have remained unaware of these blessings. And now here I am, part of this family with a child of my own, and yet somehow unable to replicate the perfect example my parents had worked so hard to set before me. Fifty years of happy marriage, still enjoying each other's company, still each other's best friend. It's hard not to feel like a disappointment. It's hard not to feel as if I've let them down.

Mum calls across the table to me. 'Everything all right, Noah? You seem a bit lost.'

I draw a deep breath and resolve to stop indulging these self-chastising thoughts. 'I'm fine, Mum,' I reply, and with that, I take another breath and dive headfirst into the conversations going on around me.

The food is as exquisite as Rosalind had said it would be. I have scallops followed by lamb, and although I'm limiting myself to water as I'm driving, everyone else comments on how marvellous the wine is. As the waiters clear our plates away in preparation for dessert I excuse myself, and when I return from the cloakroom everyone is deep in conversation.

Being temporarily outside of the conversational loop allows me to observe the Martineau family in action: the grandstanding, ribbing, posturing and good-natured debate so typical of all our family get-togethers. Not that they've ever done anything to make me feel out of place, or excluded. Not that they've ever made me feel like a stranger or an interloper. This is my family. Their anecdotes, their shared jokes, their way of seeing the world, feel as much mine as they are Charlotte's or Phillip's. And yet, as I listen to the chat and laughter I can't help but be reminded of my other family, the one I've rediscovered, the one into which I was born.

I consider Kerry and how wonderful and strange it has been getting to know this woman with whom I share so much and yet know so little about. I consider Kian, and the surprise on his face when he found out I was his uncle. I consider how much space these two former strangers now take up inside my head, and the urge I have to spend more time with them. This desire for connection, for a relationship, for a bond. What does this mean for my relationship with the people sitting around the table next to me? What does it mean for my future in this family? Is it possible for me to be both Noah Martineau and Jason Hayes? To inhabit both the rarefied world in which I'd grown up and the tougher realities of Kerry and Kian's lives?

I look over at my parents laughing as they listen to Charlotte recounting a story about one of her colleagues in the history department. How would they feel if they knew what I'd done, if they were aware of my burgeoning relationship with Kerry? Would they feel betrayed? Or would they feel I had a right to explore where I'd come from, and encourage me on that journey? There is no point going down this road, at least not yet, no point causing them unnecessary pain, at least while things between Kerry and me are at such an early stage.

Later we decamp en masse to my parents' for coffee. Once we're all inside, Dad breaks out a single malt he's been saving for a special occasion and refuses to accept no for an answer as he passes round glasses. After we've all had at least one sip, there are fresh rounds of toasts from both my mother and father, interspersed with several anecdotes culled from the Martineau family annals: the time following an air-traffic control strike that we all got stuck in an Italian airport for three days and survived solely on bottled water, bread and Laughing Cow cheese; the occasion when Dad was nearly arrested after taking particular exception to a parking ticket, which he believed he'd received unfairly, only to be saved by my mother's smooth talking; the episode when my parents lost Phillip in the National Portrait Gallery, only to be reunited with him twenty horror-filled minutes later when he was finally discovered sitting cross-legged in front of a portrait of Winston Churchill, sketching an impression of the painting into an old school exercise book. These stories are a joy to relive, embodying as they do the true spirit of what it is to be a Martineau, but there's only so much I can take. I'm so shattered that I fall asleep on my feet, the glass dropping from my hand on to the floor, and it's only then that Millie and I are reluctantly granted permission to depart.

On the drive home with the windows wound down fully, Millie, unlike me, is full of energy and still buzzing from all the compliments she's received over the course of the evening. 'The waiter thought I was eighteen and tried to pour me some wine, before Uncle Phillip stopped him,' she says gleefully. 'Wait until I tell Clemmie, she'll be so jealous. She always thinks she looks older than me.'

Millie grows quieter the closer we get to home and for a

moment I think she might be falling asleep. But as we pull into our road, she turns to me and says, 'Dad, can I ask you a question?'

'Of course,' I reply, alarm bells ringing at the change in her tone. 'What's wrong?'

'I heard you and Uncle Phillip talking about the flat. Is that going to be your new home? Are you and Mum going to get divorced?'

I bring the car to a halt outside the house. For all the make-up and the heels, she's still my baby girl and I hate the thought that she's been carrying all this worry around with her.

'Oh, sweetheart, it's not what you think. Uncle Phillip has offered me the flat while Mum and I are sorting things out. It's only temporary, but it does mean that you can stay with me whenever you want. And in the meantime, Mummy and I are going to carry on working on our problems. And then one day soon I'll be coming home for good, because it's all that I want in the world. You know that, don't you?'

Millie nods. 'I just worry, that's all. So many of my friends' parents have split up. They always make out like they're really happy because they've got two homes, two bedrooms, and get to have two Christmases, but I liked things the way they were. I don't want them to change.'

She looks so young all of a sudden, so vulnerable that it takes all that I have to resist the urge to stride back into the house and tell Rosalind that this has all been a terrible mistake, that nothing is worth putting our beloved daughter through so much pain. But that wouldn't be fair on Rosalind; she hasn't made this stand lightly, and anyway that wouldn't solve the problem between us.

Steeling myself, I turn to my daughter and offer her a reassurance I can only hope is true. 'Things won't change. I promise. Mummy and I love you more than anything in the world and there's nothing we wouldn't do for you, including fixing what's gone wrong between us. I know it's hard, but you've just got to trust us. Everything is going to be all right.'

Millie kisses my cheek, then I walk her up to the front door.

I wait while she lets herself in and hear a sleepy Rosalind call from upstairs. Millie turns to me, and I give her an extra-long hug to let her know I'll always be there for her. To reassure her that I really do mean every word I've said.

15

Kerry

Tuesday, 29th March

When Jodi throws open her front door, Kian and I practically have to cover our ears because of the piercing scream she lets out. For a minute or two it's a blur of hugs and kids and dogs, as the contents of Jodi's tiny house spill out on to the street to greet us.

When one of the dogs makes a run for it up the road, Jodi sends her eldest son Mason after it while she shoves the rest of us inside.

'It's so, so, so good to see you, babes,' she says, closing the front door behind her as her two youngest look on. 'You look great too, have you lost weight?'

Embarrassed, I pull down the hem of my jumper. I haven't lost weight at all; if anything my belly is bigger than ever. This is just her being sweet. 'I wish,' I say breezily. 'I'm trying to cut back on the rubbish and eat healthily at the minute. In fact, I'm on a bit of a diet.'

Jodi laughs. 'Fat chance of carrying on with that while you're here! Everything we've got planned for you involves food. Speaking of which . . .' Turning around, she bellows in the direction of the kitchen in that funny accent of hers. 'Stacey, put the kettle on, babes, and bring us that plate of biscuits, will you?' She turns back to me and grins. 'What's the point of having kids if they can't make you a cuppa once in a while?' She looks at Kian. 'Isn't that right, babes? I bet you're always making your lovely mum a cuppa and getting her to put her feet up, aren't you?' Kian shrugs shyly, which only makes Jodi laugh even louder.

'Look at him,' she says. 'I think I've scared the life out of him.' She gives Kian another massive hug, squeezing him so hard I think his eyes might pop out. 'I can't believe how much you've grown since the summer, you're a big lad now, aren't you?' She turns to her two youngest kids, Marley and Paige. 'You pair take Kian upstairs and show him where he's sleeping. You could show him your new *Star Wars* Lego while you're at it.' Not waiting to be told twice, the kids sweep Kian out of the room, and then the front door opens and in comes Mason, carrying a wriggling black and white terrier under his arm.

'How far did he get?' asks Jodi, taking the dog from him.

'Almost to the end of the road,' replies her son, sounding like a proper little Geordie.

I give Mason another hug and have to reach up because he's grown so tall.

'I'm already two inches bigger than Mum,' he says when I comment on his height. 'I reckon I'll be bigger than Dad by the end of the year.'

'That's if you live that long,' says Jodi. 'He came off his skate-board the other day, wasn't wearing his helmet.' Mason looks mortified. She kisses his head. 'I love him really. Right, you, go and see how your sister's getting on with that tea, she's taking so long I reckon she's gone to China for it.'

Mason leaves the room, with both dogs trotting behind him, and finally Jodi and I are alone. As we sit down on the sofa next to each other, I think how good it is to see her, and how lovely it is to have so much time stretching out ahead of us to talk. Though we chat on the phone all the time, it's just not the same as being face to face. There's so much I want to tell her, so much I want to say about Noah, about Kian, and about the thoughts that have been keeping me up at night. But for now, all I want to do is relax, yap about this and that, and enjoy being with my oldest and closest friend.

Stacey and Mason bring in the tea and biscuits. Stacey looks the dead spit of her mother, right down to her dark-brown curly hair and caramel-coloured skin. At sixteen she's so beautiful and so grown-up, it breaks my heart thinking of her mum at that age, stuck in Milread Road. I ask her how she's getting on at school, and what her plans are for the future. She tells me she's getting on well and is even thinking about going to college, doing A levels and going to university.

'She'll be the first Mitchell to ever go,' says Jodi proudly. 'I know it's a long way off yet, but I can't wait until she graduates and I can hang one of them pictures on my wall of her wearing one of those funny hats.'

Stacey laughs, looking even more like her mum than ever. 'Steady on, Mum, I've got to get through my GCSEs first!'

After a bit Stacey and Mason disappear upstairs, leaving me and their mum alone again. The moment they've gone, Jodi gets up and shuts the living-room door.

'I thought they'd never leave,' she says excitedly.

'Why, what's up?'

Her face lights up. 'I've been bursting to tell you ever since I got the news . . . I'm six weeks pregnant!'

She sits back and scans my face, waiting to see my reaction. I don't know what to say. I don't know what I'm feeling. Of course, I'm pleased for her. I can see how happy she is, but in that instant I know that there are things I can't tell her now, things I can't ask. She was busy enough with four kids, a husband and two dogs as it is. With a baby on the way, she won't have a moment to spare for anything or anyone else.

I must have let my feelings show, because Jodi looks at me all worried. 'You okay, babes?'

'Yeah, of course, I'm sorry, it's just a bit of a surprise, that's all. I thought you were all done with having kids.'

'So did we, to be honest with you. We'd even talked about Mark having the snip, then this happened and well, we're both made up really. Why, do you think we're making a mistake?'

I feel terrible raining on Jodi's parade like this. I tell myself to get a grip and stop being so selfish. 'No, of course not, this is absolutely the best news ever! I'm so happy for you, really I am. That baby is going to be loved so, so, much, not to mention spoiled by its Auntie Kerry. This has to be the best thing I've heard in ages.'

She looks relieved. 'Do you mean that? For a minute there I thought you might be thinking we were mad, adding another kid to this crazy house.'

'Of course I mean it,' I say. 'This really is the best news. You were made to be a mum. I promise you, I couldn't be any happier for you than I am right now.'

We talk non-stop about the baby, about being pregnant and how there's nothing quite so chaotic but wonderful as a house with a newborn in it. We only stop when the kids come to find us and we realise we've been so busy talking, we've forgotten all about dinner.

It's fun rustling up a quick meal for everyone with Jodi; beans on toast for seven. For dessert it's a tray of glazed doughnuts fresh from the supermarket. The kids scoff the lot down so fast that by the time we realise what's what, there's none left for me or Jodi. We don't mind though, especially when Jodi cracks open a secret supply of almond Magnums that she's had stashed away under a bag of broccoli in the freezer.

After dinner, Jodi bundles Marley into his buggy and we all head off to the local park. I help Stacey push the little ones on the swings while Jodi takes the dogs for a quick lap around the field and Mason and Kian play football. When it starts to get dark, we troop back to Jodi's and make a start on tea. This time the kids help out, chopping vegetables, setting the table and generally getting in the way until their dad comes home from work.

Mark gives me a big hug when he sees me, and when I whisper congratulations in his ear, he laughs that deep laugh of his and whispers back, 'To be honest, I didn't think I still had it in me.'

After a tea of shepherd's pie and veg, we clear the table, and Mark and I do the washing-up while Jodi gets Marley and Paige bathed and into bed. When she comes back down, we all settle in the living room and watch a movie, some kids' film that Kian's been desperate to see for months. Mark falls asleep in the first ten minutes, and Stacey and Mason are on their phones for most of it, but Kian enjoys it, and Jodi and I agree that while it wasn't exactly our cup of tea, it did make us laugh out loud a couple of times.

The kids and Mark clear off to bed not long after the film has finished, and then Jodi makes herself a cup of tea and pours me a glass of wine. I feel a bit funny drinking on my own. Normally Jodi and I polish off a bottle or two between us whenever we get together like this, but obviously with the pregnancy and everything, she can't. But I do fancy a drink, so I tell myself I'll just have the one, and as we settle down on the sofa, and Jodi lights some candles, I feel so comfortable and relaxed I almost nod off.

'So come on, then,' says Jodi, nudging me. 'I've been dying to ask you all day, how are things going with Jason . . . I mean Noah? Still good?'

I think about yesterday, when Noah took me and Kian out for the day. Although we'd planned to go to the skatepark, when I looked it up it turned out it was shut for repairs because of a water leak. Kian was heartbroken, but then Noah suggested the Natural History Museum and he cheered right up. It being Easter Monday the queue to get in was so long it took nearly an hour to get inside, but it was well worth the wait. Kian thought the dinosaur skeletons were the best thing he'd ever seen, and it was lovely watching Noah rushing round with him from one display to the next. After lunch at Nando's, we finished the day with a visit to Hamleys toy store. Noah treated Kian to some sort of mini-robot thing that you control with your phone, which totally made Kian's day. I tried telling Noah he was spoiling the boy, and that he didn't need to do anything like that, but he wouldn't listen. 'I'm his uncle,' he explained. 'Spoiling him is what I'm supposed to do.'

I tell Jodi all about the trip to Brighton, about the look on Kian's face when I told him who Noah was and, of course, all about our day out at the museum yesterday. Even though you could count the number of times we'd seen each other on one hand, it didn't seem to matter. We were getting on better than I ever could have hoped. It all just felt so easy and natural. Like all those years we'd spent apart had just begun to melt away.

'Sounds like all your dreams have come true,' says Jodi. 'I'm so happy for you, Kez. I know how long you've wanted this. I bet you couldn't have ever imagined it would work out so perfectly.'

Perfectly. Was it perfect? How could it be when I still had so much I had to tell him, so many things to share?

'Not in a million years.' I finish off my glass of wine and pour another. 'It just goes to show how things never turn out exactly the way you think they will.'

We talk until midnight, about Noah, about men, about the kids, until Jodi's barely able to keep her eyes open. She helps me make up a bed on the sofa, then kisses me goodnight. Alone in the dark with half a bottle of wine sloshing around in my belly, I can't sleep. All I can think about is Noah.

I pick up my phone. There's his name and number listed under my favourites. My thumb hovers over it. I imagine pressing down on it, listening to the ringing tone, hearing his voice when he picks up, probably half asleep by now. I imagine myself saying the words, telling him the truth about the real reason why I got in touch. But then I imagine his reaction, the feelings of hurt and anger, and I just can't bear it. I quickly switch off my phone to stop myself doing anything stupid. I know soon I won't have any choice but to tell him. I know soon I'll run out of time. But things are so good right now, I can't bear to spoil them. I just want a little more time. I just want things to be normal for a little while longer.

16

Noah

Wednesday, 30th March

'In our last session we touched briefly on your adoption, didn't we, Noah, and things seemed to get quite heated, quite quickly. Would you agree that this is something of a flash point in your relationship with Rosalind?'

It's just after eight o'clock, and once again Rosalind and I are sitting across from Elspeth. After our last experience I had rather hoped that this session might at least begin on more neutral ground, but sadly this is not to be. We've only really just sat down and already the subject of adoption is back on the table. And I wish it wasn't. I really do wish it wasn't.

It's hard not to be defensive but, remembering why I'm here, I give it my best shot.

I take a deep breath. 'Yes, I think that's a fair observation.'

Elspeth nods thoughtfully. 'And why do you think this is the case?'

'Simply because when it comes to this topic, Rosalind and I have two very different viewpoints, ones which are directly in opposition.'

'And how would you describe your viewpoint?'

'In a nutshell? That there's little to be gained from raking over the past.'

Elspeth closes her eyes and puts her hands together in front of her mouth for a moment, as if in silent prayer.

'Putting aside value judgments for the moment, what do you think would happen if you did, as you say, "rake over the past"?'

'I have no idea,' I reply. 'But I can't imagine it would be anything good.'

'And why would you imagine that? Have there been previous occasions when reflecting on the past has caused problems for you?'

I think back to my sessions with the Scandinavian-glasses chap. 'Well, yes. At Rosalind's suggestion I saw a counsellor some years ago who wanted me to explore my feelings about my past. It didn't go well at all, and in the end Rosalind was in complete agreement that I should cease attending, as it was having a some-what adverse effect on our relationship.'

Elspeth picks up a pen from the table in front of us and scrib-bles something down on the notepad that's open on her lap, before looking directly at me.

'I think that's a very interesting point you've made there. Talking about this issue in the past has had an adverse effect on your relationship with Rosalind. But the question I'd like us to explore now is: what effect do you think *not* talking about your adoption is having on your relationship?'

I have to admit Elspeth is good, very good indeed. I wouldn't be the slightest bit surprised to learn that in a previous life she too had worked in law. For all her apparent gentleness and efforts to appear non-confrontational, her question is as effective and brutal as an axe in battle, cleaving through my layers of defence and getting to the very heart of the matter.

Once again I'm aware how minuscule this room is, and I have to fight the urge to push my chair back against the wall in a bid for breathing space.

Rosalind leans forwards and puts her hand gently on my knee. 'Noah?'

I glance at her briefly, clear my throat and shift my position in the chair. I try to remind myself that this isn't an attack, that Rosalind is just doing her best to get to the bottom of the prob-lems between us so that we can repair them, so that we can move on. But it's hard, really hard.

I need to play for time. 'I'm not quite sure what you want me to say.'

Elspeth removes her glasses and gives them another one of her superfluous cleans.

'Let's try a more direct question: do you feel there's any truth behind the assertion that your being adopted has affected your relationship with Rosalind?'

I think for a moment. Whenever counselling clients about how to offer evidence in court, the golden rule is this: Say as little as possible.

'Yes.'

Elspeth smiles knowingly. 'And would you like to expand on that?'

I wipe the palms of my hands on my knees. For some reason they're suddenly slick with sweat. 'Well, yes, obviously it's had an impact,' I agree. 'A person's formative years are bound to influence who they become. But isn't that just as true for Rosalind as it is for me?'

I'm being a barrister again. I know it. Avoiding the question, the issue, because I know the answer will surely incriminate me, but as neither Rosalind nor Elspeth has said a word in response to my question, I feel a little of my confidence returning and so repeat the question.

'All I'm saying is, why should it be that the circumstances surrounding my birth have more impact on our current situation than Rosalind's?'

'Maybe because you have no idea what kind of environment you were born into,' says Rosalind, with a touch of frustration creeping into her voice. 'Maybe because you were rejected as a baby by the two people in the world who were supposed to love you unconditionally. Maybe because you were a black child from a troubled background, raised by a middle-class white family. You're surely not suggesting that none of this has the slightest bit of relevance to where we are now?'

If this cross-examination had been taking place in a court of law, then right now Rosalind's legal team would be rubbing their hands together in glee at the prospect of a win. It is virtually impossible to argue against her logic. She's made a strong and compelling argument, one I know in my heart of hearts I can't rebuff. I don't doubt that my adoption has significantly affected the way I see the world, only an idiot would attempt to suggest otherwise, but if there's ever been a dictum I've lived by, it's this: 'Never look back.'

It explains why, growing up, I'd asked my parents so few questions about my origins. Why, even when given the opportunity, I'd never contacted the Adoption Contact Register. Why, in the fifteen years we've been together, I've only discussed my adoption with my wife on two occasions – once when she met my parents, and the second after our first midwife appointment when she was pregnant with Millie. It explained my initial reluctance to meet Kerry. Why, at the age of ten, I'd begged and pleaded with my family to let me change my name. And it explained why, even though my marriage is hanging by a thread and I'm so desperate to make things right with the woman I love, I still do not want to have this discussion.

I stand up. 'I think I need some air.'

Elspeth looks at her watch. 'Of course, why don't you take five minutes, collect your thoughts and when we reconvene, I suggest we put a pin in the topic of adoption for this session and revisit it at a later date.'

I pick up my jacket, leave the room and head outside. I'm only alone for a matter of seconds before Rosalind appears.

'Are you okay?' She puts her hand on my arm, her eyes searching my face anxiously. 'I didn't mean to push so hard in there.'

'I'm fine.' Despite the circumstances it feels good to know that she still cares about me, to know that she understands how difficult this is for me. 'It just got a little intense, that's all.'

'I know how much you hate talking about your adoption,' she says. 'But surely you must see how central it is to everything we're going through. How are we going to make any real progress unless you're willing to explore this part of your life?'

For one mad moment I consider telling her the truth: that I am doing just that, exploring my past, at least that's what it feels like getting to know Kerry. And in many ways it would be a relief to share this with her. But at the same time, my worry is that if I tell her now, if I reveal everything I'm going through and all the feelings it's brought to the surface, then it won't just be my emotions I'll be dealing with but those of my wife, my parents and my siblings too. I fear the addition of all of those voices and opinions would place too great a burden on something that is still so fragile, so nascent. I need a little more time, to see where this is taking me, to understand what this means for who I am and who I might become.

'You're right,' I tell Rosalind, 'I do need to talk about this . . . and I will, I promise. It just might take some time.'

'You don't know how much it means to hear you say that.' She kisses my cheek and for the longest time afterwards I can still feel her lips against my skin. We stand in silence watching the world go by for a minute or two: a group of rowdy students on their way to the pub; a gaggle of business-suited commuters, their ready-meal suppers stuffed into flimsy carrier bags, wending their weary way home; young couples with eyes only for each other, walking arm in arm at the beginning of a romantic evening out. It all seems so blissfully normal, a window into a world I long to get back to.

As if reading my mind, Rosalind smiles. 'Millie's really looking forward to seeing you at the weekend.'

'She's been inundating me with texts about how she wants her "new bedroom" to be decorated and arranged. I have to keep reminding her that this is only temporary. It is, isn't it?'

Rosalind squeezes my hand. 'Of course it is. I just think it's helpful to have our own space while we're working things through. There's nothing more that I want than for us all to be back together again.'

I look at my watch. 'I think my five minutes are up.'

She smiles. 'Coming back in?'

'Yes,' I say. 'Let's go.'

The next couple of days are frantically busy with work, thanks to a fraud case being dumped on me at the last minute. I'm in court first thing every morning, and spend every evening trawling through the hundreds of documents relating to it. In between I'm fielding texts from Charlotte, who is upset at the unexpected news that her ex-husband is getting remarried; long-winded emails from my father about an article he's been asked to write for *The Times Literary Supplement*; voice messages from my mother asking when Millie and I will be visiting next; a steady stream of Whatsapp messages from my brother relating to the broken central heating in the flat and the plumber he's arranged to fix it; messages from Millie about her plans for transforming her room at my place; and calls from Kerry, keen to know how I'm doing and asking when we can get together.

I realise I'm lucky to have so many wonderful people in my life. But at the same time, it's hard to know exactly where I'm going to find the time to see any of them. By Friday evening, not only am I exhausted, but I've done next to nothing to prepare for Millie's visit. I look around and realise that since moving into Phillip's flat a week ago, whether consciously or otherwise, I've spent very little time here other than to sleep, or consume the odd solitary ready meal or takeaway. I suppose it's partly because I've been so busy, but mostly it's because I haven't wanted to see this as anything other than a very temporary arrangement. Looking around the flat, however, with a view to Millie's impending visit, I can see how unwelcoming this attitude has made the place appear. There are no personal belongings scattered around, no food in the cupboards, not even sheets on the bed. So setting the alarm for six on Saturday morning, I get some pressing bits of paperwork out of the way, tidy the flat from top to bottom, reply to everyone's messages and emails, before then dashing to the shops to pick up a new duvet and bed set for Millie. I return home via Waitrose with enough food and drink for an army. Finally, just before midday, I look around the flat and, confident I've done just enough to make the place look welcoming, I flop down on the sofa for half an hour before heading out in the car to pick up Millie.

When I arrive, she is waiting on the doorstep, bags packed and coat on. She seems so excited, almost as if we're going on an exotic holiday, rather than an overnight stay in Bayswater. But I know how worried she must be about what's going on between Rosalind and me, and she's probably putting on a brave face for my benefit, which is heartbreaking to say the least. I say goodbye to Rosalind and as I load Millie's things into the back of the car, some of her excitement, genuine or otherwise, about the weekend rubs off on me. I feel optimistic, enthusiastic even, rather than full of dread and worry that I might disappoint her somehow. As we pull away, I forget all about the madness of the week, and how bone-crushingly tired I am, and concentrate instead on enjoying every moment I have with my daughter.

Millie professes to love her room, even though it's not a patch on her own at home. Nonetheless, she throws herself into re-arranging the furniture and adding a few adornments that she's brought along with her. Left to her own devices I'm sure she would have spent the afternoon showing it off to her friends on social media. As it is, however, I'm aware that Rosalind will be more than a little annoyed if all Millie eats this weekend are the crisps and chocolate she raided from the cupboards soon after her arrival. So it is that, a little after five, I lure her out of the flat with the promise of pizza and all the ice cream she can eat.

We go to a quaint little pizzeria I'd read about in *Time Out* that's not far from Lancaster Gate. It's such a cliché it's almost laughable: red checked table cloths, candles in squat wine bottles, Dean Martin on the stereo and black and white photos of the old country on the wall. I order a Four Seasons and Millie, who unlike most of her peers is a raging carnivore, has a pizza chris-tened The Italian Job that comes laden with so much cured pork it's practically oinking.

I'm not sure how she does it, but somehow Millie manages to devour her meal without once stopping her constant stream of chat. In fact it's only when her ice cream arrives that she pauses, looks almost embarrassed and says, 'I'm talking too much, aren't I?'

I laugh. 'It's nice. I like hearing what you've got to say. Most parents complain that they get barely more than grunts out of their children once they get to your age.'

'I know, but like Mummy says, non-stop talking can get on people's nerves. Anyway, all I've done is talk about me. How about you, Dad? How are you really?'

It's a strange thing to be asked this sort of earnest question by your own offspring, let alone when they're twelve and sitting across the table from you, with a warning look on their face as if to say, 'and don't try to palm me off with platitudes.'

She loads up her spoon with another mound of stracciatella ice cream, so tempting I start to regret not ordering a bowl for myself.

'Actually,' I say, helping myself to a small spoonful of her ice cream. 'If you want to know, I'm feeling a bit overwhelmed.'

'Overwhelmed how?'

I think about the last counselling session: how uncomfortable talking about the past had made me feel. Maybe this is my chance to get some practice in at being more open and honest, less evasive.

I take a deep breath and look at Millie's face, so innocent and expectant, and make a decision. 'I'm going to tell you something now, something I haven't told anyone, not Papa or Nana, not Uncle Phillip or Auntie Charlotte. Not even Mum.'

Millie's eyes widen in anticipation and she even goes as far as putting down her spoon. 'Dad, what is it? You're freaking me out.'

'You know I'm adopted, don't you?' Millie nods. 'Well, recently my birth sister got in touch with me.'

I can see her brain whirring as she attempts to process this new information. 'Wait, you mean you have an actual sister that's not Auntie Charlotte?'

I nod. 'I didn't know that until she got in touch, but it turns out that yes, I have. Her name's Kerry, she eight years older than me and has a son, Kian, who's ten.'

Millie's eyes widen even further and she sits back in her chair amazed. 'You mean I've got another cousin, apart from Arthur and Emily?'

'I know, it's pretty mind-blowing stuff, isn't it?'

She thinks for a moment.

'And Mummy doesn't know? Why haven't you told her?'

The six-million dollar question. Is it because I don't want to rock the boat any more than is necessary? Is it because I want to work through this myself first? Is it because I still don't know what I feel? Or all of these things rolled into one?

'It's complicated. You know Mummy and I have been having some problems that we're sorting out? Well, we're really getting somewhere with that, but because of it, Mummy has a lot on her mind and I don't think it would be fair to give her any more to worry about. Obviously, it's up to you if you want to tell her. The last thing I want is for you to feel you have to keep secrets from her. But I'd prefer it if you could wait for a little while, until I've found the right time to tell her myself. Really though, it's up to you, I'll understand whatever you decide.'

Millie falls uncharacteristically silent, her forehead corrugated, deep in thought. Finally, she picks up her spoon again, takes a mouthful of ice cream and swallows. 'I think you're right,' she says. 'Mummy can be such a fusspot sometimes. She worries about everything and she has got a lot of things worrying her at the moment.'

I breathe a huge sigh of relief. Putting my daughter in this difficult position might not win me any parent of the year awards, but it does feel good sharing this with her. I've missed the closeness of our everyday contact, hearing about all the little details of her life, I've missed it all, I've missed her, and for better or worse this has brought us closer together. 'So, for now, it's just you and me?'

Millie doesn't say anything at first. Instead she finishes her ice cream, pushes her bowl to one side, then leans across the table and stares at me intently. 'Yes, for now it's just you and me,' she echoes with a grin. 'But this is huge, Daddy, so you have to tell me absolutely everything.'

17

Kerry

Monday, 4th April

It's early morning. I'm stuck in bumper-to-bumper traffic on my way to my first job of the day, talking on the phone with Noah.

'Blimey,' I say in surprise. 'So you told Millie? What did she say?'

'Well, nothing for a moment or two, which for Millie is absolutely unheard of, but then she asked me to tell her everything and so that's what I did.'

'And she's okay with it?'

'More than okay, actually. I think she thinks the whole thing is really exciting. Compared to lots of her friends' dads who work in film, music or TV, I think Millie's always thought me quite boring really. In her eyes, this has given me quite a lot of street cred.'

I feel a little tingle of excitement. I haven't wanted to push him, but I'm desperate to meet Millie and the rest of the family. Something about the tone of his voice, though, tells me this isn't the whole story.

'So does that mean Rosalind knows as well now?'

He goes quiet for a minute. 'No, not yet. Of course, I am going to tell her, but I need things between us to be a bit more settled first. The counselling is going well, but we're still quite a way from everything being back to normal.'

I don't want to boss him around, but I've got a bad feeling about this. I know if I were in her shoes, I'd want to know.

'Are you sure you shouldn't just tell her?'

'I will, but it's essential I choose the right time. I don't doubt for a moment she'll be supportive. She's not the problem: it's me. Telling Millie about you has made me realise there's still so much I have to work out, so much I don't know. She had so many questions, not just about you and Kian, but our mother and my father too, questions I had no idea how to answer.'

He goes quiet again like he's struggling to find the right words. 'Noah, are you all right?'

'I'm fine,' he says, sounding anything but. 'Look, Kerry, I know now's not the time . . . but would you mind if we met up soon to talk through what you can remember? You know, about those days and in particular my father . . . I don't even know his name.'

Of course, this is about his dad. I should've guessed. In all the time we've spent together he's not mentioned him once. I'd grown up never knowing my dad but at least I had Mum around, so it didn't bother me that much. But Noah had no memory of either his real mum or his real dad, and that's got to be tough.

As the traffic moves forward a couple of centimetres, I rack my brains trying to remember what I can about Noah's dad. I remember he was this big Jamaican guy with a deep booming voice. I remember he lived quite near us and everyone in the area knew him. I remember that whenever he'd come over to see Mum, he'd always chat to me but would never call me by my name; instead he'd call me 'Little Miss', and then laugh a lot like it was the funniest joke in the world.

'I can't remember his real name, Noah. To be honest, I'm not sure I ever heard it. Everyone, even Mum, used to call him something like Lucky, or Buck or . . .' I close my eyes. I can feel the name on the tip of my tongue. 'Stucky!' I shout, as it suddenly pops into my head. 'That's what everyone round by us used to call your dad, Stucky.'

'That's his name? Stucky?'

'His nickname, yeah. He was a really big guy and everyone in the area knew him. I'm sorry I can't remember much more than that, but leave it with me and I'll have a proper think and see if there's anything else I can come up with.'

★

'Hello, dear,' says Mrs Ryman, opening the door for me before I can fish my keys out. 'It's funny seeing you on a Monday, I'm all at sixes and sevens.'

'Yeah, sorry to mess you around and change your day but something came up and I couldn't shift it.'

'It's not a problem at all. Whatever it was, I hope you managed to get it sorted?'

'Sort of,' I say, feeling guilty. 'But I'll try not to let it happen again.'

Mrs Ryman smiles. 'Oh, don't you worry. I'm just getting old, that's all. Back when I was at the Foreign Office, no two days were ever the same, and yet here I am getting in a fluster about you changing your day. I need to give myself a good talking to!'

We chat for a couple of minutes and I tell her my good news about Kian getting a place at Melbourne Park.

'Oh, that is good news,' she says. 'I know how worried you were about what might happen if he didn't get in. That must be a huge weight off your mind.'

I think for a minute, but bite my lip. 'Yes,' I say. 'It is.'

Mrs Ryman fills the kettle while I get cracking with the Hoovering. I start in the massive living room and, because Mrs Ryman is proper old-school, I have to move all the heavy old furniture about to make sure I clean underneath everything. It's a really tiring job and it takes a lot out of me, which is why I always tackle it first.

As I'm puffing and panting, still struggling to shift the big leather chesterfield sofa, Mrs Ryman comes in with two mugs of tea on a tray and a plate of biscuits. Usually she just puts down my tea and leaves me to get on with things for a bit, but today she sits down in the armchair opposite me and I sense that she won't rest until I sit down too.

She picks up the plate and offers me a biscuit. 'These are far more of an exotic selection than I usually keep,' she says. 'My dearest friend's daughter came to visit at the weekend and brought them as a gift. It was very sweet of her.'

I help myself to a biscuit covered in purple foil, unwrap it and take a bite. I missed breakfast and feel a bit peckish now. It tastes delicious, more chocolate than biscuit, but I can't properly enjoy it knowing how much work I've still got to get through.

'It would've been my mother's birthday today,' says Mrs Ryman, and her eyes shift from me to a framed photograph on the mantelpiece. While dusting, I've often wondered about the stern-looking woman dressed in furs, captured in black and white. Though she's told me all sorts of stories about her life in the civil service, she's barely said a word about her family.

I pick up the photograph and we both sit looking at it for a moment, not saying anything.

'What was she like?'

Mrs Ryman smiles. 'In a word: formidable. She did not suffer fools gladly, and in her opinion a great deal of the world was incredibly foolish.'

'Were you close though?'

'My mother was from a different age,' she says thoughtfully. 'She wasn't one for what she considered excessive displays of emotion, even with her own flesh and blood. I suppose having lived, like many others, through two world wars, she had been focused for so long on simply surviving that there wasn't much spare capacity for anything else. I know she lost two brothers in the First World War but she never spoke about them, and there was a hardness about her that made it difficult to get close to her, really.'

I look over at the side table next to her, a black and white photograph of a smiling baby, dressed up in some long, white lacy affair. 'What about when you were little? Was she any better then?'

Mrs Ryman shakes her head. 'I can't imagine so. I was essentially brought up by a series of nannies and governesses and then once I was eleven, I was packed off to Roedean and that was that.'

I try to imagine the old lady sitting in front of me as the baby in the photograph, big blue eyes and bouncing curly hair. It breaks my heart thinking of her like that. Starting out life as a jolly little thing, then being looked after by a stream of people paid to do the job, before getting sent off to live with a bunch of strangers. It was almost as bad as dumping kids in a children's home. It makes you wonder why some people bother having kids in the first place.

I lean over and hold Mrs Ryman's hand. 'That must have been so hard for you.'

'It was simply the way things were in those days. I don't blame either of my parents. In a lot of ways, they were merely doing what their parents had done before them. I suppose that's partly why my late husband and I never had children. I was always afraid that I might repeat the pattern, as it were.'

Repeat the pattern. How funny that someone like Mrs Ryman, with all her education and money, felt exactly like I had before Kian. I can't help myself. I know it's overstepping the mark, but I put my arms around Mrs Ryman and give her a big hug. 'For what it's worth,' I say, 'I think you would've made a brilliant mum.'

She smiles, a tear glistening in the corner of her eye. 'Oh, thank you, Kerry, it means a lot to hear you say that.' She takes out an embroidered handkerchief and dabs her eyes. 'It's funny though,' she adds. 'In spite of everything, I still miss Mother after all these years and think of her often. I suppose you're never too old to miss your mother.'

She's right. It's a terrible thing to miss your mum. The worst thing in the world. No child should be without their mother. It just isn't right. I try to think of the right thing to say to comfort poor old Mrs Ryman, but then my phone rings.

'Is this Ms Hayes? It's Mrs Curtis here.'

I'd recognise Kian's school's secretary's voice anywhere. She always sounds like someone trying too hard to sound posh. Why's she calling me? What's happened?

'Yes, this is Ms Hayes speaking, is everything okay with Kian? He's not sick or anything, is he?' He'd said he had a bit of a stomach ache this morning, but I'd thought he was just angling for a day off school in front of the telly.

'Kian's fine, Ms Hayes,' she says, 'although he is in quite a lot of trouble, I'm afraid. Mrs Rankin has asked me to speak with you so the matter can be dealt with immediately.'

I'm in such a fluster as I sit down in the head teacher's office, and my heart's pounding so fast I have to undo my coat before I can even get a single word out. Kian's in the chair next to me with a face like thunder. Mrs Rankin is sitting bolt upright behind her desk, looking none too happy either, and Mrs Curtis is perched next to her, holding a notepad.

'What's all this about?' I ask. 'I've had to leave work for this.'

Stoney-faced, Mrs Rankin shuffles some papers in front of her. 'I can assure you, Ms Hayes, all of us have better things to do this morning. But the matter is so serious I had no choice but to take immediate action.'

I feel sick. It must be really bad. 'So, what's he supposed to have done?'

'I'm afraid, Ms Hayes, there's no *supposed* about it. I myself witnessed Kian repeatedly strike another pupil as they left assembly this morning.'

I look at Kian but he doesn't meet my eye. 'That doesn't sound like my son. If he's hit someone there must be a reason for it. He's never done anything like this before.'

'I'm sorry, Ms Hayes, but according to school rules there is no good reason for a pupil physically attacking another child. And while I agree this is completely out of character for Kian, the undeniable fact is he has injured another pupil. The boy is very shaken indeed, and I'm not looking forward at all to explaining to his parents how their son sustained severe bruising to his face and body while under our care.'

I'm furious and speechless with it. I look over at Kian in disbelief. 'What have you got to say for yourself?'

He folds his arms and pushes out his bottom lip even further, but doesn't say a word. I look back at Mrs Rankin. 'So is anyone going to tell me how this all started or do I have to guess?'

Mrs Rankin sighs. 'Neither Kian nor the boy who was struck will say exactly what happened, I'm afraid.'

I'm so mad, I'm literally shaking. I want to grab Kian and make him explain what happened, but this isn't the time or the place. I try to ignore Mrs Curtis furiously scribbling notes on her pad. 'So, what happens now?'

Mrs Rankin holds my gaze just a moment, long enough for me to know that Kian's not just going to get the usual rap on the knuckles. 'I'm afraid it's going to have to be a temporary exclusion.'

In an instant my blood boils over. 'You what? You're excluding him for one little fight? How can you do that when your so-called victim won't say how it started? It's obvious both of them are at fault. Is the other boy being excluded as well?'

'I can see how upset you are, Ms Hayes. But this is a serious matter, and I have no choice but to follow school disciplinary procedures as outlined in the home school agreement and on the website. If you're not satisfied with how I've dealt with things, you're more than welcome to take it up with the board of governors.'

I'm so angry that without another word, I get up, pull Kian to his feet and march out of Mrs Rankin's office, leaving the door wide open behind me. Kian knows better than to say anything as we walk to the car. He just keeps his head down, with his hands stuffed in his coat pockets.

I manage to keep it together until we're in the car, but once the doors are shut, that's it: I let rip.

'I'm going to give you just one chance to tell me why you hit that boy, and if you give me any of that nonsense you tried in there, I tell you now, I will take a hammer to your PlayStation.'

He looks up at me for a moment, his face all red and his eyes full of tears. He knows I'm not messing about.

'It was all his fault.'

'Whose?'

He looks down at his lap. 'Callum's.'

My heart sinks. I might've guessed. How two people can be friends one minute and enemies the next like this, I'll never know.

'Okay then,' I say. 'You explain to me why it was all Callum's fault.'

'He kept having a go at me.'

'About what?'

'About what he always goes on about. How I can't afford this or that . . . that my phone's rubbish, that I haven't got the latest games, and then this morning in assembly Mr Williams was talking about collecting money for charity, and Callum said to Arjun, "They should give that to Kian's mum, so she can buy him some decent trainers," and everyone laughed.'

I knew there'd be a reason for it. I knew Kian wasn't just acting like some thug. He'd taken it and taken it, and it was only when they'd had a go at me that he'd finally lost it. But that didn't make it right. That didn't mean he could just go around smacking anyone who started mouthing off. That's not how I've brought him up. It's not who I want him to be.

'Look, son,' I say, turning to face him, 'what you've got to think is, who's in trouble now? It's not Callum, is it? It's you, and you are all I care about. I've told you time and time again, the world isn't fair and it doesn't have to be, and the sooner you learn that the better. Bad things happen to good people, good things happen to bad. It's just the way it is. So don't think fairness has got anything to do with it. If you see trouble, walk the other way.' I feel myself starting to get upset. 'This is stuff you're supposed to know, Kian. I shouldn't need to be reminding you of things like this. What next? Are you going to go getting into even more trouble? Are you going to end up getting involved with gangs and knives and all that sort of thing? Because if you are, I'm telling you now, it's a dead end and I want more for you than that. I always have done, I always will.'

I'm not sure how much of this makes sense to him, because by the time I finish speaking I'm proper sobbing: nose running, make-up smeared, barely able to get my words out. Kian doesn't know what to make of me, but then he starts sobbing too, telling me over and over again that he's sorry and that he's going to be a good boy from now on. I know I'm overreacting. I know I'm blowing things out of all proportion. I know deep down he's a good boy but I just can't help myself: I feel like it's the end of the world.

18

Noah

Saturday, 9th April

I look across at Kerry in the driving seat, hands in her lap, staring out of the windscreen in the direction of a row of shuttered shops. We both watch as a thin, weary-looking young woman barely out of her teens trudges past, pushing a baby in a buggy, plastic shopping bags hanging from the handles, while two young children trail behind.

'Are you absolutely sure you're up for this, Kerry? We could come back another day, if you'd like?'

She shakes her head as if making an effort to bring herself back to the present. 'Sorry, did you say something?'

Something's wrong. She's barely spoken a word since she picked me up in Bayswater this morning. I wonder if she's worrying about Kian, or whether my asking her to return with me to the estate where we were born has been a bridge too far.

'Is everything okay, Kerry? You don't seem right.'

She rubs her eyes. She looks exhausted. 'I'm just tired, that's all. Haven't been sleeping much.'

'Is it Kian? Have the school said any more?'

'He's still excluded . . . but it's not that . . . well, not that on it's own. Everything's just getting on top of me a bit, that's all. But I'm all right, I promise.' She reaches across and squeezes my hand. 'Anyway, it should be me asking if you're all right, not the other way around. This is a big deal for you.'

'And you too,' I reply. 'Have you ever been back here?'

'I've thought about it a few times, but there didn't seem any point. It's not like there was anything for me to come back to.' She unbuckles her seat belt. 'Come on then, let's do this.'

I want to move but I can't. 'Are you sure we're not wasting our time?'

She shrugs and opens the car door. 'There's only one way to find out.'

Until recently, I could count on the fingers of one hand the number of times I'd consciously thought about my birth father. I didn't know whether he was black or white, rich or poor, alive or dead, and having nothing to go on, I couldn't even conjure up an image to love, or indeed hate. Like Mary had once been, he was just a shadow, a ghostly figure, insubstantial and easy to ignore. But that all changed when Kerry presented me with Mary's photograph, one half of my genetic jigsaw. Now, not only did I know exactly what one of my parents looked like, but I also knew for sure the ethnicity of the other.

The confirmation that my birth father is black has, over this past month, brought to the fore a number of long-forgotten memories. The first was a recollection of me at prep school, aged six or seven, responding to a question about my parentage from the boy who sat next to me in class. He'd asked if I knew who my real father was, and without pausing I'd replied, 'Yes, Michael Jackson,' because Charlotte had been playing his album, *Bad*, non-stop ever since it was released and she had a poster of him on her wall. The look of awe in my classmate's eyes as he asked if I could get him Michael Jackson's autograph was satisfying in the extreme.

The second memory to resurface was of a summer's day in Regent's Park a few years later. Phillip and I were kicking a ball around while my parents and Charlotte lounged on picnic blankets, reading and occasionally looking over at us. In the middle of our game, a large group of West Indian men of all ages appeared and started a game of cricket nearby, and I found it hard not to stare. Some had dreadlocks, others tall Afros, some had light-brown skin like me, while others were dark like polished ebony. I found everything about them mesmerising, from the way they spoke to one another in deep booming voices, using a language I didn't understand, through to the grace and fluidity of their movements, so different to the middle-aged men I'd seen playing village cricket while visiting family friends in Suffolk.

The final memory was from my teenage years. An evening when my father had a well-known visiting black African poet from university to supper one evening, who was in exile for his political views. Despite knowing this to be nothing more sinister than my parents extending a warm welcome to a fellow academic, as they frequently did, I had a nagging feeling that there was something else at play, and bizarrely the conclusion I drew was that perhaps this was their way of introducing me to my birth father. Of course, the evening passed without event and I never mentioned my unfounded suspicions to anyone or, feeling foolish, allowed myself to think about it again.

Of course, at other times on other days, when my efforts to deny my past were less successful, I'd imagined all manner of permutations of my parents, covering the entire racial rainbow, but after meeting Kerry and learning about Mary, it wasn't those I recalled. It was these memories, and others like them, featuring men with skin tones not unlike my own. I suppose, having discovered one half of the genetic jigsaw, it made sense to go in search of the other, which is why I'd called Kerry.

Kerry had been full of apologies when we'd met up to discuss my father. She'd had a terrible few days because of Kian's exclusion and I'd tried to comfort her as best I could. The more I tried, however, the less she seemed to want to talk about it and in the end she insisted instead that we focus on finding my father.

Unable to recall any further details about the man she only knew as Stucky, we'd turned to the Internet, but nothing of any use had come up. Eventually we decided to call it quits. I could see she was exhausted and had had more than enough for one day. But as I was about to leave, she suggested we visit The Park, the nickname for the sprawling Sixties-built four-thousand-occupancy housing estate where we were born. 'We'll go in my car though,' she'd said. 'Even if people think you're a drug dealer, there's no way your motor would last five minutes there. Oh, and make sure you dress down.'

It's a beautiful April morning, with blue skies, birdsong, and blossom in the trees lining the pavement, but the glowering squat concrete blocks somehow seem to suck all the beauty out of the day. Everything about the estate is unrelenting, from the grey bleakness of the buildings to the gloom of the covered parking areas. I don't know whether it's the graffiti, the abandoned furniture at the side of the road or the burned-out car that we pass, but all of it combined creates a sense of low-level menace and brings to mind numerous police reports I've read over the years. As we make our way through the estate towards our destination, I find myself wondering who is watching our approach and what their plans might be.

Kerry strides along with the quiet confidence of someone who belongs. I try my best to emulate her, but feel like a fraud. I feel as though my privileged upbringing and education are so apparent for all to see that I might as well be waving a flag.

The estate is such a warren of pathways and underpasses that I find it impossible to get my bearings. I ask Kerry how she knows where she's going without consulting a map, and she simply shrugs and says, 'It's like riding a bike, I suppose, it all just comes back to you.'

Another five minutes and we come to a halt in front of an ugly, grey, concrete six-storey block. It looks more like a prison than a collection of homes, and not for the first time I wonder exactly what the architects of these buildings were thinking, putting whole communities in places like this.

Kerry and I stand staring at the building for several moments. I read the name written along the edge of it in archaic Sixties-style municipal lettering: 'Lakeside'.

Kerry laughs. 'You couldn't make it up, could you?' she says, as I scan our surroundings for a body of water more significant than the oily puddle on the patch of brown grass in front of us.

She points towards the building. 'That was us,' she says. 'Third floor, second one from the left.'

I feel nothing as I stare up at the building. No flicker of recognition, no hint of familiarity, nothing. It's just a flat, and not a very nice one at that: two windows, net curtains, brown front door, nothing remarkable about it, and yet, once upon a time, this was my home.

An elderly Chinese man walks by with a small dog and I look at Kerry. 'How do you feel being back here?'

She continues to stare steadily at the building. 'Fine,' she says, not giving anything away. 'Let's just get on with it.'

As she moves on, it occurs to me that I haven't pinned Kerry down on what she has in mind for today. 'On with what exactly?'

'Knocking on doors,' she explains. 'I'm pretty sure your dad's family used to live in the next block along, so chances are there might be someone around who still remembers them.'

The block Kerry thinks my father lived in is almost identical to Lakeside, although the ground floor windows and doors are all boarded over. We climb the stairs to the first floor, Kerry taking the lead. The smell of damp and urine is heavy in the air, and it's only as we emerge on to the landing that I dare breathe through my nose again.

Assessing the row of identical front doors, it's clear that some of the residents are trying hard to make the best of their surroundings. One flat has a brightly coloured welcome mat outside, another has a collection of bird-themed wind chimes hanging from the roof of the porch. Others, however, have made no effort at all, with ill-fitting window coverings and overflowing bags of rubbish propped up outside their front doors.

Kerry knocks firmly on the first door, which has a handwritten 'Beware of the dog' sign sellotaped to it. No one answers, but there is indeed a dog inside, which hurls itself at the door, barking savagely. There's no answer at the flat next door either, or indeed the rest of the floor. In fact, the only person to respond to our knocking in the whole block is a young girl in a pink fluffy onesie, who on seeing us immediately slams the door shut.

'Well, at least we tried,' I say as we descend the stairs. 'Maybe we could come back another day at a different time and see if it makes any difference.'

Kerry sighs bleakly. 'To be honest, you could bang on my door at home all day, every day and I wouldn't answer it. People who live in places like this keep themselves to themselves. Can't blame them really.'

I can't quite work out whether Kerry is simply trying to manage my expectations or is just in a bad mood. There's something wrong, but I can't work out what.

Standing at the foot of the stairs, I think about suggesting that we try one of the other blocks on the off-chance, but then I look around and see an elderly black lady pushing a shopping trolley, coming towards us, and I have an idea.

'Good morning,' I say, giving her my best professional smile.

She scowls in my direction. 'I haven't got any money, if that's what you're after, so you can clear off,' she says in a thick West Indian accent.

'No, no, no,' I rush to reassure her. 'We're not after money, we're trying to trace someone who used to live here a long time ago. Have you lived here long?'

She eyes me suspiciously. 'Who's asking?'

'My name's Noah Martineau.' I point to Kerry, 'And this is my sister,' and gesturing to the block behind me I add, 'and thirty years ago we used to live there.'

As she looks from me to Kerry, her face softens slightly as curiosity replaces suspicion. 'You say you live there?' I nod. 'A lot of people live there. I've seen them all come and go over the years.'

'We were the Hayes family,' says Kerry.

The woman shakes her head. 'I don't remember you.'

'How about Stucky?' I offer. 'Do you remember anyone with that name?'

She permits herself the luxury of a small smile. 'You mean Jaclyn's boy?'

I feel a pinprick of excitement. 'You remember him?'

'Stucky is what they used to call Jaclyn's boy, although his given name was Paul. Is that who you're after?'

Kerry and I exchange glances.

'Does he still live around here?' I ask hopefully.

She shakes her head. 'I doubt it. I haven't seen that boy in a long time.'

'Well, how about Jaclyn?' asks Kerry. 'Is she still local?'

'No,' says the woman with a sniff. 'She moved away some years back.'

'Oh, right,' I say, trying to hide the edge of disappointment in my voice. 'I'm sorry to hear that.'

The woman regards me for a moment, not saying anything. Then, as if she's reached a decision, she adds, 'But I still keep in touch with her eldest daughter, Marcia.'

'Do you have an address for her?'

The woman scowls. I've clearly said the wrong thing. 'If you think I'm going to give out that kind of information to a total stranger, you can think again.'

I extract a business card from my wallet. 'Of course,' I say. 'Very wise, but would it be possible for you to pass along my contact details to her, please? It's very important.'

She considers the card in her hand carefully. 'I can't read a damn thing without my glasses. What does it say?'

I read it to her and her eyes light up when she hears the word barrister. 'You're a barrister and you say you grew up here?'

'It's a long story, but yes, I was born here.'

'My great-nephew wants to be a barrister, but I tell him if you want to work in law you can't spend all day playing video games. You've got to work hard and put your face in a book.'

My heart is racing. It feels like we're so close. 'Wise words indeed, well, if you'd like, you should feel free to pass my details on to him too. I'd be more than happy to give him some advice to steer him in the right direction.'

I seem to have said the magic words because the woman suddenly beams at me as though I've handed her a blank cheque. 'That boy certainly needs steering,' she says. 'I blame his mother, she's too soft on him, but you didn't hear that from me.' She sniffs again and carefully inserts the business card into her handbag.

'What did you say your name was again?'

'Noah Martineau.'

She eyes me guardedly. 'And who is Stucky to you exactly?'

'My father.' The words feel strange coming out of my mouth.

She shakes her head sadly. 'That boy, such a charmer, but always bringing trouble to his mother's door.' She puts a hand on her shopping trolley as if getting ready to be on her way. 'Well, Mr Noah, it was a pleasure to meet you and I will certainly see what I can do as regards Marcia.'

Kerry and I stand and watch as the old woman walks away.

'Well, that was a result,' I say to my sister, as she finally disappears from view.

'We'll see,' she says, looking at her watch. 'Who knows if she'll even remember to pass on your number?'

It isn't like Kerry to be so negative. There's definitely something wrong. Something she's not telling me.

'What's wrong? I feel like you've not been yourself all morning. Just tell me, it might be something I can help with.'

'I'm fine, really I am.'

'No,' I say firmly. 'You're not. Is it me? Have I done something to upset you? Is it coming back here? I'm really sorry if it's brought back bad memories, I—'

'Noah, please stop,' says Kerry. 'It's nothing to do with that.'

'Then what?'

She closes her eyes, as if trying to block out the world, and I see again just how pale and tired she looks.

'Cancer,' she says finally. 'I've got cancer.'

19

Kerry

Monday, 4th January

Ten past six in the morning, on the first Monday of the new year. It's Kian's first day back at school after the Christmas holidays but he's still fast asleep. And it's my first day back at work, and I'm standing in front of my bedroom mirror in just my bra and knickers, staring at my belly.

I'm not a vain person. I don't have time to be, and with no bloke on the scene, weeks can fly by without me bothering to shave my legs or do under my arms. But I've always liked to keep an eye on my figure. Not that I'm into all those crazy diets you read about in the papers, or exercising like a maniac at the gym. But I do like my clothes to look nice, and so I watch what I eat. I don't binge on chocolate or crisps, and while I love a good pizza or burger, it's always a treat, not something I have every day.

All this is a way of saying I don't quite understand why all of a sudden my jeans don't fit. I was really careful not to go overboard at Christmas, I didn't overdo it on mince pies or chocolates like I normally do, actually if anything I probably ate less over the Christmas break than I would at any other time of year. For some reason, I just didn't have much of an appetite.

Even so, I've been struggling to zip up my jeans for the last couple of weeks. When I first noticed it, I started cutting back straight away. Out went bread, cheese and biscuits, and in came lettuce, low-fat yoghurt and skimmed milk in my tea. It didn't make the slightest bit of difference, if anything it was worse. In fact, I could've barely touched any food at all and I'd still end up having to walk around with the top button undone because the waistband was so tight.

I mentioned it to Jodi and she said it might be IBS. Apparently some mate of hers up in Newcastle had it terrible, and was on special tablets from the doctor. I'm not sure whether it is IBS or not, but I'm beginning to get a bit worried. Perhaps this is the beginning of middle-age spread, and I've heard how hard that is to shift.

Standing sideways on to the mirror, I look at my profile and put a hand on my belly. I almost look pregnant, and as I'm not about to go out and buy a load of new jeans, I make my mind up to phone for a doctor's appointment and see if I can get it sorted once and for all.

I finish getting dressed, dry my hair and then wake Kian up to start getting ready for school. I have to go into his room every five minutes just to make sure he hasn't climbed back into bed. Kian, unlike me, is not a morning person.

By some miracle, I manage to get an appointment that afternoon, although it does mean I have to rearrange the Singhs' clean for another day. The doctor looks about twelve and has about the same amount of confidence I'd expect from someone whose voice has only just broken. He gets me to lie down on the bed and has a bit of a feel and asks me a bunch of questions about my health and what I've been eating. After all that pushing and poking, he tells me he doesn't know exactly what's wrong but just to be on the safe side, I should book in for an ultrasound. The minute he says this, I roll my eyes. That's the problem with these young GPs: because they don't know anything, they refer you to someone else at the drop of a hat. They've done it for Kian loads of times, as if it's never occurred to them that I'm a single mum and every time they send me running across town to see someone else, it means I have to turn my life upside down to get there. Just as I'm thinking there's no way I'm going through all that palaver, he tells me I can get the ultrasound done at the surgery. I still think he's wasting my time, but I'll take the ten-minute journey here over an hour's slog across town any day of the week. I have the ultrasound a week later, and then forget all about it because I've got so much on, covering shifts for a cleaner mate who is on holiday, repainting the bathroom and trying to help Kian with his science project.

A week and a half later, I'm cleaning at the Khans' when the twelve-year-old doctor calls me. Apparently the ultrasound has picked up some sort of ovarian mass. I don't know what one is. It sounds bad but he tells me chances are, it's some sort of benign cyst that can be sorted out quite easily. I still feel a bit panicky but then I remember that last summer one of the mums from school had a couple of cysts removed, and she was right as rain after a day or two.

The doctor tells me he's going to refer me to a consultant and I think to myself, Well, they can't be that worried, because that'll be six months at least. But a week later I get an appointment through to see a Mr Gauld the following week. He's a lovely bloke, with a bright and breezy manner, and he puts me at ease straight away. 'There's a good chance it's nothing,' he tells me, 'but I've always been a belt and braces sort of chap, so I'd like to run a few blood tests and book you in for a CT scan.'

My heart sinks the moment he talks about having more tests because knowing my luck, each one is going to be on a different day, and will make sorting Kian and work out a nightmare. Seeing the face on me, Mr Gauld smiles. 'I know it's a pain, Kerry, asking you to run all over town to be poked and prodded, but humour me just a little while longer.'

He manages to get me in to have my blood tests straight after seeing him, and then it's a two-week wait for the CT scan. In the end, I get an early morning appointment, which means that although I have to shift a couple of clients to Saturday morning, I'll still get to pick Kian up after school. The scan isn't as bad as I thought it might be. Really it's just me lying on a bed, going through a giant doughnut of a machine while it takes pictures of my insides. It only takes twenty minutes or so and afterwards I joke with the radiographer, a pretty Chinese lady, about whether I can get a copy of the pictures she's taken to put up on the living-room wall, and she just laughs and says stranger things have sold in art galleries for millions. Because the scan's over so quick, I even have time to treat myself to a nice coffee and a slice of cake in the hospital canteen afterwards, before making my way to my first job of the day.

While I wait for the results I keep myself busy, which isn't exactly hard. As usual I'm flying round like a nutter, catching up with all the work I've had to rearrange, ferrying Kian about between all his after-school clubs and friends' houses and keeping on top of the house-work.

Anyway, a week later I'm in the middle of running hot water into the bowl to start washing up after tea, when my phone rings. Wiping my soapy hands on a tea towel, I take the call. I half expect it to be Mrs Pryor moaning about something I've forgotten to do this morning. But it's not.

'Kerry Hayes? I'm Mr Gauld's secretary. As a follow-up to your recent tests, he's asked me to book you in for an urgent appointment. What day next week would suit you?'

My head goes fuzzy. I walk over to the kitchen door and close it, and sit down at the table. 'Urgent? Why do I need an urgent appoint-ment? It's just a cyst.'

'I'm afraid I can't discuss that with you over the telephone,' she says, 'but I assure you Mr Gauld will explain everything at your appointment.'

I feel myself starting to panic. Why would he want to see me urgently over some little cyst? 'No,' I say firmly. 'You get him on this phone now so I can find out what's going on.'

'I'm sorry, Ms Hayes, that won't be possible. If you could just let me know when you can come in, I'll get that booked in for you now.'

I feel myself getting wound up. 'Look, if you don't get him on this phone now I don't care what happens to me, I'm not coming in. It's your choice.'

The secretary goes quiet for a minute, then asks me to hold the line. As I wait, all I can hear is the sound of my heart beating and the blood rushing through my ears. It feels like she's gone ages, but then I hear a faint click and a man's voice comes on the line.

'Kerry, Patrick Gauld speaking, I understand there's a problem with you coming in to see me?'

'There's no problem,' I say. 'I just want to know what's going on, that's all. Your secretary said it was urgent, but what's urgent about a little cyst?'

He goes quiet for a minute.

'*Kerry, I'd feel much happier having this conversation face to face, so if you wouldn't mind—*'

'*What conversation?*' I snap. '*Look, I'm a grown woman. I just want someone to tell me what's going on.*'

He goes quiet again, and right there and then I know it's bad news.

'*I don't want you to panic but I'm afraid the CT scan results together with the blood tests have confirmed my suspicion that you have ovarian cancer.*'

My heart stops. Nothing seems real any more. '*But . . . but . . . my GP said it was nothing to worry about,*' *I say helplessly.*

'*That's because most ovarian masses GPs encounter do indeed turn out to be nothing more than a straightforward cyst, not ovarian cancer.*' *He pauses and takes a deep breath.* '*Kerry,*' *he continues,* '*I don't want you to worry. My plan is this: over the next couple of weeks I'd like to do some further tests to ascertain exactly what we're dealing with here. If it's a manageable size, we'll operate to remove it and then start you on chemotherapy. If not, then we'll have to reassess in the light of what we discover. But I want you to remember that you're an otherwise fit and healthy young woman, and we have an excellent team here so I'm sure we can get this sorted for you.*'

My head's spinning.

I feel sick.

I know I should be listening harder to what he's saying, but the only word that stands out is '*cancer*'.

I spend so long in my head that the next thing I hear is him asking if I'm okay. I tell him I'm fine, even though I'm anything but.

'*Kerry,*' *he says.* '*Now we've had this chat, I still need you to come in and see me so I can explain everything thoroughly to you face to face, and get you booked in for more tests. The sooner we crack on, the better.*'

None of this makes sense. I don't feel ill. I don't feel like I've got something growing in me. I just feel like me.

'*But . . . but . . . I've got a son,*' *I tell him.* '*He's only ten. How can this be happening to me?*'

'*Listen,*' *he says after a minute,* '*there's no reason for you to worry.*

As I've said, I'm very good at what I do, and you will get the best care possible.'

I try to take him at his word but it's just so hard. My head's spinning with everything he's told me. I feel myself starting to panic.

'But ... but ... I can't have cancer, I'm a single mum.' I think about Kian and get a massive lump in my throat. 'I can't have cancer. I just can't. It's just me and my boy. What will happen to him if anything happens to me?'

'I'm sure it won't come to that, Kerry. Let's just focus on getting these tests done and starting your treatment.'

'But what if the treatment doesn't work? What will happen to my boy? I haven't got any family, he hasn't got anyone else, at least no one he can depend on. It's just me and him.'

'Kerry,' he says calmly. 'I know this is a lot to process, but you need to take a deep breath and slow down. We need to take this one step at a time. And the first thing we need to do is get you in to see me and then get these tests underway.'

'But that's just it,' I say. 'I can't afford to take things one step at a time. Being on my own means I always have to think five steps ahead about everything.'

'Well, look,' he says. 'If you're worried about who will look after your son should you need to stay in hospital for any length of time, I know in some cases social services—'

'No!' Just hearing someone say those words in connection with my Kian makes me feel physically sick. 'There's no way my boy's going into care. I know you mean well and everything, but it's just not going to happen, not for a week, not for a day, not even for an hour.'

'Kerry, as I said, I don't want you to panic. You have ovarian cancer but that's not the end of the story by any means. But we do need to get moving with these tests so that we can start treatment as soon as possible.'

'I know,' I say quietly. 'But it doesn't matter what you say. I can't think about anything else, apart from what will happen to my Kian if I don't get better. He comes first, he's my world and before I do anything else, I need to know he's going to be all right.'

In the end, he only lets me go after I agree to go in and see him the following week, and afterwards I just sit there in a state of shock. I feel like nothing's real, like I'm in a dream and I'm desperate to wake up. I can't believe it. I've got cancer. It's the sort of thing I only ever thought happened to other people: friends of friends, relatives of mums at the school gate, partners of people I used to know years ago. Only last week I bumped into Bev from the supermarket I used to work at. She'd just lost her husband to bowel cancer. He was only forty-seven. I start to panic again. What if that was me? What if this cancer is worse than they think? What if there's nothing they can do? I can't leave Kian. I just can't. He needs me.

I take a deep breath. I've got to calm down. It's no good getting hysterical. After all, the consultant said it was nothing to worry about. No, I can't go to pieces, I've just got to focus on getting this sorted. I'll go and see the doctor next week like he said, and do whatever it takes to get better.

For a minute or two I feel okay. But then I get thinking how, even if this isn't as bad as I think, it's still going to be pretty awful. I think about Mrs Greig who I clean for: her sister-in-law had a terrible time with breast cancer a few years back. She's better now, but I remember her telling me how ill she was after her surgery. She was in hospital for weeks, and even when she was discharged she couldn't get out of bed for days on end, let alone go to work or look after her kids. How could I hope to take care of Kian on my own like that? It's just not possible. I'm going to need help, and lots of it.

My first thought, of course, is Jodi – after all, she is my closest friend in the world – but she's three hundred miles away and has a house full of kids of her own to deal with. My second is Kian's dad, but he can barely be relied on to send his own son a Christmas card, let alone look after him day in, day out. I think about everyone else I know: the school mums I sometimes chat to, cleaner mates who I've done favours for and old work mates who I used to get on really well with. The thing is, they're all either dealing with stuff of their own, or I don't know them well enough to even think about leaving Kian in their care. For one mad minute I even think about asking Mrs Ryman. She's one of the most capable people I know, and I'd trust her with my life, but she's in her eighties and looking after a ten-year-old boy for any length of time would probably finish her off.

This is impossible.

I'm so desperate, I even end up wishing Mum was still alive. How ridiculous is that? My mum of all people. But if she was alive, then at least I could straighten her out somehow, make her fit to take care of Kian. That would be the answer to all my problems. I think that's partly why I turn up at the cemetery, why I end up staring at a headstone, desperately wishing things could be different, wishing she'd been a real mum, someone I could've turned to when I needed her most.

That night, I chat on the phone with Jodi. I don't tell her anything yet, but instead I ask if it would be okay for me and Kian to go up during the Easter holidays. I know she's got a lot on her plate at the moment with her kids, Mark's family and everything else that's going on in her life. Still, even if there's the slightest chance she could have him, I'll take it.

I know I can't pin all my hopes on Jodi, especially when I've got no idea when my treatment will start. But even though I'm right up against it, I meant what I said to the consultant. There's no way I'm going to let social services get their hands on my son. Not while there's breath left in my body. They tore apart my family, dumped me in home after home with total strangers, and left me feeling mad and angry at the world and everything in it. There's no way I'm going to let them do that to Kian.

So I'm going to need another plan.

That's when the answer hits me: Jason.

I'd always told myself I'd wait for him to make the first move.

I'd always told myself it wouldn't be fair to just barge back into his life unannounced.

I'd always told myself that he might be perfectly happy with his lot and not be interested in digging up the past.

But this is different. This is an emergency.

And anyway, this isn't about me any more.

It's about Kian.

Later, once I'm sure Kian's asleep, I sit down at the kitchen table and write a letter to Jason. But unlike all the others I've written over the years, this one won't be going to some office, waiting to be filed away; it'll be going to his address, straight into the hands of my baby brother.

I won't tell him what I need, to begin with. I don't want to scare him off. But I'll open the door between us. Find out who he is now, what he's like. Then, as soon as that's done, I'll tell him the truth. And I'll just have to hope beyond hope that when I do, he finds it in his heart to do this one thing for me, a total stranger.

20

Noah

Saturday, 9th April

Kerry and I are sitting on a concrete bench in the closest approximation to a park this area has. There's a slide, a couple of broken swings and a climbing wall covered in graffiti. In the far corner, a group of girls no older than Kian are huddled together fussing over a small, scrawny black and white cat, while on the other side two boys on bikes sit staring at their phones, occasionally passing comment on whatever it is they're watching.

Kerry has cancer.

I can't believe it. How could this happen when we've only just found each other? How can this be fair when her life has already known so much sorrow? I think about some of the despicable characters I've met in the course of my career. Real thugs who think nothing of inflicting pain and misery on those around them, and yet somehow they get to live full and healthy lives. Why couldn't this have happened to someone who deserved it, rather than someone like Kerry who's never done anyone any harm? I feel like the ground is shifting beneath my feet. In an instant, I feel that nothing is certain any more.

Kerry lifts her head from my shoulder, dries her eyes and wipes her nose on a tissue from her coat pocket.

'I'm so sorry about that,' she says, the first time she's been able to speak since breaking the news to me. 'You're the first person I've told, and saying it out loud like that just makes it seem more real somehow.'

'I can't imagine what you've been going through. It must have been so horrible for you. When did you find out?'

'A while ago now, I just didn't know who to tell or how to say it.'

'Well, the important thing is that I know now. You don't have to deal with this on your own any more. I'm going to be with you every step of the way.' I kiss the top of her head gently. I feel terrible that I've been going on about finding my father, when all this time she's been suffering in silence. 'I can't believe I dragged you all the way out here like this. I'm so sorry, Kerry, I should've known something was wrong. I should've been a better brother to you.'

She starts to cry again. 'You've got nothing to apologise for,' she says through her tears. 'If anything, I'm the one who should be apologising to you.'

'For what? Kerry, you've been carrying around this terrible burden on top of finding out about our birth mother passing away. You must be exhausted with it all.'

Kerry cries even harder when I say this, and when I try to pull her towards me for a hug she suddenly stands up, pushing me away. 'Don't,' she says, 'please, Noah, don't be nice to me, I don't deserve it.'

Confused, I get to my feet. 'Of course you do. Why would you think you don't?'

She looks at me, eyes red and puffy. ''Cause I haven't been totally honest with you.'

'About what? I don't understand.'

Kerry dries her eyes again and takes a deep breath. 'Listen,' she says, 'before I go any further, I need you to understand something: I wasn't trying to pull the wool over your eyes or nothing. I just needed to see you, and I couldn't explain the real reason why upfront, without scaring you off.'

'Kerry, I really don't understand what it is you're trying to say. Pull the wool over my eyes about what exactly?'

'Mum.'

'What about her?'

'I . . . I deliberately let you think Mum died a few weeks back, but that's not true.' She looks down at her feet. 'Truth is . . . Mum actually died six years ago. I didn't know at the time. I only found out a few months after it happened, when one of her friends called out of the blue and said they'd been trying to track me down to let me know.'

The ground beneath my feet shifts again. I run a hand over my head. None of this makes any sense. 'But why would you lie about something like that?'

'Because I was afraid of what you'd say if you knew the real reason I got in touch . . .' Her arms drop to her sides and she closes her eyes. '. . . I got in touch . . . because I'm going to need someone to look after Kian and I want it to be you.'

She tells me the whole story of her diagnosis and the anguish that followed. How she was going to have to have an operation followed by chemotherapy. How she feared that if anything were to happen to her, then Kian would end up in care.

'So, all of this, you tracking me down after all these years, this was about getting me to look after Kian?'

She looks horrified at the suggestion. 'Of course it wasn't like that! It wasn't like that at all. The truth is . . .'

'Truth?' I snap, angry in spite of myself. 'What would you know about the truth? You've lied to me from the beginning. Why should I believe anything you say to me now?'

Kerry shakes her head. 'Please, Noah, don't twist things like that, it wasn't like that at all.' She shuts her eyes for a moment and draws the deepest breath possible. 'The thing is,' she continues, 'I haven't just found you, Noah . . . the thing is, I've known where you were for at least five whole years.'

I can barely believe what I'm hearing.

What little solid ground that is left beneath my feet gives way completely. All that's between me and the abyss below is thin air.

'Five years?' My words are so loud that the girls fussing over the cat all turn as one to look at us. 'You found me five years ago but waited until now to get in touch? Why?'

There's a long silence and then she speaks. 'Because you were happy,' she explains. 'And I felt like I didn't have the right to spoil what you had.'

★

She tells me how she tracked me down and about the day she saw me for the first time in thirty years. It was a Saturday morning, and she'd been sitting in her clapped-out Vauxhall Cavalier with five-year-old Kian strapped in his car seat in the back. She tells me about the flood of excitement that came over her as the weeks and months of sitting outside my house, waiting for a glimpse of its occupants, finally paid off.

'I can't tell you how much I wanted to get out of the car and run over to you, Noah,' she says, clutching my arm. 'It took every bit of strength I had to stay put, but I knew I had to. You weren't my little baby brother any more. You were a grown man with a beautiful family, a big house, and a posh car. And what's more, you looked happy, really happy, and that's all I've ever wanted for you. It broke my heart a million times over to be so close to you and have to keep my distance, but I didn't feel I had the right to waltz back into your life out of nowhere. All that mattered, all I cared about, was knowing for sure that you'd got the happy ending I always wanted for you.'

Neither of us speaks for a while. Instead we sit staring ahead, watching life unfolding in front of us. The girls with the cat disappear only to be replaced by a young mum and her child, kicking a plastic football to each other. The boys on the bikes are joined by several younger children, and a game of tag ensues. An elderly couple in matching jackets stroll past arm in arm, leaning on each other for support.

'I don't remember that day.'

Kerry looks at me. 'Which day?'

'The day you saw me.'

Kerry shrugs. 'No reason you should.'

'But you said I looked happy, that I looked like I'd got my happy ending. It's funny, isn't it? You can try all you want not to take things for granted, but somehow you always do.'

'That's just life, isn't it? I remember when Kian was a baby, thinking I'd never forget the sound of his laugh, the smell of him all warm and cosy when I'd lift him out of his Moses basket for his early morning feed. Or how it felt to have him fall asleep in my arms. But you do forget, don't you? Life just carries on, time keeps moving forwards and the list of things you tell yourself you'll never forget keeps on growing.' She turns to look at me. 'I know I'm asking a lot of you, Noah, really I do. And I can't tell you how much I wish I wasn't. But things are the way they are, and this is what I've got to deal with. At the end of the day, time is running out. I've got a date for my surgery now and whether you say yes or no, I've got to sort something out for Kian, even if that means him going into foster care for a bit. And while it would break my heart for that to happen, I'll do it if it means me getting rid of this disease once and for all. I want to see my boy grow up. I want to see him get married. I want to be there for him when he has children of his own. So whatever it takes to make that happen, I'll do it. All I'm asking is that you'll think about taking him in. That's all, just think about it.'

Back in the flat, having been dropped off by Kerry following a virtually silent journey back to Bayswater, I set to preparing for Millie's imminent arrival. Rosalind's bringing her round in a couple of hours and she is staying overnight again, which I've been looking forward to all week. However, despite my best intentions, I find myself wandering aimlessly from room to room, not getting much of anything accomplished. No matter what I do, I can't seem to shake the image of Kerry sitting in the cold in her car outside my house, hoping to catch a glimpse of me.

I feel ashamed and guilty, because if I had caught sight of her car that day, I probably would've been suspicious. Imagined it was someone up to no good, watching homes, waiting for them to be empty before making their move. Never in a million years would I have dreamed that, instead, I was being watched from afar by my own flesh and blood, by a sister I never even knew existed.

This little scene says so much about each of our lives. Kerry has always been on the outside in one way or another, ever since we were separated all those years ago. Abandoned and thrown into care, while I was swept up into the loving arms of my adoptive parents and handed a life of privilege.

And now she has cancer. I can't believe it. That someone who has already had to fight so many battles in the course of her life must face the biggest battle of all seems obscenely unjust.

I owe Kerry, of this there is no doubt. She has endured the life that had been meant for me too. She has suffered hardships that I too should have borne. And having never forgotten me as I had forgotten her, she tracked me down only to sacrifice her desire to be with me in order to preserve the bubble in which I existed, one inside which no bad thing ever happened, and everything went my way.

But do I really have it in me to do what she's asked? My life is enough of a mess as it is. How would I even begin to explain the sudden appearance of a nephew in my life, a new addition, to a wife who is still mourning the loss of a much longed-for child of our own, when she isn't even aware of Kerry's existence? Am I really ready to tell my mother and father that, in spite of everything they've done for me, I've secretly reconnected with my birth family behind their backs? And what of Phillip, to whom I owe the roof over my head? Or Charlotte, who has been so unreservedly supportive? How would they react to the knowledge that I'd chosen not to share this with them until I had no choice? Perhaps Rosalind was right after all: perhaps I do keep too much of myself hidden from those I claim to love.

And what of Kian? This ten-year-old boy who I've only met twice? Do I really have it in me to look after him indefinitely? A friend of Rosalind's had undergone surgery followed by chemotherapy some years ago, and at times the treatment had seemed almost worse than the disease itself, rendering her incapable of looking after herself for months on end. Taking Kian in for that amount of time would have a huge impact on my life, not to mention my relationship with Rosalind. It would be one thing telling her about Kerry, but quite another to inform her that my secret sister's son may have to come and live with me. And what about Millie? She's already been challenged by the problems between Rosalind and me; the last thing she needs as an only child is to have my attention divided even further. And even if all of these issues are somehow magically resolved, how could I possibly meet the needs of a young child whose mother is seriously ill, while working the exhausting hours so often required of me?

The welcome arrival of Millie takes my mind off these questions for a while. She's so effervescently alive, so effortlessly engaging that it's impossible not to allow myself to put aside my thoughts at least for a short time. But later that night, having kissed her goodnight and returned to my own room, the thoughts return so seamlessly it's as if they've never been away.

I want to do the right thing.

I need to do the right thing.

But at the moment I just don't know what that is.

21

Kerry

Monday, 11th April

'Kian!' I yell. 'If you're not in here in ten seconds I will flush that phone down the toilet, don't think for a minute I won't!'

I can see he believes me, but that doesn't stop him making a right performance of getting out of the car.

'Right,' I say, as he stands on the Pryors' doormat, hands shoved deep in his pockets and a sulky scowl on his face. 'Take your shoes off, follow me, and whatever you do, don't touch a thing unless I tell you.'

Since he got suspended Kian has been tagging along with me to work, and at first he'd quite enjoyed it. But the novelty of going in and out of posh people's houses has started to wear off and he's getting bored now, and restless with it.

I park him on the sofa in the Pryors' playroom, just off the kitchen. It's crammed full of toys, books, games and gadgets, and there's a massive flat-screen TV on the wall. To be honest, it's always struck me as a bit of a kids' prison, a place to keep them entertained and out of sight while Mrs Pryor bitches over coffee with her mates, and I hate it for that reason alone. But desperate times call for desperate measures, so I switch on the TV, hand Kian the remote and a bag of crisps, and tell him to keep out of trouble.

'You can watch all the telly you like,' I say, 'but do not even think about touching anything else in this room, okay?'

He looks at me all indignant. 'But what about the PlayStation? It's the new one and they've got loads of games.'

Sometimes it's like it goes in one ear and straight out the other.

'What did I just say?'

Kian sighs heavily. 'Don't touch anything that's not the TV.'

'There you go, then,' I tell him. 'There's your answer.'

Leaving the door open so I can keep an eye on him, I go back into the kitchen and sit down to gather my strength for a minute. Ever since they told me I'd got cancer, it's been impossible to know whether I'm ordinary, everyday tired or whether it's because I'm ill. Anyway, whatever the reason, I don't sit down long. I can't. Once again Mrs Pryor has left it like a right tip, and it takes me a good half hour of clearing away the breakfast things and loading the dishwasher before I can get going on my regular cleaning.

I give the kitchen surfaces a wipe down, sweep the floor, then fill my bucket with cleaner and boiling-hot water and start mopping. Mopping usually gives me the chance to switch off my brain, but it doesn't work today. Today all I can think about is Noah. Today all I can think about is how I've let Kian down. Today all I can think about is how time has finally run out.

It's been two days since I last saw Noah and I haven't heard a word from him. I'm terrified I've scared him off. Not just because of my illness, or even because of what I've asked of him. But because I haven't been honest with him. I should have told him the truth from the start.

I've lost count of how many times I've nearly called him or sent a text. I just want to tell him I love him. That even if he says no about Kian, it won't make any difference to how I feel about him. I want to say sorry for dumping all this junk on his lap. I just want to hear him say he forgives me. Anyway, like I said, time has officially run out: this morning I finally called social services about Kian.

Kian was in the car when I made the call. I'd told him I was just nipping into Tesco for a few bits, but even though I walked into the entrance all I did was walk out of the exit on the other side and find somewhere quiet to make the call.

Even as the phone rang, I still found myself hoping that Noah would call, that he'd come to the rescue, but by the time I got through to an actual human being I knew it was too late. This was it, I'd run out of time, I'd run out of options. This was the last thing in the world I ever wanted for my boy, but the situation was impossible: start my treatment and have Kian go into care or don't have the treatment and risk him being without me for good.

The woman I spoke to was nice enough. She told me that they had plenty of lovely temporary foster carers on hand for just this sort of thing. She told me not to worry about anything, took all my details and told me someone would ring me back this afternoon. As calls go, it wasn't anywhere near as awful as I thought it would be but that didn't stop me from feeling like I'd betrayed my boy, that I'd let him down in the worst way a mother can. His whole life I'd tried my hardest to be the best mum I could be, to give him everything I never had, to protect him, to be there for him no matter what, and yet here he was going into care. I couldn't help but feel like I'd failed him, failed him just like my mum had failed me. And on top of it all, I still hadn't told him about my operation.

I try my best not to think about any of this as I finish the floors. I cried all my tears outside Tesco this morning, and now the only thing left to do is just get on with things. But as I empty my mop bucket ready to fill it again, I start to feel bad about being so down on Kian, especially now I know how this week is going to play out. I fish a can of Coke out of my bag to give him as a treat, but when I go to the playroom the door's shut and I can't hear the telly. I know something's up straight away. I fling the door open to find Kian, PlayStation controller in his hands, staring up at the screen in front of him. He practically jumps out of his skin when he sees me and drops the controller on the hard limestone floor. We both watch helplessly as a massive chunk of it flies off and skids across the room.

Kian stands there staring at me with his mouth open, like he can't decide whether to run or cry.

'Mum,' he splutters. 'I can explain.'

'Explain what? I told you not to touch anything, but you went ahead and did what you wanted anyway.'

'It . . . it . . . it wasn't like that, Mum, I just wanted—'

'Not another word, do you hear me? Have you any idea how much these things cost? Have you? Where am I supposed to get that kind of money? Do you think it grows on trees?' Kian looks down at his feet the whole time, but I'm so furious I'm not prepared to let it go. 'I've asked you a question, Kian. Do you think money grows on trees?'

'No,' he says sulkily.

'So tell me then, where do you think it comes from?'

'You,' he says, still not looking at me.

'And how exactly do I get this money? From sitting on my backside waiting for magic fairies to put it in the bank?'

'No,' he says again.

'That's right, because there are no magic fairies, Kian. There's just me, getting out of bed day after day, clearing up after miserable cows like Mrs Pryor, who think that fifteen quid an hour buys them a slave. Well that's that, I've had enough! Not only are you paying for a new controller, but your days of sitting around watching TV are over! From now on you're helping me. You can start by cleaning the downstairs toilet. I want it sparkling, the sink, the seat, the bowl, everything.'

Kian looks horrified and pushes out his bottom lip. 'I'm not doing that.'

'I think you'll find you are.'

He turns up his nose in disgust and folds his arms angrily. 'I'm not touching someone else's toilet, that's rank.'

'But it's okay for me to do it so that I can pay for broken controllers that I told you not to touch? Get in there now! I mean it, Kian!'

He lifts his chin, eyes narrowed in defiance. 'I'm not cleaning someone else's toilet. It's embarrassing!' And just like that, I see red.

I've never once hit Kian. I've never had to. But in that moment, with everything that's going on, I just lose it, and smack him around the face. I don't know which of us is more shocked by the loud crack my open hand makes as it hits him. For a moment we just stand there, looking at each other, then Kian pushes past me, tears streaming down his face, and runs out of the room.

I feel awful, like the worst mother in the world, so I run after him, calling out for him to stop, calling out that I'm sorry, which is exactly the moment Mrs Pryor and her yummy mummy cronies choose to turn up.

'What exactly is going on here?' barks Mrs Pryor as Kian skids to a halt in front of her, while her friends and their children huddle behind her for protection. 'Kerry, who is this boy?'

'It's my son, Kian, Mrs Pryor.'

'Your son? What precisely is he doing here in my home?'

I have to think quickly. 'He's not well. He's got a bit of a temperature. I had to keep him off school today and I didn't want to let you down again, so I brought him with me.'

'Let me get this right: you brought your sick child into *my* house without asking my permission? How dare you?'

All I want is for the ground to open up and swallow me whole. It's like being back at school and getting told off by the headmistress. 'I'm so sorry, Mrs Pryor,' I say. 'You're absolutely right. I should've asked your permission. I promise it won't happen again.'

'You're damned right it won't,' snaps Mrs Pryor. 'Your cleaning is patchy at best, you never get round to completing half the jobs I ask of you, and now to top it all, you treat my home as if it's a day care centre for sick children! Well, this is the last straw! And to think how worried I've been about how best to get rid of you. Well, enough is enough! Get your things and go, and if you think I'm going to pay you for today, you can think again!'

I can feel all of Mrs Pryor's mates staring at me, and I don't know where to put myself.

This is a complete nightmare. And just when I thought this week couldn't get any worse. I start collecting my stuff together but no sooner have I picked up my mop bucket than I hear Kian say something. I turn around to see him squaring up to Mrs Pryor like some sort of tiny prizefighter.

'What did you just say to me, young man?' demands a shocked Mrs Pryor, hands on hips.

'I said, don't talk to my mum like that,' says Kian through gritted teeth. 'She works really hard and your house is loads messier than ours.'

Mrs Pryor is so outraged it looks as if she's about to explode. 'I beg your pardon?'

'I think he said you can shove your job up your arse,' I say, surprising myself. 'I think he said you live like a pig, your kids are spoilt, and I'm pretty sure your husband's having an affair.' Picking up the rest of my stuff, I march over to Kian and, grabbing his hand, push past Mrs Pryor and her mates and head straight out the door. I might have just lost a big chunk of regular money when I need it most, but at the very least I've kept my dignity.

That evening, I'm cooking tea when Kian knocks on the kitchen door, and asks to come in. He never knocks on any door in this flat, not even the bathroom. Normally, it being the two of us, he barges in and starts talking about whatever it is that's on his mind, but today's different. Today he knows he crossed a line.

I look up from mashing the potatoes and tell him to come in. He looks small and sad and there's no trace of the fight and the fire from earlier in the day.

Walking up to me, he holds out his hand, in which is a fiver, two pound coins and some bits of change.

'What's all this, then?' I say, putting down the masher and wiping my hands on a tea towel.

'It's for you,' he says, holding it up a bit higher. 'To make up for the money you lost today because of me.'

I can't help it. I'm an emotional wreck as it is about belting him like that. I sweep Kian up into my arms and cover his face and head in kisses. I just love him so much. It breaks my heart thinking that soon some complete stranger is going to be looking after him.

'I'm so sorry for hitting you like that,' I tell him. 'I really am.'

'No, Mum,' says Kian. 'I'm sorry, you were right. I shouldn't have got into trouble at school. I shouldn't have touched the

PlayStation when you told me not to, and I shouldn't have been cheeky to Mrs Pryor.'

I laugh. 'Well, you might be right about the first two but as for Mrs Pryor, that cow has had it coming for a long time.'

'But you've lost your job.'

'*A* job,' I correct him. 'I've got others and anyway, there's always plenty of work for a good cleaner.'

I tell him to put his money away and wash his hands so we can have tea.

He looks at me, not quite understanding. 'Are you sure you don't want the money?'

'Yes, babe, I'm sure. Whatever happens, you and me are always going to be all right.'

As a treat we eat tea on our laps in front of the TV, and afterwards I tell him to turn on the PlayStation and teach me again how to play *FIFA*. I'm still none the wiser after half an hour of him chatting away, but it's good spending time together, having a laugh and getting things back to normal between us.

After Kian's gone to bed, I think about the day again and sit down and work out how much I'm going to be down a month without the Pryors. It works out to three hundred and sixty pounds, which is a big chunk of money for me to lose. But on the other hand, it's one less client for me to find cover for while I'm getting over my operation.

I've been putting it off for far too long. I don't know what I was thinking. I suppose I've been in denial about it. But with no time left, I start ringing around all the cleaners I know, ones who I've covered for in the past, and ask them if they can take on a couple of my clients for a while. Some say yes straight away, others say they're already fully booked. But most tell me they'll need to get back to me. So when the phone rings after ten, I'm thinking it's just one of the cleaning girls, but then I look at the screen and see that it's Noah.

'I'm sorry, Kerry,' he says. 'I hope I haven't woken you.'

It's ridiculous how apologetic he sounds when the truth is I couldn't be happier he called.

'You could ring me at three o'clock in the morning and I wouldn't care. I'm just so glad to hear from you. I'm so glad you don't hate me after everything I dumped on you. I'm sorry, Noah. I should never have done that. Please just say you forgive me.'

'There's nothing to forgive. It's me who should be apologising to you: for being so wrapped up in myself all these years that I never bothered to find out you even existed. For not being there when you needed me. For not getting back to you sooner. I want you to know that whatever you need, it's yours. I'll look after you and I'll look after Kian too. I'll be with you every step of the way. And I promise you we'll get through this. We'll get through this together.'

It's like someone's lifted a ten-tonne weight off my chest. Finally I can breathe again. Kian won't have to go into care. My boy will get to stay where he belongs – with family. I look down at my hands. I'm shaking like a leaf.

'Thank you, Noah,' I say, trying to hold back my tears, 'thank you so much. It's such a relief to hear you say that. You don't know what it means to me.'

'So what's next?' asks Noah. 'We need to make plans, don't we? When exactly is your surgery?'

'Well, that's just the thing,' I say. 'It's tomorrow.'

22

Noah

Tuesday, 12th April

'So Mrs Ryman is one of your clients, isn't she?'

Kerry nods. 'Well, these days she's more of a friend really. I'd trust that woman with my life. Which is why she was the first person who sprang to mind. I just hope Kian behaves himself. She's in her eighties and she's still a force to be reckoned with but even so, if she has to cope with him for more than a few hours he'll wear her out.'

Kerry and I are in my car, heading towards Hammersmith hospital for her operation. We've both had to turn our lives upside down in a very short space of time. Thankfully I wasn't due in court today, but I've had to call the clerks and ask them to offload any work they've secured for me for the rest of the week so I can be with her. Kerry, meanwhile, has been on the phone since seven o'clock this morning, first with Mrs Ryman in order to ask her to look after Kian while I take her to hospital, and secondly with social services to cancel the emergency foster care she'd requested.

'I know I've said it already, but I really am sorry I left it so long to get back to you. It must have been horrible for you to have had to involve social services for Kian.'

'I won't lie,' she says. 'It wasn't easy, but that's all in the past now. With Mrs Ryman helping out today and you being here with me and looking after Kian while I'm in hospital, all the pressure's off.'

'And Kian knows what you're going into hospital for?'

She shakes her head. 'He knows I'm having an operation but

not what for. There's no good scaring the kid with talk of cancer and tumours. I've told him the operation is something ladies have to have sometimes, and he pulled a face and didn't ask any more questions. Anyway, once he heard it was you he'd be staying with until I get out of hospital, he was too excited to worry.'

'And you've got someone covering your clients for you too?'

She shrugs. 'Most of them, not all, so I'll just have to hurry up and get back on my feet sharpish, won't I?'

She laughs, but I can tell she's putting a brave face on things. For all intents and purposes she's self-employed just like me: no sick pay, no safety net. And now she's in danger of losing some of her regular work.

'Look, Kerry,' I say, keeping my eyes on the road ahead. 'The last thing I want is to offend you, but I want you to know I'm more than happy to help out financially until you're back on your feet. I don't want you worrying about money when you should be focusing on getting well.'

'That's lovely of you, Noah,' she says. 'And I'm grateful, but I've got a bit tucked away for emergencies so I should be fine.'

I have my doubts whether Kerry would tell me if she needed any financial help, but she's a proud woman and has enough on her mind, so I decide to let the matter rest for the time being. Instead, for the remainder of the journey to the hospital, we chat about inconsequential matters, the weather, the traffic, even our joint horror at the recent shrinkflation of our favourite snacks, all in a bid to distract ourselves from what lies ahead.

Arriving at the hospital, I try to make myself useful while Kerry is waiting in the queue at reception, by picking up a few things from the hospital shop that I think she might need. I buy a selection of women's magazines, a newspaper, a large bottle of Lucozade and some grapes, all the recovery clichés I can think of. Loaded down with my purchases and Kerry's small suitcase, filled with things for her stay, I return to her just as she's finished booking in.

'It's the third floor for the surgical ward,' she says. After scanning the lobby for signs to the lift, we make our way towards it.

'How are you feeling?' I ask. 'You must be nervous, but I've looked your consultant up online and he has an excellent reputation.'

Kerry smiles. 'What? Is there like a TripAdvisor for doctors? Has he got five-star reviews?'

'Something like that,' I say, pleased her sense of humour is still intact.

Once on the ward, Kerry is shown to a bed and told that her consultant will be with her shortly. But when after an hour there's still no sign, I make enquiries of the nurse on reception, only to be told that he is still in his morning meeting.

When another hour passes and he fails to appear, Kerry begins to worry. 'I know there's always a lot of hanging around in hospitals but this is ridiculous. Don't they know that people have lives of their own to get back to? I told Mrs Ryman you'd pick Kian up at four at the latest, and I can't let her down when she's already doing me such a massive favour. If it comes to it, you'll just have to go and leave me to it. I'll be fine as long as I know Kian's in safe hands.'

It is cruel keeping Kerry waiting like this with no information forthcoming. The least they could do is keep her up to date with what's happening. I stand up, determined to make my presence felt at reception, but as I do so, a thin, bespectacled man in his late fifties sweeps on to the ward and immediately makes a beeline for Kerry.

'Kerry,' he says, 'I'm sorry to have kept you waiting for so long. As usual we had a number of emergencies to deal with, and that always causes something of a backlog.' He smiles at me as I introduce myself, but his focus is clearly on Kerry. He draws the curtains around the bed and takes a seat. 'Aside from the emergencies,' he begins, 'another reason for my late arrival is that I've been in conference with my colleagues about your case. You remember last week having some pre-operative scans and tests? Well, the results are back from your last lot of tests and on the basis of those results, my colleagues and I are in agreement that the best way forward with your treatment now is chemotherapy rather than surgery.'

Her consultant pauses for a moment to allow the news to sink in, and I reach for Kerry's hand. Having steeled herself for this operation, the news that it isn't going to happen today must be a real shock to her.

'Kerry, I don't want you to worry,' the doctor continues. 'These sorts of things happen all the time, I'm afraid, but with the new information we have now, we will need to change our plan of attack.

'Thanks to the latest lot of imaging, we can see that the tumour is a little trickier to access than we first thought and is growing at a slightly faster rate than we anticipated. I'm sorry for this eleventh-hour change but I really do feel that, as things stand at the moment, chemotherapy is the best treatment option, followed by surgery once we've got things a little more under control. Ordinarily I'd get you booked in to start treatment by the end of the week, but your pre-op tests show that you're running a slight temperature.'

She looks at the consultant, confused. 'Am I? I feel fine, honestly. Can't we just get cracking on with things?'

Mr Gauld smiles. 'I appreciate your willingness to get the ball rolling, Kerry, and obviously you've had to make all manner of arrangements in order to be here today, but it's very important that we get this right, and unfortunately, while you're probably just nursing the beginnings of a cold, we want you to start treatment fighting fit.'

Kerry looks from the consultant to me and back again. 'Be honest, is the cancer worse than you thought?'

'Not necessarily in terms of outcomes but it is more complex than it first appeared. We're going to need to run a couple more tests over the next week or so, but the plan as it stands at the moment is to give you a good blast of chemotherapy to get things under control and then as soon as they are, we'll have you in for surgery.'

It's after one by the time I pull up outside Kerry's flat, having picked Kian up from Mrs Ryman's on the way. We've yet to talk about this new turn of events; I think we're still getting our heads around the fact that the operation we'd done so much rearranging for hasn't happened.

'I'd ask you in for a cuppa,' says Kerry, 'but I feel like I've already wasted too much of your time.'

'Of course you haven't,' I reply. 'I've arranged to have the whole day off anyway.'

She fishes a set of house keys out of her bag and hands them to Kian. 'Let yourself in and get the kettle on for me, babes. I'll be up in a sec.'

Kian takes the keys, says goodbye to me and, grabbing the small suitcase from the seat next to him, gets out of the car.

'Are you all right?' I ask, as we sit watching Kian struggling with the suitcase up the stairs. 'I'm really worried about you.'

'I'm not great, to be honest,' she says, sitting back in her seat with a sigh. 'I just can't believe it's going to take even longer to sort out. I'm starting to get scared, Noah, really scared.'

I take her hand. 'Oh, Kerry, of course you are. That's completely understandable. But your consultant knows what he's doing. And we'll get through this together. I'll be right here with you.'

Kerry starts to cry. 'But how? You can't keep dropping everything to run around after me every five seconds, it's not right. And anyway, chemotherapy's a different ball game. I know for a fact that it can make you really sick. I might not be up and about for weeks. Maybe Kian would be better going into temporary foster care after all, especially if I've got to have an operation after that too.'

'It won't ever have to come to that, I promise. You and Kian will either stay with me or I'll come and stay with you. We'll work it out. The important thing is I'm here for you both. Kian won't have to go into foster care.'

She throws her arms around me, and as she sobs into my shoulder I realise that no matter how much I want to make things better, at the moment there's very little I can do.

'You don't know what this means to me, Noah.' We part and she sits back in her seat and dries her eyes. 'I'll never be able to thank you.'

'How about starting with that cup of tea?' I joke, switching off the engine.

She smiles. 'You know I'd make you a seven-course meal if you wanted one,' she says. 'But I'm going to let you get off. It looks like I'm going to be doing a lot of leaning on you over the next few weeks, so you'd best make the most of your freedom while you've got it.'

'If you insist,' I say. I can see how exhausted she is. She probably just wants to have some time on her own with Kian. 'But if you need me for anything, even if it's just to talk, then call me, okay?'

Kerry nods, gives me a hug and then smiles again. 'I suppose one good thing's come out of this,' she says. 'At least I won't be laid up in hospital for Kian's birthday. He's been on and on at me about having a party, and it broke my heart to tell him he wouldn't be able to because I'd probably still be recovering from my operation. At least now it's not happening, I can throw something together for him. You will come won't you?'

'Of course,' I say. 'I wouldn't miss it for the world.'

Leaving Kerry's, my first thought is to call chambers and let the clerks know that I'm available for work after all, but I change my mind and instead of making my way to Chancery Lane, I head towards Rosalind's studio in Camden.

This dramatic change in Kerry's situation has put a great many things into perspective. It's never ceased to amaze me how quickly a life can be turned upside down by the utterance of a few words. The declaration of, 'Guilty,' or 'Not Guilty.' The surge of joy felt hearing, 'I love you.' The devastation wreaked by the three words: 'You have cancer.'

Words have power, and I've made a career wielding them to best effect. And yet here I am, speechless in the face of Kerry's pain. But although there's nothing I can do to help Kerry right now, there is at least one wrong that I can right with a single conversation. It's time I told Rosalind the truth: about Kerry, about Kian, but above all about myself.

Reaching Rosalind's studio, a former cloth factory backing on to Regent's Canal, I feel nervous and excited at the same time by the prospect of what I'm about to do, as I walk through the automatic doors into the lobby. Even though I haven't been here for a long while, the young woman behind the reception desk recognises me immediately and buzzes me straight through the security barriers.

Reaching the studio, I knock on the door in case Rosalind is with clients, then put my head in. Aoife, Rosalind's business partner, looks up from her laptop, arching an expensively maintained eyebrow in surprise as she does so.

'Noah,' she says. 'What an unexpected pleasure! Are you looking for Rosalind?'

'Yes, is she around?'

Aoife shakes her head. 'She called in sick this morning. Is everything okay?'

'I just wanted a word. Maybe I'll drop by the house and see if she needs anything.'

'Sounds like a lovely idea. I'd go myself but I'm pretty swamped here. Give her my love, won't you?'

'Of course,' I say, and then there's a couple of awkward moments where I realise that we haven't seen each other since Rosalind and I separated. I wonder how much she knows and what she thinks of me now. Thankfully her mobile rings before things can get any more uncomfortable. 'I'll let you get that,' I say, and then exit before she can object.

I head to Primrose Hill via Waitrose. I pick up flowers, chocolates and, as an afterthought, half a dozen herbal teas. On the way, I think about calling to tell Rosalind I'm coming but talk myself out of it. I want to make the most of the momentum I've built up and anyway, before I know it, I'm pulling up in front of the house.

I let myself in, not wanting Rosalind to get out of bed if she's resting, but in the hallway I make sure to call out to her. When she replies, however, her voice doesn't come from upstairs but from the rear sitting room, and I enter to find her hastily straightening the sofa cushions and clearing away a pile of tissues from the coffee table. She's wearing an old cardigan and jeans. She looks tired and pale, her eyes rimmed with red.

'These are for you,' I say, handing her the flowers. 'Aoife told me you weren't feeling great.'

'Thanks,' she says, as I give her the rest of my care package. 'This is so sweet of you but you needn't have worried. I'll be fine. I just need a bit of rest, that's all. Where did you see Aoife?'

'At the studio. I dropped by and—' I stop as I realise that Rosalind is crying. 'What's wrong?'

She shakes her head. I take the things from her hands, place them on the coffee table and then we both sit down.

'Please, Rosalind,' I say, holding her hands in mine. 'Tell me what's wrong?'

'I'm okay,' she says, as her tears continue to fall. 'Really I am.'

'So what is it? What's the problem?'

'Today . . .' she says, her voice barely above a whisper, 'today would've been my twenty-week scan.'

In that instant a door I've held shut crashes open, letting in wave after wave of grief, almost strong enough to sweep me off my feet. This is grief I hadn't yet expressed to Rosalind, grief I hadn't even dared express to myself. The miscarriage. The searing pain of our loss. The emptiness left behind after hope and happiness had been swept away.

I close my eyes, take a deep breath and regain my composure.

'I'm so, so sorry,' I say finally. 'I didn't realise.'

She dries her eyes with a tissue. 'There's no reason you should,' she says, and for a moment I think she's angry with me but then she squeezes my hand tightly. 'I nearly forgot myself. Can you believe it? Something that was so important to us and I forgot all about it until a reminder popped up on my phone. A bloody phone reminder!'

My mind flashes back to that moment in the GP's office when he'd confirmed her pregnancy. Jokingly she'd added a reminder of her next appointment into her phone as she did with all the tasks she needed to organise. 'There you go,' she'd said. 'Car in for service, renew house insurance, and now find out whether I'm having a baby boy or a baby girl.' It had been a funny moment and we'd both giggled like children at the wonderful shock of it all. Never did we think that a moment so filled with joy would come back to haunt us like this.

I'm not sure how long we sit there in silence, wrapped in each other's arms. Time seems to lose all meaning. But it is long enough for Rosalind's tears to subside, my own sense of shock to abate, and for something close to peace to settle on us both.

Eventually she sits upright, gathers together the gifts I'd brought and offers to make us both a cup of tea. As we stand in the kitchen, waiting for the kettle to boil, Rosalind arranging biscuits on a plate while I wrestle with the cellophane on a box of liquorice and peppermint tea, she looks over at me as though suddenly remembering something.

'You didn't say why you stopped by the studio this morning. And now I think about it, why aren't you at work?'

This should be the moment.

The one where I tell her everything, where all my secrets come tumbling out into the open. But as I look at her beautiful face, still etched with sorrow and exhaustion, I realise I can't do this to her. Not here, not now. Unburdening myself today would be an act of pure selfishness, and I love her too much, care for her too deeply, to do that. I've been keeping all this to myself for so long that I'm sure a while longer won't hurt.

'It was frustrating really. I had a case collapse at the last minute so I rescheduled a meeting over this side of things, and thought I'd drop in and surprise you. Was that an okay thing to do?'

She leans against the counter, her shoulders relaxing slightly. 'It's more than okay, it's lovely. Although I'm guessing I've made you late for your meeting now. What time was it supposed to be?'

'Don't worry,' I say, finally breaking through the cellophane on the teabags. 'It's nothing I can't sort out.'

Rosalind smiles. 'Well, even though it's probably not the afternoon you were hoping for, I'm glad you came.'

We talk for a good hour, mostly about Millie but about work and family too, until finally I tell her I have to go. On the doorstep we hug goodbye, and it reminds me how much I've missed being close to her. She must be feeling the same, as before I know it, we're kissing. Suddenly she pulls away her face, full of both longing and regret.

'I'm sorry.'

Rosalind sighs. 'There's nothing to apologise for. It feels good to be so close to you, Noah. Really good. And there's nothing I want more than to be with you, to have things go back to normal between us, but the last thing either of us wants is to jeopardise all the work we've done so far. We're so close, really we are. Just a while longer and I think we'll be there.'

23

Kerry

Sunday, 24th April

'This better not be you telling me you're not coming.'

The pause before he answers tells me everything I need to know.

'The thing is yeah—'

'The thing is what?' I snap, before I can stop myself. Kian's in the other room and if he hears me shouting he'll know it's his dad on the phone. I sneeze and wipe my nose on the tissue from the pocket of my jeans, then shut the kitchen door with my foot. 'Why aren't you coming?'

'Something's come up at the last minute. He won't mind. Just tell him I love him and give him twenty quid towards whatever game he wants and I'll pay you back next time I see you.'

'And when will that be? When hell freezes over? I have begged you about this, Steve. I told you how important it is. I even gave you a hundred quid towards that stupid phone of yours so that you'd agree to come, and you think you can back out of it, just like that? No, I mean it, Steve, absolutely not.' I stop and sneeze again. 'Kian has put up with enough of your crap over the years for you to let him down like this again.'

'I don't know what you want me to say, Kerry. I've told you I can't be there. I can't be in two places at once, can I? I'm not a magician. Anyway, I'll make it up to him. There'll be other birthdays, so it's not like it's the end of the world, is it?'

I swear, if he was standing in front of me right now, even though this bug I've got is making me feel like a limp lettuce leaf, I'd grab the frying pan from the draining board in front of me and smash it right in his stupid face, and I wouldn't stop hitting him until the handle broke or the police pulled me off him. I can't believe how furious I am. I'm exhausted, but all I want to do is let rip. But I can't. Because of Kian. Because I know that it would mean the world to him to have his dad here. Because even though I know I'm going to be okay, there's still a small part of me that's terrified about the future, and wants to make this the best birthday my boy's ever had.

I think about telling Steve about my cancer. How, once I've got this cold under control, I'm going to be starting chemo. Maybe it would guilt him into doing the right thing for once. I don't, of course, because deep down I know it wouldn't make any difference. He's never helped when I've been well, so I can't imagine why he'd do anything now I'm not. Still, I have to do something, anything to make him see sense.

'Look, if you come, I'll give you another hundred quid and I'll even say Kian's big present is off both of us. Just please say you'll come.'

He's quiet for a minute. I think he's surprised I'm not screaming at him as usual, and I can hear his brain whirring over the hundred quid.

'Nah,' he says after a while. 'Too many strings and like I said, I can't be in two places at once.'

I don't even have the energy to give him what for. I can't believe how pathetic he is. I can't believe I ever let him into my life. What was I thinking? Why didn't I just turn and run the moment he came up to me, and let him ruin some other poor sod's life? I hold the phone up in front of me and his tinny voice fills the air as he blathers on with even more excuses. But I'm done listening. In fact, I'm done with him for good. I'm never going to let him mess Kian around like this again.

Chucking the phone on the counter, I sit down at the kitchen table and have a little cry. It doesn't last long, I can't let it take over me. I give myself just enough time to get it out of my system, then I give my nose a good blow, dry my eyes, and get to thinking about how I'm going to break this to Kian, when the doorbell rings.

It's way too early for Kian's friends to turn up but, as stupid as it sounds, my next thought is that it's Steve, that somehow I've actually got through to him, that he does care. And so, as I go to open the door, my heart is practically skipping a beat at the thought that the party might not be a wash-out for my boy after all. As it turns out, I'm half right. It's not Steve, it's even better, it's Noah, and standing next to him, looking like some sort of mini-supermodel, is Millie.

'I don't understand,' I say, throwing my arms around her so tightly that she lets out a tiny squeak, half shock half delight. 'I wasn't expecting this, what a lovely surprise!' I let go of her and take a step back, wiping the tears from my eyes. 'You must be thinking you've come to a right mad house. I'm just so happy to finally meet you.' I go to give her another massive hug but then I remember my cold and stop myself. 'I've got a bit of a cold,' I explain, 'and I don't want you to catch it, so just imagine that I've given you the biggest hug in the world, and I promise I'll make good when I'm better. Honestly, you have no idea how happy you've made me. No idea at all. And Kian is going to be made up.'

I chivvy them inside the flat and call Kian to come and say hello to his cousin. Unlike me, his greeting is a lot tamer, even though I know for a fact he's been dying to meet Millie ever since he heard about her. He gives her a nod, followed by a gruff, 'All right?' Then he stands there looking at his feet, while we all take in the huge amount of gel he's used to sculpt his hair into a mess of spikes.

In the kitchen, I start to make drinks for everyone while Kian opens a bag of crisps and empties them into a bowl.

'Sorry we're so early,' says Noah, as I pour out a glass of Tango for each of the kids. 'It's just that Millie was so excited about today, I had no choice.'

Millie pulls a face. 'No, I wasn't. I just thought if we came early we could help out.'

'That was really thoughtful,' I reply. 'And your help will be much appreciated. There's not much to do: they're eleven-year-old boys and all they eat is pizza, crisps and chips. But I'm going to cut up a couple of cucumbers and some carrot sticks anyway, even if all they do is throw them at each other, so I could do with a hand doing that a bit later.'

'I'd be delighted,' says Millie, and I notice for the first time how well-spoken she is, just like her dad; in fact she might even be a bit posher. I watch as she looks around the room. 'You've got such a lovely home.'

I smile. 'That's very kind of you, but I can't imagine it's a patch on yours.'

Millie takes a polite sip of her drink. 'I like our home,' she says thoughtfully. 'But Mummy prefers things to be quite plain and I like colour, and lots of it too. When I get a house of my own, I'm going to paint every room a different colour of the rainbow.'

'Sounds lovely,' I say. 'If you like colour then you'll love my bedroom: it's bright yellow, with tiny flecks of gold glitter in it. Every morning when I open my eyes it's like the sun's exploded and splattered all over my walls.'

I make drinks for Noah and me. 'How many of Kian's friends are you expecting?' he asks, as I hand him his coffee.

'Not many, only half a dozen or so. To be honest, I'm surprised he even wanted a party at home. These days it's all about Laser Quest or go-karting.'

'I've been to loads of those now, Mum,' says Kian. 'It gets a bit boring after a while. Anyway, everyone's excited about playing on my new PlayStation.'

I look at Millie and roll my eyes, even though I'm secretly chuffed by how much he loves his big present from me. 'See what I mean? It's quite easy to please boys: pizza, chips, pop and a PlayStation, and they're happy for hours. Don't worry though, I won't leave you alone with them, I wouldn't wish that on anyone.'

This time it's Kian who rolls his eyes. 'Mum!' he moans. 'Stop being embarrassing.'

'Ding!' I joke. 'I do believe that's my first "stop being embarrassing" of the day. I'm usually up to about five by this time, so that's quite good going.' I plant a kiss on Kian's cheek before he can stop me. 'Why don't you show Millie your room before everyone else arrives?'

He looks down at his shoes and says to them, 'Do you want to?'

Millie nods. 'I'd love to,' and without another word they leave the room together.

Forgetting all about my cold again, I put my arms around Noah and hug him so tightly that he nearly drops his coffee.

'What's that for?' he asks, putting his mug down on the table.

'Don't give me that,' I say. 'You've brought Millie here. I can't believe it. Does this mean Rosalind knows?'

He bites his lip nervously. 'Er . . . well . . . not exactly . . . actually, to be truthful, not at all.' Then he adds quickly, as if he's worried I might tell him off, 'I have tried to tell her but with one thing and another it hasn't been possible. I'm taking her out for dinner next week, though, and I plan to tell her then. But when you mentioned Kian's party to me the other day, I thought this would be too good an opportunity to miss. Millie's thrilled at the idea of meeting you and Kian and anyway, after all you've been through recently, I thought you deserved a nice surprise.'

'Nice surprise?' I repeat. 'More like the best surprise ever! It means the world to have you both here. Look at us having a proper family get-together after all these years! It's like all my Christmases have come at once.'

I want to say more, lots more about how much I love him and how grateful I am to have him back in my life again, but I'm afraid of overwhelming him, and before I can say another word, the doorbell rings again.

'I guess this is it, then,' I say. 'Brace yourself, and open some windows because there's an awful lot of aftershave about to come your way.'

An hour in, and despite a few upsets, the party seems to be going well. When some of the boys got a bit bored waiting to take their turn on the PlayStation and started squabbling, Noah stepped in and sorted things out. Now, anyone who isn't playing the game is being driven round the block in Noah's flash motor, and it's hard to tell which is the bigger draw. As for Millie, she seems happy enough hanging out with Kian, and has made herself a hit with the boys. Apparently she's a bit of a whizz on the PlayStation, even beating some of them at a game she says she's only played once before.

With everything under control, I go to the kitchen to put the pizzas on and sort out the chips and while I'm at it, have a sit down. In front of Kian I like to make out like I've got all the energy in the world, but the truth is, what with this cold and everything else going on, I'm just so tired these days I can hardly keep my eyes open much past midday.

I fill the kettle and take out a mug. Perhaps a nice cuppa will pep me up a bit. I'm so glad Kian's having such a good time. He hasn't even mentioned his dad once, which is a relief. Maybe he's finally over him, just like I am. Maybe after being let down one too many times, he's learned to take all the promises his dad makes with a pinch of salt. It isn't a nice lesson to learn, especially so young, but at least now he has the comfort of two brand-new family members in his life, ones who seem to actually enjoy spending time with him.

As I finish putting the last of the pizzas in the oven, the door to the kitchen opens and in comes Millie.

'You all right, love?' I ask. 'Come out for a bit of fresh air, have you?' I wrinkle my nose and wave my hand under it and she laughs.

'Actually,' she says, 'I've come to see if there's anything I can do to help.'

My heart melts, she's so adorable, and I have to stop myself from squeezing her to death again. I open the fridge, take out a bag of carrots and two cucumbers and hand them to her.

'You can make a start on those, if you like. The peeler's in that top drawer and there's a chopping board behind the bread bin.'

Millie sorts herself out, then takes a seat at the kitchen table and starts peeling. I can't take my eyes off her. She's so beautiful. I've always wondered what it would've been like to have a girl.

For Kian to have a sister, someone he could rely on, someone he could share the burden with when I get old. I wonder if she would've been anything like Millie, or just like Kian with long hair. I suppose I'll never know now.

Millie looks up and catches me staring at her. I look away guiltily as she asks me how many carrots to cut up.

'What you've got out there is plenty. Like I said, most of them will probably just end up on the floor anyway.' I sit down in the chair next to her, and we both start slicing up the vegetables.

'This must be really weird for you,' I say, dropping a few slices of cucumber into a bowl. 'You know, finding out about me and Kian and everything.'

Millie stops chopping for a moment. 'It's like something on TV. I always thought my life was pretty ordinary, but now it's anything but. I knew Dad was adopted, but I never thought he might have this whole other family.'

'Well, it's your family too. I know your dad and I are only half brother and sister, but it's still blood. You and Kian too, branches of the same tree.'

Millie thinks for a moment and then smiles. 'I hadn't thought about it like that. But it's nice, isn't it? Even though we hadn't met until today, we've been linked together all this time.'

We sit chopping in silence for a minute, and then Millie turns to me and says: 'What was Dad like as a baby? That's one thing I've always wondered. Mum and Dad have got millions of photos of me when I was tiny – some of them are really embarrassing – and they're everywhere around the house. And Granny and Granddad have lots of baby pictures of Mum too. I've always felt sad that Dad's the only one in my family who doesn't have any.'

I tut loudly. 'Hasn't your dad shown you the pictures I gave him? Typical man. He's probably just slung them in a drawer somewhere.' I ask her to give me a minute, and then I slip out to my bedroom and dig out the Margate picture to show her. When I hand it to her, she drinks in every detail without saying a word, and I can tell that her mind is buzzing with questions.

'First thing in the morning,' I say, 'I'm going to get you your own copy, and on the back I'll write: "Dear Millie, this is your dad at thirteen months old on a day trip to Margate. He was the loveliest, smiliest, cheekiest little thing you've ever met, and I loved him more than anything else in the world."'

Millie laughs. 'I'll try to remember that, when he's telling me off for leaving my games kit in the hallway.'

We carry on chopping, chatting about school, friends and even boys but then, just as I get up from the table to check on the pizzas, the doorbell rings.

'That'll be your poor dad,' I say. 'Hopefully now the pizza's done, we can distract Kian's mates and they'll leave him and his car alone for a bit.'

On my way to the front door, I poke my head into the living room to give the boys a heads-up that the food will be ready in a few minutes and to get their hands washed. They're so into their game that they barely look up, so I yell again and finally, one by one, they start trooping to the bathroom.

Opening the front door, the first words out of my mouth are: 'That was good timing,' but the person outside isn't Noah. It's a tall, smartly dressed blonde who looks about ready to explode.

She angrily shoves her phone in my face, and in a voice that makes it clear she means business, she barks, 'Who are you? And where is my daughter?'

I stand staring at her, speechless for a second, because I have a horrible feeling I know who this is, even though I've never actually met her. But it's only when Noah appears with a gaggle of boys trailing after him, and I see the look of horror on his face, that I know for sure.

24

Noah

Sunday, 24th April

'Rosalind,' I say instinctively. But that's the only word I manage to utter as my world begins to crumble around me. It doesn't make any sense. What is she doing here? How did she know where I was? How could she have possibly found out about Kerry? My first thought is that Millie must have told her, but as my daughter appears next to Kerry in the doorway, the look of complete shock on her face makes it clear this isn't the case. My second thought, however, isn't about the how or the why, because that now seems hopelessly irrelevant given the abject rage emanating from my wife. Instead my second thought is this: 'This is bad, really, really bad.'

'What the hell is going on here, Noah?' demands Rosalind. 'What are you and Millie doing here? Who are these people? Why aren't you shopping in the West End as you said you'd be?'

'Rosalind, I know this looks bad but I can explain . . .' I begin, but then my voice falters, daunted by the scale of the task in front of me. How can I possibly say everything that needs to be said without making things worse than they already are?

My hesitation, however brief, only serves to fill her with panic, which makes its way into her voice. 'Noah, you're scaring me,' she says shakily. 'What possible reason can you have for bringing our daughter to a place like this? I don't know who any of these people are.'

Millie pipes up: 'It's nothing bad, Mummy, really it isn't.' She glances in my direction. 'Daddy was going to tell you everything next week when he takes you out to dinner. Isn't that right, Daddy?'

I look over at Millie helplessly. She is doing everything in her power to support me, but somehow I still can't say a word.

'I swear if somebody doesn't tell me what's going on right this second, I'm going to—'

The words come unexpectedly, as though they've punched their way out directly from my heart. 'I found my family,' I hear myself say. 'My birth family.'

I watch the confusion play over Rosalind's features. 'I don't . . . I don't understand. How did you find them?'

I sigh. 'It's a long story.'

'And yet that hasn't stopped you from introducing them to Millie behind my back?'

'I know this sounds terrible, Rosalind, but—'

Without another word, she furiously grabs Millie by the hand, and ignoring her protests about the jacket she's left inside the flat, pushes past me as Kian's shell-shocked friends make room for her, flattening themselves against the outside wall.

'Rosalind, wait!' I call, but she doesn't even break her stride. I run down the stairs after her, but she won't stop. Somehow I finally manage to get in front of her and block her way.

'Rosalind,' I plead, 'just give me a minute to explain.'

The look she throws in my direction brings me up short. It's a mixture of hurt, anger, disbelief but most of all disappointment. 'Don't!' she screams at me in the stairwell, much to Millie's horror. 'Don't say another word! Or I swear I'll make you regret it, Noah. I mean it, just one more word and I'll make you regret that you ever met me,' and with that she pushes past me, gets into her car and drives away.

I don't know how long I stand staring at the space vacated by Rosalind's car, but the next thing I know Kerry's next to me, a hand on my arm and a look of deep concern on her face.

'Come on,' she says, 'let's get back inside. I'll make us a brew and we'll work out how to fix this.'

I don't want to go back upstairs. I want to go after Rosalind, but I know I can't, at least not yet. I've never seen her so angry and I can't imagine that my chasing after her will do anything other than exacerbate the situation. Anyway, as it is, I need to apologise to Kerry and Kian for ruining their party.

I let Kerry lead me back up to the flat, past all the kids still wide-eyed at the live-action posh-person soap opera that has unfolded in front of them. In the kitchen, Kerry closes the door firmly behind her, sits me down at the table and fills the kettle. I'm relieved that she's not the kind of person who feels the need to fill every silence with idle chatter, and there's something oddly comforting about watching her go through the familiar ritual of making tea.

By the time she hands a mug to me and sits down opposite me at the table, I feel considerably calmer, though no more hopeful.

'I'm sorry,' I begin. 'To have landed all this at your door, and on Kian's birthday of all days.'

Kerry laughs. 'Don't worry about him, he's had an amazing day, just ask him. I know for a fact his mates will be talking forever about riding in your flash motor. They loved it.'

'I haven't broken up the party, then?'

'No chance,' says Kerry. 'If I know anything, they'll all be too busy stuffing their faces with the pizza I nearly burned to give any of that a second thought.'

I take a sip of tea, scalding myself in the process.

'What am I going to do, Kerry?' I ask eventually. 'I've made such a mess of things. I'm not sure how I'll ever be able to make things right with her.'

Kerry sighs and puts her hand on mine. 'How do you think she found out?'

I think back to the moment I first saw her: she was waving her phone angrily in Kerry's face. 'She must have used an app to track down Millie's phone. It's the only thing that makes sense.'

'But why would she do that?'

A hunch makes me reach into my pocket and pull out my phone. Sure enough there's half a dozen missed calls from Rosalind. 'She must have been trying to get hold of me for some reason, then tried Millie, then the app. We've done it before when we've become separated on shopping trips.'

Kerry smiles. 'Technology, eh? Nothing but trouble.'

I can't bring myself to join in the joke. I feel awful for burdening Kerry like this when she's already got so much to contend with. 'I ought to be going. I've caused enough trouble for one day.'

'I can't help feeling like this is all my fault,' says Kerry, putting down her mug. 'If I hadn't asked you to come today, everything would've been all right. Do you want me to talk to Rosalind, try to explain things? I'll tell her it was all my doing.'

As desperate as I am for a solution, I don't somehow think Rosalind would appreciate me hiding behind someone else. 'The thing is,' I say, 'it's not your fault, it's mine. I should've told Rosalind about you from the start, but I chose not to. Why would I do that when the whole reason my marriage is in trouble is because I keep pushing her away? It's almost as if I've got some sort of latent urge to self-destruct.'

Kerry shrugs. 'I don't know about any of that, but what I do know is that you're a good man, Noah. And whatever you did, you only ever had the best intentions. We all make a mess of things from time to time – I'm living proof of that – but it's what you do to clean it up that counts.'

I leave it until early evening before I dare to venture to Primrose Hill. While I know there's every chance Rosalind will refuse to see me, I have to try. I need to make her understand how deeply sorry I am for everything. I need to convince her that I really have changed, even though the way I've acted lately appears to the contrary. I need for her to know how much I love her, and our family, and the life we've made together. And that I'm prepared to do anything, absolutely anything I can to make things right.

My heart is racing and my palms are damp with sweat as, clinging on to Millie's jacket with my free hand, I ring the doorbell. Perhaps I should've called first, given Rosalind time to get her head around the idea of seeing me. Maybe that would've demonstrated more respect for her feelings than turning up unannounced. But it's too late for that now. What's done is done, and now I will simply have to live or die by my decision.

I hear someone on the other side of the door and know straight away that it's Millie looking through the peephole, just as we'd taught her to do before answering the door.

'Dad,' she says desperately, and in tears, she throws her arms around me tightly.

We're still hugging when Rosalind comes to the door. Millie turns to look at her mother. 'Please don't be angry with Daddy any more,' she begs. 'Please say he can come in.'

I look at Rosalind. On the surface at least, she appears less angry than she did, but there's a coldness about her now, a hardness, which is far more worrying.

She looks at me, then at Millie and shrugs. 'Fine,' she says, 'but it's still bed for you in twenty minutes . . . it's been a really long day.'

Rosalind disappears upstairs, leaving Millie and me alone. We settle in the snug, momentarily uncertain of what to say to each other. For a long time, Millie cuddles up to me with her head on my shoulder. We gaze out through the French doors at the fairy lights woven into the branches of the potted olive trees in the garden.

'I'm so sorry, Daddy,' says Millie after a while. 'I tried to talk to Mummy and explain everything but it doesn't seem to be making any difference. I've never seen her like this before. It's scaring me.'

I bite my lip for a moment, just long enough to compose myself in the face of her sadness. 'Don't be scared, sweetheart, there's nothing at all to worry about. You know as well as I do how lovely Mummy is. There's nothing to be scared of, nothing at all. Mummy's just sad that's all, and it's my fault, not yours. I should've been honest, like we've always taught you to be. I'm afraid I haven't been setting you a very good example.'

Millie shakes her head. 'But you were going to be honest. You never meant to lie. You always planned to tell Mummy, it's just that things got in the way.'

'But that's just it, sweetie. If you wait too long for the right moment to tell somebody the truth, it's practically the same as lying. I should've—' I stop mid-sentence as Rosalind calls Millie up to bed. She hugs me tightly and I kiss the top of her head, not wanting to let her go.

'Up you go then, and don't worry, everything will be all right, I promise.'

I sit looking out into the garden for a while longer, wondering if I should go or wait for Rosalind. I wait for so long that I eventually give up hope, and I'm about to leave when I hear her coming down the stairs.

'Can we talk?' I ask, before she can say a word. 'Please, it's important.'

She walks into the kitchen and starts unloading the dishwasher. I don't know whether to try and help or stay out of her way. In the end, I hover by the sink and ask her to stop what she's doing for a minute.

'How long?' she asks, putting down the dish in her hands on the counter. 'How long has this been going on? Millie's told me the little she knows, but that's the one thing I really want to know.'

'Just after we separated.'

A flash of anger crosses her face. 'So that makes it okay, does it? The lies, the sneaking around, the pretence that you were willing to change?'

'It wasn't a pretence. I am willing to change. I have changed. It was just so complicated. It felt like it was one thing after another: things between us; me moving out; worrying about how this was all going to affect Millie; and then out of nowhere, Kerry made contact. At first I didn't know where it was going, or even whether or not to believe her. But it's true, she is my sister, and it's thrown everything I thought I knew about myself into question. Worse still, she has ovarian cancer. She starts treatment this week, and apart from her son, Kian, I'm the only family she has.'

Rosalind says nothing. Instead she stands there watching me, completely unmoved. This isn't like her. It isn't like her at all.

'Aren't you going to say anything?'

She shrugs. 'Why should I? You don't.'

'But I've just explained. It was difficult.'

She straightens up, as though ready to attack. 'Difficult? Well, guess what, Noah? Life is difficult . . . and messy . . . and compli- cated . . . and inconvenient. Things rarely happen in the order you'd like them to. Things don't always follow a nice neat little plan. But that's why we're supposed to talk to each other, and support each other and be open with one another. So that we're not dealing with any of this crap on our own. But you needed to do things differently. You needed to keep your problems to yourself. Well, guess what? They're all yours now. I wash my hands of them completely. You can't have it both ways, Noah, you just can't. I've tried my best to save us – you know I have – I thought we were really getting somewhere. I thought you were finally opening up to me. How foolish of me! All this time, you had a door locked and bolted to a secret room I knew absolutely nothing about. Well, I can't do this any more. Though it breaks my heart to say this, we're over and there's not a single thing you can say that will make me change my mind.'

25

Kerry

Tuesday, 26th April

'Right, I think that's everything, Mrs R,' I say, picking up the half-drunk mug of tea in front of me. I swig back the lukewarm contents in three gulps, give the mug a quick wash under the tap, dry it up and put it away. 'Those last bits of washing are on the line and there's a bit of breeze going now, so they'll be done before you know it. I've changed your bed like you asked, and sorted out the toilet roll holder. All it needed was the screws tightening a bit.'

Mrs Ryman looks at me as if she might cry, and I have to look away because I know if she starts, then so will I.

'Kerry, I can't tell you how much I'm going to miss this.'

'Miss what? Me blathering on all the time about nothing?'

Mrs Ryman smiles. 'You know what I mean.'

'I'm going to miss you too,' I say. 'But I promise I'm not leaving you with just anyone. Janine is the salt of the earth, and I've given her strict instructions to look after you good and proper while I'm away. Don't get too attached to her, mind, 'cause I'll be back before you know it. If there's any problems at all, just drop me a text and I'll sort it out.'

I give her a quick hug and before either of us has the chance to get all emotional, I start taking my things out to the car. When I come back inside for the rest of my stuff, Mrs Ryman is standing there holding a beautifully wrapped present.

'Oh, now look,' I say, trying not to cry. 'I told you I didn't want any fuss.'

'I know you did,' says Mrs Ryman. 'And I decided I was well within my rights to ignore you. You're an absolute treasure, Kerry, really you are. You're far more than my cleaner, you're my friend and I just wanted you to know that.'

I carefully open the gift. It's a set of posh teas and a china cup and saucer. 'For when you're recuperating,' Mrs Ryman explains. 'One should never underestimate the power of a good cup of tea.'

I haven't gone into the details about my treatment with Mrs Ryman, or anyone else for that matter. All I've said is that I've got to go into hospital for a bit, and it might be a month or two before I'm back on my feet. I've managed to get cover for most of my regular clients, but there are a couple I'm still struggling to sort out, and chances are I might just have to lose them for good. The thing is, time is running out. Well, to be honest, it's pretty much gone altogether. Noah's taking me to the hospital for my first chemo session tomorrow, so today is all about making sure Mrs Ryman is sorted. Now, the only thing left is the one thing I least want to do.

I have a little cry in the car after I leave Mrs Ryman. She's so sweet getting me a present like that, and everything she said was so lovely. Drying my eyes, I start the car and, pulling myself together, head to Kian's school to pick him up. It's quite nice being early for a change. It gives me a chance to have a proper catch-up with some of the mums. Most of the time I'm flying in seconds after the bell goes, and tearing away the minute I've grabbed Kian because we're running late for his karate lesson or whatever.

One of the mums is having trouble with her next-door neighbour, so we all chip in with advice about what to do for the best. Another has started selling Avon and gives us all a catalogue to look at, and we have a good laugh about all the miracle creams on offer. And then a mum from Kian's class comes along with her gorgeous six-day-old baby boy, and we all stand round cooing over him. It's all so lovely, so normal, that for a bit I don't even think about tomorrow and everything that lies ahead. But then the bell goes, and suddenly there's Kian standing in front of me, uniform all over the place, hands delving around in my bag looking for a snack, and I'm back thinking about this thing I've been dreading so much.

The first words out of his mouth as he tears open the wrapper on the Fruit Winder he's fished out are: 'Please, please, please can we go to the skatepark, Mum?'

I give him The Frown. He knows better than to start bombarding me with questions before he's even said hello. He sighs, rolls his eyes and gives me a, 'Hello, Mum.' But then just to wind him up, I offer my cheek too, and even point to it. He's not stupid though. While I do get my kiss, he does a full three-sixty first to check that none of his mates are looking.

'Now,' I say calmly. 'What can I do for you, son?'

He rolls his eyes again. 'I've told you already,' he says. 'The skatepark. I want to go. Everyone else is going.'

I hate the skatepark. It's cold, dirty and noisy. And worse still, there's danger everywhere I look: kids flinging themselves about, trying to impress their mates by jumping off things that in my opinion shouldn't be jumped off.

I look at Kian's pleading face, only just resisting the urge to wipe the dried dinner from around his mouth.

'What's my answer every time you ask me if we can go to the skatepark after school?'

He sighs. 'You say no. You say, "Not on a school night."'

'And is today a school night?'

Kian nods.

'So why are you asking, then?'

'Because I really, really want to go,' he says. 'Come on, Mum, can we, please? I promise I'll be careful.'

I think for a moment. I'd planned for us to go straight home so I could get started on making the special tea I got in for him this morning, but I suppose that can wait.

'All right, then,' I say. 'We can go, but don't think I'm going to make a habit of it.'

Kian's whole face lights up. It's as if I've literally just told him he's been picked to play for England.

'Do you mean it?' he asks in disbelief. 'Really? On a school night?'

I laugh. 'Are you trying to get me to change my mind again? Because if you are, you're going the right way about it.'

Always the clown, Kian mimes zipping his lips and then starts to run off to tell his mates the good news. He only manages a few steps before he suddenly stops, turns around and yells at the top of his voice: 'You're the best mum in the world.' All the mums standing near us laugh, and I do too, because kids say that kind of thing all the time when they get what they want. But inside, I am absolutely glowing with pride. I love my boy so much. He's my world. My most precious thing.

It's after six when we get home from the skatepark and Kian is ravenous, even though we stopped on the way and picked up a cereal bar and a couple of bananas to tide him over. Walking behind him up the stairs to the flat, I notice that his trousers, which were brand new at the beginning of the term, are already skimming his ankles. He'll need a new pair soon. It feels weird not knowing if I'll be well enough to take him shopping for another pair, because right now I don't actually feel so bad. Yes, I'm tired all the time, yes, my back aches, but other than that I feel okay. I don't feel like there's something inside me trying to kill me.

While I get cracking with tea I let Kian watch a bit of telly, even though he's got spellings he needs to practise for his test tomorrow. Tonight we're having barbecue ribs, potato wedges and coleslaw: his favourite. Once I've got everything in the oven I set the kitchen table, even though Kian will no doubt complain that we're not eating in front of the telly.

With a few minutes to myself, I go into my bedroom and get out the folder I've been hiding in my underwear drawer. Over the years Kian has pretty much discovered all of my hiding places for Christmas and birthday presents, and he isn't opposed to a little bit of snooping every now and again when he's bored. But now he's reached an age where even the thought of my bras and knickers is enough to terrify him, so I know for sure this is one place that is safe.

I spread out on the bed all the letters, leaflets and information I've collected together since my diagnosis. Searching through them, I pick out the leaflet I'm looking for. It's called: *Talking To Children and Teenagers When An Adult Has Cancer*. I hold it firmly in my hands but I can't actually bring myself to open it. Because it's chemo and not surgery, because chances are I'll be sick and weak and might even lose my hair, rather than just be laid up in bed for a few days, I'm going to have to tell Kian the truth. I want him to know that the treatment I'm about to have happens to millions of people, every day all around the world. I want him to know, even though it might make me sick for a little while, this treatment is actually going to make me better. I want him to know I'm going to be okay, that before he knows it, I'm going to be back on my feet, and moaning about the state of his bedroom. I want him to know that even though things will be different for a while, one day soon everything will get back to normal. But despite all this, there's something about having it all written down in front of you in black and white that feels a bit too real, a bit too terrifying.

I shove everything back in the folder. I will tell him, but I'll do it my way, using my words. I put the folder back in my underwear drawer, go to the kitchen and call Kian for his tea.

Trying to pick the right moment to tell him is even harder than I imagined. I try over tea, but he is still too excited about the skatepark and all the stunts he's seen the bigger kids do. I try again while we are doing the washing-up, but then one of his mates texts just as I'm about to start, and he disappears into his room for half an hour and only comes out again because he wants to know if we have any ice cream. I even try to tell him while we are on our way back from the corner shop with a pack of Magnums, but he is too distracted watching some of the neighbours trying to catch a stray Alsatian that is causing havoc on the estate.

Now, we're sitting side by side on the sofa with our ice creams, watching endless YouTube videos of skateboarding tricks on the laptop. It's only now I realise that I've run out of time. That there isn't going to be a perfect moment. I'm just going to have to grit my teeth and get on with it.

'Kian,' I say, pausing the video, freezing some kid on the screen, not much older than he is, in mid-air. 'I need to talk to you about something.'

He stops licking his ice cream and looks at me. 'Is it about Dad? I sent him a text last week and I still haven't heard back from him.'

It's been all I can do not to spit every time I've thought about Steve. After the way he'd behaved over Kian's birthday, it didn't surprise me that he was keeping a low profile. But even then, I thought he might have the decency to at least pick up the phone to his own son and apologise for not turning up to his party like he'd promised. But there's been nothing. Not a word. And now – scumbag that he is – he's ignoring him completely.

'No, darling,' I say, putting my arm around him. 'It's not about your dad.'

'It's not about Callum, is it?'

I feel my heart sink. 'What's happened now?' I say sharply.

'Nothing, I promise, Mum,' he says. 'It's just that he's started trying to wind me up again. And I've told Mrs Watson like you told me to, but he keeps threatening to say I've pushed him when I haven't. I promise, Mum, I haven't touched him. It's just that he knows it will get me into trouble.'

I let out a sigh. How am I going to sort this out? I'll have to ring his teacher first thing in the morning and make sure she's on top of it. I'm not having this all start up again.

'I know you haven't done anything, son,' I reassure him. 'You know better than that now. I promise I am going to get it sorted but in the meantime don't let him rile you, okay?'

Kian nods. 'Thanks, Mum.' He stops and thinks for a moment. 'If it's not Dad, and it's not Callum, then what is it? Is it about Uncle Noah or Millie?'

I kiss his head gently. 'No, sweetheart, it's not about them, it's about me.'

And then taking a deep breath, I dig right down into myself, collect together every last bit of strength I've got, and tell him.

26

Noah

Tuesday, 26th April

'Hi, Rosalind. It's me again. Look, I know what I did was wrong. I accept that one hundred per cent, and I'm absolutely committed to making things right. Please, can we just find a way to talk about this? I'm happy to meet wherever and whenever you want, just say the word. Right, well that's all really. Give Millie a kiss from me and hopefully I'll see you soon.'

This is the fifth message in a row I've left for Rosalind and I've yet to hear back from her. I'm worried, really worried. I'd never seen her as hurt or as angry as she was on Sunday night after Kian's party. But I had thought that given a little time and space, she would've calmed down sufficiently for us to be able to talk things through by now.

As shocking as her words were, I'm sure they were born out of nothing more than her frustration with me. I can't blame her for lashing out like that, it was everything I deserved. But even so, we still need to talk. There is too much at stake – Millie, and the life we've built together over the past fifteen years – to throw it all away. If only we could just sit down face to face, I know we could make things right. I know that I could make her see that though my actions might appear careless and deceitful, there were compelling mitigating circumstances and my intentions had been anything but malicious. All I'd wanted was to protect her, not burden her with things I hadn't even managed to sort out in my own head.

Although I've taken part of the week off so that I can be on hand if Kerry needs me to do any last-minute jobs before her chemotherapy starts, there are still cases that I have to prepare for. I look over reluctantly at the large pile of folders on the kitchen table, untouched since I'd brought them home at the weekend. I know I should try to tackle them. I know leaving them unopened is eventually going to make my life even more difficult than it already is, but I just can't seem to find the motivation. With things the way they are, it all just seems a bit futile, a bit hopeless. I can't work while I know that my marriage is on the verge of collapse, but I can't do anything to save it without risking making the situation worse.

I sit down on the sofa, head in hands, trying to think my way out of this mess. If only I could go back in time, I would do things so differently. I'd be honest and open with Rosalind from the start, and at least then we could face whatever came our way together. Rosalind was right. I have always kept her at arm's length. I have always kept difficult things locked away in their separate compartments, on the pretext of protecting those I love. But instead, all I've been doing is giving myself permission to hide from issues in my life that I haven't wanted to face up to. Clearly if I am going to put things right between Rosalind and me, I am going to have to start facing things head on, and if right now that can't be with Rosalind, then I'll have to start somewhere else.

'Noah,' exclaims my mother, as she opens the front door. 'What an unexpected treat! Come in. Shouldn't you be at work?'

'I've taken some time off this week but I'm doing a little prep for my cases from home.'

'You should do that more often,' she says. 'I don't know how anybody commutes these days. Even in the middle of the day, travelling across London can be an absolute nightmare, so I can only imagine what it's like for you.' She kisses my cheek. 'Funny thing is, I've been deliberating all morning about whether or not to go to my life-drawing class today – you'd be surprised but the naked form can be very exhausting when you have to stare at it for several hours at a stretch – and you've just helped me make up my mind.'

Before I can think of a suitable response, my mother has whisked me off to the kitchen, and I barely get a word in edgeways as she tells me about all of the characters in her life-drawing class.

'And don't get me started about my watercolour group,' she says, filling the kettle, as my father pops his head around the kitchen door. 'You'd think it would be all genteel ladies in pastel scarves, but far from it. They're quite a racy bunch, I can tell you.'

My father does a double-take. 'Hello, son,' he says. 'I was wondering who your mother was talking to. I never know from one day to the next who I'm going to find in this kitchen. The other morning she had the Amazon delivery chap in here in tears, telling her all about his family in Romania. Lovely chap he was, but still, it's not what you expect to find when you're shuffling through in your dressing gown in search of breakfast.' He comes over and gives me a hug. 'Anyway, I'm glad it's you. I was just in the middle of writing an outraged letter to the *TLS* about yet another one of their spurious headline-grabbing articles on the origins of Shakespeare's first folio. I won't go into details but I wouldn't mind your casting a legal eye over my second paragraph in particular, just to be on the safe side.'

I smile. My parents are being their glorious eccentric selves, which is both amusing and comforting in equal measure, and for a moment it makes me question the course of action I've decided upon. Seeing them like this makes me realise all over again how fortunate I've been to have them as my parents. The last thing in the world I want to do is hurt them. And yet here I am, and if I'm really serious about making a change, then I have no choice but to follow through.

'Of course I'll take a look at it,' I say, 'but before that, there's something I need to talk to both of you about.'

My parents exchange concerned glances but say nothing.

'Do you remember a while ago I asked you if I had any natural siblings? Well, at the time I told you I was asking out of curiosity, but that wasn't true. The truth is, I'd received a letter from a

woman claiming to be my birth sister, and over the course of
the past few months I've got to know her. Her name's Kerry, she
has an eleven-year-old son and they're both really lovely.' I stop
and examine their faces, but it's impossible to tell what they're
thinking. Perhaps this is a moment they've been expecting to
happen since adopting me, one they'd rehearsed in their heads
many times over.

'I want you both to know that I never intended to keep this a
secret from you,' I continue. 'It was all just so confusing and
unsettling, and I've been trying to work out my own feelings about
a lot of it, which is why, I suppose, I didn't confide in you or
even Rosalind. I wanted to be sure in my own mind about what
I felt before involving anybody else in the equation. But then at
the weekend Rosalind found out by accident, and she's so hurt
and upset by it all that she won't even speak to me. I couldn't
bear it if my actions caused either of you to feel the same. So
that's why I'm here. To say sorry, to ask your forgiveness.'

The two of them stand staring blankly at me for a moment
and then as one, without a word, they enfold me in a joint
embrace. When Mum finally lets go, there are tears in her eyes.
'Oh, Noah, there's no need to ask for forgiveness, no need at all.
Of course you haven't done anything wrong. When your father
and I adopted you, things were very different than they are now.
We were only given the scantest of details about your early life.
We didn't even know where your sister had been taken, let alone
that she was still in London. We have always tried to encourage
you to be curious about your past but you've always seemed so
adamant, so absolutely sure that you weren't interested, and over
the years we've tried to respect that. But we've always hoped that
a day would come when you'd change your mind. No matter
who you are, or what your background, I've always felt it important to know your history.'

'*There is a history in all men's lives,*' says Dad, with a smile.

I look at him. I know it's a quotation but have no idea where
from. I take a stab. 'Swift?'

'Shakespeare,' he replies. '*Henry IV part II.*'

Mum takes my hand and her eyes search my face. 'There's something else, isn't there?'

I nod, and then without further hesitation I tell them everything. They listen intently without interruption.

'So you'll effectively have sole responsibility for the care of Kerry's son if she's too ill to look after him?' asks Mum when I finish.

'That's the plan,' I reply. 'We just don't know how badly the chemo will affect her.'

'I can't quite believe it,' says Dad. 'How dreadful for you all. Is there anything at all we can do? We could help with transport or even help with Kian if you need us to.'

I shake my head. 'As it is at the moment, there's barely anything I can do to help. Kerry won't let me. She's had to spend her whole life taking care of herself, I don't think she's used to letting herself be taken care of. I practically had to fight to get her to agree to let me take her to hospital tomorrow.'

Mum reaches over and squeezes my hand. 'Well, I don't want to get in the way but if you do think of anything, shopping, cooking, cleaning or looking after Kian, just say the word.'

'Thanks, Mum,' I say. 'But to be honest, I don't think any of us really know what the next few weeks will bring. I'm just glad I can be there for Kian.'

I know they must have lots of questions. Questions about how all of this will affect my job, Millie and, of course, my marriage, but for now they don't ask them. Instead they just let me talk about everything I'm feeling and thinking. All the confusion and worry I've kept hidden. It's such a relief to finally be able to talk about it freely. I don't think I quite realised until now how difficult it's been carrying all this around with me, how draining it is trying to compartmentalise that which refuses to stay in its box.

At Mum's insistence I stay for lunch, and afterwards spend some time admiring her most recent paintings. I check over Dad's letter, which is indeed highly libellous, and suggest a number of ways he might like to tone it down. By the time I'm ready to leave, things seem if not quite back to normal, then something not far off.

'You'll let me tell Charlotte and Phillip about everything, won't you?' I ask, after hugging them both.

'Of course,' says Mum, 'we won't say a word, will we, Geoffrey? And don't worry, I know they'll be supportive, and will want to help.' Mum gives me a final kiss and looks up at me. 'We're so proud of you, Noah, we always have been, and we always will be. I know things look bleak at the moment, but whatever happens, please promise me that you'll always remember we're here for you. You don't have to go through any of this on your own, you'll always have us, your family. We'll always be here for you.'

Though the journey back to Bayswater takes forever, I barely notice as I'm so wrapped up in my own thoughts. It's such a relief to have finally unburdened myself. I'd been so worried about how my parents might react, that they'd somehow feel betrayed, and hurt by my desire to get to know Kerry. I suppose that's always the fear lurking in the back of the mind of anyone who has been adopted: if one family can give you up, what's to stop another doing the same?

Suddenly a memory surfaces from my days at prep. I'm seven or eight, and I'm standing outside the headmaster's office, my parents are on the other side of the door and I'm straining to hear what's being said. I'm here because I'm in trouble. I'm here because I so desperately want to fit in. I'm here because my friends dared me to set off the school fire alarm and I did it, hoping it would make them like me.

The headmaster told me I was in very serious trouble, but it wasn't until he informed me that he'd called my parents in for a meeting that I fully realised the magnitude of what I had done. They would be disappointed, how could they not be? I'd let them down, and they would be angry and upset. And the longer I stood outside that room the more convinced I became that this was it, the moment they realised they had made a terrible mistake in adopting me, the moment it dawned on them that the best thing they could do would be to return me to wherever it was they'd got me from.

Even though my parents had never given me any cause to doubt their love, these fears must have been lurking beneath the surface for years because by the time they emerged from their meeting with the headmaster, I was so distraught as to be inconsolable. That was the first and the last time I ever misbehaved at school, from then on all I ever did was shine. Perhaps this was why I'd always worked so hard to please them, been so desperate to do the right thing, been so scared of disappointing them.

It is this sort of breakthrough in my thinking that I should be sharing with Rosalind, I tell myself. But even as I pull up outside the flat and check my phone anxiously once again, there's still no message from her. On any other day this would have been a real blow but today, buoyed by my parents' acceptance, I feel hopeful. If they can find it in their hearts to understand why it has taken me so long to confide in them, then perhaps, given time, Rosalind can too.

On the way up to the flat I grab my mail from the pigeonhole, and as I wait for the lift I sort through it. There are a few things for me to forward to Phillip, a handful of takeaway menus, a notice from the residents' committee about the date of their next meeting and then finally a thick white envelope, on which is franked the name of a well-known firm of solicitors. I know what it is without even opening it, and yet even once I've read the contents, I still find it impossible to believe. In one fell swoop all my earlier optimism vanishes without trace: Rosalind has filed for divorce.

27

Kerry

Wednesday, 27th April

The flat feels weird when I get in from dropping Kian off at school. Normally I'd be crawling across west London by now, on my way to my first job of the day, Mariah Carey cranked right up on my little car stereo and my head buzzing with everything I have to get done before picking Kian up at the end of the day. I don't often get to be on my own in the flat at this time on a weekday. It's quite nice actually. The sunlight streaming in through the window makes everything glow a lovely colour, and it's nice and quiet because all the troublemakers round here are still in bed. I'm tempted to make myself a cuppa and sit and enjoy the peace for ten minutes, but I can't. Noah will be here soon to pick me up, and I don't want to keep him waiting. Anyway, seeing as I'm twice as nervous as I was going in for the operation, I doubt I'd be able to sit down for more than a few seconds. I still can't believe this day is finally here. I still can't believe that today is the day I start chemotherapy.

In the bedroom I stare at my wardrobe, trying to work out what to wear. One of the leaflets I'd read said to wear something comfortable with loose sleeves so the nurses can do what they've got to do. I try on a few outfits that do the job but I don't like any of them. They all make me feel a bit wrong. A bit too casual, like I'm just nipping out to the shops, and that's not how I want to feel. I want to feel strong, smart and ready for anything. Like someone who means business, which I do. I haven't put myself through the torture of telling my only son that I've got cancer, just to let it win. When I told Kian that I was going to fight this illness with all the strength I had, I meant every single word. There's no way I'm going to let this thing beat me. There's no way I'm going to let it get the better of me. Suddenly I know exactly what to wear, and so I lay it all out on the bed and then go to the bathroom for a quick freshen-up.

I'm fully dressed and halfway through putting on my make-up when the doorbell rings. I check the peephole through force of habit, and spy a smartly dressed Noah looking back at me.

'You look great,' he says when I open the door, but then he looks sort of embarrassed. 'I mean . . . I'm sorry . . . that's not something you say on a day like this, is it?'

I smile to myself. The trouser suit that I wore when I met Noah for the first time and my new emerald green top were definitely the right choice. 'You don't need to walk on eggshells around me, Noah.' I give him a kiss on the cheek. 'And anyway, you're right, I do look great. If you're serious about kicking cancer's arse, you've got to look the part, haven't you?'

I tell Noah to make himself at home while I finish putting on my war paint. I never normally wear a lot of make-up but today I go full-on: foundation, blusher, mascara, lipstick: the works. When I stand back from the mirror I hardly recognise myself, and I half wonder if that isn't the point. I don't want to look like someone who's scared or nervous. I want to look like someone who's got everything under control.

Even though I haven't always gone the right way about it, control has always been important to me. It has been from the day I left the children's home and my life was finally my own. All those years as a kid, having people who didn't know me from Adam making decisions about my life: where I should live, who I should I live with, whether I was allowed to see my own flesh and blood. That's why I like working for myself so much. I suppose that's why I never let Steve properly move in with me, even when things were going well. I suppose that's why I enjoy cleaning, it's me putting chaos in order, making sure everything has its place. Maybe it's why this cancer scares me so much.

Because I haven't got control over it, it's got control over me. And I hate it, I hate it more than anything.

I slip on my shoes, a smart black patent pair with a bit of a heel that I picked up in the sales, grab my bag and go in search of Noah. I find him sitting at the kitchen table, fiddling with his phone.

He looks up when I come in. 'Ready to go?'

I start getting a bit emotional, even though I'd promised myself I wouldn't. 'You know how much I appreciate you coming today, don't you? I know how busy you are. You must have loads to do and just so you know, I'm more than happy if you need to get off at any point. I'm a big girl, I'll be all right and anyway, thanks to Kian, I've got an Uber account now, so it'll only take me a couple of clicks to get home.'

Noah stands up and puts his hands on my shoulders. 'How many times do I have to tell you?' he says. 'I don't have to be anywhere else. I don't want to be anywhere else. I want to be with you. As I said last time you brought this up, my cases are being covered and right now you're my number-one priority.'

'I know,' I say. 'I just worry.'

'Well, there's no need.' He gives me a smile. 'I'm here and I'm not going to let anything bad happen to you.'

He checks his watch. I feel sick with nerves. It's time to go.

'Right,' he says, 'now we've got all that sorted, we probably ought to be getting off. Are you ready?'

I want to say no. I want to say I'll never be ready. I want to say that even though I know this is all for the best, I'm scared of the treatment, of the side effects, of it not working at all. Of the cancer. But then I catch Noah looking at me, and I can see from his face that I don't have to say anything. That without me saying a single word, he somehow knows exactly what it is I'm feeling.

Unlike last time, when we reach the hospital I immediately sense a change in Noah. Suddenly he's not just my little brother any more, he's more what I imagine he's like at work. On every other visit to the hospital I've had to stand around for half an hour while I work out where it is I've got to be, but as I start looking through my paperwork, Noah is off talking to a porter. When he comes back he knows exactly where we've got to go, and he leads me away from the crowds in the main lobby to a set of lifts off a long corridor, which take us to the second floor. When the lift doors open, it's like we're in a completely different world to the one we left behind. It's much quieter and calmer up here than it was on the surgical ward, let alone the hospital concourse. There are potted plants and comfy chairs, and the woman at the reception desk even greets us with a warm smile.

I give her my paperwork and she checks through it with me and then tells us to take a seat. Noah and I don't talk much while we wait. I'm too nervous and I think Noah is too, although you wouldn't know by looking at him. Anyone looking at the two of us would probably think he's my consultant or something. It's not so much the way he's dressed, as how he carries himself. Like he knows exactly what he's doing, who he is and what's going to happen next. I feel better just knowing he's beside me, but when I pick up a magazine from the table in front of us I can't even bring myself to open it. Instead I just sit staring at the cover. I can't concentrate. I just want to get this over and done with. I just want to know what I'm going to be dealing with.

After a bit, a young girl in uniform comes over to us holding a clipboard. She checks my details again and then takes us along another corridor into a large, bright sunny room. It looks a lot like a hospital ward, but with the beds taken out and replaced with loads of big armchairs. There are about fifteen people dotted around the room, men and women, young and old, some alone and some with friends and family. Some of them give us the once-over like we're the entertainment, but I'm not bothered. I'm sure given a couple of weeks of this, I'll be doing the same.

If it wasn't for the drips all the patients are hooked up to, the stacks of cardboard sick bowls and the blood-pressure monitors, this could be one of those fancy spas you see advertised in the back of magazines. The ones where people with more money than sense go to have massages and some woman put hot stones on their backs to get rid of stress.

The young girl in the uniform passes us over to a smiley Indian nurse. 'Morning, you must be Kerry,' she says in a chirpy sing-song Welsh accent. 'I'm Narinder, and I'll be looking after you this morning.' She looks at Noah and smiles. 'And you're here to support Kerry, are you?'

'This is my brother,' I say proudly. 'He's a barrister.'

The nurse gives Noah a cheeky once-over. 'Don't suppose you're single, are you?'

She means it as a joke but I still don't know for sure how things are between him and Rosalind, and so I say, 'He's taken,' quickly, before he can get embarrassed.

'The good ones always are,' says the nurse with a comical sigh. 'Right then, let's get down to business.'

She sits us in chairs near a window overlooking a pretty little garden and explains what's going to happen. 'I know you've probably had all the information you can take but if you've got any questions at all, that's what I'm here for. In a minute I'm going to hook you up to a drip, which has got all of your chemotherapy drugs packed into it. The whole thing should take about three hours in total, after which we can release you back into the wild. Eating and drinking is no problem while you're having your treatment and there's a tea trolley that comes around in about half an hour, but if you can't wait, there's a vending machine just down the corridor that does a lovely cappuccino. Does that all sound okay?'

I nod, even though I feel like running out of the room. 'Sounds fine,' I tell her, but all the same I take hold of Noah's hand and give it a squeeze.

The nurse disappears for a while and when she comes back she's pushing a drip stand with one hand and pulling a small metal trolley with the other. She tells me to make myself comfortable and so I take off my jacket and pull up my sleeve.

I don't quite know what I expected, but it isn't this. There's a little scratch when the chirpy nurse puts the needle into my arm, but apart from the stuff going in being a bit cold I feel just fine.

When she's finished, she hands me a call button.

'Just in case you need anything before I come round again,' she says. 'You shouldn't need to use it but if you do spot any nice single men, feel free to give me a buzz.' With that she gives Noah a saucy wink and she's off.

I sit and stare at the drip for a bit. It's funny, it doesn't look like much, this stuff that is supposed to make me better. It could be water for all I know. You'd think they'd dye it a bright colour or something, make it look a bit more special, like it's magic or something. Still, as long as it's doing the business and attacking the thing that's attacking me, what do I care?

After the nurse comes round to check on me, Noah goes to get us both a coffee, and I relax a bit and look around the room at the other patients. I reckon the woman on the left of me is in her mid-sixties, although with her headscarf and pencilled-in eyebrows it's hard to tell. She and her husband are obviously old hands at this. They've brought all sorts of snacks and entertainment with them and are sitting with headphones on, watching what looks like a wildlife programme on their iPad. On the other side of me is a young woman in her twenties with her mum. The mum is chatting away for England as she knits, but the young woman doesn't say a word or look up from her phone once. At one point, during a bit of commotion when a pigeon flies into the window next to me, I accidentally catch the young woman's eye, but when I smile she just scowls and stares at her phone. She's not here to make friends. She's here because she has to be. She's so young. I can't help but feel sorry for her. If I was her age, I don't suppose I'd feel like smiling either.

Despite Miss Grumpy, it looks as if some of the other patients have made friends. Odd couples brought together by sitting here hour after hour. For instance, in the far corner there's an old Indian man who seems to be getting on like a house on fire with a big bloke with a quiff and tattoos all up his arms. In fact, at one point they're laughing so loud that the chirpy nurse has to ask them to keep it down. Across the way, there's a young kid barely out of his teens chatting with the elderly lady next to him. She's showing him photos of her grandchildren and instead of looking bored, he's smiling and nodding in all the right places. All these people, all these lives, crossing over each other in this one room, and now I'm one of them.

PART
3

8th September 2000

Hi *Jason,*

   Before I go any further I want to wish you a happy eighteenth birthday!!! There's a card in with this letter, but if you're reading this first I didn't want you to think I'd forgotten!

   I can't believe you're so grown up already. Are you tall? I bet you are. And I bet you're good-looking too and have got all the girls chasing after you! I hope you've got a nice girl, it makes me happy thinking you might, and I hope you treat her right too.

   Now you're eighteen and a proper adult (I'm twenty-six now by the way and I'm still not sure I'm an adult! Ha! Ha!) I hope you're doing a lot of thinking about your past and where you came from. More than anything, I'm hoping this thinking will make you get in touch with the Adoption Contact Register because there's a whole stack of letters from me waiting for you there.

   Anyway, I really just want you to know that I'm always thinking of you. And I hope you have the best birthday ever. And I really, really, really hope that today is the day you begin your search to find me. I've got a good feeling about this, a really good feeling. I think we're going to find each other really soon.

   Love you to the moon and back,

   Kerry xxx

28

Noah

Wednesday, 8th June

'So I think that's everything, Mr Martineau, I'll get the ball rolling and obviously keep you up to date with how things are progressing. Divorce is never a very pleasant experience, no matter how amicable the parties involved, but I assure you I'll do my utmost to make the process as painless as possible. Any last questions?'

Without speaking, I study the face of the chic middle-aged woman sitting across from me. Caroline Hawley came highly recommended by a colleague who I knew could be relied on for her discretion. I'd wanted somebody capable and efficient but nothing like the notorious bulldogs whose names always cropped up whenever legal professionals like myself found themselves in need of representation. I don't want this to be a war, I don't want there to be casualties. In fact I don't want this at all. But after weeks of trying to change Rosalind's mind about the divorce, I finally had to admit defeat, and having received yet another letter from her solicitor, I knew that if I didn't respond she would undoubtedly see this as an act of aggression on my part. My choice then was the lesser of two evils, but that doesn't mean I'm happy about it. I love Rosalind and I don't want us to get divorced, but if she doesn't share my feelings and won't give me the opportunity to change her mind, then there's little else I can do.

I tell Caroline that I don't have any questions for the moment and, thanking her for her time, exit her office. Back outside on the street with people rushing by on every side, I feel momentarily adrift. There's an hour to go before I need to pick up Kerry from the hospital. There isn't enough time to go into chambers or indeed return home and I'm not sure exactly what to do. I make up my mind to go to the hospital early and pick up some flowers for Kerry on the way, when Charlotte calls.

'So how was it?' Charlotte asks. 'Was it grim? It was, wasn't it? How could it not be?' She laughs. 'I'm so sorry, Noah. You'd think having been through this myself I'd know exactly what to say.'

'It was as I expected really. She's a good solicitor and I don't doubt that she'll be more than a match for Rosalind's guy.'

'I know it's hard, but you have to be sensible. I know Rosalind's not a vindictive person but divorce does funny things to people, so it's worth having a decent sort representing your interests.' Charlotte pauses. 'And how's Millie holding up, poor thing?'

'She's okay, or at least that's the impression she's giving me. Rosalind and I have both made it clear to her that this has nothing to do with her and that we love her very much, but you know what she's like – bubbly on the outside, worrier on the inside – so it's hard to know for sure.'

'Well, I'm looking forward to seeing you both for lunch on Saturday and perhaps if you make yourself scarce for a while, I can have a bit of a chat with her.'

'That would be great. She's far more likely to tell you what's really going on in her head than she is me.'

'Right then,' says Charlotte. 'I'll make it my mission. And isn't it Kerry's last session of chemo for this cycle today?'

'Yes, it is. In fact that's where I'm heading now.'

'Well, give her all the family's regards, won't you? Tell her we're thinking of her.'

Much like my parents, my siblings had both taken the news that I'd made contact with my birth sister in their stride. Charlotte's initial reaction had been to say, 'That's fantastic, I've always wanted another sister to balance out all the testosterone in this family.' While Phillip's had been, 'We're all coming over later in the year anyway so let's fix a date for us to meet up.' And that was that. There was no angst, drama, or even the slightest, 'Why didn't you tell us earlier?' Instead there was just love and lots of it. They wanted nothing more than to meet Kerry, and I had gently floated the idea past her but she'd declined. 'I can't have them seeing me all worn out and scraggy like this,' she'd protested. 'Let's wait until I'm back on my feet.'

When I arrive at the hospital, it's clear Kerry isn't yet ready to leave. Though she's finished her treatment she's deep in conversation with Mrs Sutton, a plump woman in her sixties wearing an outrageously bright pink ensemble with matching shoes and headscarf.

'Noah,' says Kerry, looking up. 'You remember Ida, don't you?'

'Of course,' I reply. 'How are you, Mrs Sutton?'

'All the better for seeing you,' she says with a suggestive smile.

Kerry playfully taps Mrs Sutton on the elbow. 'Stop it you, I've told you he's off limits.' She turns back to me and says, 'I don't know what it is about this place that gives everyone the hots for you.'

As if on cue, the cheerful Welsh nurse appears to attend to Mrs Sutton's drip. 'Oh, hello, handsome.' Kerry and Mrs Sutton immediately fall into a fit of giggles like two schoolgirls.

'Honestly,' says the nurse, shaking her head, 'I don't know what they put in this stuff but this pair have been like this all morning.'

'Sorry,' says Kerry, pulling herself together. 'This one sets me off every time.'

As I help Kerry collect her belongings together, I think about how much things have changed over the past five weeks. In this short space of time she's gone from the new kid on the block to being on first-name terms with pretty much everyone on the ward, staff and patients alike. She knows everyone, even the scowling twenty-something with the knitting mother, managing to win them all over with her trademark combination of humour and straight talking.

But as she struggles to put on her coat, it's also impossible not to see the havoc her treatment has wrought on her body so far. She was fairly slim to begin with but now, following two cycles of chemotherapy, her slight frame is beginning to look frail. The effect is magnified by the hair loss she experienced towards the end of her first cycle. Although initially subtle, within a short time she was left with so little hair that in the end she chose to shave off the remainder, opting to wear a scarf instead.

She catches me staring. 'Don't worry,' she says, 'I know I look a state but I'm all right. It's like morning sickness when you're pregnant. They reckon the sicker you are the stronger the baby is, which was definitely true with my Kian. Sometimes I couldn't take more than a few steps without throwing up. It's just the same with this treatment. Yeah I'm sick, but that just means the treatment's doing its thing.' She looks over at Mrs Sutton. 'Isn't that right, Ida?'

Ida laughs wickedly. 'Absolutely. When we're all better, me and your sister are going on a cruise and I'm paying! We're going to do the whole of the Caribbean, bag ourselves a couple of toy boys and live life to the full. Blow leaving everything to my children. I'm going to really kick up my heels and Kerry is going to help me.'

Kerry laughs. 'I haven't even got a passport, Ida!'

'Don't you worry about that,' says Ida, tapping her nose mysteriously. 'I've got it all covered.'

Kerry gives Ida a kiss on the cheek and then, as it's the last time she'll be in for three weeks, does a circuit of the room to say the rest of her goodbyes. I think to myself how difficult this must be for Kerry, knowing that some of the people she has grown so close to in such a short space of time might not be here when she returns: some because their treatment has worked and others because it hasn't and perhaps isn't going to.

'Right then,' says Kerry to Ida. 'I've got to go, but I promise I'll try and pop in next week and see how you're getting on.'

Ida takes Kerry's hand. 'You see how you are first, my darling,' she says. 'You need to rest and get well. I don't want you being too poorly for our trip.'

I offer to bring the car around or fetch a wheelchair, but Kerry is insistent that she's fine to walk. She's noticeably weaker now than she was even a few days ago, although she'd never admit it. She no longer protests when I arrive to take Kian to school or turn up with bags of shopping and make supper for us all. She no longer tells me off for running the vacuum cleaner around the flat, even though I know how galling this is for her. Stubborn though she is, the treatment has forced her to finally accept there are things that for the moment she can't do, no matter how much she might want to. She has, however, drawn the line at coming to live with me so that I can look after her and Kian properly. Regardless, I restate my offer once more.

'You're worrying again, aren't you?' she says. 'What have I told you about worrying?'

'That it doesn't get you anywhere,' I reluctantly reply, parroting Kerry's words back at her. 'But perhaps I'd worry less if you came to stay with me,' I suggest with a smile.

'Nice try, barrister boy,' she says. 'But your legal trickery won't wash with me. I'm fine in my own place. I know things look bad now, but I really do feel like this is working and it'll all be worth it in the end.'

I decide against pushing any further and instead, for the rest of the way home, I get her to tell me the stories of all of the people she's met on the ward. Some make me laugh, others are very sobering, but all of them make me want to hold on to the people I love and never let them go.

We make it back to the flat at just after two. Despite Kerry's protests that I should go home, I stay for an hour, make lunch, prepare her something in case she's hungry later on, and then get her settled on the sofa. With Kian going to a friend's house for tea after school, I know Kerry will at least get a good few hours' rest but only if I leave her to it. If I've learned anything over the past few weeks, it's that Kerry is an impossible patient and if I stay, she is bound to fuss over me when I should be the one fussing over her.

That evening, I pick Millie up from school as arranged and take her back to mine. For supper we have a pasta dish, the recipe for which she'd seen in one of Rosalind's food magazines. I allow myself to be bossed around, chopping vegetables and stirring saucepans as and when instructed. It's good fun, and it seems to make her happy, which is all I want.

The food isn't half bad and is distinctly improved by the addition of capers that hadn't been part of the recipe, but which she'd added to the dish on a whim. She really is developing a very good palate and as we eat, she informs me that she's now added chef to her long list of possible careers.

'So how many is that you're considering now?'

She counts them out. 'Artist, interior designer, historian, actor and vlogger. Chef makes six.'

'What about law?'

She pulls a face. 'The thing is, Dad,' she says with all seriousness, 'I think law is quite dry and I don't think I'm that sort of person.'

'Thanks very much,' I laugh, but even as she moves the conversation on, I can't help but be struck once again by the difference between my daughter and nephew. Millie has a quiet self-assurance about her, born out of the privilege and opportunities she's enjoyed over the course of her life. Not that she is in any way spoilt or ungrateful, but rather she never once questions the likelihood of being able to achieve her goals. But having spent so much time with Kian over the past few weeks, I know that he is completely different. He's far less certain about his future, far less self-assured, and it is impossible for me not to wonder what my dreams and ambitions would've been had I not been granted the privileged education I'd received.

After supper, Millie and I clear the table and then watch a little TV, before she declares she's off to do homework. I decide it's probably time for me to do some work too, but as I reach for my briefcase my phone rings.

'Uncle Noah.' It's Kian, his voice shaky and scared. 'You've got to come quick, it's Mum, she's not well, and I don't know what to do.'

29

Kerry

Wednesday, 8th June

'Okay, Kerry, I'll love and leave you now, but don't forget first thing in the morning, pop in and see your GP and get him to give you the once-over. Other than that, just get plenty of rest. So that's no more cartwheels for you, my love, okay?' The paramedic gives me a cheeky wink. 'And no more housework either, you can get that boyfriend of yours to run around after you, for a change.'

'He's . . . he's not my boyfriend,' I croak. 'He's my baby brother.'

The paramedic raises an eyebrow, as most people do whenever I explain to them that Noah and I are related. 'In that case,' he says, handing me an envelope to give to my GP, 'tell him he's got to look after his big sister for a bit.'

The paramedic packs away the rest of his kit, drains the last few drops from the mug of tea Noah made him and tells the operator on his radio that he's finished and ready to leave.

'I'd see you out, but I don't want to go falling over and making a fool of myself again,' I say.

He laughs. 'I'm pretty sure I'll be able to find my own way,' he says and then, picking up the empty mug, flashes me another wink and he's gone.

Seconds after I hear the front door close, Kian comes rushing in like a lunatic and goes to throw his arms around me but then stops himself at the last minute.

'It's all right,' I say.

He looks unsure. 'I'm scared I might hurt you.'

'You could never do that,' I say, opening my arms up for a hug. 'Not in a million years.'

As I hold him, I can feel his heart racing as he tries not to get upset. 'I'm sorry I gave you a scare like that,' I say, covering his head in kisses. 'But I promise you, the paramedic was really brilliant. He's given me the once-over and he says I'm fine. I promise.'

Kian doesn't move or say anything, he just hugs me tighter, but eventually he sits up. 'When I saw you lying there, I thought you were . . .' He doesn't finish the sentence. I suppose there's no need. I'd given him the fright of his life. I pull him in close to me again, breathing in the smell of him, taking it deep into my lungs. 'I must have looked like the Wicked Witch of the East, lying there with my legs poking out from behind the sofa like that. But I promise you I'm all right. I just got a bit dizzy, that's all, and bumped my head. There's absolutely nothing to worry about, okay? Your old mum is invincible. I'm like that superhero you like . . . you know, the one with the red and gold suit . . . what's-his-name with the funny beard plays him in the films.'

Kian smiles. 'Iron Man,' he says. 'But you're not a man.'

'In that case,' I smile. 'You can call me Iron Woman, I'm just as good as regular Iron Man, but unlike him I like to clear up after myself.'

I give Kian another kiss and send him off to fetch his Uncle Noah. It's getting late and he and Millie have both got school in the morning. I want to tell Noah he can get off home. I've already caused everyone enough trouble for one night.

It was my own stupid fault really. After Noah left this afternoon I must have nodded off for a couple of hours, and when I woke up I didn't know where I was or what time it was for a minute. I think I must've got it into my head I was picking up Kian or that I was late for something important. I must have stood up too quick because the next thing I know, I'm lying on the floor and Kian's standing over me, saying Uncle Noah's on his way and he's called an ambulance.

I'd tried getting up but my legs wouldn't move. They were like lead and I had a massive headache too, and when I touched my head it was bleeding, so I must have bashed it somehow when I went dizzy. I could see how worried Kian was, but no matter how hard I tried I just couldn't seem to get off the floor. The paramedic was great though. Kian let him in and he sorted me out right where I was and then once he was sure I was okay, got me up and into bed. It wasn't too long after that Noah turned up. When I saw that he had Millie with him I felt even worse, knowing he'd had to drag her all the way over here, but no matter what I said to him he wouldn't leave.

'How are you feeling?' asks Noah, poking his head around the door.

'Awful,' I say. 'But not because of the bump on my head. It's just I wish you'd go home and get Millie to bed. She's got school tomorrow, and I bet she's got loads of homework as well. The last thing she needs is to be sitting round here twiddling her thumbs.'

'Millie's fine,' he says, sitting on the edge of the bed. 'It's you I'm worried about.'

'The paramedic said I'm fine. All I need to do is see my doctor in the morning and I'll be right as rain. I just had a dizzy spell, that's all. It's nothing to worry about.'

'I beg to differ. What if Kian hadn't come in when he did? What if he'd been at a sleepover? What if it had happened while he was at school? Who knows how long you'd have been lying there, and in your condition too?'

'But I'm fine,' I say. 'It's not as though I knocked myself out or anything.'

Noah gives me a stern look that I reckon he must use in court. 'But what about next time? Look, Kerry, I know you find it difficult to accept help from anybody but I'm not anybody, am I? I'm your brother and I want to look after you. So I'm going to give you a choice: either you let me move in here until your chemo is over and you're all better, or you and Kian come and stay with me in Bayswater. I don't mind which option you choose, but those are the only ones on the table.'

If it had been anyone else trying to tell me what to do, I would've told them where they could go. But like he says, he isn't just anyone, he's my brother, and though I might not like it, he's got a point: me trying to do this by myself isn't working. As it is, I'm going to be haunted forever by the look on Kian's face as he stood over me waiting for his uncle and the paramedic to arrive. He'd looked absolutely petrified, like he was watching his worst nightmare come true. I can't put him through that again. I just can't. But the thought of uprooting him in some ways seems just as bad, and I can't ask Noah to give up his bed and move into my pokey little place. And anyway, he's got Rosalind to consider. I can't imagine she'd be very happy for her daughter to be living part-time on a council estate.

I just don't know what to do for the best.

'Noah,' I say, 'it's really kind of you, but—'

'You're worried about Kian's schooling?' I nod; it's hard enough getting him to school on time as it is, let alone having to travel across London.

'If you come and live with me, I'll make sure he gets to school on time and I'll bring him over this way to see his friends whenever he wants.'

'But what about Millie, if you—'

'If I move in with you, then I'll arrange for someone from an agency to be here on the nights I'm with Millie back in Bayswater.'

'But then you'll be spending money you don't need to spend. Not to mention living out of a suitcase.'

He smiles. 'It looks like we've got our answer then.' He takes my hand in his. 'You and Kian will move in with me. You'll have my room, Kian will have the spare room, I'll sleep on the sofa bed in the living room and I'll get a put-up bed for the living room for when Millie stays over.'

'But Millie will hate that,' I say. 'You've told me how much she loved getting her room just how she likes it. She'll hate giving it up.'

'It's her idea,' he says. 'She's as worried about you both as I am.'

I'm lost for words. Noah's prepared to turn his whole life upside down just for me. Before I know it, tears are rolling down my cheeks.

'Hey, come on,' says Noah gently. 'There's no need for that. You'll be back here in no time.'

'It's not that,' I say. 'It's you, doing all this just for me. This time last year you didn't know me from Adam, and now look where we are.'

'We're exactly where we should be,' he says. 'Where we would've been if we'd had a better start in life. I'm not doing this out of guilt, or even out of sympathy. I'm doing it because you're family, and this is what families do.'

The next morning before school, while Noah and Millie finish getting ready for the day after their night spent topping and tailing on my sofa, I call Kian in for a chat. He looks shattered and there's still a trace of worry in his eyes. I give him a big squeeze and make him sit on my lap to show him that a little cuddle isn't going to break me.

'Your Uncle Noah and me have been talking and we've decided that it might be a good idea if you and me went to live with him for a little bit. It won't be forever, just while I'm getting better. You'll have your own room there and you can take whatever you want from here with you. So, how does that sound?'

He doesn't say anything for a minute. He just sits there blank-faced, mulling it over. I can't tell whether he's sad or whether he's happy. I can't tell what he's thinking at all.

He takes a breath, then looks at me. 'I think that sounds good.'

'You're not upset?'

He shakes his head. 'It's like you said, it's not forever, it's just while you get better. And anyway it'll be fun, like being on holiday.'

That afternoon Noah picks Kian up from school, brings him back home and together we help him pack everything he'll need for the next couple of weeks. I know if I left him to do it on his own, the only things in his suitcase would be his PlayStation and half a dozen T-shirts. As it is, we manage to get all of that in along with the boring stuff like school uniform, extra clothes, books and of course underwear. It doesn't take us long, and with my case already packed and waiting by the door, all that's left to do is make sure everything is switched off and left tidy.

It's after five by the time we're ready to leave and as I lock up, I can't help but feel a little bit weird. I know it's only temporary, I know we'll be back soon, but it still feels strange. This place is my home, somewhere I'd worked hard to make nice, and leaving it behind like this feels wrong, like I really am saying goodbye for good.

Kian's thrilled to bits with his new bedroom. Because it's about a million times bigger than his and has even got a telly in it, he hasn't noticed that the curtains are flowery or that there's a fluffy rug next to the bed. In fact, he loves it so much that he only comes out when Noah tells him the pizzas have arrived. Even then all he does is wolf down his tea, before disappearing back where he came from.

'Well, he seems happy,' says Noah, collecting together the last of the leftover pizza and putting it in the fridge. 'How about you? You didn't eat much.'

'I never do these days,' I say. 'I either feel too sick or too tired to eat, but they reckon that's normal when you're having chemo.'

'You should've said,' says Noah. 'I could've got you something more appetising.'

'More appetising than stuffed-crust pizza?' I smile. 'As if.'

I try to help Noah clear the table but my legs feel a bit wobbly, so I sit down before he sees. 'How are you doing? Having us here must be really putting you out.'

'Far from it,' says Noah, and he sits down opposite me. 'To be honest, I'm glad of the company. With things the way they are I really miss family life and anyway, having you guys here is special.'

I laugh. 'You won't be saying that when you're tripping over Kian's school bag, or finding that you can't get near the telly half the time because I'm catching up with my soaps.'

'But you're forgetting this is the first time we've lived under the same roof since we were kids. How amazing is that?'

My hand goes up to my mouth. I can't believe I didn't think

of that. Me and my baby brother, back together, like a family. Before I know it the tears are back.

'I don't know what's got into me lately,' I say, drying my eyes. 'Must be all this medicine I'm on making me soft.'

Noah's phone rings, and before he can say anything to stop me, I'm on my feet. 'You get that,' I say. 'I'm going to go and unpack my things.'

I manage to put a few of my clothes away in the drawers, but then I come over all tired so I lie down on the bed to rest my eyes for a minute. As I feel myself drifting off, I remember that I haven't taken my medication yet.

I force myself to get up, even though all I want to do is sleep. But then on the way to get it from my handbag in the kitchen, I pass the living room and see Noah. He's still holding his phone but he's not talking into it. He's just sort of standing there looking like he's in shock.

'What's the matter? Is everything okay?'

He turns to me, still wearing the same look of disbelief. 'Do you remember when we went to The Park looking for my dad? How I gave my business card to that woman we met? Well, she must have passed it on because that was her.'

'Who?'

'My aunt,' he says. 'My birth dad's sister.'

30

Noah

Saturday, 18th June

With even the most humble of London boroughs packed to the rafters with hipster coffee bars and vintage tearooms, I'd almost forgotten that places like Dot's Café on the Bethnal Green Road existed. With its chipped Formica tables, squeezy tomato-ketchup bottles and a hot drinks menu limited to either plain tea or instant coffee, it could easily have been mistaken for one of its trendier cousins making something of an ironic retro statement. The grim-faced overall-clad woman behind the counter, however, makes it clear that this is indeed the genuine article.

Even though I'm early, I scan the faces of the other Saturday morning customers looking for signs of recognition. An old Sikh gentleman sitting at a corner table looks up briefly but then returns his attention to the newspaper in front of him. One of the three elderly Caribbean ladies at a table near the window casts an appraising glance in my direction, but she doesn't even pause for breath and continues her conversation in a thick, hurried patois that's impenetrable to my ears.

I order a tea, a scalding dark-brown liquid served in a mug advertising a nearby taxi firm, take a seat at a table to the rear of the room, which has a good view of the door, and settle myself down to wait.

As I make a study of the sticky laminated menu, while keeping one eye on the door, it occurs to me that I'm becoming something of an expert at meeting long-lost relatives. While the surroundings are very different to where I waited for Kerry, the feelings I'm

experiencing – a mixture of excitement, fear and nervous anticipation – are exactly the same.

My aunt's call had taken me completely by surprise.

'Am I speaking to a Mr Noah Martineau?' Her voice had been
formal and polite with a slight but unmistakable Caribbean under-
tone. 'I believe you asked my friend Mrs Powell to pass on your
business card. I was out of the country at the time, looking after
my mother in the West Indies. I've only just returned and had
your card brought to my attention.'

With everything that has happened lately I'd all but forgotten
my encounter with the elderly lady with the shopping trolley who
promised to pass on my details.

'So you must be . . .'

'I'm Marcia,' she'd said with a sigh. 'And if what you said to
Mrs Powell is true, my brother Stucky is your father.'

She had been reluctant to go into any further details on the
phone, instead suggesting that we meet face to face and so here
I am, sitting in a greasy spoon café, waiting to meet my father's
sister.

Having exhausted the menu for distraction, I turn to my phone
and send Millie a text wishing her good luck with her piano
exam this afternoon. Although things are still frosty between
Rosalind and me, she is always diligent about keeping me in the
loop where Millie is concerned. As I'm about to tuck away my
phone again, I receive a text from Kerry: 'Hope it's going okay.
Let me know when you're on your way back and I'll get some
dinner on. xxx.'

If I hadn't still been in shock when Kerry came into the room,
I'm not sure I would have told her about the call from my aunt
straight away. She looked so frail, so ill, that the last thing I wanted
to do was give her anything else to worry about. But as it was,
the words just sort of tumbled out of me unbidden.

Typical of Kerry, she'd been very supportive and had even
offered to come with me this morning. I told her, however, that
I'd be fine, that whatever I learned about my father, I'd be okay.

Even so, for the rest of the week she's been even more attentive
and protective than usual. Fussing that I'm working too hard,
not eating enough or drinking too much coffee. All of it is her
way of saying she is on my side, that whatever happens we will
still have each other.

I start to tap out a reply but don't get very far before the door
opens and I automatically look up, to see a tall woman in her
mid-sixties, with short neatly styled jet-black hair. She's wearing
gold-rimmed glasses and sporting a navy-blue raincoat and grey
trousers. The moment our eyes meet I know that it's her, and I
see that she knows who I am too.

I stand up. 'Marcia?'

She nods thoughtfully as she studies me. 'It's plain as day,' she
says, as if to herself. 'You're Stucky's boy all right.' She holds out
her hand. 'Pleased to meet you, Mr Martineau.'

'Please,' I say, 'call me Noah,' and then I gesture to the table
and we both take a seat.

'Have you come far?'

She shakes her head. 'I only live around the corner, have done
for nearly thirty years. This place isn't much to write home about
but it's cheap, and they do a good Jamaican Bun. Don't ask me
how, I don't think that Dot has seen beyond the end of this road
her whole life, but there you go. Things aren't always what they
seem.'

I offer to get her a drink and a slice of the aforementioned
bun. 'Yes to the tea,' she says, 'but I'd better leave off the bun,
I'm watching my figure.'

I order two drinks from the unsmiling woman behind the
counter, wait while they are made and then return to the table.

'Thank you for coming to meet me today,' I say, with what I
hope is a winning smile as I present Marcia with her tea. 'It's
very kind of you.'

'It's not like I had much choice,' she says grimly. 'That Stucky,
he's always been a bad one, causing trouble wherever he goes.'
She takes a sip of tea. 'So tell me then, who is your mother?'

'Her name was Mary, she died a few years ago. I think she

got to know your brother when you and your family lived on The Park estate.'

Her face softens. 'So your mother's passed on? I'm sorry to hear that. No matter how old you are it's never easy losing loved ones. I just lost my mother . . . your grandmother.'

'I'm so sorry,' I say, wondering whether this news should affect me more than it does.

'It's all right,' she says. 'It's a blessing really. She'd been ill for some time and I was with her at the end, which was important to me.'

'You talked about having been overseas. Was that where you were, looking after your mother?'

She nods. 'Do you know Jamaica at all?'

I think about the various Caribbean islands Rosalind and I have holidayed on over the years, but Jamaica had never been one of them. 'No,' I reply. 'But I know from friends that it's an incredibly beautiful country. Whereabouts did she live?'

'Mandeville,' she replies. 'She never settled properly here in London really. I think she liked the country air too much. First opportunity she got she moved back home. That was fifteen years ago now.' She takes another sip of her tea. 'Your mother was Irish, wasn't she? Pretty girl she was, dark brown hair, lovely smile.'

I sit forward. 'So you knew her?'

Marcia sighs. 'Only a little. By the time she met my brother I'd long since moved out of home and was working as a nurse at Hammersmith Hospital. I'd only ever hear about what Stucky had been up to when I came to visit my mother, and more often than not it was bad news. The thing about your father was that he needed taking in hand. He was the youngest of the five of us, with me as the eldest. My father died just before Stucky turned fifteen and with my mother working all hours, there was no one around to keep him in check.' She reaches into her handbag, takes out a dog-eared photograph and slides it across the table to me.

'If you're interested,' she says. 'This is him.'

I turn the photo around and study it. It shows a young, handsome black man with a short Afro and an athletic build, leaning against a wall. He's grinning from ear to ear and is dressed casually in a black leather jacket, white shirt unbuttoned at the collar, jeans and Adidas trainers. For a moment I'm lost for words, searching as I am for signs of myself in this young man. I see elements of myself in him when I was that age. We have the same almond-shaped eyes, the same full lips and a similar build.

I think of the photos of my mother Kerry gave to me. I imagine the two sets of photographs side by side, the first and only time I'll see my parents together.

'How old is he here?'

She takes the photo and scrutinises it for a moment or two. 'Seventeen, maybe eighteen,' she pronounces eventually. 'By this time he'd already gone bad: hanging around in all the wrong places with the wrong people. And then of course there were the girls. He seemed to have a new one every time I saw him. It was hard to keep track. But your mother I remember, because she lived close by and I'd seen her around. I warned him, you know. I warned that boy not to mess her around. I said to him, "She already have one pickney to look after, the last thing she needs is more trouble brought to her door." She eyes me carefully and slides the photo back to me. 'Keep it,' she says. 'I've got no use for it.'

I slip the photo into my inside jacket pocket, intrigued by the strength of her anger towards her brother, but before I can consider it further there's a flurry of activity as a morning delivery arrives. We both look on, using it as an excuse to collect our thoughts for a moment.

'How long ago did you say that she died?' she asks, returning her attention to me. 'Only you talk as though you barely knew her.'

'I didn't,' I reply. 'I was taken into care when I was eighteen months old, my sister too. Mary just couldn't look after us any more.'

Marcia shakes her head sadly. 'Well, that is terrible,' she says, staring down into her tea. 'That brother of mine has a lot to answer for.'

'Are you still in touch?'

She tuts loudly. 'Not any more than I can help.'

'But you have an address for him?'

She nods. 'So is that your plan, to see him? If it is, I wouldn't get your hopes up. Stucky is no one's idea of a good father. You sound like you've been brought up well and Mrs Powell said you're a barrister. Is that right?'

'Yes, I've been very lucky.'

'Well, if you want my advice you're best off counting your blessings and giving Stucky a wide berth.'

'I'll bear that in mind,' I say. 'But I really would appreciate an address for him if you have one.'

'An address?' she says with a bitter smile. 'How about this for an address? Her Majesty's Prison Nottingham.'

'He's in prison?' gasps Kerry and then, conscious that Kian is in the next room, she lowers her voice. 'What for?'

'Armed robbery,' I reply, watching her stunned reaction. 'Despite being old enough to know better, apparently he and some of his associates conducted a series of raids on security firms delivering cash to various retail establishments. Given their previous convictions they got thirteen years apiece.'

Kerry tries to rearrange herself on the sofa and I help by adjusting the pillow at her back. Though I'd suggested she stay in bed, she'd insisted on getting up and dressed even if she was only going to sit on the sofa.

'I can't believe it,' she says, rearranging the plush velvet throw covering her legs. 'I was worried that he'd turn out to be a wrong 'un, but armed robbery? I just can't believe it.'

'I know,' I say. 'His sister didn't have a good word to say about him.'

'And what was she like?'

'Nice enough,' I reply. 'A bit guarded, understandably I suppose. I get the impression that she's been clearing up after her brother her whole life.'

'And are you going to see her again?'

'I doubt it. There wasn't that same connection we have. Reading between the lines, I think she's had a pretty tough life herself. She's only in her mid-sixties and she's already a great-grandmother so I think she has more than enough to be getting on with, without adding any more waifs and strays into the mix. And anyway, before we parted she told me she's seriously thinking about moving to her mum's old place in Jamaica for good.'

Kerry sighs. 'Well, I suppose that's that then.' She looks at me and I pull a face. 'Oh no,' she says, with a horrified expression. 'You're not seriously thinking about . . .'

I nod. 'I've come this far, I might as well finish the job.'

Kerry sits forward on the sofa. 'Noah, listen to me: you do not want to get mixed up with someone like him. He'll clock your suit and hear your voice, and all he'll see is an opportunity to get something for nothing. Just stay away, it's not worth it.'

'I hear what you're saying,' I say, touched by Kerry's fierce concern for me. 'But you're forgetting what I do for a living. I deal with people like him all the time. I know how they work, how they think; he's not going to get anything past me. I just want to see him, that's all.'

'And then what?'

I shrug. It's a good question, one which thankfully I'm saved from answering by the appearance of Kian at the door.

'Uncle Noah!' he exclaims. 'I wondered who Mum was talking to. He tugs my arm urgently. 'Come and see where I am in the game you got me for my birthday, it's the furthest I've ever managed to get.'

Before I can resist, Kian's dragged me to his bedroom and there we remain, him talking ten to the dozen, trying to explain the intricacies of a game I can barely understand. As he talks I can't help but think about Kerry's warning to stay away from Stucky, echoing that of my aunt. She's probably right, and if our positions were reversed I'd be advising her to do exactly the same. And yet regardless, this is something I feel I have to do. I think about the young man in the photo and how even though we've never met, we're still connected. I'm not expecting any major revelations. I'm not expecting him to be the missing piece of the puzzle that is my life. I'm not expecting much of anything from him at all. But for better or worse he is my father, I am his son, and if for no other reason than this I feel I need to see him.

Later that evening, after Kian has gone to bed and Kerry and I are sitting watching TV, she picks up the remote and mutes the sound.

'I've been thinking,' she says, 'about what I said earlier, and it was bang out of order. I've got no right to be telling you what to do, especially when I know if it was the other way round, I'd have done the same. I just worry about you, that's all. And I don't want you to get hurt. But if seeing him is what you want to do, then I'll absolutely support you in that, okay?' She smiles. 'I'll even take you there, if you like.'

31

Kerry

Tuesday, 28th June

Until I started my treatment, I don't think I'd ever quite realised how many hair ads there are on TV. There are ads promising to cover up the grey, ads promising stronger hair because of some special vitamin or other. Ads for miracle hair-straighteners, ads for miracle hair-curlers; and then of course there's a million and one ads for shampoos, all with fancy scientific diagrams and beautiful women with perfect teeth and hair down to their ankles, laughing to themselves because their hair looks so good.

The advert on right now is for a new shampoo that's supposed to be able to reverse the damage done to your hair from a thousand blow-dries or something ridiculous like that. A couple of months ago I probably would've been tempted. I've always liked to keep my hair nice, and I've got enough shampoos, lotions and sprays in my bathroom cupboard to open a small branch of Boots. But now I've got no use for any of it. I might as well just throw the whole lot away.

I switch off the TV and go and stand in front of the mirror in the bathroom. I take off my headscarf and have a good look. Even though I know what to expect, it's still quite a shock. I barely recognise myself. I've got dark circles under my eyes, my cheeks are sunken in and my lips are all cracked and dry. With all this and a bald head, I look like an alien or someone back from the dead. It's a wonder I don't give Kian nightmares looking the way I do.

When my hair first started falling out I could barely bring myself to look in the mirror. It was awful. Proper heartbreaking.

Even though they'd warned me it might happen, I'd convinced myself that somehow I'd get away with it. But then when my hair started coming out in clumps it was horrible, worse than the throwing up and the tiredness and the headaches, because day after day it was like losing a little bit more of myself. In the end I couldn't face it any more and so I just shaved the whole lot off. I felt sick looking at it, all piled up in the sink like the sweepings off a busy barber's floor. I thought about all the effort I'd put into looking after it over the years, all the money I'd spent on potions and lotions and having it cut, and now it was gone, and the face looking back at me without it was strange and unfamiliar. I didn't know who that person was and I'm not sure I wanted to know either. After that, I stopped looking in the mirror altogether. I stopped doing my make-up too. Told myself there was no point when I didn't have any eyebrows or eyelashes. Told myself all that mattered was getting better.

I've tried to convince myself that it's nice not having to worry about my looks. Over the years, I don't know how many hours I've spent staring at my reflection and trying to make improvements on what I saw. I'm sure if I added all the minutes into one big lump it would work out to be days, maybe even weeks, just spent staring in a mirror. What a waste of precious time, time I'll never get back. But the thing is, I actually miss doing my hair. I miss that time spent taking care of myself. I even miss inspecting my face for all the little lines and wrinkles and stray hairs sprouting out of nowhere. I used to think taking care of myself was a hassle but looking in the mirror right now, I can see it for what it is: a privilege.

Enough is enough.

I slather on a load of cleanser, wash it off and then slap on a big dollop of moisturiser. My skin is so dry and sore that it practically drinks in the cream like it's parched sand. In my bedroom, I dig out my make-up bag from the bedside cabinet and then stand in front of the hallway mirror where the light's a bit kinder. I start with a bit of foundation, which I normally only use if I'm going out somewhere special, but my skin's so rough I have to go back into the bathroom, wash it off and start again.

I carefully apply a bit of blusher to my cheeks. My mouth's too cracked and dry for lipstick, so I rub in a bit of Vaseline instead, then stand back and take another look at myself. It's not brilliant, but it's better. It's like someone's breathed a bit of life into me, like I've got some of my old self back.

I think about drawing on some eyebrows, even though I'm not sure I've got the skill. In my head I'm imagining Cindy Crawford, all perfectly defined and sophisticated, but I'm scared I'll end up looking like it's my first day at clown school instead. Nervously I reach for my eyebrow pencil, but then my phone rings. It's Kian's school.

'Is that Ms Hayes? It's Mrs Curtis here from Saint Nicholas Primary.'

My stomach flips over. 'Is everything okay?'

'As Kian hasn't made it in for the register this morning, I'm just calling to check whether he's not coming in today or is just running late.'

Straight away my heart starts pounding in my chest. It's the strongest I've felt it in weeks. 'Running late? He's not running late. His uncle sent me a text less than an hour ago to say he'd dropped him off. Are you telling me he's gone missing?'

There's a silence and I can almost hear her scrabbling about in her brain for what to say next. 'I'm sure there's a perfectly reasonable explanation. Perhaps it's simply an oversight. I'll go and speak to his teacher immediately and get back to you.'

The second she's off the line, I'm straight on to Noah in a blind panic. This isn't like Kian at all. Granted he's not a massive fan of school even at the best of times, but he's never bunked off, not like I used to. It's just not in his nature, and anyway I've warned him off it. The places I used to go when I skipped school. The trouble I used to get into. I feel sick just thinking about it.

My call to Noah goes straight to his voicemail and I remember he's in court all morning, and that's when I really start to freak out. Still panicking, I call Kian's phone next. It rings out then goes to voicemail. And so I try it again and again and again but there's still no answer.

I think about what to do next. I can't just sit here like a lemon waiting for someone to tell me they still can't find him. So with one hand I start calling Noah's chambers, and with the other I grab my coat and start searching for my shoes.

It takes three goes to get through and by then I'm dressed and ready to leave. I try to tell them what the problem is but I'm so worked up, I'm barely making any sense.

'I need Noah,' I say. 'You've got to get to Noah. I need him quick—'

The footsteps are the first thing I hear, then the scratch of keys in the lock. I drop the phone and rush to open the door. My brain is so muddled I think it must be Noah come to help me, but it isn't.

It's Kian.

'Mum!' he says, his big blue eyes full to the brim with tears. He flings his arms around me, almost sending me flying.

'What do you think you're playing at?' I ask, once I've recovered myself. 'Have you any idea how worried I've been? Why aren't you at school?'

'I dunno,' he sobs, and tears start streaming down his face. 'I'm sorry, Mum, I just wanted to see you.'

He's so upset, there's no point in trying to get any sense out of him yet. So I get him to hang his coat up and go and wash his face while I call the school and Noah's chambers, and then we snuggle up on the sofa.

We sit and watch TV for a while, one of those DIY programmes that are always on, and by the time it's over he's a lot calmer and thankfully I am too.

I look over at him again, trying to work out what's going on in his little head. 'So come on then, you,' I say, pausing the TV. 'Tell me properly what happened. And don't leave anything out.'

He looks at me all worried. 'Am I going to get in trouble with school?'

'Course not,' I reply. 'It's all sorted. As far as they know you felt ill and your uncle brought you back home but forgot to call them.'

'And what about Uncle Noah? Didn't you say you had to call him at work? Was he mad?'

'No, he was fine. He was just happy you're okay. So come on then, Kian, stop stalling. What went on?'

'I dunno,' he says, 'I was okay all the way to school, and even after I waved goodbye to Uncle Noah. But then I just got this horrible feeling in my tummy, like when you've got a big maths test or something. I tried to ignore it, I promise, I tried really hard, but when the bell went . . . I can't explain it really, I just missed you. So I came home.'

'But how did you even get here? It's not like it's down the road, is it?'

He looks at his lap. 'Uncle Noah gave me some money to keep in my bag for emergencies. I bought a Tube ticket and then used the map on my phone to work out where to go.'

Even though I know he's streetwise, it still makes me shudder thinking about all the things that could've happened to him on a journey like that, with no one in the world knowing where he was.

'Did no one even stop you or ask why you weren't at school?'

Kian shakes his head. 'I had my cap pulled right down and anyway, everyone was too busy to notice me, I think.'

I give him a big squeeze and kiss the top of his little head. 'I'm really glad you got here in one piece, you know that, don't you? But if you ever, and I mean ever, do anything like this again, I will absolutely make your life not worth living. I mean it, Kian, if you think you've seen me angry, just try and pull a stunt like this again and I'll show you what angry is like.'

I can tell just by looking at him that the message has got through. He even volunteers to go back to school. But I tell him no, he doesn't have to, and instead we're going to spend the day together like we used to when he was little.

'Really?' he says, and his eyes light up. 'Do you mean it?'

'Of course,' I say, close to tears. It's my fault it's come to this. I should've realised before now how hard this has all been on him. I should've realised that even though he's been really brave these past couple of months, it must have been taking its toll somehow. The poor kid's had his whole life turned upside down. Of course all he wants is a bit of comfort and normality. Of course all he wants is a little cuddle. It's all I want too.

I reach for my phone and start looking something up.

'What are you doing?' he asks.

'Ordering pizzas,' I reply. 'I'm having a Margherita. What do you want?'

His eyes widen. 'But Mum,' he says, laughing. 'It's only half ten.'

'I know, but sometimes you've just got to do what you've got to do.'

The pizzas take about forty-five minutes to arrive, but Kian manages to polish off his *and* half of mine in under ten. Afterwards, completely stuffed, we decide we fancy watching a film, and so Kian slips to his room and comes back with a few of his favourites for me to choose from.

'I don't mind,' I say, as he spreads out a dozen or so DVDs in front of me: a mixture of Pixar movies, superhero films, a couple of *Star Wars* ones and some Harry Potters, 'The important thing is that I get to cuddle you on the sofa while we watch it.'

He picks up one of the Harry Potters, *The Prisoner of Azkaban,* loads it into the DVD player and then settles back down with me on the sofa.

'Ready?' I say, pressing play. He nods and cuddles up to me, and the film starts. I'm pretty sure I've seen this one before, I think we might even have watched it last Christmas, but I must have fallen asleep because I can't remember anything about it. It's exciting though, and I'm desperate to know what's going to happen next, but in the middle of a really good bit Kian says: 'When you're better I'm going to take you to Harry Potter World.'

I pause the DVD. 'You what?'

'I said, when you're better I'm going to take you to Harry Potter World.'

'Are you now?' I ask, wondering where this has come from. 'Well, maybe when I'm better I'll be taking you.'

Kian shakes his head. 'You can't. It's supposed to be a surprise but I can't keep it in any more. I've already started saving up and I've talked it over with Uncle Noah too.'

'Is that right?' I say. 'Well, in that case I can't wait.'

For a moment I think that might be it, but I can see from his frown that he's still working something out.

'What is it?'

He shrugs.

'Come on, Kian. You can tell me anything.'

He thinks again. 'When?'

'When what?'

'When will you be better?'

I close my eyes. I have to. He's completely blindsided me. How long has he been thinking about this?

I take a deep breath and open my eyes. 'Soon,' I say, trying to sound cheery. 'Very soon.'

'Yeah, but when?' He sighs. 'I want to get Uncle Noah to book the tickets for me, so I need to give him a date.'

You don't have to be a genius to work out what he's really asking. This isn't about a day out at Harry Potter World or surprising me or anything else. This is about a little boy wanting to know when his life is going to get back to normal. When he's going to get his mum back. When he's going to be able to go out and see his mates and not worry that when he comes back he'll find me lying face down on the carpet. All he wants is a bit of security, to know that it's not going to be like this forever. All he wants to do is get back to being an ordinary kid.

It breaks my heart that he's thinking about stuff like this.

All I've ever wanted to do is to protect him from all the horrible things in the world. Never once thinking that I was carrying one of those horrible things around inside me. I don't want to lie to him. But I don't know what the truth is either. Instead I smile and give him a hug, and say, 'I'm not sure I can give you an exact date, but I promise you this with all my heart: I'm working on it.'

32

Noah

Friday, 1st July

'Okay then, I'd better be getting off. There's leek and potato soup in the fridge and I picked up some nice fresh rolls this morning to go with it, which I've left on the counter. There are three ready meals in the fridge for supper, but you and Kian go ahead and have yours without me if I'm not back before you get hungry. I'm hoping to be home for seven at the latest, earlier if I can. I'll have my phone on the entire time, but obviously not while I'm actually in the prison. But I've spoken to my mum and she said if you need anything, then give her a call.'

'That's lovely of your mum,' says Kerry. 'But I told you, I'll be fine. You're going to Nottingham not New York. Now get a move on or you're going to miss your train.'

I pick up my briefcase but don't move. I don't like the idea of being so far away from her, even if it is only for a few hours. 'All right then,' I say, 'but don't get doing anything silly again like trying to defrost the freezer or change the beds. I'll get all that sorted, okay? Just promise me you'll have a lazy day and concentrate on keeping your strength up.'

Kerry offers me a comical salute. 'Yes, sir!' she replies. 'Anything else?'

'I'm sorry,' I say, detecting her sarcasm. 'I don't mean to be bossy, I just want you to get better.'

'I know you do,' she says. 'But don't forget I worry about you too. Don't let him take advantage of you, all right? Don't make him any promises. And whatever you do, don't invite him to come and stay with you when he gets out. You've got enough long-lost relatives living with you as it is.'

It's hard to believe that in a matter of a few hours I will finally meet my father. The process so far has been relatively straightforward. I'd contacted Marcia again and told her that I'd like to see my father, and she in turn had contacted him. A week later she'd called to tell me that he'd agreed to add me to his visitor list, then I filled out a visitor order and a matter of a few days later received email confirmation that it was all arranged.

The train journey to Nottingham passes without incident. Enjoying the comfort of a first-class carriage, which I virtually have to myself, I manage to plough through more work than I could ever have imagined doing in chambers with its constant interruptions. Perhaps, however, it is not the surroundings spurring me on to lose myself in work, so much as the desire to distract myself from the enormity of what I'm about to do.

At the station I get a cab to take me to the prison. Whenever I make such journeys for work, the mere mention of a prison destination to a taxi driver is enough to fuel our conversation the whole way, and this time is no different. Although initially confused by the colour of my skin and my casual attire, after hearing me speak and spotting my briefcase my cab driver makes the assumption that I'm here on legal business and I don't correct him. Once these basics have been established, he then launches into a ten-minute diatribe on the failings of the criminal justice system, with particular emphasis on the sentences meted out to rapists, child molesters and murderers. It's a tirade I've heard many times in many different guises over the years, and I've learned the hard way that the best thing to do in such situations is just to sit back and listen.

A short while later, we're pulling up outside HMP Nottingham visitors centre. Reluctantly the taxi driver draws his rant to a close, takes my money and scribbles out a receipt. He jokes through his open window: 'Let's hope they let you out again!' and then drives off.

Although it's my first time at HMP Nottingham, it's far from being my first visit to a prison and so I know the drill well. Inside the visitors centre I join the long queue at reception made up predominantly of women: wives, girlfriends, mothers, sisters. When my turn comes, I hand over my visiting order and ID to one of the guards sitting at a desk behind a perspex screen.

Next I'm ushered into a room where my photograph is taken, my irises scanned for biometric ID, and then finally I'm shown to the lockers where I store my briefcase, jacket, wallet and phone. Once I'm done, I'm herded towards the main prison to join the queue waiting to be searched and I think how similar this process is to airport check-in, albeit without the promise of a summer break on the other side.

The visitors hall looks much like a school canteen, even down to the vending machines positioned against one wall. The similarities stop there, however, as the seating arrangements say anything but school. There are lines of about thirty clear perspex tables, some with three red seats on one side, others with two, but all of them facing a solitary yellow chair on the other side, the chair specially reserved for the inmate.

As we wait in line, we're given strict instructions about where we should sit. I'm shown to a red seat at a table in the middle row, towards the back of the room. Without my phone or anything else to distract me until the inmates are allowed in, I take the opportunity to observe my fellow visitors. To the left of me are two Chinese women, who I suspect are mother and daughter; to my right is a thin, middle-aged woman with blonde straggly hair, who is biting her nails nervously; and directly in front of me is a small heavily tattooed white-haired man sitting next to a young Indian woman barely out of her teens, who is slim apart from her burgeoning baby bump.

Not long after everyone is seated and the guards have taken up their positions around the room, a bell sounds and everyone looks expectantly towards a large grey door to my left. A guard enters first, followed by a single file of inmates. Some spot their loved ones straight away and wave excitedly. Others stare at the floor and wait until they're told to move by the prison officers.

But as the inmates begin to be seated and the noise levels rise, it's as if everyone forgets where they are for a moment. It's as if in the intensity of their greeting, the prison walls fall away.

I spot my birth father immediately, recognising him in part from my photo of him, but also from the various newspaper articles about his case that I've looked up online. He's tall and broad-shouldered, with a shaved head and neat beard that's now entirely white. Even though he's no longer the smiling young man in the photo, it's easy to see traces of the man Mary fell for.

He offers a perfunctory nod as greeting as he sits down in the yellow chair opposite me.

'So Marcia tells me you're Mary's boy, is that right?'

His voice is deep and rich, but he speaks quietly as though accustomed to commanding his audience's full attention.

'That's right,' I say, 'and yours.'

He smiles at my directness. 'You know,' he says, 'you're not the first one of me pickney to show up looking for me . . . but you're the first one to turn up talking like you Prince Charles.' He laughs hard at his own joke as I reel inwardly at what he's just said. Perhaps naïvely, it hadn't occurred to me that I might have other half-siblings out there aside from Kerry. It hadn't occurred to me before now that my own story has most likely been one often repeated across his lifetime. The thought that there might be other relatives, more half-brothers and sisters, out there is a strange one, and difficult to process. 'How come you talk like you do?' he asks, when he finally recovers himself. 'You didn't learn that living with your mother.'

'I was adopted,' I say, and wait for his reaction.

'Seems to me like you landed on your feet.'

I nod and look pointedly around the room. 'Yes,' I say. 'I suppose I did.'

He laughs again. 'Not all of us are so lucky.' He pauses and considers me carefully. 'You have a job?'

I nod. 'I'm a barrister. A criminal barrister to be precise.'

Stucky raises his eyebrows in disbelief, as though he thinks

I'm joking, but when I remain straight-faced he bursts out laughing again.

'A child of mine a barrister!' He laughs again. 'Why you couldn't find me sooner and keep me outta this place?'

I smile in spite of myself but say nothing.

'You wait 'til I tell them back on the wing about this,' he says. 'They'll never believe me.'

'How long do you have left to serve?'

He sighs. 'Why you ask? You want me to come and live with you when I get out?' I don't react, but he laughs nonetheless as though I have. 'Didn't think so.' He leans forward, elbows on the table, chin in hands, a grin on his face like he's really finding this amusing. 'So tell me,' he says, 'what you here for? You want me to say sorry for not being around? You want backdated child support? Tell me, what a big man like you would want with me?'

'I don't want anything,' I reply, and as I say the words, I realise I mean them. 'I'm here out of curiosity, no more, no less.'

He laughs again. 'And now you've met me, what do you think?'

I consider his question and take a moment to study his face. 'I can see we look a little alike, around the eyes and the nose for instance. I think we might even have the same build too, but that's pretty much where our similarities begin and end.'

He eyes me carefully, uncertain of what to make of me. Perhaps before I arrived he'd made up his mind to try to unsettle me, whether for sport or cruelty, it didn't matter. But what did matter was that I'd sat across from men far more dangerous, intimidating and unsettling than him, and had bested them all. The fact that he was my birth father made no difference whatsoever.

'So,' I say, looking him directly in the eyes, 'it seems clear that you're not at all interested in me, and now I've met you I feel able to say that the feeling is mutual. But given that we've got fifty minutes of our visit left and after today we're never going to see each other again, why don't we make the best of a bad situation? I'll get us something to eat and a coffee, and then we can have ourselves a decent conversation.'

I don't know whether it's my directness, confidence or even

my accent, but when I return to the table bearing coffee and two pre-packed blueberry muffins, it's as if he's a different person. Between sips of coffee he tells me stories from his past: about when he was a child, about when his father died, about how he fell into crime. Even about the first time he saw Mary.

'She was standing at the bus stop, on her way to work. She was pretty, and kept herself good, and so we got to talking and we realised we lived around the corner from each other. It turned out we'd even gone to the same school, but I didn't remember her. I wasn't serious about her, it was just a little fun, and anyway she had a kid of her own and I wasn't interested in getting involved in any of that. But then one day she tells me she's pregnant and I told her to her face, it was her business not mine. What she do is up to her.'

He doesn't blink an eye when he tells me this story. It's as though it doesn't even occur to him that I might find his attitude repellent. He is who he is, he's done what he's done, and everything that happens as a result is of little consequence to him.

He goes on to tell me other stories from his life, some of which are incredibly funny, others shocking in their callousness, and I wonder whether any of them are entirely true. More than likely they are nothing more than craven attempts to rewrite history, to present me with a version of himself he's happy for me to take away. When the bell rings signalling the end of visitation, I think we're both surprised by how quickly the time has flown.

He stands and gives me a look that if I didn't know better, I'd say was one of begrudging admiration.

He grins. 'You take care, Prince Charles,' he says, shaking my hand.

'You too,' I reply, and then I watch as he joins the line of inmates and then disappears through the large grey door through which he came.

33

Kerry

Friday, 1st July

'Okay then,' says Noah, 'I'd better be getting off. There's leek and potato soup in the fridge and I picked up some nice fresh rolls this morning to go with it, which I've left on the counter. There are three ready meals in the fridge for supper, but you and Kian go ahead and have yours without me if I'm not back before you get hungry. I'm hoping to be home for seven at the latest, earlier if I can. I'll have my phone on the entire time, but obviously not while I'm actually in the prison. But I've spoken to my mum and she said if you need anything, then give her a call.'

'That's lovely of your mum,' I say. 'But I told you, I'll be fine. You're going to Nottingham not New York. Now get a move on or you're going to miss your train.'

He picks up his briefcase but then just stands there like a lemon. I can see he's in two minds whether to go or not, and part of me wants to tell him to stay here and not go anywhere near that scally of a dad of his. But I can't. This is something he needs to do.

'All right then,' he says in the end, 'but don't get doing anything silly again like trying to defrost the freezer or change the beds. I'll get all that sorted, okay? Just promise me you'll have a lazy day and concentrate on keeping your strength up.'

I nod my head and give him a quick salute. 'Yes, sir! Anything else?'

I think he must feel a bit bad because he comes over and gives me a peck on the cheek. 'I'm sorry,' he says. 'I don't mean to be bossy, I just want you to get better.'

'I know you do,' I say, fighting the urge to beg him not to go. 'But don't forget I worry about you too. Don't let him take advantage of you, all right? Don't make him any promises. And whatever you do, don't invite him to come and stay with you when he gets out. You've got enough long-lost relatives living with you as it is.'

After he's gone, I go and stand by the big window in the living room like I do every day when he goes out to take Kian to school. I like to wait and watch them come out on to the street and then cross the road at the traffic lights in front of the building and make their way to the Tube. I like to watch them chatting away together, although to be honest, Kian barely lets Noah get a word in edgeways. Who knows what he's talking about? PlayStation games, skateboarding, space exploration, I never really know what's going to come out of his mouth from one minute to the next. I just like watching them walking along in a little world of their own. It's the next best thing to being right there with them.

I lose sight of Noah and Kian when a couple of buses pull up across the road, and by the time they've driven off they're nowhere to be seen. I stay standing, looking out of the window anyway. Most days what's going on out there is much better than what's on the telly. There's never a dull moment. Argy-bargies between motorcyclists and taxi drivers; delivery vans holding up the traffic and causing chaos; people rushing to work here, there and every-where; young mums taking their kids to school. I see it all from up here, just like I could if I stood staring out of my front window at home, I suppose. Not that when I was back there I had the time, or the inclination. I was always too concerned about the state of the inside of the flat to worry much about what was going on outside. Which is probably just as well, considering some of the hair-raising stuff that goes on around there.

Through the window, I spot a couple of regulars: people I've made whole stories up about just to entertain myself. There's Jogging Man With Dog, who comes by at exactly the same time every day with a filthy great big Labrador attached to him with some sort of funny belt. I've told myself that he's a personal trainer to the stars and by the time I see him I reckon he's already done a full day's work shouting at rich people in their home gyms, and running with the dog is his way of relaxing. Then there's Old Guy In A Mac. He walks really slowly but ramrod straight and always pulling a shopping trolley behind him. I reckon he must be a retired professor or something, who misses being around people, so every morning he packs a shopping trolley full of books and goes and sits in the café across the road and reads. Just as I'm about to sit down, I spot the Rich Widow. She's my absolute favourite. She's about my age but wears completely mad clothes: leopard-print fur coat, red leather trouser-suit tight enough to make your eyes water, and always heels like stilts. She totters by every day, clutching a massive handbag I reckon is stuffed full of cash her mad millionaire husband left her in his will. I like to think she's got a Latvian lover or two, and spends her day shopping and living the life of Riley.

I could stand here people-watching all day but I feel guilty if I do it for too long, so I come away and start tidying up a bit. I can't do much because Noah will have a right go if he sees I've not been resting, but I can't just sit and see things that need doing. I tidy up the kitchen a bit, but have to stop every five minutes for a breather. Then I try to put on a load of washing, but just bending down to empty the clothes basket is enough to send me dizzy. I even have a go at tackling the nightmare that is Kian's room, but I don't get much further than putting a few things away before I feel so tired that I have to lie down on his bed.

I only mean to rest my eyes, not fall asleep for two hours, but that's exactly what happens. For a minute when I wake up, I've got no idea where I am, and it takes me a while to get my bearings. I'd been dreaming something rotten, but it was a nice dream, not a nightmare. Me and Kian were sitting on a beach having a picnic; I think we must have been on holiday or something. We were laughing and joking and then Noah and Millie turned up, and I remember thinking to myself that I was really happy, and never wanted it to end.

★

I'm halfway through my soup and roll when Jodi calls. I only told her about my cancer the day after I started chemo. I don't know why I left it so long, I suppose it was because I knew that the moment I did, she'd drop everything and come and see me. And as much as I wanted to see her, what with her being pregnant and Mark's mum's dementia getting worse by the day, I knew she already had more than her fair share to deal with and I didn't want to add to the load. Plus my consultant had warned me that with the chemo, my immune system wouldn't be up to much. So it's just been one of those things. Either I've felt too rough to see anyone, or she's had to steer clear because one of the kids has got some bug or other and she's scared I'll catch it.

It's lovely to hear her voice and we chat for ages: about her pregnancy, the kids and Mark's new job. I even tell her about Noah going to see his dad today and how worried I am. The one thing we don't talk about is the cancer, because she knows I don't want to think about it too much. I just tell her that I'm feeling good, and keeping positive, and I leave it at that. But I know, in that way you do when you're talking to someone who knows you inside out, that all the time we're talking she's reading between the lines, using all her powers to try to work out whether or not I'm telling her the truth.

It feels good talking to Jodi, really good, and it perks me right up. Though I can't manage the rest of the soup and roll, I do at least finish making Kian's bed before my batteries start to run low again. Sitting down on the bed for a minute, I look around the room at his things. When we came to stay with Noah, he'd insisted on bringing his action figures, his Lego and his Nerf guns, even though I hadn't seen him play with them for a year or more. These days it's all about his PlayStation, his phone and his skateboard, so you'd think he was too big for toys. But any time I mention getting rid and putting them on eBay, he has a right strop. I suppose that's the thing about growing up when you're his age. It's one thing growing out of something, it's another letting go for good.

I make myself a cuppa. I'm into green tea at the moment, after finding a box tucked away at the back of Noah's cupboard. It tasted like grass cuttings to begin with but I quite like it now, and it's supposed to be good for you so I reckon it's worth a go.

I flick on the TV but there's nothing much on. I watch half of an old *Columbo*, but when the adverts come on I flick over to another channel and end up watching a repeat of *Escape To The Country*. The old couple on the show are downsizing because their kids are all grown up. Mind you, the place they're looking at is twice the size of mine. They're a funny pair. She likes modern stuff and he likes old-fashioned things, and I can't see any way that they'll both be happy. But the show gets me thinking about houses, and what a lick of paint can do.

I love living with Noah, and I know Kian does too, but I miss my little flat and I can't wait to go back. I remember the day I got the keys. I'd only seen it the day before, and I knew I had to act fast or it would be given to someone else. The place was a right mess; I think the previous tenants had been kicked out, and there were still a load of rubbish bags and junk piled up in the living room, waiting to be taken away. Most people would've turned their noses up at it, but I had a real picture in my head of what it could be like with a good scrub and a coat of paint.

I couldn't afford to do all the things I wanted to do straight away, but bit by bit, month by month I made it better, until one day I looked round and it was exactly how I wanted it. I was so proud of it that when I bumped into the bloke from the council who'd first shown me round, I couldn't help myself, I practically dragged him off the street and showed him everything I'd done. I was so chuffed when he told me that he wouldn't have recognised the place. All I could think was: 'I did this, turned a dump into a proper home!'

I pick up my phone and flick through my photos until I find the ones I'd sent to Jodi a while back to show her my new bed set. Seeing my room like this makes me feel a bit homesick, but I tell myself that me and Kian will be back there in no time. For now, I've just got to concentrate on getting better.

★

Mid-afternoon I get myself ready to go out, as Noah's booked a taxi so I can pick Kian up from school. I told him I could manage on the Tube but he was having none of it, and now as I bend down to tie my shoelaces, I'm actually quite glad he bullied me into it. I feel shattered. Absolutely worn out. Like I could fall asleep on my feet, given half the chance.

The traffic is terrible, so when we pull up outside the school gates we're so late that there are already kids streaming every-where. For a minute I panic that I might have missed him. But then sure enough, I spot him coming round the corner chatting to his mates like he's got all the time in the world. As I watch him, just like I watched all those different people this morning, I imagine what sort of stories I'd make up about him if he wasn't mine. I look at his messy hair and his shirt all untucked. I look at his bag half open and slung over his shoulder. I look at the cheeky smile on his face and the mischievous glint in his eyes. From the outside I don't think I'd imagine him to be anything but trouble. From the outside I'd probably name him Scruffy Kid and imagine him running rings around his poor mum all day every day. But then he looks up and catches sight of me, and I can't help it. I can't look at him from the outside any more. He's not some stranger. He's my gorgeous boy.

Just like that, I feel my heart swelling with gladness.

For him.

For love.

For life.

For everything.

And it fills me with the kind of hope I haven't felt in a very long time. Hope that I'm going to beat this disease. Hope that I'm going to see my boy not just grow up and become a man, but have a family and kids of his own. And suddenly I'm not worried about the appointment with my consultant next week, because I'm just so full of all this hope. Hope that the treatment I've suffered through has done its job. Hope that I'm on the mend. Hope that I've finally beat this thing for good.

PART 4

8th September 2003

Dear Jason,

You're twenty-one today! Happy birthday! I really do hope you're having an amazing day. As always, there's a card that comes with this letter (Ha! I never forget!).

Twenty-one was a bit of an odd one for me. I didn't have a bloke or a family and to be honest, not much of a life. Because of this, I did a lot of thinking about where I was going and how I wanted things to be.

Now I'm twenty-nine, of course I know it's not that big a deal. You don't have to have all your ducks lined up in a row to be happy. You just have to live life well, and that's exactly what I try to do every day.

So how is this big birthday for you? Is it making you think about your life? I don't mean this horribly, but I really hope it is. Of course I want you to be happy. It's all I ever wanted. But I'm still here, Jason, and I'm still waiting for you to come and find me. I know you'll do it someday, I just know you will, but sometimes I wish you'd hurry up so we can get on with being a family again.

That's the thing I miss most of all, I think: family. The thing that no one really tells you is just how lonely life can be without it. Of course I've got mates, I've got a job that I sort of enjoy, and I've got a place to call home, but I'd give the whole lot up like a shot just to have someone to belong to.

Sometimes I think about just having a kid. I think being pregnant would be amazing. I think having a tiny human being growing inside me would just be so wonderful. And then when it's born I'd get to look after it, and give it all the love and care it needs. How great would that be? A son or daughter for me, a little niece or nephew for you. Could you imagine how happy we'd all be?

So what's stopping me? I don't know if this will make much sense, but the truth is you're stopping me. I feel like if I have a kid, if I just get on with the rest of my life, it'll be like giving up on you, and I don't ever want to do that.

I'm sorry to be rambling on like this on your birthday. It's probably the last thing you need. I just miss you, Jason. I just miss you so much.

Kerry xxx

34

Noah

Tuesday, 6th September

I don't quite know what I'd imagined it would be like. Perhaps something more medical and austere, akin to some of the hospital rooms that Kerry has been in and out of over the course of the past few months. But the room we're now standing in couldn't be more different. It's more home than hospital, with the emphasis on comfort and calm rather than brutal medical efficiency. It overlooks a sunny garden packed with flowers and shrubs, some of which, even though it's September, are still in bloom. There's a small ornamental pond to one side complete with a gently flowing water feature, the restful sounds of which can be heard through Kerry's open window.

The accommodation itself is unexpectedly generous and is kitted out like a smart studio flat. The walls have been painted in muted lemon tones with flooring and soft furnishings to complement. It has its own front door and entrance hall, a small sitting area complete with television, a kitchenette with a microwave, hob and, much to Kerry's delight, a dishwasher. At the end of the hall is a small guest room with a double bed, and next to that is Kerry's bedroom. Like the sitting area, Kerry's bedroom also overlooks the garden but has the benefit of the shade cast by a large oak tree. Although she has been given a hospital bed, it's been heavily disguised with all manner of cushions, throws and blankets so that it resembles something one might have at home. Although Kerry can bring in as many personal items as she chooses, there are already a number of tasteful paintings depicting peaceful country scenes, along with a scattering of homely ornaments.

I look over at Kerry sitting in her wheelchair by the bedroom window, Kian standing next to her, his arm around her shoulder. The two are gazing out of the window, Kerry's slight frame bent forward so that she can better see the trio of chaffinches squabbling on the bird feeder hanging from one of the branches of the oak tree. They remain enrapt, pointing and laughing at the antics of the birds, until sensing me watching, Kerry turns her head and smiles.

'It's beautiful, isn't it?' she says. 'I'm going to have a lot of fun watching those cheeky fellas.' She laughs to herself. 'Who'd have thought it? Me, Kerry Hayes, former teenage tearaway, a birdwatcher?'

Kian laughs. 'Don't worry, Mum, *EastEnders* is on later if you get bored.'

Kerry gives Kian a playful swipe. 'You're lucky I can't move as fast as I used to or I'd give you a smack for being cheeky.' She pulls him to her and plants a gentle kiss on his cheek. 'You're right though, I can't imagine I'm going to spend all day just watching birds. Nice as they are, they're not that interesting.' She looks up at me, a big grin on her face. 'This place is perfect, Noah, thanks so much for sorting it out.'

I nod and smile. 'It was nothing, really.'

'Don't give me that,' she says. 'I know the trouble you've gone to and I know that this wasn't what you wanted for me. But I'm telling you now, this is even better than what I had in mind.' She gives Kian another peck on the cheek. 'Right then,' she announces, 'no point standing around like lemons, let's get me moved in properly so I can sort us all out a nice cup of tea.'

When the consultant broke the news back in July that Kerry's treatment hadn't worked, that the tumour had resisted the chemotherapy, that there was nothing more they could do beyond helping to manage her pain, I was stunned. In the days leading up to her appointment, Kerry almost seemed to have turned a corner. She'd been so much brighter and happier than I'd seen her for weeks, so optimistic about the treatment and her future that I was convinced she was getting better. With her appointment looming, I think we'd both assumed it would be good news. I'd even planned to take us all out that evening for a celebratory meal. So to hear those words, to see the disbelief and shock on Kerry's face, to digest even partially the meaning of her consultant's prognosis felt totally and utterly unreal. So much so that the first words out of my mouth were: 'This can't be happening,' and the next were to tell Kerry that the consultant must be mistaken and we'd seek a second opinion.

I think, in the end, Kerry only agreed to see the private consultant I'd arranged for my benefit. Of the two of us, she has always been more of a realist, she's had to be, and so in the days between her prognosis and the private appointment, I think she'd come to accept reality. Something I had no choice but to do, once the second doctor pronounced his complete agreement with the conclusions of the first.

Despite all the medical team's best efforts, Kerry's cancer had continued to spread. It had now infiltrated her bowels, bladder, the lining of her abdomen, and had begun to affect her liver too. Kerry had asked her consultant, as I suppose everyone does in situations like these, how long she had left, and his reply had been infuriatingly vague: 'It's difficult to say, it could be weeks, it could be months, but what matters most is that you enjoy the time you have.'

That evening, after Kian had gone to bed and I sat on the sofa next to Kerry, frantically trawling the Internet for news of experimental treatments, Kerry told me she had something urgent to discuss. As I closed the lid of the laptop, I knew exactly what it was.

I held her hand. 'You don't have to worry for a single moment. I'll look after Kian and love him with everything I've got. You don't need to worry at all.' All at once the magnitude of what was happening hit me and though I tried my hardest not to cry, I couldn't help it. I couldn't believe this was happening. We still had so much lost time to recover, so much left to talk about and discover. It wasn't fair that her life was being cut so short when she still had so much living to do.

Kerry squeezed my hand tightly and I could see that she was crying too.

'I'll get a new place,' I said, forcing out the words as I struggled to maintain control. 'Somewhere with a garden so Kian and I can play football. And I'll make sure he goes to school, I promise. He'll get a good education and . . . and . . .' I didn't finish. I couldn't. Not when Kerry was holding me so tightly. Not when all I could hear was the heartfelt relief as she whispered again and again, 'Thank you, Noah, thank you.'

I wasn't at home the following evening when Kerry told Kian. I'd offered my support of course, but she had insisted that this was something she needed to do alone. So I'd busied myself with meaningless errands until she told me it was done. With adults bad news seems to age them, but children seem to regress to an earlier, more vulnerable stage, something I had witnessed first-hand when encountering the families of victims or indeed of clients I was defending.

Kian was no exception, and in the hours and days that followed he was noticeably clingy, unable to fall asleep unless she was in his bed, anxious whenever she was out of the room.

In an effort to distract him, I involved Kian in making plans for some of the things Kerry said she would like to do with the time that remained. Together we looked at holiday cottages by the sea, booked a tour of Buckingham Palace, organised a carriage ride around central London, and even investigated the logistics of flying her to Mexico City so that she could see her beloved Mariah Carey perform live. As it was, however, Kerry's health deteriorated far more quickly than any of us expected. And following an infection that led to her being hospitalised on a number of occasions, we soon realised that none of our plans were going to come to fruition. Instead we turned our attention to making Kerry as comfortable as we could. I arranged for more of her things to be brought over to the apartment, Kian helping me to choose bits and pieces he thought would make her feel at home. On the day they were due to arrive, however, Kerry sat me down while Kian was at school and told me that she wanted to start looking at hospices.

'I know what you're going to say,' she said. 'You're going to say that you want me to stay here. Or even that you'll move with me back to my flat, that wherever we are, you'll make it all nice, and I'm grateful, Noah. You know I am. But I've got to think about Kian. Let's face it, we don't know how bad things are going to get or for how long. If I stay here with you guys, you'll be stuck with me, you won't be able to relax, escape, or have any sort of breather. It'll just be me, me, me, twenty-four seven and I don't want that for either of you. If I go to a hospice, you can come and visit, and Ida told me there are ones where friends and family can even stay overnight. But the important thing is that you can always leave, that your home remains your home. That my little place remains in Kian's memory the home where we had so much fun. That's what I want, just to keep things nice and simple.'

I started the search for a hospice the very next day and although I'd been prepared to pay whatever it took to get Kerry the best care possible, it turned out that the one recommended to her by Ida was exactly what she had in mind. A week after our visit I received a call to say that a space had become available and we accepted immediately.

It doesn't take us long to bring in Kerry's things. All she has is a couple of suitcases, some framed photographs and a box of knick-knacks that Kian and I had collected from the flat the night before.

Once everything is put away Kerry insists on making us a pot of tea, while Kian and I figure out how to put the TV on. When she's finished in the kitchenette we get her into bed so she can rest, and then arrange a pair of chairs so that we can sit and talk.

We chat about the chaffinches again, about the dinner menu that has just been brought in by one of the care assistants, about Kian's homework that Kerry is worried he isn't keeping on top of. In fact we talk about everything apart from the one thing on all our minds: that this, right here, right now, is our first step towards saying goodbye.

After about an hour, Kerry starts to look tired, and so I tell

Kian that it's time we made a move. Kerry gives us each a kiss and a hug, and for a moment I think that Kian might cry, but before he has time Kerry, clearly far more attuned to what her son needs than I am, starts to berate him about his homework again and it seems to do the trick.

By rights Kian should have started at Melbourne Park, Kerry's chosen secondary school for him, by now, and he'd even attended their induction day back in July, but with Kerry's condition worsening by the day, a decision was made that for the time being at least, he should spend as much time as he can with his mum. And so it was agreed that the school would give him a number of projects to do when and if he had time, of which the Tudors was his least favourite.

'I'm warning you, Kian,' she says, making an effort to put on a stern face, 'if Uncle Noah tells me tomorrow that you still haven't finished your Tudor project I will go absolutely mental. Do you understand?' Kian nods. 'Right then,' she says, 'come and give me a kiss and go and wait in reception while I have a quick word with your Uncle Noah.' She reaches into her handbag, takes out a purse and empties out some change. 'Get yourself some crisps or something from the machine while you're waiting.'

She listens carefully for the sound of the front door closing before she speaks. 'Listen,' she says, 'I don't want you going home and worrying about me. It's lovely here, the doctors and nurses are ever so kind, and I'm really looking forward to the aroma-therapy hand massage I've got booked in for tomorrow. So you and Kian need to go and do something nice. Don't sit around the flat moping, don't feel guilty for having a good time. All I want is for you both to be happy. And if I know you're working on that, then I can relax.' She smiles. 'And you want me to relax, don't you?'

I wonder just how it is that she manages to make something that's of benefit to me seem like it's doing her a favour. If circumstances had been different, I have no doubt she would have made a brilliant advocate.

'Of course I do,' I say. 'But in return you have to promise me that if you need anything at all, or change your mind about being here, then you'll let me know.'

'Scout's honour.'

I make sure she's comfortable, kiss her goodbye and then go out to find Kian. He's standing at the reception desk, chatting away to the old lady on duty.

I smile at the woman behind the desk and she smiles back. The reception here is staffed by a small army of elderly ladies, who I imagine are volunteering their time as a way of saying thank you for the way their relatives and friends have been cared for here.

'This is my Uncle Noah,' says Kian, offering her a crisp. 'He's a barrister, which means he has to do things in court and sometimes he wears a wig.'

'Is that right?' The old lady smiles. 'He must be a very clever man.'

'I don't know about that,' I say, looking at Kian. 'I suppose I've just been lucky.' I take a crisp from Kian, ruffle his hair and say, 'How do you feel about a quick visit to the skatepark before we crack on with your project?'

He looks at me anxiously. 'But what about Mum? She doesn't really like me going on a school night.'

I think for a moment about going back inside to check that this is okay with Kerry but stop myself. This isn't a drill, this isn't a rehearsal and there isn't going to be a last-minute reprieve. A time is coming soon when I'll have to make countless decisions like this for Kian, decisions without clear guidance, decisions where all I'll have to go on will be my own judgment. With this in mind I realise that I have to start as I mean to go on, to project a certainty to Kian that I might not feel, but owe him nonetheless.

'I know,' I say, 'but everything's a bit upside down right now. So I think she'd say that it was okay, just this once.'

35

Kerry

Thursday, 29th September

'Are you sure I can't get you another cuppa or anything?'

I squeeze Jodi's hand. Bless her, she's trying her hardest not to cry. 'No, love, you get off or you'll miss your train.'

'Maybe that's no bad thing,' she says. 'Mark and the kids are doing all right without me, and I could bunk down in that spare room of yours again. I know you weren't up for much last night, but you're looking a lot brighter today. Perhaps tonight after Kian and Noah have gone home, we could have a proper girls' night . . . a couple of glasses of wine, a nice box of chocolates and some crap on the telly that we can have a laugh at . . .' She starts to cry then, in spite of herself, like she's remembering all the good times we've had over the years.

'Now stop that,' I say, as a wall of tears builds up in my own eyes, 'or you'll have me at it.'

'I'm sorry, Kerry,' she says. 'It's just . . .'

'I know,' I say, giving her a smile. This is our goodbye. The end of our story, and we both know it.

I point to her belly. 'Listen,' I say. 'You've got that baby to think about, as well as all the rest of them. You need to get back home. But I'm so glad you came. I'm so glad we've had this chance to have a proper catch-up. I know how hard it's been for you to get away, but this time with you, talking about the old days, laughing 'til my sides ache, has done me the world of good.'

She doesn't say anything for a minute. She just bends over the bed and puts her arms around me, holding me tight like she's never going to let go. I feel like we would've stayed like that, but then there's a knock at the door and a nurse comes in to give me my medication.

Jodi kisses my cheek. 'I'll love you forever, you know,' she says, and then she finally lets me go.

When she's gone, I look around the room. It's jam-packed with plants, flowers and cards, enough for me to open a florist's of my own. I've said a lot of goodbyes over the past two weeks but this, well this has been the worst yet. There's been a steady trickle of people popping in to see me. Neighbours, girls I used to work with, school mums, and a couple of people I met through chemo, including Ida, who's looking really well at the minute. Even a couple of my clients have stopped by: Mrs Greig and her husband came with flowers and a tin of home-made biscuits; Jane Edwards visited after work one night and gave me some of those gorgeous scented candles that cost an arm and a leg. Even Mrs Ryman, bless her, though she hasn't been too well herself, has phoned at least half a dozen times and sent over a posh basket of fruit from Fortnum & Mason of all places.

I'd put Jodi off from coming for as long as I could, because I knew it would be hard for her to see me like this. I can't get out of bed at all now, haven't been able to for over a week. I just feel so tired all the time, and my mind is constantly wandering, making it hard for me to concentrate. I know it's not going to be long now. I've accepted that. That's why I gave Jodi the green light. I didn't want her running up and down the country every five minutes. She's got enough on her plate as it is. No, if I had to say goodbye to Jodi, I was going to do it once and do it properly, and last night was it.

Once the nurse has cleared off, I close my eyes for a bit just to rest them, but I must have nodded off because the next thing I know, there's a knock at the door and when I glance at the clock on the wall, I can see I've been asleep for a good two hours. I'm still rubbing the sleep out of my eyes when Millie trots into the room, followed by Rosalind. For a minute I think I'm seeing things. The night before I could've sworn I saw a girl I used to go to school with in my room, still looking exactly as she did back in the Eighties, but I must have been dreaming.

But then Millie rushes over to me clutching a huge bunch of flowers, so pretty and lively, just like her. She rests them on the bed and then puts her hands on mine and I feel their warmth and realise this is no dream.

'Hi, Auntie Kerry,' she says, 'Dad's running late so Mum offered to bring me.'

Rosalind smiles shyly at me from the doorway. 'I hope you don't mind.'

'Mind? I'm over the moon. It's lovely to finally get to meet you properly. Come in and sit down.' I think back to the first time we met on the day of Kian's party and how furious she'd been. She looks like a different person now. Still gorgeous and stylish as ever, but without the anger I can see the gentleness in her face, and the kindness in her eyes.

Without letting go of my hand, Millie takes a seat and Rosalind sits next to her. She's wearing a simple denim jacket over a plain white cotton dress, and yet somehow she still manages to look like she's just stepped out of the pages of a fashion mag.

Millie chats away at me ten to the dozen, hardly pausing for breath. She tells me so many stories it's hard to keep up. She tells me about her school Latin trip to the British Museum; some friend of hers who broke her arm roller-skating; a new girl in her class who has been winding her up something rotten; and lots more that I can't remember. She's such a lovely little bundle of energy. Such a sweet little girl. And I adore her. It's hard to imagine that this time last year we were total strangers.

Rosalind smiles. 'Are you sure we're not wearing you out?'

'Absolutely not,' I reply, and I let Millie finish telling me all her news before I send her off on a mission.

'I need you to go and find me a purple vase,' I say.

'Purple?' Millie pulls a face. 'Why's it got to be purple?'

'To go with those gorgeous lilacs,' I say, nodding to the bouquet. 'And while you're at it, ask Karen on reception if they've got those new fancy chocolate biscuits back in the shop yet, and if she has, get me two packets, please. There's some money in a pot near the door.'

As Millie leaves the room I turn to look at Rosalind.

'Thank you so much for bringing her,' I say. 'She always cheers me up. You and Noah have done such an amazing job with her, you really have. She's an absolute credit to you both.'

Rosalind smiles. 'Thank you, that's very kind of you.'

'I'm just being honest,' I say. 'Which sort of brings me to why I've sent Millie on a bit of a wild-goose chase.'

She raises an eyebrow. 'A goose chase?'

'The vase cupboard is pretty big,' I explain. 'She'll be ages sorting through that, and the women on reception never stop talking so it should give me enough time to say what needs to be said.'

'About what?' She looks down and tucks a stray strand of hair behind her ear.

'About how sorry I am. I feel terrible the way I've turned your life upside down. I want you to know that I never wanted to come between you and Noah. Not for a minute. I'm sorry.'

'Oh, Kerry,' she says, 'you've got nothing to apologise for. Noah and I had problems long before you came back into his life.'

'I know, and that's sort of what I want to talk to you about too. I don't want to speak out of turn but please, please give him another chance. I know he's got his faults, and from what I understand those faults have made him difficult to live with, but I just want you to know that there's a reason he's like he is.'

'Because he was adopted?'

I shake my head. 'I haven't told Noah this. Somehow I don't think he wants to know. But in lots of ways he had a much worse start in life than I did. Even though he was young, and probably can't remember the half of it, those things are in there somewhere, and they always come out.'

Rosalind looks at me intently. 'What happened?'

I think about all the times I'd gone to tell Noah this, times

when I'd felt guilty keeping it from him when he had every right
to know. I almost told him that day when I said about my cancer.
I thought to myself, why am I keeping this one thing back when
I'm coming clean about everything else? It made no sense. But
I just couldn't do it to him. Not on top of everything else. Anyway,
if he'd really wanted to know, it wouldn't have been that hard to
find out. I know for a fact it's all there in black and white in the
reports the social workers had written about us, because a few
years back I'd seen them for myself. But for whatever reason,
Noah had chosen not to dig too deeply into his past and who
was I to argue?

I look at Rosalind, the woman at the centre of my brother's
world, and I realise as if for the first time that even though we
couldn't be more different on the surface, we do have one thing
in common: our love for Noah.

So I take a deep breath and I tell her everything.

The story of our childhood.

The reason Noah and I were taken into care.

The reason I am the way I am and he is the way he is.

And by the end of it we're both in tears.

'Oh, Kerry,' says Rosalind when I've finished. 'I had no idea. It
must have been so hard for you. And to think you went through
all that and you were even younger than Millie is now. I can't
bear it.' She gets up and stands by the window, looking out into
the garden without saying a word.

'I'm so sorry,' she says eventually. 'It's just so shocking. Poor
you. Poor Noah. I just don't know what to say.'

'Say you'll give him another chance. He's a good man, and
you and Millie are his world. You can make him right, I know
you can. If anyone can make this mess right, it's you and your
love for him.'

By the time Millie finally returns, proudly clutching a dusty
purple vase and two packets of chocolate biscuits, Rosalind and
I have both dried our eyes and pulled ourselves together. I don't
know whether what I've said will make a difference. It might be

a case of too little too late, but I'm glad she knows the truth, whatever she decides to do with it.

Millie, Rosalind and I chat for a bit longer over tea and biscuits, but somewhere along the way I must nod off again, because when I open my eyes they've gone and it's dark outside. For a minute I think I'm on my own, but then I spot Noah and Kian in the kitchenette. Kian notices straight away that I'm awake and rushes over to say hello and give me one of his lovely big cuddles. All his embarrassment about giving me hugs and kisses in public has gone out of the window now. He can't get enough these days. First thing in the morning, last thing at night, and everything in between, I absolutely get more than my fair share.

'Mum,' he says, 'you will not believe what happened to me at karate today . . .' and he goes on to tell me a long story about how he nearly got picked to compete in his first karate competition and only just missed getting a place. His teacher has told him that if he practises really hard, he'll definitely get to be in the next one.

It's lovely to see him so happy, so full of beans, and I let him snuggle up in bed next to me while he tells me who did get picked, and all the argy-bargy it's caused. As we talk, Noah watches. He looks tired, like he could do with a decent night's sleep. I do worry about him. I feel like this is tearing him apart but he just won't admit it. Any time I try to talk to him about it, he just says, 'I'm fine, don't you worry about me,' and then carries on as normal, as if his heart, like mine, isn't breaking in two.

'Are you hungry?' I ask.

Kian nods, but Noah says, 'I'm fine, thanks, Kerry.'

'Course you're not,' I tell him. 'If you don't eat, you're going to waste away at this rate.'

Noah pulls a face. 'Okay,' he says with a smile, 'I'll sort something out.'

Keen to help, Kian follows his uncle into the kitchen and the two of them start preparing a meal: getting the food out of the fridge, searching for plates and cups, working out how to use the microwave. It's nice watching them together like this, standing side by side at the kitchen counter, chatting away to each other.

This is how it's going to be from now on.

Kian and Noah.

Noah and Kian.

The two people I love most in the world, coming together.

On paper you wouldn't think it would work, what with them coming from such different worlds. But they're connected through things much more important than what school you went to, or what your mum and dad do for a living, and I don't doubt for a moment that it'll be enough to get them both through whatever this life throws at them. Noah will be there for Kian in all the moments I always hoped I would be. He'll be there to talk him through first loves and heartbreak; he'll be there to keep him on the straight and narrow, should Kian ever be tempted to wobble; he'll be there to celebrate all the birthdays, the milestones, the successes that I know are coming Kian's way. And it doesn't bother me that he won't always do it my way, because what matters most is that he's there at all. My boy won't ever have to be alone, he won't ever have to feel like it's just him against the world. He'll always know that he's got someone in his corner, someone who's got his back, someone he can rely on even when times are tough. That's all I could ask for, all I could hope for, for my beautiful boy. It gives me all the peace I need.

36

Noah

Sunday, 2nd October

'Uncle Noah,' says Kian, as we watch a squirrel raiding one of the bird feeders hanging from a branch in front of us. 'Do you think Mum can hear us when we talk to her?'

I consider Kian and his question carefully. 'Yes,' I say. 'I'm sure she can.'

'But I don't see how, when she's asleep all the time.'

'The human brain is truly amazing. It can do lots of different things all at the same time. And because of that, it means that even though your mum looks like she's asleep, she's still taking in all the sounds, and the smells, and the feelings that she would do normally.'

He thinks for a moment. 'Do you think she's scared?'

'Not at all.' I bite my lip, then continue. 'There's nothing to be scared of. Not that I can imagine your mum being scared of anything much, can you?'

Kian raises a small smile. 'When I was in year two, an animal man came into school with a massive tarantula. None of the other mums would touch it but Mum did. She even let it walk all the way up her arm.'

'Exactly,' I say. 'That's your mum all over: absolutely fearless.'

Kian sighs heavily and kicks a stone at his feet. 'She's not going to wake up, is she?'

I put my arm around him. It's such a difficult question to answer. I'm terrified of saying the wrong thing but at the same time, I'm all he has. Since he has been brave enough to ask the question, the very least I can do is offer an answer.

'No, I'm not sure she is,' I reply. 'But she knows we're here, and she can feel us holding her hand and hear us telling her how much we love her. So that's what we need to carry on doing.'

It's been three days now since Kerry has been conscious for any longer than a few minutes at a time, and even when she is awake, she seems confused and incoherent. Partly it's because she's getting gradually weaker, and partly it's because her pain medication has been increased in an effort to make her as comfortable as possible. Although the doctors and nurses haven't said as much, it seems obvious to me that Kerry hasn't long left and because of that, Kian and I have stopped returning home at night and have now moved into the guest room. With the exception of the occasional spell in the grounds to clear our heads as we're doing now, sitting on a bench, soaking up the early-morning October sun while the nurses attend to Kerry, we haven't left her side.

It would have been easy to feel overwhelmed by the massive responsibility of caring for a child I'd known for such a relatively short space of time. But these aren't normal circumstances, and Kian and I have become incredibly close in the face of our shared sorrow. It is as if we are the only two people in the world who truly know how the other is feeling, without having to explain. We've both watched Kerry grow weaker by the day, we've seen her struggle, and we've both had to stand helplessly by as the woman we love, who has embodied life and spirit, has begun to slip away from us.

As a result we've clung together all the more tightly, neither of us daring to think much beyond the day that lies ahead. Each morning when we wake, sometimes still in the chairs by her bed, others lying fully clothed on top of the bed in the spare room, the first thing either of us do is check on Kerry. Make sure that we haven't lost her, that she is still hanging on. The relief we feel to be given another day with her is the fuel that is getting us through this nightmare. In the long term this is, of course, unsustainable, we know that, but for the time being it is all we have.

Over the days since she had begun to fade away, we've

established a routine of sorts. We'll sit by Kerry's bedside, telling her and each other stories, learning each other's histories, trying desperately to hang on to some semblance of normality in a situation that is anything but. The visitors who arrive help lessen the sense that we're simply filling in time. They help us remember that there's life outside the hospice, that Kerry is more than her illness, more than just a woman lying in a hospital bed. More even than just a sister or a mother, she is a confidante, a mentor and a friend.

We sit for a little while longer, enjoying the peace of the garden, then in silent agreement we stand up and go back indoors. As we pass the reception desk, the lady on duty tells us that Kerry has a visitor and looking through the glass doors of the day room we spot a smartly dressed elderly lady sitting in an armchair, with a walking-frame positioned to one side. I have no idea who she is and I'm about to ask, when Kian exclaims, 'It's Mrs Ryman,' and then runs in to see her.

I follow Kian into the day room, and when I reach them the elderly lady is beaming at Kian and telling him how much he has grown since she last saw him.

'I'm sorry,' I say, 'I don't think we've met. I'm Noah, Kerry's brother.'

Despite my protests, Mrs Ryman reaches for her walking-frame and struggles to her feet. 'I like to do things properly,' she says, shaking my hand. 'Although the truth is, I feel as if I know you already. Kerry's told me so much about you. She's so very proud of you, Noah.'

'Thank you,' I reply. 'I forget – how do you know Kerry?'

Mrs Ryman laughs. 'There are many different ways to answer that question, but I suppose the most straightforward response is that she's a very dear friend.'

Kerry doesn't stir as I help Mrs Ryman into one of the chairs next to the bed, while Kian busies himself in the kitchen making tea for us all. I can see that she is shocked to see Kerry's deterioration, although she quickly recovers herself. 'I'm so sorry I haven't been able to visit before now, but I've been in hospital myself. I had a rather nasty fall, and this is the first opportunity I've had.' She reaches across and touches Kerry's hand gently. 'Poor, sweet thing, we have a lot in common she and I. I've always admired her fighting spirit. But I suppose there are some things that can't be fought off forever.' She looks through the doorway into the kitchen and then lowers her voice. 'She doesn't have long, does she? Such a brutal disease. I lost both my parents to cancer. It's never easy.' She puts a hand on mine. 'And how are you managing? I know how close you two have become in such a short space of time.'

'Fine,' I say, automatically, and then I correct myself. 'Actually, that's not true at all. I'm doing terribly.'

'Letting go of somebody you love is never easy,' she says, 'and I think it must be especially difficult given your and Kerry's circumstances.' I nod, momentarily unable to speak. 'Being reunited with you made her so happy. I could see the difference in her immediately. Next to Kian, you are her dearest treasure.'

'Thank you,' I say. 'It means a lot to hear that.'

Kian calls from the kitchenette, asking if Mrs Ryman takes sugar in her tea.

'Sweetener if you have it,' she replies, and as Kian searches through the kitchen cupboards she leans over to me. 'And how's the young man holding up?'

'As well as can be expected.'

'I lost my father when I was young,' she confides, 'and it wasn't considered appropriate for me to see him in his last days. I suppose back then it wasn't the done thing, but it's something I've always regretted. So however hard this is for Kian, please know that you're doing the right thing. A child needs to be able to say goodbye when the time comes. They need to know that they were there for their loved ones when it mattered most.'

When Kian finally brings in our tea, Mrs Ryman tells me the story of how she first met Kerry. 'I wasn't of course as decrepit then as I am now,' she says, 'but the size of the house and my arthritis made it very difficult for me to keep on top of things. The moment I met her I knew we'd get along well. She was just so matter-of-fact about everything. One always knows where one stands with her, and she doesn't suffer fools gladly, which is one of the many traits we share. Her cleaning is always impeccable, and I think it's because she sees her work as a reflection of her own moral standards: it's perfection or nothing. But she is so much more to me than a cleaner. She's a confidante, a comfort and a friend. Nothing is ever too much trouble for her, and no matter how busy she is, she always makes the time to talk. I remember one occasion when I was having a particularly difficult time with one of my neighbours, and Kerry sat talking with me for two solid hours after she was due to leave. Of course, I tried to pay her for her troubles but she wouldn't hear of it. She'd always say, "I know you'd do the same for me," and even though it was true, I really was very grateful.' Mrs Ryman puts an arm around Kian. 'Your mother is a remarkable woman,' she says, addressing him. 'And you are going to be a remarkable young man. Do you know how I know that?' Kian shakes his head. 'Because I can see her in you. Whatever you choose to do in life, young man, I'll tell you this: you will make your mother proud.'

Mrs Ryman stays for an hour in total before she asks me to call for a taxi to take her home. When I receive the text to say that the taxi has arrived, I help her to her feet, and then, leaving Kian holding his mother's hand, I walk her back to reception.

As I stand watching the taxi drive away, I can't help but think of all the lives Kerry has touched and the difference she's made to people like Mrs Ryman. Of the streams of people to have visited, no matter what their background or social status, the common theme of all their commentaries is of Kerry's willingness to help, to listen, to go the extra mile. Obviously I know this from personal experience, but there is something lovely about hearing it from complete strangers, something inspiring, something that makes me want to draw a line in the sand, to be a better person from now on.

As I turn to go back into the building, my phone rings. It's Rosalind.

'Is this a bad time?'

'It's fine. Is everything all right?'

'Everything's fine,' she says. 'I'm just calling to see how things are.'

'Much the same. It won't be long now.'

There's a pause. 'I'm so sorry, Noah. Please let me know what I can do to help.'

'Thank you, I will. It's been so good to have you to talk to these past few days. I think without you, I would've felt like I was losing my mind.'

Ever since I'd told Rosalind that Kerry's cancer was terminal, she had been nothing but supportive. She'd offered help, made food, and had obviously spoken to her solicitors, because mine informed me only last week that she hadn't had a communication from them in weeks. Over the past few days, there's been a subtle but significant shift between us, a depth of feeling, an intensity that hasn't been there for the longest time. I'm not sure what's caused this change – perhaps I'm just misinterpreting her sympathy for something else – but whatever the reason, I've decided not to question it too closely, and instead just be thankful that it's there at all.

'I'm here whenever you need me,' she says, as the call draws to a close. 'But I know you can't talk for long. I just wanted to check in with you, that's all. Mills sends her love and she's asked if she can come and visit at the weekend if possible, but I said we'll have to wait and see.'

'That would be lovely,' I say, 'but, yes, we'll have to wait and see.' She's silent for a moment and I think that's the end of the call, but then she stays on the line and I do too, and we remain that way, connected but silent for several moments more, until finally, after telling me she loves me, she ends the call.

37

Noah

Wednesday, 19th October

'There you go.' We both stare at our reflections in the mirrored wardrobe doors: black suits, crisp white shirts, matching silver sparkly waistcoats and bow ties. 'We look a bit mad, don't we?'

Kian smiles sadly. 'A bit.'

There's a knock at the bedroom door. Millie comes in wearing a long, glittery blue dress, with a matching bow in her hair. 'Mum said to tell you the cars are here.'

'Thanks, Mills. We'll be down in a minute.'

She leaves the room, wafting a trail of her mum's perfume behind her. I sit on the edge of the bed, pat the space beside me and Kian sits down.

'How are you holding up?' I ask, putting an arm around his shoulders.

He shrugs. 'I'm okay.'

'You don't have to be, you know. It's okay to be sad. It's okay to cry, or be angry, or to let out anything else that you're feeling.' He nods but says nothing. 'I suppose what I'm trying to say is that nobody is expecting you to pretend everything's okay. We're all here for you, Kian, all of us, and I'll be right by your side the whole time. You won't be going through any of this on your own. And if you feel like it's all getting a bit too much, if you want to up and leave at any point, then that's fine too. There's no right or wrong on a day like today, we're all just trying to get through it.'

Together Kian and I make our way downstairs, where Rosalind and Millie are waiting for us in the hallway. Rosalind is wearing a black knee-length dress embroidered with silver beads and sequins. Her blonde hair is swept up and held in place by a sparkly silver hairclip.

'Don't they both look handsome?' she says to Millie, and then noticing a strand of white cotton on Kian's lapel, she reaches out and gently brushes it away. 'I've spoken to the driver. He says there's no rush but they're ready whenever we are.'

As we step outside into the thin mid-morning sun, me holding tightly on to Kian's hand, with Millie and Rosalind following closely behind, I wonder what our neighbours make of the sight of us, dressed as we are. With our mix of formal attire and sparkly accessories we could easily be mistaken for a family magic act, but for the hearse and funeral car parked up and waiting in front of the house.

As we walk towards the car, our driver opens the rear door but Kian stops suddenly, his eyes fixed on the hearse in front. Kerry's coffin has a large sparkly silver cloth draped over it, on top of which has been placed a single wreath made up of cream and purple flowers.

For a moment I think this is all going to be too much for him, and I'm about ready to turn around and take him back inside, but then he looks away, squeezes my hand tightly and steps into the car. Once we're all inside, the driver makes eye contact with me in the rear-view mirror and, checking once more to see that Kian is okay, I give him an infinitesimal nod, and we pull away.

Kerry passed away at just after ten o'clock on the morning of Tuesday 4th October. Kian and I had been in our usual seats next to the bed, and he was holding her hand and telling her about our morning walk around the garden. The mischief the squirrel had been up to emptying the bird feeders in preparation for winter; how all the leaves had started changing colour; and how a nice lady on reception had brought in some homemade biscuits and let him choose one. While we'd been made aware that Kerry didn't have long left, it was still a tremendous shock to us both when she finally stopped breathing. Far from being dramatic, it was horribly unremarkable, a shallow breath, followed by another and then nothing. Not knowing what to do, I had pressed the buzzer to summon the nurse, who'd confirmed our worst fears: Kerry was gone.

Still holding his mum's hand, Kian sobbed uncontrollably and all I could do for the longest time was let him. I couldn't take it in. I couldn't believe that the line between life and death was so flimsy, and all that separated the two was the space of a single breath. As the nurse withdrew to give us some privacy, I put my arms around Kian and allowed myself to join him in his grief, and there we remained, united in sorrow, neither of us quite able to comprehend that it was finally over.

I'm not sure how much time passed between that moment and Rosalind's arrival but the next thing I knew, my wife was there carrying the food and clean clothes she'd brought for Kian and me. Finding us like that, adrift and in shock, it had been she who had taken control. Leaving us to say our goodbyes to Kerry, she'd quietly packed our things before taking us home, not to the Bayswater flat but to Primrose Hill.

'You can't be on your own at a time like this,' she'd explained. 'You don't have to go through this alone.'

It was Rosalind's quiet strength and determination that saw Kian and me through the dark days that followed. While we were still lost in the hopelessness of it all, it was she who cooked every meal, handled every difficult phone call, and dealt with all the necessary paperwork. In a sea of confusion and doubt, she was an island of calm and comfort, helping and guiding Kian and me through the seemingly endless decisions that needed to be made. Never once did she allude to the problems between us. Never once did she remind me that this was no longer my home. Instead she held me up, kept me going, and stood by my side, thereby enabling me to do the same for Kian. We were both in her debt, of that I had no doubt, and yet never once did she ask for anything in return.

On our arrival at the crematorium, we are greeted by a sea of glitter and sparkles that lifts my spirits just as Kerry knew it would. I'm pleased to see that all the other mourners have joined in with the spirit of how she had imagined this day. 'I want everyone to shine,' she'd told me, when we were chatting one day at the hospice while Kian was out of the room. 'I want everyone to sparkle. I want there to be light and brightness everywhere Kian looks, not gloom and doom. I want him to remember me like I used to be, not like I am now. I want him to know that no matter how dark things seem there's always a little glimmer of light if you look hard enough.'

And she was right, of course.

Her glitter idea is the perfect metaphor for the day. I've been to enough funerals over the years to know what sombre affairs they can be, but as we get out of the car, and I spot my dad sporting a glittery bowler hat, Mum next to him with a shimmering pink scarf draped around her shoulders, and Charlotte behind them both in a silver sequined top and black suit, I know it was the right decision. Even prim and proper Mrs Ryman, who I suspect has never owned such an item of clothing in her life, has donned a sparkly red jacket over a sensible blouse and tweed skirt. I can't help but smile. Rather than being solely an occasion to mark her death, with just a touch of glitter Kerry has transformed it into an opportunity to celebrate her life and legacy.

Once we're all out of the car, we stand still as Kian takes in the scene before him. In spite of all the glitter and sparkle, it's hard to ignore the strength of sorrow in the air from those gathered outside the chapel. All eyes are on Kian, a little boy without his mum, and among the sadness I can feel everyone willing him on, step by step, moment by moment, wishing him all the strength he needs to get through a day like today.

The service seems to go quickly, with a short address by the vicar, followed by a few words from Jodi and me. I'd spent several days trying to compose the words I was going to say today, but in the end I don't manage much beyond thanking Kerry for being a wonderful friend and sister. Jodi, however, clearly shares a great deal of Kerry's strength and determination. Eight and a half months pregnant, wearing a maternity dress that she's adorned with sequins, she has everyone in the room simultaneously crying and laughing with tales of mischief and heartbreak from their time as teenagers in care.

As the service draws to a close, there's one last surprise for everyone as we leave the building: Mariah Carey's 'All I Want For Christmas Is You'. Kerry had been insistent that no matter what time of year it was this would be the right song to play everyone out to. 'You can't feel sad when Mariah's belting this one out at the top of her lungs,' she'd assured me with her trademark grin. 'It's like a blast of pure happiness.'

It's a bit cooler than it was when we go back outside; the sun is hidden behind clouds and there's a cool breeze, but that doesn't stop people from lingering to chat. Everyone wants to speak to Kian, to tell him how brave he's been and what a wonderful person his mother was. He holds my hand the entire time, never once letting go, as though anchoring himself to me for comfort, as though he's afraid that without me there, he might be in danger of drifting away.

I recognise a few of those who come to see him but not all. There are mums who knew Kerry from the school gates, neighbours from around the estate, people she used to work with and many more besides. A couple of women in their forties introduce themselves as former residents of Kerry's children's home, and through this I discover just how hard Jodi has been working to fill the chapel with people who knew Kerry.

In spite of exhaustive efforts on both our parts, however, there is no sign of Kian's father, just as Kerry had predicted. I'd left messages on every number I could find for him. I'd even been around to his last-known address, only to discover that he had moved several months before. I didn't doubt for a moment that news of Kerry's passing had made its way to him somehow, and the fact that he hadn't been in contact with Kian even to offer a word of comfort spoke volumes about his character.

At the first opportunity I lead Kian away from the crowds and over to see Jodi, so that I can thank her for her kind words and make sure she has directions to our house. She's standing with her family, but the moment she see us heading towards her she waddles over, throws her arms around Kian and covers him in kisses.

'You did really well in there, little man,' she says, fighting back her tears. 'Your mum would've been so proud of you.'

Jodi hugs me too and introduces me to her family. 'You all know Kerry was like a sister to me,' is her opening gambit, 'well this is her baby brother, which in my book makes him part of our family too.'

38

Noah

Wednesday, 19th October

'Are you sure you won't stay, Narinder? The caterers are just about to put out the food.'

The lovely Welsh nurse who'd been so kind to Kerry during her chemotherapy smiles and shakes her head. 'Believe me, I'd love to,' she says, pulling on a black woollen coat over her red sparkly dress. 'I caught a whiff of something delicious as I passed through your beautiful kitchen, and it was all I could do not to scoff whatever it was straight out of the oven. But my shift starts in less than an hour so I'd better get a move on. But thanks ever so much for inviting me and making me feel so welcome. It's been a beautiful day, you've really done your sister proud.'

It had been difficult to decide where to hold the reception for Kerry's funeral. We'd obviously considered her flat, but reasoned it might be upsetting for Kian. We'd also considered hiring some anonymous function room, but that hadn't felt right either. In the end it was only when Rosalind suggested having it here in our home that I finally felt like we'd hit on the perfect solution. There is more than enough room to accommodate all the guests for the day, especially now that the sun has come out again and most people are in the garden. And more importantly for Kian, unlike his home, or for that matter my brother's flat, there are no unhappy memories of Kerry's illness here.

Once I've shown Narinder out, I head into the garden in search of Kian. Although there had obviously been tears during the funeral itself, he's been surrounded by people ever since, talking to him and making sure he is okay. I've assured him several times that he can come and find me whenever he wants, and although if it had been up to me I wouldn't have let him leave my side, I'm conscious that I need to let him do things his own way.

As I stand on the patio, scanning the garden for signs of Kian, Mum appears beside me and puts her arm through mine.

'If it's Kian you're looking for,' she says, 'there's no need to worry. He's with Millie and some of the other children. They're at the bottom of the garden playing with next door's cats.'

'Maybe I should check on him,' I say. 'Make sure he's okay.'

Mum shakes her head. 'I tried myself but believe me, Millie's got it covered. She's really taken him under her wing.'

'She's a good girl,' I reply. 'I don't know what I would have done without you all, these past few weeks.'

'I know, darling,' says Mum. 'It must have been so hard for you.'

We find a couple of empty garden chairs and sit down next to each other in silence as people mill around chatting. I spot Dad talking animatedly with Jodi's partner, and Ida deep in conversation with Mrs Ryman: strange pairings that I can't imagine happening anywhere else but here. How odd to think that the connection between all these people is Kerry.

Mum turns to me. 'You've done a tremendous job, you know, you really have. It can't have been an easy thing to do, organising your own sister's funeral like this. It was hard enough for me when I had to arrange your grandmother's, I can only imagine what this has been like.'

'Rosalind's been the one dealing with the arrangements really. This is all down to her.'

'She's a special girl, all right.' She puts her hand on mine. 'How are things between you both?'

I consider her question carefully. 'To be honest, Mum, I don't know. Things have been so raw, so frantic, that I'm not really sure either of us could answer that at the moment. I know we still love one another, I know she cares for me as much as I care for her. Part of me thinks that maybe the fact she's being so caring is her way of saying there's still hope. But then another part is equally convinced this is simply Rosalind doing what comes naturally to her, nurturing, coping, healing. As for what any of this means for our future, I have no idea.'

'And now there's Kian to consider too. I take it you've discussed his future with Rosalind?'

'I had to. Even if Rosalind and I never get back together, the fact that I now have responsibility for Kian impacts all of our lives.'

Mum nods. 'And how did she respond?'

'She was just so terribly sad about the whole situation, and with everything else that's been going on it's been impossible to talk about it any further. I suppose we've all just been in crisis mode really.' I look at Mum. 'But yes . . . I do know that we can't go on like this indefinitely.'

'All you can do in a situation like this is take things one day at a time,' says Mum, and she gently pats my hand. 'Right,' she says, and kisses my cheek before standing up and looking in the direction of my father. 'I'm afraid I'm going to have to love and leave you. I can tell just from his body language that your father is on one of his rants again and that poor man who came with Jodi appears to be bearing the brunt of it. I'll go and tell him the food's ready, that should do it.'

Most of the guests have gone by six but Jodi and her brood stay on a little longer, determined to help clear up in spite of my protests. There's not that much to do as the caterers have taken care of most of it, but nonetheless Jodi orders her extensive family to stack away the remaining hired chairs, ready for their collection in the morning, while we search the garden for empty cups and discarded plates.

There are so many hands helping that we're done in no time at all but even so, Jodi immediately looks around for more to do. I sense she's reluctant to leave, almost as though her departure will sever the thread connecting her with Kerry for good.

'You know you're welcome here whenever you want,' I say,

taking her to one side. 'It's like you said earlier, we're family, and Kian for one needs all the family he can get.'

Jodi gives me a hug worthy of Kerry herself. 'You can see right through me, can't you, pet?' She plants a lipsticked kiss on my cheek. 'Thank you, Noah.' Drying her eyes, she calls her family together. 'Right then, we'd best be off to let these lovely people have some time to themselves.'

Standing on the doorstep, Millie, Rosalind, Kian and I watch as they drive away, waving until their car turns the corner at the end of the road. As I close the front door, I can't help but feel odd at the thought that this day I've dreaded for so long is finally drawing to a close. It's the end of a chapter, one that has seen an incredible amount of change in a very short space of time, and as yet I have no idea what will be written in the next one.

I catch sight of Kian as he follows Millie into the kitchen. He looks exhausted and after Rosalind has poured them each a glass of chocolate milk, I suggest to him that it might be time for bed. He offers no protest; instead, clutching his glass tightly, he makes his way upstairs, assuring me he'll call me to come and say goodnight once he's brushed his teeth.

Millie, Rosalind and I finish clearing up the kitchen, and once we're done I head upstairs to check on Kian's progress. There's no sign of him in the family bathroom and so I put my head around the door of the guest bedroom, assuming he's become distracted playing on his phone. Instead I find him lying on top of the bed, fully clothed, toothbrush in hand and snoring softly. He looks so peaceful, so lacking in cares, that I haven't the heart to wake him. Easing the toothbrush from his grasp, I cover him with a blanket from the end of the bed, kiss his forehead and turn out the bedside light.

As I leave the room, half closing the door behind me, I find Millie standing on the landing, brushing her teeth despite having been told countless times only to do so in her bathroom.

'But I like doing it out here,' she explains, her mouth full of toothpaste. 'There's more going on.'

Responding to my raised eyebrows, she disappears back into

her room and I follow, studying the walls while she finishes brushing her teeth. It's still all cute animal posters and inspirational quotes, but I know that won't last for much longer. Soon enough she'll dismiss these as being too childish for her sophisticated palate, and they'll go the way of all her cuddly toys and baby dolls.

Emerging from her en-suite, she wipes her mouth with the back of her hand, something else Rosalind and I have told her off about.

'What?' she says knowingly, but I haven't the heart to reprimand her. She's been so thoughtful, not just today, but throughout this whole ordeal. Instead I wrap her in my arms and hold her tightly.

'Is Kian okay?' she asks, looking up at me. 'I was going to see if he wanted to borrow a book to read. I loaned him the *Diary of a Wimpy Kid* last week and he told me he was really enjoying it.'

'I don't think he'll be doing any reading tonight, sweetheart,' I say. 'He's out like a light, but it was kind of you to think of him.'

Breaking free of my embrace, she sits down on the edge of her bed.

'Thanks for today, Mills,' I say, sitting down next to her, 'and not just today but for everything. I know the past few months have been crazy and you've had a lot to take on board very quickly.'

'It's okay,' she says. 'I just wanted to help. Auntie Kerry was such a lovely person, you must miss her very much.'

'I do,' I say, and I feel myself wobble slightly at the thought of a world without her. 'I just wish we'd all met her years ago. It's my own stupid fault.'

'What do you mean?'

'Nothing really, it's just I keep thinking to myself if only I hadn't been so stubborn all these years, if only I'd looked into my own history earlier, then maybe I could've found Kerry, instead of her having to find me.'

'But you weren't to know,' says Millie. 'Mum always says you have to make the best decision you can at the time with the information you've got, or something like that. You didn't even know you had a sister, so how could you look for her?'

I smile at her wisdom, so grateful to be back living under the same roof as her no matter how temporarily. 'Thanks, Mills,' I say, and I put my arm around her shoulders and kiss the top of her head.

'Dad? Can I ask you something?'

'Of course,' I reply, turning to face her. 'Anything.'

'What's going to happen next? Are you and Kian going to stay? Are you and Mum getting back together?'

I so want to reassure her about the future, to let her know in the light of all this chaos that finally everything will be all right. But I can't, as I still don't know myself. I think about changing the subject, making a joke or just glossing over it, but in the end I opt for openness. I choose honesty.

'I don't know yet, darling,' I tell her. 'I wish I did, but I don't.'

We chat for a while longer, and then I kiss her goodnight and head up to the attic room that used to be my study and which, since my return, we've turned into a bedroom for me. There's not much in it, just a desk, a futon and a few things of mine draped over the back of a chair. I grab my toothbrush and head down-stairs to the family bathroom. When I'm done, I look at myself in the mirror. I look tired and drawn, and I wonder where exactly I'm going to find the energy to carry on. Turning out the bath-room light, I'm about to go in search of Rosalind so I can say goodnight, when I find her sitting on the stairs up to the attic.

'I was just about to go looking for you.'

She smiles, softly. 'Great minds think alike.'

'I just wanted to thank you for everything you've done today. You've been amazing, absolutely amazing. I'd never have got through any of this without you.'

She stands and joins me at the foot of the stairs, slipping her arms around my waist as she does so. 'It was nothing,' she says, 'at least no more than I know you'd do for me.'

We remain locked in an embrace, neither of us wanting to let go. I want so much for things to be right between us, I want so much for all the bad things that happened to stay in the past, but I know that's too much to ask, at least right now when there's still such a lot to sort out.

I kiss her cheek and turn to go, but she takes hold of my hand and stops me. We stand for a moment, my eyes searching hers, trying to make sense of what's happening. But then she pulls me towards her and kisses me, and as she leads me to the room that used to be ours, I stop trying to make sense of anything at all.

39

Noah

Friday, 28th October

'The removal guys are all done,' says Rosalind from Kerry's kitchen doorway. She walks over to me, her footsteps echoing around the empty room, and puts her arms around me, resting her head against my chest.

Today has been tough, watching Kerry's home gradually stripped of its personality, as her carefully chosen furnishings and belongings are loaded into the back of a van. Kian and I had been here earlier in the week, chiefly to clear out his room but also to collect a few small items from around the flat that are special to him. I would never have guessed that a mirrored vase with artificial flowers, a bowl of orange-scented pot pourri and a fluffy cushion would be among the things he'd select, but they were, and I suppose each, in some way I may never fully understand, reminded him of his mum and the happy years they'd spent together here.

My job today is more prosaic, the overseeing of the emptying of the flat, the contents of which I've assured Kian will be kept safely in storage until such time as he feels ready to make a decision about what to do with them. I'm glad he's decided not to be here this morning, choosing instead to remain home with Millie and my parents. There's something painfully poignant about seeing a life dismantled in this way, and I'd rather Kian remember the place as it was when he and Kerry were here, than the empty shell it is now.

Rosalind looks up at me, stroking my arm tenderly as she does so. 'Why don't I give you a moment?' she suggests. 'I'll be in the car if you need me.'

It is still impossible to say exactly where Rosalind and I are. Since the funeral and our night together just over a week ago, we've continued to share the same bed night after night, and are always in each other's company, so much so that it feels as though our getting back together is a done deal. And perhaps it would've been, if I'd still been the old me, the one who always chose to bury his head in the sand. But I'm not that man any more and I don't think I have been for a long time. I am a new man, a new creation, thanks in no small part to the events of the past six months.

I take a final walk around each room of the flat, partly to check that I haven't overlooked anything, but mostly in the hope of seeing, not Kerry's ghost exactly, but some small glimpse or reminder of the sister I miss with all my heart.

Leaving the keys on the kitchen counter as instructed by the housing association, I walk to the front door and open it, take one last look around before leaving for what will be the last time.

Rosalind is sitting behind the wheel of her car, a cream-coloured VW Beetle, and as I climb into the passenger seat beside her, she puts a comforting hand on my knee. 'I can't imagine how difficult that must have been for you,' she says. 'Are you okay?'

I nod, because the words don't seem to be there, but when some moments later I finally do speak, what comes out of my mouth is completely unexpected.

'I think we need to talk,' I say. 'About us, about the future, and about how sorry I am for the mess I've made of everything. But before that, there's something I need to do. And I'm going to need your help to do it.'

Ever since my conversation with Millie on the evening of Kerry's funeral, I've been thinking about the details surrounding my adoption. How even though I've been offered the opportunity to find out more, I've always been so focused on the present that it's never once occurred to me that the past may have any relevance. But I realise now you can't escape your past, no matter how hard you try. One day it will catch up with you, as it had with me. Meeting and getting to know Kerry had been one of the most surprising and wonderful periods of my life. I'd learned so much about myself from her stories of our childhood, stories that would've been lost to me forever without her. Even then, there was still part of me that hadn't wanted to know the full story. I can think of a number of occasions when I sensed that Kerry had wanted to talk to me, to tell me something about our past and would have, if only I'd probed a little deeper, seemed more willing to learn, more eager to uncover the truth of our beginnings. But there were questions I deliberately hadn't asked, conversations I'd cut short, avenues I had chosen to leave unexplored, all for fear of finding out truths I wasn't yet ready to learn. But those days are over, and my desire to turn away from the truth has vanished. If I really want to have a future with Rosalind, if I'm to be the best father to Millie and uncle to Kian that I can be, if I really do want to honour Kerry's memory, then I need to discover, I have to discover, the story of my past once and for all.

Friday, 4th November

The London branch of the Henderson Foundation, the charity responsible for arranging my adoption, is housed on the third floor of an unassuming 1960s office block overlooking the Hammersmith flyover. From the moment I'd contacted them, it had taken a week to process my application, and another to set up an appointment for today. I'd been on my way to court when they'd telephoned with a date, and the very first thing I did was call Rosalind to ask if she would go with me. 'Are you sure you really want to do this?' she'd said. 'You know you don't have to?'

'But I do,' I'd replied, conscious of the worry in her voice, guessing she thought she'd somehow managed to guilt me into doing this. 'And I need you with me. I want you with me.'

We don't have to wait long in the agency's small reception area, with its artificial potted palms and piped-in easy-listening classical music. Within a few minutes of our arrival, a door to a side office opens and a middle-aged woman with a kind face and short dark hair emerges. She ushers us into an even smaller room, in which has been crammed a table and three chairs.

'I'm Amanda,' says the woman. She shakes my hand and then Rosalind's. 'I think we spoke on the phone. As I explained, we can get you copies of all your documents but it will take some time. I'm afraid you can't take them away with you today but you are welcome to stay for as long as you need. Please don't feel you have to rush.' She leaves the room and returns moments later carrying several thick files, which she places on the table in front of us.

'They're arranged chronologically,' she explains, separating out the files and tapping a slender green document wallet with her index finger. 'In this top one you'll find the social worker's summary report, which was used as the basis for your adoption. It's only three pages long, but touches on all the significant events that took place, so I'd start there if I were you.' She picks up a pale-blue wallet file that's about an inch thick and sets it to one side. 'This one is different to all the others, and you can take it home. It came straight from the Adoption Contact Register, and contains personal letters and correspondence from anyone who has attempted to get in touch with you in the years following your adoption.'

In an instant I recall my conversation with Kerry, how she told me that from the age of eighteen she'd written to me at least once a year, hoping the letters would one day find their way to me. And now here they are, messages from the past made all the more precious by the fact that she is no longer here. I pick up the file but make no attempt to examine its contents. I haven't the strength for this yet. It's a job for much later. Instead, I hand it to Rosalind and wordlessly she slips the file into her bag.

'I'll leave you to it,' says Amanda.

Once she's gone, Rosalind and I sit side by side, staring at the files in front of us. The only sound is the ticking of the clock on the wall and the muted noise of traffic outside.

Rosalind takes my hand. 'Noah . . .' she says hesitantly. 'Before you go any further I need to tell you something . . . I already know what's in these files.'

'What do you mean?'

'Before Kerry passed away, she and I talked. She wanted me to understand . . . well, why you are the way you are, I suppose, and so she told me the truth about your beginnings . . . and how you came to be adopted.'

My eyes rest on the folders in front of me for a moment and then I look back at Rosalind.

'You know I believe in being open,' she says. 'You know that nothing matters more to me than honesty. But I've really struggled with trying to work out the right thing to do here. If I'm honest, I'm glad Kerry told me, because I had the opportunity to thank her for everything she did for you. It was incredible. Truly incredible. But knowing what happened left me with a dilemma: not just when I should tell you but if I should say anything at all.' She puts her hand on mine. 'What's in these files is going to be difficult to process and I wouldn't wish this knowledge on my worst enemy, let alone the man I love. Much to my shame, I finally get it now. I now understand your need to keep doors closed was never to keep me out but to protect me and Millie from the demons behind them.' She squeezes my hand. 'I'm so sorry, Noah. I fought you on this for so long, only to realise now that you were just doing what you thought was best.'

It's impossible to know what to make of all this. Rosalind doesn't just know what's in these files, she also finally understands exactly what it's like to be me. To have to wrestle with the past, to have to strike a balance between honesty and the desire to protect those you love.

My gaze flits down warily towards the files, as though they have developed some sort of supernatural power. 'You really think I shouldn't read these?'

Rosalind nods. 'But this is your decision, not mine, it has to be.'

It would be so easy to stand up, take Rosalind's hand and walk away from all this. We could return to our lives, our family, and never have to think about the past ever again. It's tempting. Really tempting. But I feel like I've come too far to turn back now. Whether this Pandora's box heralds my downfall or salvation, I have to open it and finally face up to what's inside. Snatching a last reassuring look at Rosalind, I take a deep breath, open the first file and begin to read.

40

Noah

Friday, 4th November

The story that unfolds is one at once familiar and yet completely alien. I'm no specialist in family law like some of my colleagues but in search of mitigating circumstances for those I'm defending, I've read many official documents like this over the years. So the format and phrasing is familiar, which somehow adds to the feeling that I'm reading the story not of myself, but of a stranger.

I was born on 8th September 1982 in Hammersmith maternity hospital at 2.22 p.m. My mother, Mary Anne Hayes, was a twenty-three-year-old single parent with a daughter, Kerry Lisa Hayes, who was eight at the time of my birth. Mary had no contact with the father of either of her children, and neither were named on her children's birth certificates.

The social worker's report reveals that while mine and Kerry's early life could at times be chaotic, we were initially well looked after by our mother. But following the sudden death of her own mother a year after my birth, Mary became depressed and alcohol-dependent. Some time later she met and fell under the influence of a local drug dealer and soon after that, became an addict herself.

I pause, and realise for the first time that I haven't taken a breath since I started reading. Rosalind, who has been holding my hand throughout, grips it a little tighter, reminding me that she's there, reassuring me that I'm not in this alone.

I don't quite know what I'd imagined Mary's problems to be. I suppose I hadn't allowed myself to dwell on it in any detail, but seeing it here in black and white makes it somehow all the more shocking. I'm no naïf, I'm well aware of the various factors that lead to parents losing custody of their children, and compared to some of the cases I've known the situation described here is relatively tame, and yet I feel like a bomb has just been detonated somewhere deep in my subconscious, firing shrapnel of the past into the present. My professional ability to compartmentalise won't save me here, because this isn't just another case file I'm reading. It isn't just another pitiful account of life at the bottom of the pile that will be my focus for a short while before I move on to my next case. This is about me, it's the story of my life, and the world into which I was born.

Reading on I discover that over time, as Mary's drug dependency increased, ten-year-old Kerry took over the role of my primary carer, feeding, changing and washing me whenever Mary was incapable of doing so. Then when Mary began to absent herself from the family home (initially for a few hours at a time but eventually whole days), Kerry began truanting from school in order to look after me. Feeding us both with whatever tinned and packet food she could find in the kitchen cupboards, Kerry held the fort until our mother's return. Then as time went on, and Mary's absences lengthened, Kerry was forced to resort to shoplifting for food and nappies.

I have to stop reading for a moment. It's all too much. I have a sudden image of a tiny ten-year-old Kerry, a girl a few years younger than my own daughter, pushing a pram up and down the aisles of a supermarket, anxiously looking around her as she hides food and baby supplies in the basket underneath me. My heart breaks again and again for this girl, for her courage, for her strength, for her fierce love for me. Why did no one try to help? Why did no one intervene? What were her teachers doing all this time, as day after day her classroom chair stood empty? How had social workers, who must surely have had Mary on their radar at some point, not picked up on what was happening? And what about neighbours, what about friends, what about family?

I feel angry on Kerry's behalf.

I feel guilty that she had faced this alone.

But most of all I feel thankful, down-on-my-knees grateful, for this amazing, self-sacrificing, extraordinary act of love.

For the sake of this little girl and the woman she became, I force myself to carry on reading, even though my every instinct is telling me to stop. I don't need to continue reading to know that Kerry is a hero, I don't need to read another word to see my life of privilege – my loving parents, my education, my idyllic childhood spent in blissful ignorance of the harsh realities of this world – in a different light, and although a thousand experts on this sort of thing would insist I need closure, I know in my heart of hearts that the short time I'd had with Kerry is all the closure I need. But regardless I read on.

The final part of the report outlines the events that led to our finally being taken into care. With Mary having been absent for a fortnight, our situation was becoming increasingly desperate, as money to pay for the gas and electricity meter ran out. In the midst of these circumstances Kerry did her best to keep things going, but a week later she fell ill with a raging fever and was unable to leave the flat in search of food. It was only then that a neighbour, on hearing my constant crying, broke into the flat and found us in our mother's bed, huddled together on dirty sheets soiled by my leaking nappy. The police were called and we were immediately taken into care. The report concludes that had it not been for Kerry, there is little doubt that our situation would have ended in tragedy.

Reaching out, I carefully close the file.

And then I fall to pieces.

She'd saved my life.

Kerry had saved my life.

And all these years she'd kept it to herself.

An hour later, Rosalind and I are sitting in a busy café not far from the adoption agency. All around us people are talking, laughing, carrying on as though this is just another ordinary day, when for me it's anything but.

I put my face in my hands, overcome once again by waves of

gratitude, sorrow and guilt, all at once. Rosalind reaches across the table and takes my hand in hers and I lift my head to look at her.

'I can't believe it,' I say. 'I just can't believe all that was in my past.'

Rosalind nods. 'I felt the same way when Kerry told me. It doesn't seem real, does it? She was so brave, so selfless, it just breaks my heart even thinking about what you both went through.'

I lean forwards, still holding her hand. 'I owe Kerry everything. Absolutely everything. She saved my life and yet I'll never get to thank her.'

'But that's just it,' says Rosalind. 'You did thank her. She told me so. All the thanks she ever wanted was for you to have a good life. And by being the man you are, building the life we have, taking care of Millie and Kian, you're thanking her in a way words never could.' She's crying now, we both are, in the middle of this bustling café in a sea of strangers we're sure never to meet again.

'I'm sorry,' I say, pressing her hand to my chest. 'I'm so sorry for shutting you out for so long.'

'You were just doing what you had to do,' she counters. 'I should never have pushed you so hard. I should have tried harder to understand.'

'No more than I should've tried with you, when it came to losing the baby.' My voice cracks on that last word, as finally I push open the door that's been closed for so long.

'I was devastated.' My voice is so quiet I can barely hear myself above the hubbub in the café. 'Although I didn't allow myself to acknowledge it at the time, I wanted our baby so much it hurt. And to have it not happen was like having my heart ripped out.' I look down at the table that clearly hasn't been cleaned for some time, at the tiny grains of sugar someone has spilt. Against the dark wood of the table they sparkle like fragments of diamond. 'It feels mad to say this after all these years, but I think part of me has always longed for a big family. For our house to be filled with noise and mess and laughter.'

Rosalind lifts her head, her face full of surprise. 'You've always wanted more kids?'

I shrug. 'I know, it's news to me too. But I think yes, I did . . . I do.'

A solitary tear forms in the corner of Rosalind's eye that she quickly wipes away. 'But how . . . but you never . . . why didn't you say anything?'

I smile. 'Well . . . that's sort of my thing, isn't it? Not talking. Not speaking. Not sharing. Anyway, how could I say anything when I didn't even know myself until a few moments ago? But it makes sense. It makes complete sense, now I think about it. Most men finding out that their girlfriend was pregnant just before finals would've been panic-stricken, but I was over the moon. And it wasn't just that for the first time in my life I'd have someone who was related to me by blood; thinking about it now, I can see that it was also because she, our daughter, would be just the beginning.'

Rosalind is stunned, and incomprehension stalks her every word. 'But . . . but . . . if that was how you felt, why weren't you keener on IVF?'

My gaze drops to the table again. 'How could I be? You were so against it, so worried about the impact it might have on us, so fearful that the emotional stress of it might tear us apart, that I couldn't ask you to go through with it just for me. So I suppose, me being me, I just put all my energies into looking forward, into building a happy future for the three of us.'

I look at Rosalind, uncertain of what she is thinking, afraid that this might be a confession too far, that her disbelief might be about to turn into anger.

'I'm sorry,' I say. 'I can see now how damaging my approach to life has been. I should've been more honest with you, I should have been more honest with myself.'

She bites her lip, her eyes filled with tears. 'Oh, Noah,' she says, without a trace of ire. 'I only said that about IVF because I was afraid of pushing you into it. You're always so concerned about my happiness, about what I want, the last thing I wanted was for us to go down that route knowing it was only me taking us there.' She bites her lip again, and then fixes her gaze unswervingly on me. 'Are you saying that you want us to try for another baby?'

I draw a deep, fortifying breath before speaking. 'You and Millie . . . you are all I need, and if you're all I get in this lifetime, then so be it, I'll still have won the lottery. But yes, even though we now have Kian . . . especially now we have Kian, it is something I'd like us to explore. I want Millie and Kian to have all the family they'll ever need and more, I want them to never doubt they belong. I want them to have what I had with Kerry, people in their lives they can always count on, no matter what.'

It's a little after four when Rosalind and I arrive home. We call out from the hallway but there's no reply, and we search through the ground floor of the house until we spot Kian and my parents out in the garden, wrapped up against the November chill.

Seeing us, Kian rushes into the house holding something in his hand, while my parents amble in behind him.

'Look at this,' he says, thrusting the rank-smelling object towards my face excitedly, 'it's dog food . . . but it's not for dogs, it's for hedgehogs!'

I look over his head at my parents for explanation.

'We spotted one in your garden at the weekend but I forgot to mention it,' says Dad. 'Anyway, while young Kian and I were out there clearing leaves I told him all about it and how scrawny the poor little chap looked, so Kian suggested we give him a good old nosh-up.'

'We looked it up on the Internet,' says Kian. 'They eat slugs and snails but they really love dog food. Your dad said that if we go out with torches a bit later, we might see them.'

The front door slams shut, rattling the kitchen windowpanes. Millie's home from school.

'Have we finally got a puppy?' she exclaims, spotting the dog food in Kian's hand straight away. 'I knew you'd change your mind. Where is it? In the garden?'

I smile at her boundless optimism. I've lost count of the times her mother and I have explained that we're not getting a pet of any kind for the time being.

''Fraid not, darling,' says Rosalind. 'Apparently the dog food is for a hedgehog in need of sustenance.'

'A hedgehog? Oh, how cute!' she exclaims without missing a beat. 'I love hedgehogs. Where is it? Let me see it.'

'It's too early for him yet,' says Kian, 'but come outside and I'll show you where I put his food.'

Millie whizzes past so quickly that she almost knocks me off my feet and as she hurriedly kisses her grandparents, my mother says in a stage whisper, 'Hedgehogs are great. But keep trying on the puppy front, they're much easier to get a lead on.'

Later, after a supper of sausages and jacket potatoes, at Kian's behest we all troop outside with torches in search of the hedgehog. When he fails to materialise, my father suggests that we wait in the shed in case our presence is putting him off. So that's exactly what we do. Clearing a space for us all, armed only with our winter coats and steaming mugs of hot chocolate made by Millie and Kian, we await our nocturnal visitor.

As we stand in the growing darkness, whispering and giggling with each other, it's impossible not to reflect on the precious nature of this moment: I have two healthy parents, two excited children, and a wife who, even without being able to make out her expression in the shadows, I can tell is just as content as I am.

This moment couldn't possibly be of greater contrast to the rawness and the sorrow of earlier in the day. Such an intense low, followed by a life-affirming high produced by nothing more dramatic than a shed, a hedgehog and the people that I love. It's these small moments that make life worth living. The moments you take for granted. The ones you think will always be in plentiful supply. But if this past year has shown me anything, it's the need to cherish each and every moment, whether good or bad, whether joyful or painful, as the precious fleeting gifts that they are.

ONE YEAR LATER

41

Noah

'Come on, guys!' I shout up the stairs for the fifth time in as many minutes. 'We should have left half an hour ago. Let's not be the last ones there again.'

I wonder sometimes exactly how long over the course of my life I've spent waiting in this very hallway for my family. If I were to hazard a guess, I'd say at least a month, or that's what it feels like.

First to come down the stairs is Rosalind, sporting a new hairstyle sculpted by Millie, who is suddenly into all things fashion and beauty. I knew that she had been nervous about letting Millie loose with her curling tongs on the basis of a handful of YouTube tutorials, but actually it doesn't look half bad.

'How do you like it?' asks Rosalind, giving me a twirl. 'Life's going to be a lot easier with my own live-in hairdresser.'

I smile as I gently pull her towards me, wrapping my arms around her. 'All we need is for the next one to be a builder, and if Kian makes it as a professional footballer we'll have all of our hair, home and football-ticket needs covered for life.'

Deciding to try for another baby was one of the big decisions we made following our talk the day I read my adoption records. A few weeks later we went to see a fertility specialist, and Rosalind began a course of treatment designed to increase our chances of conceiving naturally. Although it hasn't happened yet we're still hopeful, and determined not to let this get us down. In Millie and Kian we have a wonderful family, the best family, and the feeling of desperation I once had, but could never voice, has abated. But that doesn't mean that more children wouldn't be wonderful. Rosalind feels the same and we've agreed that if there's no change come the new year, our next step will be IVF. It will, of course, be a challenge for us, a testing of our reforged bond, but we're not daunted by the prospect. The events of these past two years have seen to that. We've been through the fire and as a result we're harder, tougher, more resilient. There's nothing that can break us now. We're stronger together than we've ever been.

Next to appear, descending in a cloud of Lynx Africa, is Kian, who by the looks of his gelled hair has been watching some YouTube tutorials of his own. Though he's still as skinny as a rake, he must have grown a foot at least in the past year and currently shows no sign of stopping. Just last week, Rosalind had to take him shopping for new school trousers as all the ones he owned seemed suddenly to have shrunk.

'Like the hair,' I say, in an attempt to acknowledge his efforts, but Kian turns crimson and rolls his eyes.

'I haven't done anything to it,' he protests, in direct contradiction of the evidence before me. 'I always look like this.'

Rosalind turns away to hide a smile and I dig my hands down into my pockets and nod in all seriousness. 'Sorry,' I say, 'my mistake.'

I look at my watch again. Now we really are late. I'm about to bellow up the stairs one last time but then Millie appears, and for a moment I'm speechless. Even though our destination is only a casual family celebration at my parents', Millie is dressed as if she's going to a rock concert, in ripped jeans, silver eight-hole Dr. Martens boots and black leather jacket, a slick of thick black eyeliner finishing off the look.

'Nice outfit,' I say, well aware that anything further will cause more trouble than it's worth.

'Dad!' she says exasperatedly. Clearly even the little I have said is too much.

As she finally joins us, I allow myself a moment to take in this, my family: my beautiful wife, teenage daughter, and twelve-year-old nephew. A motley crew to be sure, but all mine, and even though we're late, it's all I can do not to hug and kiss each and every one of them. They're my reason for being, my comfort and strength, and I'm thankful for every day that I have them in my life.

It's been just over a year since we lost Kerry, a year in which there has been a lot of heartache along the way. Christmas for Kian without his mum was particularly difficult, as was his birthday. And even though we're all still adjusting to our new life together, we've managed to establish some new traditions of our own. Friday nights are now takeaway night, as instituted by Kian, and once a month at the weekend it's kids' takeover night, where Millie and Kian not only cook the family meal but also decide on the evening's entertainment.

Just two weeks ago, we commemorated the first anniversary of Kerry's passing. We spent the weekend at a rented cottage on the Devonshire coast, going on walks, playing board games and eating good food. In the evening I hooked up my laptop to the TV and, gathering around it, we looked through old photographs of Kerry and Kian that I'd scanned on to my hard drive. Emotional though it was, I think Kian enjoyed it, reliving those memories, sharing his stories of Kerry, remembering who she was and how she'd lived. And later that night, after everyone else had gone to bed, Kian and I sat up until late, trading anecdotes we hadn't had time to share, telling stories of Kerry that made us both smile.

I still miss Kerry and the connection we had, and frequently find myself thinking about her, wishing I could tell her about my good days and bad, imagining the advice she'd give, and the no-nonsense way she'd deliver it when the occasion required. I know I'll always miss her and be beyond grateful for all she has done for me, but I am glad I had the opportunity to know her, albeit for such a short time.

As predicted, we are indeed the last of my family to arrive at my parents' home. Dad, whose birthday it is, greets us all with a bear hug, ushering us through the house into the conservatory where the rest of the family are gathered. Charlotte introduces us to her new boyfriend, Nick, a fellow academic she met online, while my mum and sister-in-law Cassie begin setting out a huge feast. Despite the chill in the air, Phillip's children are playing out in the garden, but the moment they spot Millie and Kian they race full pelt inside, keen to spend time with the glamorous older children.

The meal itself is wonderful, far more food than even twice our number could hope to demolish. Afterwards, once Dad has made his customary birthday speech, peppered with literary references no one but he and Mum understands, I grab the bag I'd brought with me from the front room, and ask Kian to join me for a walk.

He looks a little exasperated at my request, reluctant to leave his cousins behind, but I assure him it won't take long, and together we head away from the house to a bench tucked right at the bottom of the garden.

'I've got something I want to show you,' I say, reaching into my bag. I take out a white envelope and hand it to him.

'Is that Mum's writing?' he asks, studying it.

I nod. 'Do you remember how I told you that after I was adopted, your mum wrote letters to me that were stored at a special place until I was ready to find my birth family? Well, about a year ago Rosalind and I went and collected them. Until a couple of weeks back I hadn't felt able to read them, because I missed your mum so much, but after we got home from Devon I decided to look through them. There's eighteen in all and I've been reading one a day ever since. Anyway this morning, before everyone got up, I sat in the garden at home and picked another out to read, and while all of them are special, I really think you need to see this one. Your mum wrote it when she was pregnant with you, and I think it's something you'll treasure.'

As I sit watching Kian read Kerry's letter, listening to the sound of the children playing in the distance, I think again about what a remarkable person my sister was and the amazing sacrifices she made to save me. One day I'll tell Kian just how much of a hero his mum was, but for now it's enough he knows that from the moment he was conceived, he had been loved and wanted with a passion and a fervour that knew no bounds. A love that not even death could destroy.

28th September 2005

Dear Jason,

I know I usually write to you on your birthday but I couldn't wait. I've got some massive news: I'm pregnant! It's early days yet but I've been so sick that the midwife told me she reckons this baby's a strong one. I haven't told anyone else yet, not even Jodi, because I want you to be the first to know.

I know I'm old enough to know better. It's not like I'm some kid pregnant at fifteen or whatever, I'm in my thirties, and by rights I should've been settled down with a nice house, a fella and a couple of kids by now. But you know as well as I do that life doesn't always work out the way you want. Sometimes you've just got to play the hand you've been dealt.

The baby's dad, Steve, isn't up to much, to be honest. Sometimes he's sweet but more often than not he's hopeless, and I'd be surprised if he sticks around once I break the news. But even if he does do a runner, not even that could take the shine off how over the moon I am about becoming a mum.

This is my chance, Jason, my chance to do things right. To raise a little boy or girl and for them to know that no matter what happens, they are truly loved. I already love this little bean with all my heart, and I know my love will only get stronger as the days go by.

As long as there is breath in me, my kid won't ever know what it's like to be scared, or hungry or feel like nobody cares. They won't ever have to struggle, or fight to survive. They will always be surrounded by people who love and care for them no matter what.

And I want you to know that even though it's been years

since I've seen you and you might be a million miles away, when my baby arrives there will always be a place for you with us, because you're family, pure and simple. And even if I never get to see you again, I'm going to make sure that my kid knows all about you, and how lovely you are, and how in a world full of darkness you were always the bright shining light that kept me going.

All my love always, your sister, Kerry

Acknowledgements

For their time, kindness, advice and general aceness huge thanks are due to the following: Everyone at Hodder, everyone at UA, Matt Whitehead, Chris McCabe, Adam Marley, Nick Sayers, Alice Morley, Ariella Feiner, Louise Swannell, Cicely Aspinall, Simon Purkis, Chris Manby, Roxie Cooper, Manpreet, The Sunday Night Pub Club, The Brum Radio Book Show, Dr Simranjeet Kaur, Katie Fforde, The Board (in all its guises), Jenny Colgan, Marian Keyes, Lisa Jewell, Zoe Ball, Amanda Ross (and all at Cactus), Tracey Rees, Miranda Dickinson, Freya North and Ruth Hogan.

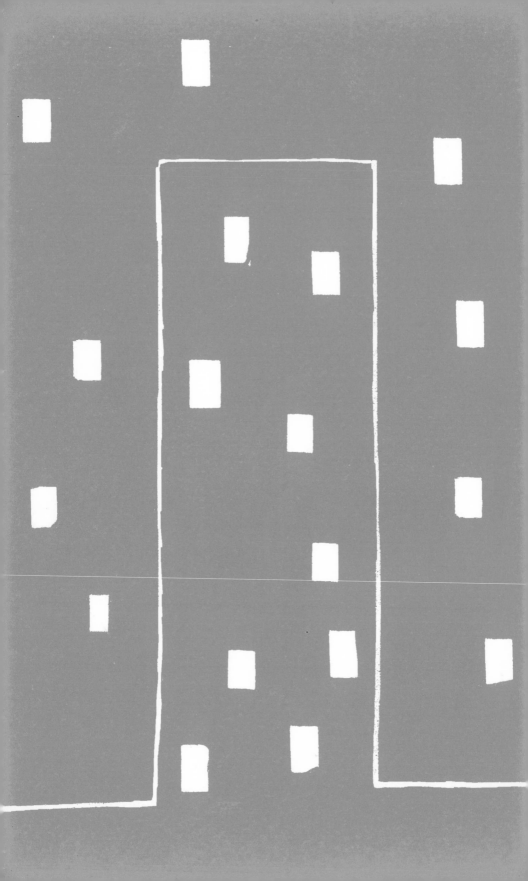